With the release of *Standoff*, David Rollins is the author of nine international best selling novels, six of which feature OSI Special Agent Vin Cooper, OSI.

He currently lives in Sydney, Australia. Want more? Visit davidrollins.net.

Standoff

David Rollins

First published by Momentum in 2013
This edition published in 2013 by Momentum
Pan Macmillan Australia Pty Ltd
1 Market Street, Sydney 2000

A CIP record for this book is available at the National Library of Australia

Standoff

EPUB format: 9781760080549
Mobi format: 9781760080556
POD format: 9781760080938

Cover design by XOU Creative
Edited by Jo Lyons
Proofread by Hayley Crandell

Macmillan Digital Australia: www.macmillandigital.com.au

To report a typographical error, please visit momentumbooks.com.au/contact/

Visit www.momentumbooks.com.au to read more about all our books and to buy books
online. You will also find features, author interviews and news of any author events.

For Sam, my biggest fan and greatest critic.

'Don't let it end like this. Tell them I said something.'

— Pancho Villa

Prologue

Six hours ago

The glossy red Learjet was parked on the ramp beside a Winjeel, an old orange and white single-engine flight trainer with faded Royal Australian Air Force markings on the wings and fuselage. Bobbie Macey, the Lear's pilot, patted the old timer's dusty skin with the flat of her hand. "You're a long way from home, babe."

A cab pulled up. Macey's co-pilot, Rick Gartner, got out and wandered over. "That ol' girl's had a hard life," he said with way too much cheer for the hour. "Bit like you."

"Watch it, sonny," said Macey.

"Sleep okay?"

"Fine. You?"

Gartner slipped her a sly grin.

Macey sighed. "Local girl?"

"Not saying."

"Struck out, huh?"

Gartner kept up the grin but the edge had come off it.

"Thought so," said Macey.

The two pilots had an easy relationship, all business in the cockpit and all banter out of it – most of it good-natured. At

1

forty-four, Macey was the captain and Gartner, in his early thirties, her co-pilot. Over the past few years they'd flown quite a few charters together and knew the routine like it was scripted. If there was occasional friction between them it stemmed from Gartner's habit of chasing skirt even though he was married with a kid. A gigolo had written the guy's moral code, Macey had decided, and it rubbed her the wrong way. But he was easy to get along with otherwise, once the ground rules had been set out during a two-day layover in Panama. That night, after putting away a skinful, he'd cupped her breast as she passed him on the way to the john. She'd stopped, looked down at his hand like it was a food stain on her shirt and said, "You want a bottle broken over your frikken' head?" Later that night, she'd said, "Pull that shit again I'll have you fired. I'm your boss, get it?" After that, no further trouble. Nevertheless, it still bugged Macey when Gartner left a bar with some floozy under his wing, and that happened often enough.

Macey ran her hand down the riveted skin of the old trainer's flank. The aluminum was cooler to the touch than the ambient air temperature, which the local weather report on her cell phone told her was hovering just above seventy degrees Fahrenheit. Comfortable.

"Not much going on around here," Gartner commented, hands on hips, surveying the surroundings. "Might go see if I can rustle up some coffee."

"Not for me, thanks," said Macey.

"Bladder can't cope, eh?"

She grunted. "I'd like to see you pass a kid the size of a submarine."

The younger man snorted as he walked off. "Too much information, boss."

"Be back here in thirty," Macey said to Gartner's back, the co-pilot raising his hand above his shoulder in acknowledgment.

With Gartner gone, the pre-dawn quiet returned. Macey did a few stretches, using the Winjeel's wing for support. A pickup pulled off the access road and motored slowly into the facility. Despite the early hour, there were still plenty of people moving about this small privately owned airport – early risers.

Here and there were single-engine aircraft: Cessnas, Beeches, a few twins and several gliders – this place was big on those. It was Macey's first time at this facility. She'd run charters in and out of El Paso often enough in the past, operating from the international airport ten miles across town to the northwest. But Horizon Airport looked and felt home built. The single runway was narrow and lumpy like it had been rolled straight onto the desert floor, the sand and rock nibbling at the edges of the asphalt. And getting in and out of this place was different to what she was used to. After flying for United back in the day, and the Marines before that – KC-130s, tankers, airborne gas stations – you got used to a certain level of infrastructure. This place had almost none. No radar, no control tower. Around here it was all see-and-avoid, which wasn't ideal when you were flying a jet with a stall speed equal to the cruise of the average single-engine plane frequenting this chunk of sky. What troubled Macey most about Horizon, though, now that she thought about it, was the almost complete lack of security. A little chain-link fencing enclosed the back of the facility and that was pretty much it. Anyone could just wander in and do whatever they liked. It was for this reason that she'd slept aboard the Lear. The passenger seats went back horizontal so it wasn't so bad. Lord knows she'd slept on aircraft most of her adult life.

Macey took a stick of cinnamon gum from her pocket, called it breakfast and popped it in her mouth. She walked past the trainer toward the Lear. A 35 model. Compact, yet with ample room for eight passengers. Agile too, like a sports car, and cruised comfortably at a little over Mach 0.8 at forty thousand feet, performance roughly equal to that of a big commercial airliner. Worth a few mill. A nice prize if someone cared to steal it.

She walked around the aircraft, giving it a casual pre-flight, looking over the control surfaces and landing gear. Chocks up against the tires: check. Tags on the pitot tubes to keep out the sand and bugs: check. Covers on the engine intakes for same reason: check. Nothing amiss. Macey examined the front hatch: locked, just as she'd left it.

Today's charter was to take a local well-to-do rancher, his wife and two young children, to Orlando, Florida. They were spending the day at Disneyland, a birthday present for one of the kids from what she'd been told. At 7 pm, they were to return the family to Horizon before heading back to the charter company's HQ at LAX.

Macey's watch read 5:09. The family wasn't scheduled to turn up till 5:45. It would still be dark then, but they wanted to get an early start. So, in other words, Macey told herself, you got time to kill, babe. She gazed up. The stars directly overhead were dimmer than the points of light down on the horizon, the larger ones twinkling like the landing lights of faraway inbound aircraft. She dug her hands in her pockets and started walking along the short taxiway, toward the runway. Somewhere unseen within the facility, a single-engine aircraft fired up and then settled back into an easy idle. A Lycoming 320, her educated ear told her. A lizard, startled by her footsteps, skittered for cover into some low scrub. Macey walked into and out of a cool band of air. She enjoyed this time of the morning. It was peaceful, quiet.

*

Gartner strolled to the terminal building and tried the front door. Locked.

"Great," he said. He put a hand against the glass and peered inside to make doubly sure that the place was empty. Dark, no movement. He went around the corner of the building and was startled by a large black man sitting on a side doorstep. The man stopped what he was doing, which was aimlessly lobbing pebbles collected in one hand into a tin.

"Hey," he said looking up.

"Hi," Gartner replied.

"You work here, man?"

"No, just having a look around."

"Know if I can I get a plane outta here?"

"It's not that kinda airport. A charter flight maybe. You might get lucky ..."

The man grunted and turned away without further acknowledgment and went back to lobbing pebbles.

Gartner walked around him and meandered back behind the building toward a row of Quonset huts. Several had lights on. The sound of an angle grinder coming from one of them cut through the silence. A pickup motored slowly by, muffled country and western music on its sound system. Despite the early hour, people were already here earning a buck. An old Piper Cub was hangared in one of the Quonsets, a Cessna 172 in its neighbor and an auto body shop in the one after that. He stopped in front of the body shop. A shower of sparks from the angle grinder sprayed from the shadow behind a '69 Mach I Mustang. The space around the old classic was filled with used auto parts: panels, axles, differentials and suspension components. A guy in dirty blue coveralls stood up behind the car, a cigarette attached somehow to his upper lip. His sudden appearance caught Gartner by surprise.

"Morning," Gartner said, adding a wave.

The guy repositioned the protective glasses on top of his faded Las Vegas ball cap. "Mornin'."

"Say, where can I get a coffee around here?"

The man walked to the front of the Quonset. He was in his mid-forties, of medium height with longish brown hair hanging down either side of the cap and a face streaked with black dust. He puffed on the cigarette before pulling the butt off his lip. He dropped it on the ground and stood on it. "Now? Not a chance."

"The sleepy end of town, eh?" said Gartner more to himself, looking around. This adventure was a dead end. He told himself he should just go back to the Lear and fire up its cappuccino machine. And then he remembered Bobbie had the keys.

"Ah can fix ya some if yer desperate, long as ya don't mind it black," the man said helpfully. "Cain't get m' heart started 'thout it."

Gartner thought about saying no, but the minutes were dragging. A coffee and a word or two would pass the time. "Know what you mean. Black's good, thanks."

"Don' got no sugar, neither."

"That's how I take it."

"Shouldn't be more'n a minute or two. Just had a coffee masef." The man laid the angle grinder carefully on a mat protecting the car's hood, went to a side bench cramped with a jumble of auto-electrical components and flicked a switch on a white plastic electric kettle smeared with greasy black fingerprints. "Ya'll own that Lear up on the main ramp?"

"I wish."

"But ya'll's the pilot, right?"

"One of 'em."

"Needs two pilots, eh? Nice plane."

"Nice car," Gartner countered.

The man unscrewed the red lid from a jar of Folgers and shook some granulated coffee into a foam cup.

"Will be when ah'm finished. Juss 'bout ready to take 'er over t' the paint shop. Not mine, though – a customer's. She been givin' me the hurry up for weeks."

"She?" In Gartner's world a Mach I Mustang was a man's car, though probably Macey would have something to say about that, he thought.

"Yeah, she – Gail Sorwick. Anniversary present for her ol' man."

"Some present." For some reason the name was familiar to Gartner but he couldn't place it.

"Some lady – ya know what ah mean?" In case Gartner didn't, the man made a gesture with his hand like his fingertips were burning and then shook them to put the flames out. "Drives a Porsche herself, a Cabrio'. Every time she come roun' here the place kinda stops and a lotta male traffic starts walkin' back an' forth out front here tryin' t' look busy, borrowin' shit. Funny as hell."

"Hot women have that effect on the world. An immutable law of the universe."

"Yep."

The lid on the jug danced excitedly before the unit turned itself off with a loud click. The man poured boiling water into the foam cup and handed it to Gartner. "There ya go."

"Thanks. This'll help."

Close by, a Lycoming roared into life and then settled back into an idle. Gartner glanced in the direction of the sound and saw the red beacon rotating on a Piper Warrior. "What's down the far end of the road?" he asked.

"Not much. Trucks an' trailers, mostly. Whole yard full of 'em out back. All the action's right here." He confirmed that with a yawn. "Don' get many Learjets. Why ya' here?"

"Got a charter. Off to Disneyland for the day." Gartner sipped his coffee. "Happiest kingdom of them all."

The man grunted. "So they say. Well, ya'll have a nice day."

"You too," said Gartner. "And thanks for this." He held up the foam cup and gave it a nod.

The man went back to the Mustang and his angle grinder and Gartner walked toward the Piper, thinking that the people round here were pretty friendly. The single-engine aircraft began to move, its landing lights chasing away the darkness in its path. Red light from its tail beacon swept the low buildings while its strobe light fired flashes of hard white light that hurt his eyes. A refueling truck drove a short distance and parked against an office. The lights went on in the building beside it and Gartner heard music or a television, he wasn't sure which. The place was waking up. He glanced at his watch. Still had a good fifteen minutes. He gulped down a mouthful of the Folgers and followed the Piper. It turned and disappeared from view until Gartner walked further onto the ramp, opening out the angle. The lights outlining the runway came on. He concluded that the Piper's pilot would've flicked the switch remotely with his radio to activate them.

*

Bright white lights suddenly came on, outlining the runway. Macey turned and watched the aircraft swing onto the taxiway. It motored slowly west, coming her way, heading for the beginning of Runway 08 and a take-off into the soon-to-rise sun.

She stepped off the asphalt and walked in the flinty dirt, giving the aircraft coming up behind her plenty of room. Something small and frightened jumped out of her path and dived for a burrow; some kind of gopher, she imagined.

The aircraft – it was a Piper Warrior, she now saw – turned off the taxiway and onto the runway. Half a dozen seconds later it ambled past her, strobe lights flashing and its beacon washing her in red light. The pilot raised a hand to Macey, giving her a departing wave. She returned the gesture and went back to keeping an eye out for gopher holes.

Up ahead, the Warrior stopped briefly. It then turned sharply through one-eighty degrees and faced back down the runway, its landing lights powerful and blinding. Macey put her head down and watched her feet kicking up the dust as she walked. The Warrior's engine note climbed rapidly, its throttle open. She didn't have to look up to know that the plane would be stationary, its handbrake on while the pilot performed final engine checks. Its racing Lycoming and prop noise died away for a few moments before it began all over again. But this time the plane began to move, handbrake off, the engine and propeller reaching a higher, louder, more serious note this time, throttle wide open.

It eventually howled past her – no wave from the pilot this time – and bounced down the asphalt, lined up perfectly between the two rows of lights. The small aircraft lifted off when it was roughly adjacent to the terminal building and climbed out at a shallow angle. Macey savored the smell of burned aviation fuel reaching her nostrils. The lights beside the runway turned off, leaving behind blue and orange floaters that swam in her eyes.

The night quickly returned and the sound of the single-engine plane dwindled to nothing after a minute or two. Macey stood in the darkness and took it in, her hands deep in her pockets, playing with spare change in one and the packet of Big Red in the other. She took a deep breath. Better head back and pre-flight the Lear, she told herself. Their charter would be turning up soon.

It was then that she heard aircraft engines. This note was totally different to the Warrior's. These engines were distant, the hum carried by the night air, and the sound faded as the currents shifted. But then they came back again, distinctly louder this time. Macey peered into the night, searching for landing lights. She couldn't see any. The engines were turboprops. The rapidly growing volume of sound told her the aircraft were approaching fast and it was disorienting not knowing the direction they were coming from. And troubling. Aircraft approaching a facility like this had to do so with at least fifteen hundred feet of air under their wings, their strobes and running lights illuminated. An inbound radio call would have automatically triggered the runway lights. The fact that the runway was still darkened informed her that the mystery aircraft hadn't made –

A black shape exploded from out of the darkness and roared past low overhead, interrupting her thoughts.

"Shit!" she exclaimed, ducking involuntarily as the blast of propeller and turboprop roar enveloped her. "Hey!" she shouted at it as the shape disappeared in the blackness. Macey's muscles relaxed as she stood up from the crouch, the hair raised on the back of her neck, her spine tingling with shock. Then a second aircraft, lower than the first, almost took her head off, the pressure wave coming off the backs of its wings buffeting her. Like the first aircraft, this second one was almost instantly swallowed by the night. She peered into the darkness, trying to locate them. After a dozen seconds, as if to help her out, their landing lights and strobes came on, pinpointing them against the stars, one three hundred yards behind the other. They were coming in to land.

The fright Macey experienced almost being chewed up by low flying propeller blades ebbed away leaving indignant anger in its place. She was gonna have some serious, mother-lovin' words with those pilots. But almost immediately she decided that probably wouldn't be too smart. There was only one reason for coming in low like that: to avoid the radar at El Paso International. The aircraft seemed to have come from the southwest, the direction of Mexico. The border was barely seven miles away, only a couple minutes' flying time with the ass those turboprops had been hauling. Macey watched the aircraft lights enter the landing pattern. Her hands were clammy. Everything told her that what she was witnessing had a dangerous quality about it.

The runway lights finally came on. Macey started walking toward the facility, turning to look back over her shoulder at the inbound aircraft. They were approaching fast, the wash from their powerful landing lights already shimmering and flickering on the ground around her. After a few steps she broke into a jog, which turned into a sprint. She was running hard, wanting to get back to the Lear, find Gartner. She stole another glance over her shoulder. The aircraft were coming in hot. Her foot went into a hole. It went in deep. She stumbled. Macey knew she was in trouble. Her momentum propelled her forward, all the strain of her weight on a point against her shin pressed against a rock, her knee joint overextended. She knew it was coming, nothing she could do to stop it … The *crack* was like a dry tree branch being snapped over someone's thigh, her bones breaking as the ground rushed toward her outstretched hands.

Macey lay facedown in the dirt for several seconds, groaning, dreading the worst – *knowing* the worst – before rolling slowly to the side. The change in body position released the pressure on her foot and it popped out of the gopher hole. She pushed herself up on an elbow and saw that her lower leg was bent in an odd way, a right angle in it halfway up the shin like she had a second knee joint there. She rolled all the way onto her back and grunted, holding her leg below the break, swearing angrily at her own stupidity.

"Now what the hell are you gonna do?" Macey said aloud and brought her foot back down on the dirt, feeling the ends of the fractured shinbones grinding against each other. This should feel worse than it did, she thought, but knew the real pain was yet to come.

The lead aircraft touched down and then its engines shrieked and propeller blades snarled in full reverse thrust. Macey turned her head to the side to watch it go by, to identify it. It flashed past, lit up by the runway lights. A turboprop with a T-tail – a King Air. The whole thing was painted flat black. Macey hadn't seen too many King Airs painted flat black. Or any, come to think of it.

She groaned and let her head fall back onto the ground. Then the second aircraft thundered past, sounding the same as the first. Another King Air. The facility's buildings were a good thousand feet away across the dirt and rock. "You're gonna have to crawl or hop to get there," she told herself. "What's it gonna be?" Macey decided on the latter; too many critters on the ground, some of them with stingers or fangs.

The effort that went into standing up made her eyes water, but she eventually made it, her foot, held off the ground, swinging uselessly in midair. She had a cell phone in her breast pocket. Call Gartner, she told herself, and patted both pockets – empty. The damn thing must be on the ground somewhere. She looked around but couldn't see it. Get back to the Lear, was her next thought, and the quicker the better. But then the runway lights went out again, plunging the world into darkness. "Fuck," Macey grunted.

*

"It's a Piper Warrior taking off. Nothing to get excited about," said Gartner to the night air. He decided to head back to the Lear, but there was plenty of time, no need to hurry. And Macey was probably already there, taking charge as usual. Flinging what was left of the coffee on the ground, he dropped the cup in a trash-barrel. It was only when he heard the Piper's engine racing out on the end of the runway that he picked up the pace. The aircraft was already moving when he walked around the corner of a building to bring it into view, its landing lights dancing in the darkness out on the end of the runway. The thrill of flight still excited Gartner and, though it was only a Warrior, he paused to watch it inch down the runway and eventually, finally, lift off. A jet it wasn't.

A few minutes later Gartner arrived back at the Lear and now there was a mini hub of activity going on around it. A refueling truck was topping up the Winjeel's tank, its pilot discussing something with the mechanic. Their charter was also waiting, the family sitting in a white Suburban with the motor running to power its AC, a muffled song from *The Lion King* playing on the DVD for the kids. As Gartner approached the vehicle, the driver's door opened and a fit, forty-something male in Levi's and a crisp blue shirt hopped out and came to meet him.

"Barney Sorwick," he said. "You the pilot?" He tilted his head at the Lear.

"Co-pilot." Gartner held out his hand. "Rick Gartner."

Barney shook it. "We're a bit early."

"No problem, sir. Good to get an early start. The boss will be back in a minute and we'll take off shortly after that."

"Call me Barney, okay?"

The passenger door opened. Mrs Sorwick climbed out and walked over: long tan legs, khaki shorts, suede boots and a loose white cotton top. *Gail* Sorwick. It clicked – the woman giving her husband a Mach I for an anniversary present. Gartner felt he already knew her. And yeah, he could see what all the fuss was about: tall and slim with olive skin, dark eyes and dimples. Her straight black hair was in a tight high ponytail. It swung from side to side as walked toward him, seemingly in slo-mo. The Gail Sorwick Effect.

"This is my wife, Gail," said Barney.

"Hi." She smiled warmly.

"Rick Gartner, your co-pilot for the day."

"Dad ..." a whining kid called out from the Suburban. "Can you tell Amie to stop?"

"Excuse me." Barney sighed deeply. "Duty calls."

Gartner was happy to be left alone with Mrs Sorwick, only she seemed to be distracted by something in the night sky. "What's that noise?" she asked.

Gartner realized that the sound of approaching turboprop engines had been in the background for a while. He hunted around in the sky for the source but couldn't locate it. The aircraft – was it more than one? Yeah, two. They were close, *very* close. And low. Gartner frowned with confusion. Why were aircraft buzzing the airport at night with their lights turned off? He subconsciously scratched his head while he searched the sky again, at a loss. Gail Sorwick was having similar problems. Then, above, aircraft landing lights came on. There were two sets, almost directly above them, climbing. The runway lights came on next.

"They're landing," said Gartner, thinking aloud.

Mrs Sorwick stood beside him. "Do planes usually fly like that? With their lights off?"

"No," Gartner replied, uneasy about it, same as she was. He hid it with shrug. "But I'm sure there's a good reason – emergency training procedures ..." Of course, that was complete fabrication.

Mrs Sorwick changed the subject. "So, I checked the weather in Florida and looks like it's going to be hot, steamy and overcast. I hope that doesn't affect the flight home."

"No, but it's going to provide plenty of excuses for ice cream," Gartner ventured.

"Trust me, our kids don't need *any* excuses when it comes to ice cream."

Gartner glanced across at the Winjeel and the Lear, the refueling truck having finished with the old RAAF trainer and starting to move. The pilot was in the truck, hitching a ride somewhere. Gartner noticed a lightening in the eastern sky, the black sliding into a thin dark-blue band at the horizon. Time was marching on. He'd happily stand around for hours doing small talk with Gail Sorwick, but duty called. He wondered where Macey had gone. "Well, you'll have to excuse me, ma'am. Gotta go do my thing."

"Sure," she said. "When can we come aboard?"

"Whenever you're ready."

Mrs Sorwick gave him a nod and went back to the Suburban to organize the kids, World War III having broken out between them and their father.

Gartner walked to the Lear. The landing lights of inbound aircraft were now lined up with the runway – the mystery turboprops. One was a mile out, the other two miles behind it. "Bobbie?" he called out. Silence. He went past the back of the Lear to the edge of the ramp. Perhaps Macey had gone for a walk in the desert. He scanned the darkness for signs of her, but there weren't any.

The first aircraft touched down, its propeller blades snarling when reverse thrust was selected. It slowed quickly, using very little runway, and turned off onto the taxiway. The second aircraft landed moments later, as economical as the first in the amount of runway used. Gartner focused on the plane coming toward him, wondered what type it was and who might be at the controls. The mystery only deepened when the lead aircraft was close enough for him to get a good look at it. A King Air. It was painted a dull, flat black all over. The second aircraft, also a King Air, had caught up to the lead plane and he saw that it, too, was painted up just like the first: black.

This little airport was suddenly getting busy. A large truck had pulled up behind the Suburban, which the Sorwicks were in the process of moving to a spot around the back of the parking lot. The air was now full of turboprop noise, and beams from the two sets of landing lights. The aircraft came off the taxiway and continued on past the Lear and the Winjeel. The lead King Air turned ninety degrees so that it faced the access road and the truck parked on it, extinguished its lights and shut down the engines. The second aircraft pulled up beside the first and its lights and engines died. The deafening roar of the turboprops ceased almost immediately and simultaneously, replaced by a *whoosh* of the windmilling blades. Despite the imminent arrival of dawn, the two aircraft on the ramp were congealed remnants of midnight.

The sudden silence increased Gartner's unease. Where the hell was Macey? She was ex-military. Maybe *she* could explain this. He took the cell phone out of his pocket and was about to speed-dial her when the door behind the cockpit of the lead aircraft opened, the action mirrored by the King Air behind it. Ladders came down. And then men spilled out of the first aircraft. Gartner swallowed. They were all wearing ski masks and carrying guns.

They fanned out across the ramp. Some were shouting. And before Gartner could move, two of the masked men ran up to him, yelling. He froze. One of them slapped the cell phone out of his hand and stamped it into the asphalt. The other bashed him in the side of his face with a swipe of his gun. Gartner fell to the ground in a state of shock, his face numb and his mouth full of blood. Jesus Christ, a tooth was loose.

The two men were talking at each other excitedly. Gartner couldn't understand them. He thought that his brain had come loose, like his tooth, or that something had broken inside his head. Then he realized that they were speaking a foreign language – Spanish. Were they Mexican? He began to sit up and one of the men pointed a gun at him and shouted. Gartner lifted his hands up above his head and moved slowly as he got to his knees. Then he saw the Sorwick family being herded toward the Lear by two armed men. The kids were bewildered, crying. Gail was trying to comfort them while Barney attempted to reason with their captors. One of the men grabbed a kid by his blond hair, pulled a heavy Bowie knife from a scabbard on his belt and held the blade against the boy's throat. He wanted silence. Barney Sorwick gave it to him.

Gartner knew enough Spanish to order a tortilla, but that was about it. He couldn't communicate with these men. And he'd seen the reaction when Barney Sorwick tried. Two more masked individuals walked almost casually over to the Sorwicks. One of them was dressed in military camouflage pants and shirt. He was short – maybe only a little over five feet tall, and stocky. The shape of that well-fed body told Gartner that he was older than the men around him, all of whom were fit-looking and mostly dressed in faded military gear. The men who had accosted him and the Sorwicks all seemed to defer to this man, standing aside for him when he approached. He reached Barney and Gail. He spoke to them in Spanish and Barney replied in Spanish. The man laughed, made a gesture and, in response to it, Gail was separated from her husband. The man with the Bowie knife offered it to his boss, who shook his head. He turned to Gail and assessed her as he removed his own knife from the scabbard on his belt, a knife with a long thin blade and mother-of-pearl handle. Then he cut Gail's top off her body. Just like that. Gartner's mouth fell open. Gail screamed and the man slapped her, hard. He then grabbed her by the ponytail, cut the straps of her bra and the cups sprang away from her breasts. The sight of them, now exposed, terrified Gartner. The situation was fucked up to the nth power. What was happening? This wasn't reality.

Gail whimpered. Barney yelled something and then lunged at the uniformed man, hoping to grab him, to stop him as-saulting Gail. The man responded by taking a pistol from a holster on his hip, cocking it and pointing it at Barney's little girl, who was facedown on the tarmac crying her eyes out. Barney backed off and started sobbing, holding his hands over his face. He fell to his knees and bent forward so that his forehead almost touched the ground.

"I'm sorry. I'm sorry. I'm sorry. Please ..." Barney begged between the sobs, his voice cracking.

The uniformed man ignored him and, using the knife's long blade, traced the undersides of Gail's breasts, taunting Barney to do something stupid.

Gartner watched, immobilized by fear, as the point of the blade scratched a white line in Gail's skin all the way down to her exposed belly button. The man then pulled the zipper down on his fly and extracted his erection. He yelled something at one of the men who rushed in and forced Gail down onto her knees in front of his curved member. He held the knife under her chin and she looked up at him, her face twisted with fear. She trembled as she opened her mouth.

That was when the shooting started. *Brraat ... brraat-dat-dat-dat. Brraat ...* It came from somewhere behind the terminal building where the Quonset huts were. There it was again – *brraat ... brraat-dat-dat-dat* – individual bangs followed by automatic fire. There was a lull, and then the shooting seemed to be coming from everywhere. The uniformed man barked a few words at his people, his prick still in Gail's mouth, his hand wound tightly around her ponytail.

Gartner watched Barney Sorwick, could see that he was about to make some kind of move, his eyes darting left and right, his hands and shoulders twitching. Suddenly, he broke free of the men holding him and lunged at the monster forcing himself on his wife. But the man moved at the last instant and all Sorwick managed to get was a finger hooked in the mouth opening of the ski mask the man was wearing. And then it was ripped away, revealing the uniformed man's face.

The subordinates held their breath, along with Gartner, waiting for the reaction. It was a *mestizo* face, wide and flat with high cheekbones. Gartner placed him in his forties. As faces went it was brutal and cruel, the face of nightmares. Large blue tattooed tears dropped from the corner of an eye and grew larger as they ran down his cheek and neck. He sneered at Barney and made a gesture to the man with the Bowie knife, who then threw the heavy weapon at Barney. It flew through the air and hit Barney's forehead with a *thunk*, the blade quivering above the left eye, four inches of the polished steel embedded in brain. As Barney fell backward on the asphalt and began to convulse, the tattooed man drew his holstered pistol and began shooting the children.

And that was all Gartner saw as a spray of lead smashed into his spine at the base of the neck and returned him to the night.

*

Bobbie Macey wasn't covering a lot of distance. She hopped a few times and then stopped. The pain in her broken leg was different now. It had an edge to it. The nerve endings were waking up to a serious problem, and they were ringing alarm bells. She went down on her hands and knees and crawled, braved the critters and made reasonable ground. It was that or stay put and wait for Gartner to come looking for her. She realized that she could see her hands in the darkness now. Dawn was on the way. With around a hundred yards covered down on all fours, she stopped to rest and give her knees a break.

"Lord, don't let me faint," she said aloud after a sharp stab of pain caused her to catch her breath. Macey imagined herself lying here in the heat of the day, dehydrated, discovered by ants and scorpions long before Gartner got to her. The taxiway was still another three hundred yards ahead.

It was then that she heard the gunfire. *Brraat ... brraat-dat-dat-dat ...* She'd heard it before, as a Marine in Iraq. From a distance it crackled, sounding like bubble wrap being squeezed. "What's happening?" she asked the night. Another pain spike shot up her leg, convincing her to lie down. Macey's eyes rolled back in her head.

When she opened them again, the sky above her was blue, her mouth was full of dirt and the pain in her leg was unbearable. An awful noise filled her head. She turned it to the side and saw a black bird streak past not more than thirty yards away, followed by a second black shape.

"Buzzards," she mumbled before again slipping into unconsciousness.

One

I was earning an honest day's pay as a special agent in the Office of Special Investigations, doing my best to apprehend Senior Airman Angus Whelt, officially AWOL from Lackland Air Force Base roughly three hundred miles to the east. Whelt wasn't inclined to make it easy for me and my current partner, Hector Gomez – not the Hector Gomez who plays shortstop for the Colorado Rockies but the carsick Texas Ranger Hector Gomez who was throwing up onto the floorboards in the passenger seat beside me, making the cabin reek of regurgitated spicy ground beef, corn chips and refried beans as we bashed along a dirt trail close to the US–Mexico border.

Whelt wasn't making it easy for us because if we caught up with him he'd soon thereafter be doing a big slice of federal time. He was on the run because OSI had closed in on his narcotics operation. "Doctor" Whelt and his partner, Airman First Class William Sponson, also AWOL, were, according to various sources, the dealers of choice at Lackland until someone tipped them off about OSI closing in on their asses. So they fled. The Air Force grinds its heel on drug dealers and neither man was too keen about becoming something sticky on the bottom of the Air Force's boot. We knew where Whelt was – playing hard to get on a dirt bike at our eleven o'clock. Sponson's whereabouts were presently a mystery.

Ahead, an overhang in the bend jutted out suspiciously – a root ball maybe. I yanked the wheel hard over to clear it. Our rental – a Jeep Patriot from Thrifty – hit it anyway. Or maybe the damn root ball hit us. The impact jarred like an uppercut and pitched the vehicle on its side, up on two wheels. We teetered there like a stunt car, on the verge of rolling over while I wrestled with the wheel. Gomez was thrown sideways against the window. He left behind a smear of something on it: either bile or banana smoothie, I was too busy to make a positive ID either way. Fortunately, nudging the opposite berm jolted us back down onto the relative security of all four wheels.

"Je ... sus!" Gomez said, bouncing around beside me, one hand braced hard against the ceiling.

Whelt was on what looked like a Honda motocross bike. He'd chosen to make his escape on it with good reason: the asshole rode like a Crusty Demon. His record said that he'd been some amateur national motocross champion before joining the service. Any moment I fully expected him to loop his bike in midair and flip us the middle finger.

He suddenly speared off the trail and took to the virgin bush, the bike's rear wheel spewing a rooster tail of rock and sand as he rode a divergent course from ours, away from the trail. Shit, I'd known he was gonna do that eventually. I glanced across at my partner, the Ranger, fighting the heaves. He was a mess. And, yeah, re window smear: banana smoothie.

If we were going to catch Whelt, we had to follow the guy into the rough. Gomez looked over at me, read the play instantly and shook his head, his eyeballs large. Like we had a choice.

I turned into the low dirt wall that bordered the trail we were on. The jeep's front wheels hit it with a sickening *graunch* and the hood reared up as the front wheels clawed at the sky. The rear wheels punched into the berm next and the vehicle reacted, bucking viciously fore and aft. When everything settled a little I stood on the gas pedal and steered for the crest, the tires scrabbling for traction while the front air dam smashed into rocks and low bushes.

My hope was that Whelt would make a mistake and put his bike down so that we could catch him, cuff him and take him in, but that hope was fast disappearing over the hill in front of us, standing up on the footpegs, the bike leaping and bounding over the terrain as it was designed to do. Behind Whelt meanwhile, the Patriot, designed for Walmart parking lots, didn't at all appreciate the treatment we were giving it.

"Hey!" Gomez said, pointing.

He was indicating the US–Mexico barrier fence in a depression below us, an eighteen-foot-high, rust-colored steel mesh barricade that looked about as solid as a parked freight train, one that snaked across the land as far as I could see.

"What's he ... up to?" Gomez wondered aloud.

"The Great ... Escape."

The pounding, crazy ride was making talking difficult.

"What's . . . that?"

"The Great ... Escape ... with Steve McQueen. Movie."

"So?"

"McQueen's running from the N ... Nazis. Steals a bike, makes a break for Switzerland ..." I swerved to avoid a boulder and ran the jeep nose first into a ditch. A thick wave of dirt spewed up and over the hood and windshield. "Only the border's ... fenced – like we got here," I continued.

"Lemme guess, he jumps the fence," said Gomez. Whelt had stretched his lead, almost gone. "You think that's what this guy's gonna do?"

I doubted tunneling was on his mind.

Ahead, another hill. Whelt was already beyond the crest, only his dust visible.

Gomez shouted: "It's a movie, so ... he makes it, right?"

"No, he gets ... hung up on the fence."

I wasn't ready to give up. And anyway, it was this or paperwork. I steered toward the crest, foot to the floorboards. We came over the rise, the jeep's motor racing, tires spitting gravel, the dust thick inside the cabin.

"Whoa!" Gomez yelled, bracing for impact as we shot over the crest.

My left boot beat him to it, standing on the brake pedal. The jeep slid sideways one way and then the other as we ploughed down the hill, coming to rest while a rolling ball of our own dust overtook us. Below, in the crook between the hill we were on and the one beyond it, was a crowd of people and vehicles. A crowd of illegals – Mexicans. Significant numbers of Border Patrol Agents were marshaling them together. There were well over fifty people and a dozen off roaders down there, out in the middle of nowhere. The attraction that brought everyone to this particular point appeared to be a break in the fence, a five-by-ten-foot section of the steel mesh simply cut out by an oxyacetylene torch. On the other side of the fence, the Mexican side, were chewed-up tracks of numerous vehicles that, pre-sumably, had brought the illegals to this point. A departing dust ball on the southern horizon confirmed it.

Several of the BPAs were looking up at us, presumably wondering who we were and what the hell we were doing. One of them was starting to move in our direction, hand on the butt of the pistol on his hip, coming to investigate. I scanned the area for Whelt and found him on the crest of the hill opposite. He'd stopped and was looking back at us. Okay, so the guy wasn't upside down in midair but he was still flip-ping us the bird. No way were we gonna negotiate our way through this parking lot and catch him.

Gomez wiped his mouth clean with a wad of Kleenex. "Shit."

"You were saying about real life?" I asked him.

My cell was buzzing in my pants pocket. Taking it out and looking at the screen, I saw I had half a dozen messages from a familiar Maryland number: Andrews AFB, home of the people keeping me in the style to which I ought to have left far behind by now at age 34 – the OSI. Gomez wandered down to talk with the BP Agent coming up the hill, his ID and badge held above his head, while I checked in. My supervisor and buddy, Lieutenant Colonel Arlen Wayne, picked up after a ring and a half.

"Vin …" Arlen said, the signal sketchy. "Where are y …"

"Where am I?"

"…"

"I can't hear you," I said. "I'll call you back later."

"… NO …"

There was a bar and a half of signal strength registering on the display. I walked around, trying to find another bar or two. "That better?"

"Yeah. Where … you?"

"On the border with Gomez letting Doctor Whelt slip through our fingers."

I noticed a major dent in the Patriot. The panel just below the front fender had been stove in. I bent down to have a closer look and saw a pool of hot engine oil spreading on the gravel between the front tires, ants running from the steaming black tsunami. I hoped I'd checked the insurance box on the rental agreement and, if not, that Thrifty were a bunch of understanding folks.

"For … bout him," Arlen said.

"Did you just say forget him?"

"They . . . his buddy, Spon …"

"They found Sponson?"

The rest was even more garbled though I gathered he wanted to know how far away from El Paso we were. "Thirty miles, give or take," I told him.

Arlen sounded like he was in a dentist chair, a drawer full of cutlery in his mouth. But I caught the key message: Get to Horizon Airport at El Paso and monitor the El Paso Sheriff's Office radio in the meantime. "We'll hurry. Call you when we get there," I confirmed.

Just before the line went dead I heard him say, "Vin ... slaughter. Jesus, some real bad shit."

Our other runaway, Whelt's pal Airman First Class William Sponson, had turned up in less than ideal circumstances. Arlen didn't often swear. It had to be some extra fucked-up ass-burger to move him into four-letter-word territory. Unlike me. A wisp of steam escaped through the jeep's grille. Fuck, shit and urination. This pile of spot-welded horse flop was going nowhere in a hurry. "Do you remember checking the insurance box on the rental agreement?" I asked Gomez as he walked back up the hill toward me.

"Nope."

Two

The jeep made it to the Interstate and expired there on the side of the road, smelling of fried engine oil, the needle on the temperature gauge buried in the dead zone. I called a local towing company and a couple of Border Patrol Agents offered us a ride to El Paso. They told us they had round-ups every other day like the one we stumbled across.

"I'm sure you read the headlines," said Agent Willow Schwinn behind the wheel, a chubby talkaholic. "Keepin' illegals out is like trying to hold back the sea. On the bright side, ain't no damn computer stealin' *this* girl's job."

"We might'a stopped those folks just now," continued her equally chatty male buddy in the front passenger seat, whose name I didn't catch, "but half a mile along the barrier fence could'a easily been another breach, a bigger one maybe, with trucks pulling up to take a hundred or more illegals. What you saw today might even have been a decoy, a diversion. Happens all the time. They used to pull the same shit with drugs till we wised up to it – send a small shipment through and set it up for a bust so that the real haul sneaked past while your back was turned filling out the paperwork. Sometimes we get lucky, like last month. Found thirty million dollars in cocaine inside bags of chicken manure – fertilizer. They thought the smell would fool the dogs. Didn't."

"That was a mother lode, not a decoy. The seizure would'a hurt 'em for sure."

"Hurt who?" I asked.

"One of the cartels – Sinaloa, Juárez or Chihuahua, not a hundred percent sure. Drugs or illegals, the aim is the same: get the goods to a city with a big population. Do that and they're gone."

"We seen every trick in the book. Illegals pack 'emselves into everything from suitcases to containers," Schwinn said. "Opened the hood on an SUV once and found a guy tucked in beside the carburetor."

"I seen a woman squeezed herself into a filing cabinet," countered Agent Passenger Seat.

"Under 'B' for 'Busted', right?" said Schwinn with a smirk. "One of these days I swear I'm gonna find one hiding in the bottom of my Slurpee."

Ha ha ha …

The guy sitting next to me in the back looked Mexican and his name sure sounded Mexican. Maybe the folks riding in front could only spot the ones playing hide and seek. I glanced at Gomez.

He looked at me and shrugged, seemingly unaffected by the slurs, his face a mask. He asked, "Would you folks mind tuning your radio into the local police frequency?"

"Sure, no problem," Agent Passenger Seat responded happily. He leaned forward, punched a button on the system and dialed in a freq. After a few seconds of air came continuous short bursts of frantic communications. It was all centered around a crime scene at Horizon Airport. Nothing specific, mind, but some real bad shit appeared to have gone down at the place, as Arlen had said. There were requests for multiple ambulances, forensics teams, mortuary services, the coroner's office, investigators, patrol vehicles – essentially all available mobile units from the El Paso County Sheriff's Office were to pedal their asses to the facility, pronto.

"Shee-it," said Agent Passenger Seat, sharing a look with Schwinn.

Fifteen minutes later we turned off the Interstate, heading north, and then east onto Pellicano, the road alive with El Paso Country Sheriff's Office and El Paso Police Department vehicles, as well as ambulances. About a mile from the highway a police roadblock had been set up on a minor sandy side street off Pellicano. I couldn't see any signs indicating the presence of an airport anywhere hereabouts. A chopper coming in to land and the roadblock itself, clotted as it was with various media vans and trucks that were being denied access, were the only indications that we were getting warmer on the airport location front.

On the other side of my window a knot of media photographers clicked away at us like we were stars arriving at a red carpet occasion.

"Says here that Horizon was built by a local fella by the name of Phil Barrett, now deceased," said Gomez, reading from his iPhone as we waited in the queue of official vehicles. "His family still owns the place."

"A private airstrip?" I asked.

"Nope, public."

Could be that the facility was in the Barrett family's backyard. I looked around. The terrain was about as dry and sun-stunned as any desert I'd ever seen and growing an airport out here had a lot more chance of surviving than grass or plants.

Gomez was on his cell. "Calling in," he said, meaning Ranger HQ in Austin. "Get some clearances happening."

Agent Schwinn showed the police officer her ID.

"Border Patrol, eh?" said the heavy-set guy, dark-blue sweat stains under his armpits and a face that looked like he'd just bathed it in cooking oil. "Names."

Schwinn provided them and the officer jotted them into a logbook.

"You got business here?" he asked.

Gomez lowered his window, still on the phone to Austin. "Hector Gomez, Rangers, and Special Agent Vin Cooper, Air Force OSI. We're looking for a deserter. Got word he turned up here."

"IDs," he said.

Gomez and I passed them over.

"Yeah, well, if he's here the only thing he'll be turning up is daisies." Finished jotting down our details on his clipboard, the officer handed back our credentials.

"This is the Sheriff's jurisdiction out here, ain't it?" Gomez asked, now off the phone and giving me the thumbs up on those clearances.

"Yeah, but as you're about to find out, things are a little messy around here at the moment." Then to Schwinn he said, "Go straight ahead. A deputy will show you where to park. You need to check in with Commander Matheson from the Sheriff's Office. There's an Emergency Operations center parked behind the terminal building. You can't miss it." He pulled his face away from the window, leaving behind a few sweat drops on the sill, and tapped the roof with his hand.

Schwinn motored forward, taking it slow. A sign by the side of the road – finally – announced Horizon Airport and welcomed us to it, obviously not party to the circumstances of our visit. A little further along, the road, bordered on one side by a neat row of trees, widened into an impromptu parking lot of EPCSO black and whites, blue and whites from the local PD, plus assorted forensics vans and ambulances. A frustrated-looking deputy, head cocked to one side and hands on hips, pointed at a slice of sand for us to occupy.

"We'll leave you guys to it," said Schwinn, coming to a stop but leaving the motor running. "This one's a little beyond our job description."

We thanked the agents for the ride, got out and checked in with the deputy.

"Rangers in on this now too, eh?" he said, nodding at the polished silver "cinco peso" on Gomez's chest, the famous five-pointed Texas star worn by the Rangers, punched from an original Mexican silver five-peso coin. "Not surprised. This is some bad shit."

He told us to display our IDs and then provided directions to the operations center parked behind the departures building.

Out of the AC in Schwinn's vehicle the sun beat down with a physical force that made my shoulders slump. Marshmallows could roast in the hot air hitting the back of my throat. I glanced at the runway, the far end of it disappearing in a puddle of shimmering mercury. After a couple of minutes, my underarms were already starting to look like dark ponds.

Behind the makeshift parking lot, a line of yellow crime-scene tape cordoned off access to the ramp beyond it, as well as to the paths leading to several homes and trailers on the desert sand. The place was crawling with law enforcement. Around these residences, heavily armed PD and Sheriff's Office tactical response personnel, as well as K-9 deputies and their dogs, searched the low sand ridges and bushes. Other police and deputies walked a grid laid out on the sand, looking for what would fall under the general headline of Clues. A Texas Department of Public Safety chopper was arriving, landing down the far end of the runway in the mercury puddle. Other helicopters hovered stationary at around five hundred feet over the desert half a mile away. Media choppers, I guessed, keen for the story behind whatever the hell had happened at Horizon.

Gomez and I headed in the direction of the airport's main buildings. Crime scene tape extended out onto the ramp. An old military aircraft was parked inside the tape, a kangaroo in its roundel – Royal Australian Air Force. A bright-red Learjet sat fifty feet beyond it, also inside the tape. Between the aircraft, several portable sunscreens had been placed over various groups of forensics people to provide them with a little relief from the sun's assault. They were dressed in blue coveralls and wore facemasks and white plastic booties over their shoes, CSI written on the backs of the coveralls. Some were kneeling over four or five bundles of clothing dumped on the asphalt. Others were making notes, speaking into digital recorders or standing around chatting. I'd been in this game long enough to know it wasn't piles of discarded laundry they were photographing.

I didn't need to prompt Gomez. He saw what I saw and neither of us liked what we were seeing.

The police tape continued all the way to the terminal building. Along the way we passed at least another half dozen tactical response officers and CSI people from both the PD and the Sheriff's Office, their heads down, deep in thought, heading back the way we'd come.

The tape went around the rear of the airport terminal, a small low-roofed shed clad with corrugated steel. Twenty yards behind it, a number of police and SO deputies were hanging around a Winnebago – the op's emergency command center. Gomez and I walked up to the door, excused ourselves and squeezed in. A man and a woman, both in the gray uniforms of the EPCSO, had their backs to us, discussing a large overhead photo of Horizon Airport taken from a height of around fifteen hundred feet, propped on an easel in front of them. Drawn with felt pen at various places all over the picture were red circles, each given a number and a two-letter code. There were quite a few of these circles. Seeing four of them in a cluster drawn on the ramp, where the old air force trainer and the Learjet were parked, I knew each circle represented a fatality. I found a circle numbered 19, then saw another numbered 27.

"Jesus," I muttered.

A burst of comms came through a police radio.

The female deputy turned around. Three stars adorned her collar. According to the silver tag on her shirt, her name was Foote. She was a short, barrel-shaped woman with full lips and puffy black rings around her eyes that told me she was either an insomniac or played contact sports. I decided either could have been the case. "I'm Chief Deputy Foote," she said. "Can we help you gentlemen?" The subtext of the way she said it informed me that their help was unlikely to be forthcoming and that calling us "gentlemen" was not because she thought we were. The information I skimmed from various badges and the nametags on the man beside her told me he was Operations Bureau Commander Matheson, the number two in the room. Like his boss, the Chief Deputy, Matheson was also short. He kept himself in shape, though, and I guessed his age at about forty. A roll of thick blond curls crowned his pudgy red face. He reminded me of Richard Simmons. I wondered if he took aerobics classes.

"Ranger Gomez and Special Agent Cooper, OSI," said Gomez, parrying Foote's tone with practiced dull efficiency. "We've been informed through channels that Airman First Class William Sponson, AWOL from Lackland AFB, had been picked up at Horizon Airport. We're here to check on that report."

Gomez's subtext: *I'm a Texas Ranger. Fuck with me at your peril.*

"Don't you Air Force people wear a uniform?" Matheson inquired, frowning at me.

Subtext: *I wonder what you'd look like in Spandex.*

"Of course, we welcome Ranger support," Foote added.

Subtext: *I'm not going to fuck with you. It's just that me and this guy beside me are completely out of our depth, and I was hoping to keep the people who are aware of that to a manageable circle I can browbeat.*

"Washington sent me here, but I'm guessing if my deserter's around, the only place he's headed is the morgue," I said. "And I'm further guessing along with twenty-six others."

"Can you give us the specifics of what's happened, ma'am, sir?" I asked when there was no response.

"We're working on it," said Matheson.

Subtext: *We've got no idea whatsoever.*

But then the Chief Deputy sighed, glanced at Matheson and said, "Look, your summary's on the money. But there are no witnesses and there are also no surveillance cameras so therefore no surveillance footage. If it sounds like we don't know what happened here, that's because, honestly, right at this point we don't know."

Subtext: *No more subtext, fellas.*

"Almost all of the 27 DOAs have multiple gunshot wounds," she continued. "Whoever did this even went into homes. We've got men, women and children murdered. And the information you have about your airman is correct. We found him – he's dead. His identity is yet to be positively confirmed with your personnel department, but he was carrying his Air Force photo ID card."

Maybe I was wrong about Foote. It had been known to happen. "So, everyone present at this facility was murdered sometime last night?" I asked.

"We've narrowed the attack to between four-thirty and six this morning," Matheson answered.

"And we do have one survivor," said Foote. "We believe it's one of the Learjet pilots."

"Is he talking?" asked Gomez.

The Chief Deputy shook her head. "We wish. He's in a coma. They – whoever *they* were, and there had to be quite a few of them given the area covered by this attack – shot him in the back and left him for dead. His spinal cord's smashed, but he's alive. Barely."

There was a knock on the partially closed door behind us. A woman in a blue CSI suit stepped in, the white booties still on her feet.

Matheson raised his chin at her. "Give us a minute, Liz."

Subtext: *Let's not give these out-of-towners anything we don't have to.*

"No, tell us what you've got," Foote said to her, countering the commander, sticking to her earlier decision to play it straight.

Liz was about five foot four, in her late twenties. Her hair was wavy, dark and cut shortish, presumably so that she wouldn't inadvertently dip the ends of it into her work. Her gray eyes were clear and intelligent, her casework yet to etch its lines around them. "Chief, I can confirm that vic 5AF was also sexually assaulted," she said. "Semen and blood in the mouth and the back of the nose passage."

"Blood?" Foote asked.

"Yes, Chief. Quite a bit."

"Hers?"

"No way to know until we test, though preliminary examination hasn't found any wound."

"What are you thinking?"

"She bit whoever assaulted her, and she bit him hard."

"Anything else, Liz?" Matheson asked her.

The question appeared to deflate her. "No, sir."

"Okay, well …"

It's fair to say I wasn't much liking Matheson.

He looked at Gomez and me with a dopey smile and said, "Well, anything you need, please don't hesitate to ask."

Subtext: *Goodbye. And don't come back with any demands.*

"Thank you, Commander," said Gomez, "For your help and assistance."

Subtext: *Fuck you.*

To Foote, I said, "Thanks, Chief."

Subtext: *Thanks, Chief.*

"Liz," said Foote, "can you please take these gentlemen to DOA number one?"

"Yes, ma'am," Liz replied.

Gomez and I followed her outside, into the furnace.

"No one got off a call before they were killed?" I asked.

"No. Maybe someone tried, but whoever hit this place cut the power and took out the cell tower. They knew what they were doing."

"You mind explaining the number and lettering system?" Gomez asked our guide as we power walked to keep up with her toward the main terminal building.

"Five AF – the fifth victim logged," she said. "AF for adult female. Your man was victim number one – 1AM. The first victim – an adult male. We found him slumped on the terminal building's doorstep."

I'd seen other victims on the overhead photo of the facility with the suffixes "MC" and "FC", which I could now decipher to mean male child and female child. Jesus …

"Who did the logging?" Gomez asked.

"We did – EPCSO forensics with some help from PD. The woman who runs the café in the terminal building called 911 when she arrived for work and found everyone deceased." I was about to ask where the woman was so that we could talk to her, ask a few questions, when Liz added, "She's under sedation."

We came around the front of the building. A shade tent had been erected over the DOA. A couple of crime scene investigators in their coveralls and booties were standing under the tent, talking quietly, while a photographer, also in CSI gear, changed camera lenses. A bloated fly flew around my face in a big hurry to join a dozen others circling the large bloody morsel curled in a ball on the stoop – Airman First Class Sponson. Numbered tags placed on the ground around him indicated the places where shell casings had landed. I counted nine tags. The photographer casually resumed what the lens change had interrupted – documenting the evidence.

Gomez and I stood in the sun, out of the photographer's way so as not to interfere or contaminate the evidence.

"Hey, Alice," Liz called out. "You about done?"

"Almost," replied one of the CSI twosome. "A few more snaps for the album and we can bag and tag him."

"Same MO as most of the others?"

"A spray on full auto; in this instance by two perps, we think. Nine millimeter rounds fired at close range – no more than ten feet from the vic. MP-5s, probably; certainly a submachine gun. We dug a slug outta the doorway. The shooters stitched him up pretty good across here and here." She drew a line with her finger from her shoulder to hip one way and then the other – a cross. From the wide pool of blood around Sponson he hadn't died fast, despite the amount of lead pumped into him.

A familiar-looking fly crawled into his nose and then out again, rubbed its legs together – possibly with glee – turned and went back in.

"Anything else?" Liz asked.

"Picked up a cigarette butt. *Faros,* a Mexican brand – might be the perp's, might not. Otherwise, *nada.*"

"Looks like your guy, Vin," said Gomez, getting down on his haunches to get a better angle on the DOA's face.

"Uh-huh." I pulled out the photo I had in my pocket and showed it to Gomez.

"Yep," he said, coming up. "Might'a come here hoping to fly out under the radar. Head south over the border. Wrong place, wrong time."

"What's gonna happen to him?" I asked Liz.

"We have to finish doing our thing. The tape won't come down for another 24 hours at least. Maybe you should go talk to the guy taking the lead, Lieutenant Carlos Cruz. I'll take you to him. Once we're done here the deceased will make the trip to the mortuary for autopsy. At that point County Coroner Sue Flores is the person to speak to."

"Got her phone number on you?" Gomez asked, taking notes.

Liz read it off her phone contacts.

I gazed down on Sponson. He was a big African-American: two-thirty pounds, give or take. I wondered if he hadn't spent so much time and money supersizing himself whether he might have taken a ride on the back of Whelt's bike instead of coming here. In which case he'd also have had the opportunity to give us the finger instead of entertaining the flies.

Three

Two AM, 3FC, 4MC and 5AF were under the shade tents Gomez and I had seen when we first arrived: they were the victims near the Learjet and the old Aussie trainer. Milling around the area were more than a half-dozen law enforcement officers, a mixture of CSI, medical examiners, and homicide, the latter distinguished from the rest by the word INVESTIGATOR printed on the backs of their coveralls. One of these, a tall sallow guy, had the words LIEUTENANT on his back to avoid confusion.

"What do I get if I guess which one's Lieutenant Cruz?" Gomez asked.

"A banana smoothie," I replied.

Liz, our tour guide, caught Cruz's eye and he came on over. "You pass that information about 5AF to the Chief Deputy?" he asked her.

"Yes, sir."

He gave a long sigh of frustration. "I'm sure hoping we get a match on the perp's DNA, 'cause so far we got dick."

Given the alleged source of that DNA, the detective's choice of words was a long way from sensitive, but then I'm the last person who should throw stones.

"We sure could use a break," he continued.

"Sir," said Liz, "Ranger Gomez and Special Agent Cooper here wanted a word with you."

"Federal," he said, instantly on his guard, scowling at me, thinking I therefore had to be FBI.

"OSI," Gomez informed him.

The Lieutenant visibly relaxed – OSI, unlike the Bureau, not being in the takeover business.

"We were in the area when we got a call," Gomez continued. "One of Agent Cooper's deserters turned up here."

"Yeah, that's 1AM," he said, "outside the terminal building."

"You got no idea what happened here?" I asked, "Other than a bunch of murderers arrived by aircraft and went through the place hunting down folks and killing them?"

Lieutenant Cruz flipped his sunglasses on top of his head and squinted at me. "That's some interesting speculation you got there, Agent ... er ..."

"Cooper."

"Mind telling me what inspires it?"

"Which part?"

"How they arrived."

"That's what folks do at airports, Lieutenant. They fly in and they fly out."

"They could've bussed in."

Yeah, and they could've arrived on a herd of dromedaries.

"Look, I know that the killers flying in makes sense. And we have made formal requests for assistance to the FAA and air traffic control at El Paso International. I'm just trying to keep the options open here. We don't know anything for sure yet."

Fair enough, but I doubted ATC at the main airport would be able to help. Air traffic control was once my gig back in my Combat Controller days – jumping in behind enemy lines with Special Forces, laying beacons and other nav aids for

fighters and bombers. So I was aware that even a cheap on-
board GPS had the precision to get an aircraft in and around
civilian airspace. A half decent pilot could land a plane just
about anywhere these days without tripping any alarms or the
suspicions of local ATC, but I said nothing about that. The
detective would find it out for himself soon enough, if he did
his job.

I gazed at the blankets covering the children and parents
murdered there on the ramp. The heat was accelerating the
leaking of body fluids, the smell beginning to rise off the asphalt. Forensics was working hard to document the crime
scene and get the deceased refrigerated.

"Lieutenant, we're gonna need some closure here. Your
DOA 1AM was trafficking drugs," said Gomez. "So head
office wants us to stick around."

"Head office" meant Austin – Texas Ranger central. No one
argued with Rangers. The business with Whelt and Sponson
was my first case with Gomez. He didn't ask permission, he
took it. I liked that. We were gonna work out just fine.

"Just clear it with the boss," he said.

"Sure," Gomez replied.

"So victim 5AF. Why was she singled out for special treatment?" I wondered aloud.

"Her name was Gail Sorwick, married to Barney Sorwick."
He pointed at one of the blankets. "That's him there – 2AM.
From the photos in her purse she had two young children –
Ryan and Clare." His finger moved on, pointing them out on
the ground. "The whole family, murdered. The kids were five
and seven years of age. Mrs Sorwick was a looker. After she was
sexually assaulted, she was shot and subsequently mutilated."

Lieutenant Cruz stepped over to one of the blankets and
lifted a corner. The dead woman was naked from the waist
up. Her face was clear and placid and, yes, he was right about
Gail Sorwick being a looker. "She fought back."

The woman had bitten her attacker, drawn blood, cut him down to size.

"She's lucky that they didn't mutilate her while she still breathed," Cruz mumbled, leaning over her, talking to himself.

A police K-9, a big German shepherd, was barking incessantly at something out toward the runway. I looked over in that direction. Nothing.

"Her killer wanted to make a statement," said Gomez. "Send a message."

Cruz looked at him.

"Why go to so much effort to murder everyone in the area, being careful not to leave any evidence behind," Gomez continued, "and then lace a mutilated corpse with your jism. It's a message. Doesn't make a lot of sense otherwise."

I had to agree, it didn't. "What's the message?" I asked him.

"Add it to the list of questions."

Lieutenant Cruz nodded. "Well, we're rushing to check the DNA profile against our records. But I doubt we'll get a hit."

I nodded, the lieutenant's turn to get some agreement.

The dog was still barking, at ghosts apparently. A black Labrador had joined the chorus, straining at the leash, its handler getting curious.

"What about your sole survivor?" Gomez continued.

"The Learjet pilot? Still in a coma. We're not expecting him to come around."

"Where's the other pilot?" I asked.

The sheriff's investigator looked at me, licked his sunburned lips and swallowed. "What other pilot?"

"A Lear usually flies with two."

"We, ah ..." Cruz massaged his chin and put a hand on his hip. "Hey, Belle!" he called out. "You found anyone else with an FAA commercial ticket in their wallet?"

Belle, a middle-aged, prematurely gray-haired woman with glasses and lines like trenches through her cheeks, glanced up from her discussion with a crime scene investigator and shook her head. "Nope, just the one."

The lieutenant turned briefly toward the dogs, distracted by the racket they were making, then turned back. "You said it *usually* flies with two? So it can also fly with one, right? Maybe on this flight, there was only the one pilot."

"Maybe," I agreed without commitment because maybe the killers had abducted the other pilot; or maybe the missing pilot had something to do with the slaughter at Horizon Airport; or maybe the Sheriff's office just hadn't found him/her yet.

Those dogs were making a hell of a noise. There was something out there in the desert. Their handlers had given in and were walking them over to an opening in the fence, going to investigate nothing. The desert was as empty as my bank account.

I moved toward the edge of the ramp, away from the tents and the bodies, my hand shielding my eyes from the glare of the sun. Sand, rock and low scrub – nothing else out there. The end of the runway shimmered in quicksilver. A couple of birds circled the desert a hundred or so yards away. *Nope, nothing.* I turned away just as a mound of sand appeared to move beneath those birds. I looked back, but I couldn't place the movement.

"You saw something," said Gomez coming up behind me, squinting into the distance, also shading his eyes. "Me, too."

Whatever it was, it moved again.

"There!" he said, pointing.

We both started to run toward it. At first I wasn't sure what it was, but then it flopped over onto its back. Jesus, it was human.

Four

It was also a woman. Gomez and I were first to reach her. She was filthy, dehydrated, exposed skin burned red by the desert sun. She was barely alive. From the angle of one of her legs I could see that it was badly broken. Gomez began cutting away the pant leg with a small buck knife. A stick of bone appeared. It was covered in coagulated blood. Shredded muscle, dirt and ants erupted from a weeping red crater midway between her knee and ankle. I had no idea where she'd crawled on her hands and knees from, but it had to be a reasonable distance given her state. She was clearly in a lot of pain, drifting in and out of consciousness.

"The buzzards ... the buzzards," she said, head rolling from side to side like she was having a nightmare, her tongue thick in her mouth. "Black buzzards ..."

"Did she just say black buzzards?" Gomez asked.

"Yeah." I had a small bottle of water in my pocket. Taking off my shirt, I poured water on it and wiped the dirt off her face before drizzling some more water on her tongue and cracked lips.

Lieutenant Cruz arrived, panting, and pulled Gomez and me away from her. "Give us some room."

The room we gave up allowed a couple of crime scene investigators to swoop down on her. They undid her shirt, examined her quickly for other damage while she looked at them wild-eyed. Behind us, an ambulance came bumping across the desert, taking the shortest route, red lights flashing.

"Black buzzards!" she cried out. "No!"

The ambulance pulled up, the medics jumped out and raced to her side. The CSI backed off and let them through.

"Looks like her lucky day," I said.

Gomez nodded. "Had a few of those yourself I see."

He was frowning at my bare skin, my back puckered where bullets had entered, the scar tissue ragged where they'd exited. A swirl of burned skin here, a knife cut there, mementos from various cases gone by. I put my shirt back on, feeling self-conscious.

"So what happened to you?" he asked.

"Life."

"What about your partners?"

The question made me think of Anna Masters and mostly, unless reminded, I was successful at locking any thoughts of her away in a private vault. And I wanted the door to remain firmly bolted shut. She'd been my former partner in all the roles that counted, killed not so long ago. And no matter what the forensics report said, it was my stupidity that had pulled the trigger and blown a hole in her chest. So much for not thinking about her ... History showed that most of the people around me seemed to come off second best, which was why I preferred to work solo, though that wasn't always possible. Like now. "Do you really want to know?" I asked him.

Gomez thought about it. "You just answered the question."

The medics lifted the woman onto the gurney and then hoisted it into the back of the ambulance. One of them climbed in with her. The doors closed and the remaining guy ran around to the front and jumped in behind the wheel.

"Who is she?" Gomez wondered as the ambulance moved off.

"The missing piece, maybe," I said.

Cruz came over with a wallet – the woman's. He pulled a credit card-like ID from the wallet. "Well, well – FAA license. Your second pilot."

Gomez looked sideways at me.

I shrugged.

"Wanna go double or nothing?" he asked.

"Hit me."

"What are those buzzards?"

"Birds," I said. "Black ones ..."

He shook his head.

"I know, you wonder how I do it ..."

There was a slight change for the better in the mood, but it wasn't my banter that had done the trick. We'd found a *survivor*. Life had triumphed. I almost felt light-hearted.

"Hey, Lieutenant. Where you taking her?" I asked.

He was speaking on his cell with his back to me. Holding the phone against his chest he replied over his shoulder, "Thomason Hospital. And we're gonna give her an armed guard."

"We're coming along. Got some questions for her," Gomez told him.

"You'll have to stand in line."

"We're cutting in," I said.

The lieutenant nodded, world-weary-style. "Jesus, you Feds are all alike."

*

"She's exhausted, in shock and she's on a morphine drip," said Doctor Monroe, a thin black woman with heavily lidded eyes and the look of terminal tiredness about her. "I don't know how much sense you'll get out of her. Keep it as brief as possible."

Gomez, Cruz, Matheson, Foote and I all ignored that.

The doctor checked left and right and came in a little closer, something on her mind. Dropping her voice, she said, "Is it true what they're saying on TV?"

"What are they saying?" Chief Foote asked her.

"There's been a massacre. They're saying it might be Mexicans – from across the border. Is that true?"

"We're not in the rumor business, Doctor," said Foote, deftly palming off the question.

I moved to the patient's bed. I'd already learned, with as much digging as the intervening hour would permit, that the Learjet pilot's name was Roberta E. Macey of Venice Beach. She was forty-four, married to a civil engineer and had three kids, two of whom had left home. She was the senior pilot at California Executive Jet and a US Marine KC-130 aerial tanker driver before that. I also knew that, having survived at least five hours under the sun with no water or shelter and the temperature for most of it hovering around 110 degrees Fahrenheit, all while enduring a compound fracture of her tibia and fibula, she was no cream puff.

Monroe loitered.

The Chief glared at her. "If you don't mind, doctor," she said, "Police business."

The doctor returned a look as if she'd just been told she had unseemly body odor. "Five minutes, no more," the women said, her nose a little in the air. "I'll be just outside."

With a glass against the door.

Macey was propped up in bed, the veins in her wrists attached by lines to various bags held aloft from a stand. A monitor with a sensor clipped to her index finger beeped away quietly to one side. She appeared to be asleep, though she was frowning. Her face had been cleaned up but it was badly sunburned and there was a deep gash across a cheek now covered by a gauze bandage. Anti-bacterial wash gave her an all-over orange pallor. Her broken leg was in a temporary cast and raised above the bed, held there in a sling suspended from an overhead pole.

"Ms Macey?" said the Chief Deputy, leaning over the bed. "Roberta?"

The patient groaned, swallowed drily and opened her eyes. She appeared a little disoriented, unsure of the surroundings and the people in her face.

"Ms Macey, we're the police. We'd like to ask you a few questions."

"What happened?" she asked dreamily.

"We were hoping you'd be able to tell us," said Foote.

"You might let her in on what we know," I suggested. "Give her some context. Might help." And might not. Being told what had happened could just as easily push her over the edge, if she was close to it.

"There was some kind of a raid on the airport this morning," said Cruz. "A lot of people have been killed."

Macey closed her eyes slowly and then reopened them. "I heard it. The gunfire. Like Iraq." She closed her eyes again briefly. "Who?"

"We don't know," said Foote. "Do you remember anything?"

Gomez chipped in. "When we found you, you said something about black buzzards."

"I said that? Don't remember. They were King Airs; painted black. Two of them. Looked like buzzards. Maybe that's what I meant. They came in low from the south – real low – avoiding radar." Macey again swallowed with some difficulty, her lips cracked, swollen, burned. Foote took the glass of water with a straw in it off the breakfast tray pushed back against the wall. She held the straw to Macey's lips and the patient took a few sips, after which her head fell exhausted back onto the pillows. "I heard the shooting," she repeated, tears growing in the corners of her eyes.

Foote rested a hand on her shoulder. "Did you see anyone?"

"No. Heard the gunfire and started running."

"Away from it?" Matheson asked.

"Toward it."

I was pretty sure I knew which direction Matheson would've headed.

"What were you doing way out there?" Cruz asked.

"Had some time before the charter arrived. Went for a walk ... wanted to look at the stars." Macey scowled, a sudden thought occurring to her. "Gartner, Rick Gartner. Is he ... ?"

"He's alive," said Foote.

He was, yes, at least technically. But I agreed with the Chief's half-truth. Knowing your partner's dead – or close to it – doesn't help all that much when you're alive and kicking, relatively speaking, and aren't sure if you have the right to be.

"We were going to Disneyland, taking a young family."

Macey must have read something in Chief Foote's face. "Did they kill the family?"

"The Sorwicks?" said Foote.

Macey nodded.

"Yes, they did."

The pilot's forehead became a brace of deep, parallel lines. Her eyes closed and the lines disappeared and she appeared to drift off to sleep. But then she said, as if from a rapidly increasing distance, "How many people did they kill?"

"'They' – you keep saying 'they'," Cruz said. "Who's they?" The lieutenant was hoping to coax something more from the only potential witness we had, but the Learjet pilot was snuggled up to the poppy.

"Ms Macey?" Foote prompted. She gave the pilot's shoulder a gentle shake, but got nothing in return.

Doc Monroe arrived. She opened the door to the room and held it open, leaning against it, her body language saying, "Okay, everyone out."

Foote, Matheson and Cruz held an impromptu meeting in the hospital parking lot, Gomez and I spectating.

"We're going to have to go public," said Foote.

"I agree," Matheson agreed, happy to let the Chief Deputy take the lead now, and any career bullets later.

"I think we should wait until we have some idea about who did this and why," said Cruz.

"You heard the doctor, Carlos," Foote reminded him. "There are rumors. If we don't fill the vacuum someone else will. It's already a media circus." She put a hand to her forehead and smoothed the hair back from her temples. "Look, more than anything, we need to make some progress. If you've got any ideas, Matt, let's hear 'em. We need to claw something back here, and fast."

Matt Matheson? Even the guy's name lacked imagination. I felt sorry for the Chief. She was doing her best, but it was like watching someone attempting to start a car with a dead battery on a cold morning.

Matheson stroked his chin, said nothing, no current in the wires.

"So what do we know?" Foote asked, looking at everyone in turn, including Gomez and me. "An unknown number of assailants flew in to Horizon Airport before dawn this morning, and killed everyone they could find. Only two people are known to have survived. Automatic and semi-automatic weapons were used ..."

"We've collected DNA evidence and we're talking to the FAA about identifying the aircraft," said Cruz.

"That's something – a start," said Foote. "What else? Anyone got any theories? Right about now, I'll listen to *anything*."

Crickets.

I had a question. "Why two aircraft?"

The corners of Foote's mouth sank like they were supported by quicksand.

"The attack wasn't random," Gomez said. "Lieutenant, you said you thought it was carefully planned and executed. I agree."

Cruz nodded, grateful for the support.

"And for some reason the plan called for *two* aircraft."

Gomez looked at me. "How many passengers can you put in a King Air?"

I'd worked with several variants in the past. "Depends on the configuration," I replied. "Ten or more?"

"Lieutenant, you got an estimate of how many killers you believe were running around the airport?"

I sensed that Gomez had maybe sniffed something out.

Cruz held his forehead in his fingertips and massaged it. "Nothing definitive, no, but given the area, the number of deaths, the spread of the casings and the variations in striations on them – best guess so far is up to maybe fifteen."

"Around fifteen people arriving in relative comfort, split between two aircraft ... Why not twenty or more killers, fill the planes up with them and do the job in half the time with twice the numbers?"

"Maybe all the assailants were squeezed into one plane," I said, headed to the same place Gomez was going. "Because there was something else in the other aircraft."

Gomez scratched his chin. "This is about drugs. The hit squad in one aircraft came along to ensure there were no witnesses to the cargo brought in on the other."

No one had anything to say. The air was tense, all of us testing the theory internally, looking for holes. That is with the possible exception of Matheson, who was maybe thinking about what music he was gonna put on for the evening's floor class.

"Would've been a big load," said Foote, climbing on board.

"Does El Paso still get a lot of drugs coming across the border?" Gomez asked.

"Yes, but nothing like Laredo."

"Didn't you make a big bust here not so long ago? A thirty-million-dollar haul?"

Foote, Matheson and Cruz all nodded.

"Maybe this time, whoever made this shipment – maybe they wanted the delivery assured," I said.

"Jesus," said Foote.

Gomez turned to me. "What's the cargo payload of a King Air?"

I was paid to know these things. I took a guess at it. "Over a ton."

"They land, the hit squad deplanes, disburses, kills all possible witnesses to the offload and flies away."

"What do they offload into?" Foote asked.

"A truck, or perhaps several vehicles," Cruz suggested. "Y'know, split up the load. One or two get caught but the others sneak through. Your standard decoy run."

"That makes sense," said Foote.

"We got evidence that any of this is anything other than guesswork?" asked Matheson.

"*Educated* guesswork," Cruz corrected him.

I wondered whether Matheson might need the word educated spelled out. "What's a thousand kees of cocaine worth on the street?" I asked. "A hundred million?"

"In these parts, somewhere around one hundred and thirty million dollars," said Foote. "Lieutenant?"

Cruz nodded, backing her up.

"So where's it gone?" I asked. "El Paso?"

Foote replied. "No, the market here's too small."

"Five hours after it's landed and transferred," Matheson added, "those vehicles are gonna be halfway to Dallas."

"Why Dallas?"

"Biggest distribution point in north Texas for drugs coming up from this part of Mexico," said Gomez. "Anything major heads to Dallas for dispersal – it's a transport hub for the rest of the country."

"We been to a conference hosted by the DEA 'bout it," Matheson added. "You can hide in Dallas, but you can't hide in El Paso."

The way he said it, sucking something from between his teeth, made it sound like El Paso wasn't an option for drug dealers, not when ol' Commander Matheson was on the job.

"What time did the sun rise this morning?" Gomez inquired.

"Six twenty-one," Cruz answered. "According to our survivor, the killers were gone by then. That was roughly six hours ago. So if you're right, the shipment will be more than halfway to Dallas, but not too much more."

Gomez was pulling out his cell. "If they're on I-20, they'll have come through Odessa. Maybe we can stop 'em this side of Abilene. But they also could've taken the long way round, I-10 through San Antonio," he said, thinking it through on the go. "DPS can cover both routes."

Foote acknowledged the help and also fired up her cell, as did Matheson who turned his back on us, I assumed to play a level or two of Angry Birds in private. Cruz consulted his notes. I twiddled my thumbs.

Gomez finished his call as a cab drove slowly up to the hospital entrance drop-off. Our transport had arrived. All twiddled out, I gestured to the Chief that the Ranger and I were leaving. Foote excused herself to whoever was on the other end of the line and pressed the cell against her chest. "Thanks for your help. You both staying in town?"

I told her that we were. She asked for our cards and told us she'd be in touch.

A few minutes later we were in the cab, heading for our motel, an old-style two-star cinder block sandwiched between the highway access road and the railroad tracks, complete with stained carpet and walls no thicker than the beige-colored wallpaper covering them. I needed to take a shower, or maybe a dip in the outdoor swimming pool.

"You gonna report in?" Gomez asked when we got out of the cab.

"Yeah, gimme forty minutes."

"I'll call Thrifty, break the good news to 'em and pick us up another jeep."

I took that shower, the outdoor pool being a little bigger than a bathtub, but then I thought that maybe I'd made the wrong choice when the drain beneath my feet in the shower recess exhaled something that made me think of what was rising off the asphalt out at Horizon. I gave the cold tap a few extra turns but the water pressure couldn't wash away thoughts of the slaughtered family left on the ramp, or any of the many other victims unfortunate enough to be early starters out there, murdered so that some rich college kid in LA, Frisco, New York or wherever could get his hands on a gram of blow and maybe get lucky at a party with some drug slut in the john. I wasn't a fan of Class A drugs, and I didn't care too much either for the people who thought taking them did no harm. The sight I caught of Gail Sorwick when a corner of the blanket lifted was going to stay with me for some time. What a way to go, to see your children and your husband gunned down in front of your eyes while the killer made you swallow his poison. She'd tried to balance the account with her incisors, but it was a final small act of defiance. The animal killed her and then mutilated her. If I ever got my hands on the fuck who did that, I made a silent promise to Gail Sorwick that I would make him pay.

I eventually got out, toweled off and dressed – dark-blue T-shirt, jeans and all-terrain boots. My cell rang, the tone telling me that I'd missed a call. The screen informed me that it was Arlen, so I rang him back.

"Vin, how was it?"

"Heavy."

"I know. It's all over the news. Turn on your TV."

"It's locked on the porn channel," I said.

"So you'll be staying in tonight?"

"I've never seen anything like this down here."

"I know," he said. "The networks have all got their birds in the sky. Tweets leaked the story after some of the relatives were informed. The Mexicans are being blamed. Some think it's the violence from Juárez spilling across the border. It's virtually a failed state over there. Could be a gang called the *Barrio Azteca* involved in some payback, or maybe the *Los Zetas*. There are a dozen theories floating around. No one's sure, but everyone's guessing. The FBI is gonna get involved."

"So we can all relax then," I quipped.

"And maybe the CIA."

"Cancel all relaxation."

"No one likes where this is headed; gonna bring all the vigilante crazies out of the woodwork looking for revenge. I just heard a couple of Mexican-Americans were shot at a Texaco up in Seattle. The word 'payback time' was spray-painted on the wall behind them. The last thing anyone wants is open season on US citizens who don't have blue eyes. Do you know what happened? Other than what's playing on CNN?"

I gave him a rundown up to the point where Macey made her late entrance, followed by the subsequent deductions in the hospital parking lot.

"Drugs will bring in the DEA," Arlen said, more to himself. "And you've got a witness?"

"I'd call her a survivor. It's the Lear pilot. She saw two black King Airs arrive, heard the shooting, and then saw the aircraft depart. Didn't witness much else. She was out walking the desert, star-gazing."

"Too bad."

"Yeah." It was, though if Macey had been close enough to see anything else it would've been the last thing she saw.

"What about the other Lear pilot? What's his name ... ?"

I heard paper being shuffled: Arlen had briefing notes.

"Rick Gartner," I said. "As far as I know the guy's still in a coma. No one's taking odds on him snapping out of it."

"Well, if you hear anything come of those roadblocks ..."

"I'll let you know," I promised.

"What about our deserters?" Arlen asked once the bigger picture had been dealt with.

"I'd say Angus Whelt is checking into a suite in Cancún by now. And, as you know, Sponson's lining up with twenty-six others at the medical examiner's table. We'll have to pick him up from the country coroner's office when they're done."

"I'll make the arrangements."

"What do you want me to do?" I asked. I couldn't chase Whelt south of the river. As for what was happening at Horizon Airport, being federal and limited to the affairs of the Air Force, OSI had no jurisdiction in what was a local, civilian investigation. Those facts put me right out of the picture.

"I'll see you back here tomorrow."

"Here" was Andrews AFB, in DC. I said goodbye and tossed the cell on the bed, exchanging it for the TV remote. I turned on the set bolted to a caged bracket on the wall and up came the picture of two women working on each other furiously with all the affection of a couple of carpenters hand sanding a cabinet. I changed channels and got a flicker of black before the picture returned to the two women rubbing each other raw. Forty minutes were about up anyway. I turned the thing off. Maybe Gomez and I could find someplace around here where we could get seriously tanked.

Five

Gomez was drunk. That made two of us. The Ranger waved a shot of tequila around in front of his shiny face.

"An Arab, a Frenchman, an American and a Mexican are ridin' down the Interstate," he said. "The Arab picks up an AK-47, shoots some rounds and then throws the gun out the window. The American asks him why he did that and the Arab says, 'We got so many of these where I come from, I don't care what happens to it.' Next, the Frenchman picks up a bottle of wine, drinks a little and then throws it out the window. The American asks him why he did that and the Frenchman says, 'We got so much wine in my country, I don't care what happens to it.' Then it's the American's turn: he picks up the Mexican and throws him out the window."

Gomez laughed and it *was* funny and it was *his* joke and there *was* plenty of Mexican in him; so what was I gonna say? You can't tell jokes like that?

A couple of other Hispanics in the bar fixed him with expressions that gave away nothing.

"That's a good one," he continued a little too loud, raising his shot glass and toasting it.

Gomez was smart, he could laugh at himself and he knew how to drink to excess. His performance review was certainly shaping up nicely.

"Next one: Why doesn't Mexico have an Olympic Team?" he asked, believing he was on a roll. "Because anyone in Mexico who can jump or swim is in the United States. Heh heh heh ..." He waved at a Mexican-looking character seated down the far end of the bar who gave him no reaction whatsoever. "Your turn, Cooper," he said.

"Okay ..." I said, checking the immediate area. Gomez was the center of attention and, given that no one else in the place was smiling, I figured the natives probably weren't all that happy about the roast.

"I'm waiting ..."

I had to think and there was a lot of tequila getting in the way of that. Something popped into my head. "Okay – two nuns. They're riding down the back streets of Rome. One says to the other, 'I haven't come this way before.' The other nun says, 'It's the cobblestones ...'"

Gomez stared into the middle distance, processing the joke and failing to get it. But then a grin spread across his face, his eyes disappearing behind slits. "Ya got me – I was waiting for the racial epithet," he said.

"I'm slurring religion today. Open season on nuns."

"Jesus, Cooper. Gimme one fuckin' good Mexican joke, for Chrissakes."

I looked at him.

"*Give* it to me. I can take it," he insisted.

I sighed. How far was I supposed to push this? "Okay ... Why are there no Mexicans on *Star Trek*?"

"I dunno. Why?"

"Because Mexicans don't work in the future, either."

He frowned at me, which made me think that maybe I had, in fact, nudged it over the edge. I didn't know Gomez that well. "Hey," I told him. "You asked for it."

At which point he broke into a grin. "Gotcha," he said. "Hell, this shit don' worry me. There are *millions* of illegals in America. *I'm* American and I don' like that as much as any other American."

"This doesn't get under your skin?"

"Could be worse."

"You could be a gay Mexican-Irishman," I said.

He sniggered. "Look, the jokes are funny because there's a grain of truth in 'em. And they hurt for the exact same reason. There's a poor country next to a rich one; what do people reckon is gonna happen? And when you add drugs to the picture ..." He tossed back one shot and then another and followed it with a suck on a lemon, which made him pull a face like he just sucked on a lemon. "Ughh – I hate this shit. Gives me the shakes. Can we switch to bourbon now?"

I raised my eyebrows at the barman, pointed at a quart of Jack among the bottles lined up on the shelf in front of the mirror beside him and waved two fingers at the bar in front of us.

The drinks sorted out, I asked Gomez, "How long you been here? Your family ..."

"My father immigrated in 1941, after Pearl. He joined up the day they gave him citizenship and he fought on the beaches of Normandy. His youngest brother, my uncle, fought in Nam. I'm just following the leader 'cause I'm not smart enough to pull the rug out from under Warren Buffett. What about you, Cooper? What's your story?"

I shook my head. "Nope, got no Mexican in my family tree."

"Shit, Cooper ..."

Gomez's cell rang, distracting him. He picked it up off the bar, looked at the number. He didn't recognize it but shrugged and answered anyway.

"Gomez," he said, followed by, "Uh-huh, uh-huh, yeah. Okay, thanks." He ended the call and put the phone down. "The Sheriff's Office." He reached for the shot of bourbon in front of him and threw it back. "The road blocks on 10 and 20. They got nothing."

The TV monitors scattered around the bar were tuned to the local news, which had spent the best part of the day re-hashing what the Sheriff's Office chose to divulge about the events out at Horizon. From what I could see through my tequila goggles, it wasn't much – just the bare facts: there'd been a massacre; 27 people shot and killed; no suspects taken into custody. And that was the burr in the shoe right there. Where was the guy who'd run amok with a semi-auto before turning it on himself, the way these things usually went? There were suspicions that persons from across the border had perpetrated the crime, which wasn't being denied in the TV news report. Just as I was thinking this, Matheson's red face and curly blond locks bounced in front of the cameras. He began deflecting the only two questions anyone cared about: who did this, and why.

I gestured at the bartender and he hit us again.

"You still agree with the drug delivery theory?" Gomez asked, throwing back the shot.

"Senseless otherwise."

"Still think it was ..." He waved his shot glass around. "You know ..."

I didn't know. I looked at him. He was swaying.

"Think I have to go," he said, belching wetly, sliding off his stool like something made of rubber and wiping his mouth with the back of his hand.

I followed, finding my feet with some difficulty and only after I realized they were at the end of my legs where they usually were.

"Floor's moving," Gomez said, leaning to one side while we both fished around in our pockets for cash to leave on the bar. "I need one more for the road." He slapped a wad of ones and fives on the counter.

"Shhure," I slurred, adding to the pile and signaling the bartender.

"No, no. Not a drink, a joke. C'mon, hit me. A Mexican joke. I'm religious. No more poking fun at nuns." He grinned at his own drunkenness and then stumbled toward the door buried in darkness below a couple of faintly illuminated exit signs.

"Two Mexicans in a car," I said, the bourbon coming back up and scalding my throat. "Who's driving?" I pushed open the door, noise from the highway hitting us and causing me to stumble a little.

"Dunno. Who?"

"A cop," I said.

Gomez cackled. "Heh heh heh … That's one of mine." His eyes slid off my face, the grin fading. "Going back to the motel to throw up in private. You?"

The thought of lying down on the sidewalk and closing my eyes was overwhelmingly appealing; but then just as I was considering what to use as a pillow, a cab pulled up beside us.

*

I woke, head pulsing like it was expanding and contracting, bladder brimming with cold acid, tongue thick and dry. I stumbled out of bed, made it to the toilet and leaned against the wall with an outstretched hand, a warmth spreading through my groin as I stood there, head back, letting go into the bowl. "God," I said aloud to no one in particular and for no reason other than acknowledgment of the simple heavenly relief of taking a piss.

Next stop, the sink. I washed my hands and face and drank four glasses of water, stripped off my shorts and took a shower. It was only then that I looked at my watch: 4 AM. I stood under the steaming jet, waited for the pounding in my head to become bearable as the nightmare images from Horizon Airport once again began to play across my mind. From there, I moved to the hospital and then out into the hospital parking lot. Largely because of Gomez and me, the resources of Texas law enforcement had been uselessly diverted to stretches of highway over four hundred miles away. Had we missed something? Or had we just read the signs wrong? Or was this about something other than drugs? El Paso sat on the Mexican border and yet somewhere I'd seen a sign proclaiming that it was "the safest city in America". How had it managed to pull that off with Juárez, the second-most violent city in the world, sitting literally a stone's throw across the dry ditch grandly known as the Rio Grande? For sure El Paso would have its share of stash houses full of drugs, cash and weapons, its cartel-paid stooges, Mexican-Americans acting as hit men, go-betweens, drug smugglers and fixers operating on both sides of the fence. Maybe what had happened out at Horizon was just a new phase in El Paso law enforcement's corner of the war on drugs.

I belched tequila with a bourbon chaser. Fifteen minutes had passed under the shower and I was no closer to any kind of revelation. I was, however, more or less sober. I turned off the hot tap and wound on the cold.

A short while later, I threw on my standard non-uniform uniform – a navy polo shirt, khaki chinos, low-cut walking boots, followed by an ankle safe holding a pair of Smith & Wesson cuffs. The Sig came aboard next, but not before a run through the usual checks ensuring a full 13-round mag with one in the pipe, ready to fire. The Sig Sauer 228 was the standard OSI issue. It was a heavy weapon – far heavier than a Glock, say – but it felt good in the hand. I slid the weapon into the Raven concealment holster clipped to my belt in the region of the small of my back, made sure the shirt wasn't hooked up on it, and checked the weapon's positioning. I used a left-hand holster, but located the pistol so that I could reach around, like I might be getting my wallet from my back pocket, and draw it right-handed.

I took a cab ride in darkness out to Horizon. The driver sat on the other side of a Plexiglas shield, which kept the questions to a minimum, like why I was going to the site of the massacre. He dropped me at the airport's access road where a black and white was parked. I got out and walked. A flashlight came on and a female deputy approached. She was compact and round-shouldered with a large head and no neck to speak of and reminded me of a clothed basketball, but the image may have been prompted by the name on her chest – Wilson. She was young, maybe twenty. A light was on inside the vehicle and another young deputy was occupying the passenger seat, head tilted back like he was inspecting the lining. I heard snoring. This was the graveyard shift, so probably these were the SO's youngest, rawest deputies, paying their dues.

"I'm sorry, sir, but this facility is closed," Deputy Wilson said.

I handed over my credentials. "Much going on?"

"What's your business here, Agent Cooper?" she replied, examining the ID under the flashlight and ignoring the pleasantries like she was the one who was hung-over.

"I'm already on your clipboard, Deputy."

She went to the cruiser, retrieved it from the roof and rolled on back, flipping through a couple of pages as she walked. "Here you are ... OSI, working with the Rangers. Why so early, Mr Cooper?"

"I left something lying around here yesterday."

"Oh, what did you leave? Someone might've handed it in ..."

"My common sense. You find one with a few holes in it, it's mine."

The deputy turned the Maglite in my general direction. I gave her a smile. "I can't put that down, sir ..."

"I'm just walking the crime scene, Deputy. Having a second look. We lost a man here."

"We?"

"The Air Force."

"Well, I suppose that's all right. But stay out of the taped-off areas. Forensics hasn't finished yet. It'll start getting busy again here around first light. That's in …" she checked her watch, "… 45 minutes from now." She handed back my badge wallet. "Any theories about what went down here, sir, other than it was drug related?"

I shook my head and told her I had nothing. I hadn't changed my mind about the special delivery, but I was equally sure that something important had been missed, or maybe misinterpreted. I doubted forensics had overlooked anything, but I have found through the years that going over old ground can sometimes help, or at least didn't hurt. I told the deputy to have a nice day and she told me she'd keep an eye out for that thing of mine with holes in it.

It was a few minutes after five and there was no hint of the coming dawn as I headed for the ramp. The area itself was dark but I could still make out the pale shapes of the shade tents hovering like ghosts over the places where the victims had had their photos taken. A low chain separated the access road from the tarmac. I stepped over it and kept walking toward the runway. The cool desert air was still and quiet. I tried to imagine the airport as Bobbie Macey might have seen it before all hell broke loose here almost exactly 24 hours earlier. This small, cozy family facility didn't have a tower or even a permanently lit runway. Macey and her co-pilot had split up prior to the flight for some reason, Macey going for a stroll out to the end of the runway, while Rick Gartner – the man in the coma – had stayed close to the Learjet.

I walked west, toward the airport's few buildings. Sometime before first light, the two King Airs had arrived from the south at low altitude, flying nap-of-the-earth to avoid radar detection. Once on the ground they'd taxied to the ramp where their passengers had dispersed to kill everything that moved. It made sense to me that the shooting had started once the invaders were spread throughout the facility. Having reconnoitered what they were up against, they'd probably then just worked their way back to their aircraft on the ramp, taking care of business as they moved.

I crossed one of the few roads in the facility. Nothing to my left but black empty desert, lit with the occasional insufficient light. To my right was a row of Quonset huts. One of them had a shade tent set up out front, indicating a DOA. From this angle I could see some kind of vehicle in the hut, something classic that reminded me of my own car, a Pontiac Parisienne. This was a long way from the runway. Whoever hit this place was very thorough about it. I kept walking, kept mulling everything over. There was a chance that the bad guys had flown in prior to the assault and cased the joint. If so, there was a chance the aircraft registrations would be recorded either digitally or in a log or ledger. Equally likely, they could've driven here and had a look-see. In that instance there'd be no record – nothing.

I found myself in a paddock of sand, and stopped. The morning was utterly silent, nothing to disturb the high-pitched whine of tinnitus in my head, the legacy of too many explosions and a long period of incessant calling from my ex-wife's lawyers. Though it was still relatively cool, a single droplet of sweat trickled down my temple and the Sig felt clammy in the small of my back. I flopped my shirt back and forth to get some ventilation going. Still no sign of the coming dawn except that the stars had vanished, frightened off by the coming white-hot furnace just below the horizon.

Coming into view in front of me were the unlit shapes of semi-trailers. Recalling the overhead photo of Horizon and the placement of bodies, there weren't any victims indicated among them, but I was here now so I pushed on.

Down the back of the facility it looked less like an airport and more like a boneyard for old long-haulers. At least thirty trailers were lined up in rows while others were parked at random angles. In another fenced-off area beyond, an unimpressive sign announced that this was the headquarters of the National Truck & Transport Company.

I went up to a couple of trailers and slipped between two refrigerator units, the air in the confined space smelling of grease and brake dust. Nature was calling so I took a leak on a tire, second for the morning, and allowed my mind to drift. The killers had swept through the area while the cargo was offloaded. They murdered everyone in the area to make sure there were no witnesses. Keeping the assumptions going, I imagined the perps also wouldn't have been happy for the type of transport vehicles they used to be common knowledge. Or the time the vehicle or vehicles had departed to be known. But were there other cards the killers were keeping close to their chests?

I zipped.

The assumption that sent the DPS off to Abilene on I-20 was the one that the perps were driving their cargo to Dallas. No doubt, DPS had also covered I-10. I kept moving between the trailers. And then it hit me. Maybe there was another reason. Maybe possible witnesses were killed not just to keep them from informing authorities about the transfer of drugs to vehicles that could be identified, but that the transport vehicle or vehicles *had never left the airport at all*. And what triggered this sudden revelation? The fact that I had just come around the end of a trailer to find myself face to face with two young guys dressed in oversized gangsta chic, bandanas on their heads and jeans belted tight halfway down the backs of their legs. They were twenty years old, maybe less, and were the image of Mexican gangbangers. And the other dead giveaway to this epiphany of mine? Heckler & Koch MP-5 submachine guns hung off their shoulders.

The three of us looked at each other for what seemed like a full minute, but was probably closer to a second or two. They knew who they were. And they knew I knew who they were. They reached for their MP-5s and I went for the Sig. My fingers found its handgrip and I pulled the weapon clear as my legs got themselves pumping. I moved to the left, putting one shooter in the way of the other while allowing me to fire with my right arm extended.

One of the men panicked and began firing his weapon in my general direction, before it was properly aimed, half a dozen rounds drilling into the dirt maybe ten feet behind and beside me. The other man, the one who was obscured, was trying to untangle his weapon, which seemed to have been caught up somehow in the deep open scallops of his tank top. I got off two shots as I ran. One of these rounds smacked the guy wrestling with his weapon in the cheek. I knew that from the way a hand went to his face, and from the way he fell to his knees and discharged his weapon straight into his buddy. I couldn't see the specific damage but I knew it was fatal by the way the second guy fell.

And the need for me to run ended, just like that. I went into a crouch. My heart was now competing with my breathing to give the tinnitus a run for its money. The survivor was on his knees beside his dead pal. Keeping low and my Sig aimed, I moved in and kicked their weapons clear. I pushed the man holding his face headfirst down into the dirt, planted my knee firmly in his back, and pulled one of his hands behind him and reached for my cuffs. A loud noise distracted me. Looking up, I scanned the area. It was a trailer twenty yards away. One door had banged open. The second door was following, swinging wide. Two dark shadows jumped down from the trailer. I heard them whispering hoarsely in Spanish to each other. I holstered the Sig. The guy beneath my knee – I snapped Smith & Wessons on his wrists.

One of the shadows had a flashlight, which also meant they probably had lights on inside their trailer. That suggested there was a good chance their night vision was shot. And if that was the case, it meant I would have an advantage for a small period of time. The guy face down in the dirt started groaning, the pain making itself known. Time to move. I crawled over to the MP-5s in the dirt, took one, dropped the magazine out of the other and shoved it in a pocket. I then ran at a low crouch toward a group of three trailers parked on the far side of the area.

"Aemellio! Crisanto! Aemellio … !"

It was the shadows calling. The gunshots had made them nervous and they ran back and forth, sweeping the area with their flashlight, searching for their pals, both of whom were immobilized, one permanently. The deputies on the front gate would have heard the gunshots along with anyone else in the vicinity. And pretty quickly this truck stop would be crawling with law enforcement.

The flashlight beam eventually found what they were looking for. The shadows raced up to their buddies, shouting and swearing in Spanish and English. Meanwhile, I came around the other side of the lot behind them and headed for the trailer they'd been occupying, the doors of which were wide open. I reached the trailer without being spotted, the shadows preoccupied. Inside, I could dimly make out chairs, bedrolls, food packaging and water containers. There were also boxes stacked to the roof. I didn't have to wonder too hard about what might be in them.

The Sig was suddenly ripped from the holster in the small of my back. Shit, so much for the preoccupation.

"Hey, you gringo fuck. You gonna die for this. Shoot you with your own stupid gun."

The guy's breath smelled of Cheerios, beer and cigarettes.

"Drop it," he said, referring to the MP-5. I set it on the ground with one hand, the other raised a little above my head. In the space between the two trailers, I saw a couple of patrol cars come power sliding from out behind the airport buildings two hundred yards down range, their rooftop LED lights firing rapid staccato flashes of red and blue into the night. The lead vehicle hit its high beams, washing the truck stop with a blaze of blue-white light. Whoever was driving knew where to come. The cavalry was on its way. All I had to do was survive another dozen seconds or so, which maybe wasn't gonna to be so easy.

"*¡Chingao!*" snapped the guy who wasn't pushing the Sig into my kidneys. "*¡Dispara al cerdo!*"

I had enough Spanish to translate his suggestion that the pig – me – needed to be shot. Any subtext, I missed it.

But then, perhaps glimpsing the reality of their predicament, his pal hissed in English: "No! We go' need his pig ass!"

The guy with the gun was considering a hostage situation, using my life as a bargaining chip, negotiate for their freedom. I could almost hear the gears turning. How else were they going to get away? But after the violence done here at Horizon, I didn't like their chances – or mine – of coming out of that negotiation alive. Pretty soon there'd be a lot of angry lead flying around and not all of it would be carefully aimed. So I pushed back against the Sig, which only made the guy reciprocate with a push of his own, digging it hard into my flesh.

"They're gonna kill you after what you did here," I said.

"We're American just like you, *chocha*. We have rights," snarled the jerk, the one who smelled like he poured Budweiser over his breakfast cereal.

"You're gonna die here, fool," I whispered. "And maybe sooner than you think."

"Kill him," hissed the asshole who wasn't holding my Sig.

"Yeah, you know what? Fuck you, *cerdo!*" sneered the guy who was.

He forced the weapon into my back harder, just the way I wanted it. And then the trigger was pulled. I heard the hammer smack the stops as the shockwave of metal hitting metal snapped through the barrel, leaped the thin polo-shirt barrier and bit into my skin. But there was no blast, no bullet ripping through my kidneys.

There was nothing at all. And I knew why.

The guy holding the Sig was momentarily confused, which maybe gave me a couple of seconds before he pulled the trigger again. I turned and grabbed the gun with my right hand. As I spun, lifting the weapon and twisting it hard in a clockwise direction, his index finger became trapped inside the trigger guard. Bones snapped like fresh carrots as I kept the turn going. The man had to bend forward to take the pressure off his rotating hand and arm. But his pal had no such inconvenience. He raised the MP-5, brought its ugly short barrel up. So I whipped the Sig around, squeezed the shattered finger against the trigger and this time the weapon fired, as I knew it would, the round hitting the man just below the sternum. It seemed to happen in slo-mo. As he died his muscles contracted, squeezing the trigger of the MP-5 in his hand. The submachine gun discharged, and a short subsonic burst of lead ripped into his buddy's thigh and groin. I felt the impact of the absorbed rounds jumping through the man's hand and into my own as he screamed.

The Sheriff's cruisers skidded to a halt in the gravel behind me and the doors flew open.

"DROP THE WEAPON!" a man shouted.

This time I wasn't going to argue. I twisted the Sig and felt the weight come off it as the man fell away to the ground and kept up with his screaming.

"On your knees!" the shouting continued. "Hands where I can see 'em!"

He meant mine, so I put my hands behind my head, interlocked my fingers and got down on my knees, like I've made folks do a hundred times. He didn't know that I was one of the good guys, and opening my mouth now in this highly charged situation might get me shot.

The deputies felt confident enough to approach, and rushed at me with their weapons raised, one either side of me.

"I know this guy," said a woman.

I recognized the voice. It was Deputy Basketball.

"He's OSI," she said.

"What the fuck's that?" replied the guy who seemed in some kind of command.

"OSI – United States Air Force," I answered.

"Shut the fuck up," he said. "Who asked you?"

"I'm gonna get my ID," I replied. "It's in my back pocket."

"You ain't gonna do shit. Don't fuckin' move. Not a fuckin' muscle."

I heard more voices through the radio in one of the Sheriff's vehicles.

"What are you doing?" the boss behind me wanted to know.

"Calling this in, sir," came the reply.

BRRRAAT!

Automatic fire.

I turned in time to see the deputy in the car lose the side of his head and slump sideways out of the car, toppling onto the dirt. The shooter was the guy giving the orders, a Sheriff's deputy. He had one of the MP-5s, and he was bringing it round, looking for more targets. He found one.

BRRRAT!

Deputy Wilson's mouth was open. I watched her fall down dead, one of her eyes a black hole.

BRRAT! BRRAT!

The weapon discharged a couple more times, but I didn't see who wore the rounds as, at that moment, I was diving between the wheels of the trailer. I crawled forward as fast as I could, my hands, knees and feet kicking up the dust. What the fuck was going on? I asked myself. I didn't need to think too hard about that to come up with an answer. In the trailer above me was over a hundred million dollars' worth of reasons.

I scrambled out from under the chassis and crossed beneath another one beside it, went forward and crossed again, putting as much distance and metal as possible between me, the killer and his Heckler & Koch.

A flashlight beam swept beneath the trailers. "You can't hide forever, asshole," the rogue deputy called out. "Gonna be just you and me out here for another ten minutes at least."

A burst of automatic fire exploded and a spray of jacketed rounds rattled and pinged off heavy metalwork somewhere nearby. The deputy was firing randomly, spraying the shadows beneath the trailers, hoping for a low percentage shot to take care of business.

"You a cop killer, Mr OSI!" he shouted into the night. "Ought'a be ashamed of yourself. They gonna hunt you down, gonna kill you right back for what you done here."

I crawled out from under the trailer and rolled beneath its neighbor as another burst of machinegun fire shredded the quiet. The flashlight beam played beneath the trailers was reaching out for me, its thrust blunted in a brown halo of dust. I sat with my back to a tire and caught my breath, each exhalation a hoarse wheeze, my throat constricted and raw, coated by the same fine dust diffusing the flashlight beam. I coughed to clear my throat, spat on the ground and sat there for a minute, listening, the noise of my thumping heart obscuring almost everything. I looked down at my hands and saw the Sig cradled in my left. I couldn't think when I'd had the opportunity to grab it. I'd been lucky, the weapon's weird design foible saving my life. I pushed my palm against the end of the barrel, which shifted the slide back. Doing that had the effect of putting some distance between the hammer and the round's primer cap, preventing detonation. By jamming the weapon hard into my ribs, the shithead had handed me a chance. I love the Sig.

A burst of fire. This one was close. Lead slammed into the tire close to my feet. The flashlight beam snapped on, bathing me in light. I'd been found. Dust kicked up all around me, the rounds sparked against steel chassis members and buzzed like angry insects as they ricocheted, leaving trails in the suspended dust lit up by the flashlight. Down on my back, I fired wildly at the ball of light between my boots – three, four, five shots. My eyes closed on those last couple, blinded by the dust. The beam went out suddenly, a man screamed and the shooting stopped. The threats also came to an abrupt halt. Had I killed the guy? I worked my way backward on my elbows until I felt the security of a wheel and tire behind me, the pumping of my own blood roaring in my ears.

I dropped the magazine and counted. Eight rounds fired, six remaining.

Noise crackled through the police radio. The sound was close by, closer than I thought. "Officer down! Officer down!" the deputy yelled breathlessly. There was stress in his voice. He was wounded. Badly, I hoped. I pictured him with the mike at his mouth, slumped in the cruiser's open door, leaking blood from a mortal wound, talking with a last breath over the dead bodies collected around him. "Horizon Airport, near the trucking company," he gasped. "Suspect is a white Caucasian male, thirties, fair complexion, over six foot, two-thirty pounds, wearing chinos and a navy shirt. Suspect has departed the scene and is armed and dangerous.

Approach with extreme caution. Repeat, approach with extreme caution."

In other words, if you see this guy, shoot first and maybe get around to asking questions at his funeral.

The dispatcher garbled something unclear.

"You're fucking dead, motherfucker!" the deputy yelled out, stronger than he'd sounded talking to the dispatcher.

A police siren. It was distant but approaching, the volume of the sound building. Time was running out. I glanced around the side of the tire at my back. Open ground and fresh air lay beyond. I crawled out of the shadow, got up and ran, the desert beneath my feet now a grey monotone in the dim awakening of first light.

Six

Joe Battle Boulevard ran from right to left directly in front of me across a mile or so of flat desert given over to various tire and auto graveyards. Butting up against the other side of that raised boulevard was a desert of the light-industrial variety. If I could just make it across the road and hide out in those concrete canyons, I had a chance of avoiding capture, assuming my ass wasn't nailed walking around out in the open in what was fast becoming broad daylight. First order of business, I killed my cell before anyone with half a brain got the idea that I could be located by tracking its position.

Streaming along the highway, hurrying to the Horizon Airport turnoff, was a constant parade of black and whites, El Paso Police Department blue and whites, and ambulances, all of which were operating under a Code Three – lights flashing and sirens screaming. Any trust I might have had in the El Paso Sheriff's Office would soon be carted off to the morgue in the back of those ambulances. I figured that the shootout could be pinned on me without too much trouble, mostly because the deceased had all been holed by an MP-5, and just my luck it would be the weapon I'd handled. If so, my prints would be all over it. And, of course, I'd shot and wounded the deputy with my own service weapon. If it came to a courtroom showdown, it would end up being my word against his – the real killer's. And while I might make a case about having no motive for those slayings, a convincing fairy tale would no doubt be constructed to give me one. And in the meantime, if I happened to get myself shot dead because I was armed and dangerous and should be approached with extreme caution, the deputy's word would never be called into question. In short, surrendering to local law enforcement was not on the table.

It took an hour to walk at a slow crouch across the desert and reach the boulevard, but I made it and managed to slip safely into those concrete canyons. In the shadow of a dumpster behind a Pfizer warehouse, I turned on my cell long enough to collect messages. Showing on the screen was a notice that several SMS messages had been received, but the only one I was interested in had come from Arlen Wayne. "Call me. Now!" it said, but I had to wait till a phone I wasn't connected to in any way happened along. I smashed the cell on the corner of a step and left it.

*

"Hello?" said Arlen.

"Hey, Arlen, it's Vin," I said turning away from the window as a PD cruiser motored by in the adjacent lane.

"Oh, it's you. Didn't recognize the number."

"Belongs to a guy by the name of … Roberto Munoz." I read the name off the driver's registration card.

"Who's he?"

"I don't know, which made him ideal."

"Whatever. So you wanna tell me what the hell happened down there?"

"Bad news travels fast."

"Ranger Gomez called. The County Sheriff's Office questioned him about you."

"What's the story?"

"That you allegedly ran amok and killed some suspects and cops."

"Deputies."

"There's a difference? Jesus, it sounds like there was a second massacre down there, and the only information we're getting is that you caused it. Tell me it wasn't you."

I told him what he wanted to hear: it wasn't me. Then I went on to outline events as they unfolded, starting with my pre-dawn arrival at the crime scene and concluding with the escape beneath the trailers. "I saw the son of a bitch do two of his fellow deputies," I explained. "And one of the suspects accompanying the drugs was alive when I got outta there, so he killed the guy in cold blood."

"Jesus, Vin ... Wait a sec, the story's just come up on screen." He mumbled something like he was reading, then paraphrased, "Says here over a hundred and thirty million dollars' worth of cocaine was seized after a shootout at El Paso's Horizon Airport in a dawn raid this morning. They believe the murder suspect – you – took several kilos of the contraband."

There it was: the fairy story. "Does it mention whether I go on to live happily ever after?"

"What?"

"The motive's fiction, Arlen."

"It says here four suspects connected with the seizure were killed by you, along with three Sheriff's deputies."

"It's in print so it must be true."

"According to this, you shot the surviving deputy in the shoulder and left him for dead."

"Him I *would* have killed if I'd had the chance. He was trying to kill me like he murdered his chums from the office. Does the report give his name?"

"Says here Deputy Kirk Matheson."

"Richard Simmons' brother?"

"Who … ? Vin, hey, I'm late for a briefing about all this with the DEA and the FBI. Stay low. I'll call you back at ten-thirty. Can you move around?"

"That's what I'm doing."

"Then get to Gomez's room at the hotel."

"That's where I'm going."

"Good."

The line went dead. I told Roberto Munoz thanks and passed his Nokia back to him through the slot in the Plexiglas. We were coming up on the motel, only there was a small problem: an unmarked white police Dodge Charger parked at reception – two heads silhouetted in front with a steel mesh grill caging off the rear seats. "Hey, changed my mind about the motel," I told Roberto. "You can drop me off at the Taco Bell."

The cab driver acknowledged the change in plan by driving past the old Best Western and nosing into the fast-food joint's parking lot. I paid for the ride and the use of his phone and went in to buy some cover.

*

The unmarked was parked so that the motel's reception could be kept under surveillance, along with my room situated conveniently beside it. Gomez's room however, was in the opposite wing behind the Dodge, on the ground floor and almost in the vehicle's blind spot. Had he been allocated the adjacent room closer to the end of the wing, movement to and from it would've been completely obscured by the motel's end wall. So basically, getting to his door was going to be risky and I'd be in an exposed position for maybe half a dozen seconds. But then a couple of motel guests returning from a late breakfast happened by while I was working up the courage to make a break for it. So I buried my face in the burrito, caught up and strolled along beside them, around the wall dividing the motel from the Taco Bell's drive-thru.

A newly washed black Jeep Patriot rental was parked between the lines outside Gomez's room. I went up and knocked on the door. It opened the inch or two allowed by the safety chain, Gomez's face appearing briefly in the dark slit. The door closed, the chain rattled and the crack reappeared, this time wide enough for me to slip through.

"There's a warrant out for your arrest," the Ranger said.

"What are you gonna do about it?" I asked.

"Make some coffee. How do you take it?"

I relaxed. "Black, no sugar."

The jug had already boiled the water. Gomez took another cup from a cupboard while I went to the window and took a peek out at the surveillance.

"Fill me in," he said.

"Well, a funny thing happened on the way to work," I began. But before I could elaborate, I felt the Sig ripped from the holster in the small of my back. *Jesus, not again …*

"Hands behind your neck, Vin, fingers interlocked. Do not turn around."

I took a deep breath. There was a chance – a good one – that I was about to get a pillow placed against the back of my head, followed by a bullet fired into it. I was almost relieved when Gomez shoved me against the door, cuffed one of my wrists before dragging it down behind my back, then told me to lower my other hand. I complied, mostly because he showed me a Government Model 1911 .45 Auto – a nice weapon, unless you happen to get shot by one. He patted me down, took my wallet and ID.

"Okay," he told me, "turn around."

I turned and found myself staring into the .45's unblinking black eye, my Sig stuffed in his waistband. "Is this you or your hangover speaking?"

"Funny." He wasn't smiling. "Take a seat." He pushed a chair my way with his foot and then transferred the Sig to the back of his pants.

"I'm still alive so I'm thinking this is unnecessary."

"Interesting statement. You wanna explain what it means?"

"Because if you were bent, like I suspect half the cops around here are, you'd have taken the opportunity to park a bullet in my back teeth."

"The walls are thin. Gunshots would draw attention."

No argument there. "So what now?"

"Like I said, there's a warrant issued for your arrest. I'm a Ranger, arresting people is what pays my rent."

"So arrest me."

"What does it look like I'm doing?"

"You gonna read me my rights?"

"I'm waiting for someone."

"Do I have to wait for longer than that coffee you were gonna get me?"

"No coffee, Vin."

My cell didn't ring at ten-thirty when Arlen Wayne said he'd call back. But I wasn't surprised. The DEA liked to talk as much as the CIA so his meeting with the both of them would probably go well into lunch. So, to pass the time, I filled Gomez in on the events of the morning.

"That ain't the version I heard," the Ranger said when I'd finished.

"Which one do you believe?"

"To be honest, Vin, you seem straight up and we worked well together, but I'd trust you more than I do if you were a Ranger. A lot of drugs are moving through this part of the world, and the money that comes with it has rotted out enough of the law enforcement in these parts to matter. None of us knows who to trust. You're not from around here, and that's to your advantage."

I tried to move my cuffed hands. "Some advantage."

He shrugged. "You say the deputy killed all those people this morning. The warrant says different. It's your word against the deputy's."

I should be a courtroom strategist. "Wouldn't you like to know who was in charge of clearing and securing the trailer park?" I asked him. "The drug shipment was just sitting there, guarded by folks who probably took part in yesterday's raid. The whole area should have been thoroughly searched."

"Yeah, you'd think," Gomez agreed. "From memory, there were no DOAs found in that truck yard. Maybe that's the reason it wasn't cleared."

"Shouldn't have made any difference."

"No, it shouldn't."

"Maybe whoever conducted the raid had any bodies moved," I speculated. "Or maybe the people who leased that part of the facility were tipped off."

"I like the way your mind works, Cooper, but you're still not going anywhere."

A soft tapping on the door distracted me.

"Is that who we've been waiting for?" I asked him, my back clammy with sweat.

"Maybe." Gomez stood and went to answer it, keeping the .45's watchful eye on me. There was nothing I could do about who was gonna come through that door. My hands were secured behind my back and Gomez knew what he was doing. I'd waited for some kind of an opening, hoping one would come along, but nothing had presented itself. Ranger training.

"Be cool, Vin," he warned, meaning that he was about to take his focus away from me for a few seconds and that he knew I might try something dumb. Maybe because he already knew from first-hand experience that dumb often seemed my first option. The door opened. My heart rate rose into triple figures, bracing for the next surprise of the day.

"You must be Ranger Gomez," said Arlen Wayne as he breezed in, showing his ID. He shook Gomez's hand, giving it a hearty pump. Moving on, he said, "Hey Vin, how you doin', bud?" He said it like he was excusing himself for being a little late for racquetball.

"You got here fast," I said.

"They briefed me on the plane."

Spotting the S&Ws on my wrists seemed to confuse him. He glanced at Gomez, looking for an explanation.

"You told me to detain him." Gomez shrugged.

"Yeah, but cuffs?"

"You didn't say make him a nice brunch and put on sports."

"Jesus, Arlen. This is *your* suggestion … ?" I complained.

"Nice work, Ranger," said another familiar face coming in behind Arlen. "Best not to take any chances." A preppy Tommy Hilfiger face beneath perfect JFK-style hair … If I remembered correctly, the last time we saw each other the mouth in that familiar face promised "to fucking get me". I noted he walked with a limp from an injury, I was pleased to say, that he blamed me for.

"Berkley Chambers," I said. "How unpleasant to see you again."

"See? Already it starts," the man complained in mocking fashion to no one in particular.

"Got something in your shoe, pal?" I asked him. "Looks to me like you're walking kinda funny."

The upturned corners of his lips headed south.

"Vin, I see you remember CIA Crime and Narcotics Deputy Chief *Bradley Chalmers*," said Arlen, stressing the asshole's correct name and title.

"What's *he* doing here?"

"We'll get to that," he said, and then introduced Chalmers – whom I knew as the philandering former deputy Assistant Chief of the CIA's Tokyo station – to Gomez.

When I'd crossed paths with Chalmers a couple years back he was the CIA's point man in an attempt to stymie the investigation into the bombing of the Transamerica Pyramid building in San Francisco. The ploy to throw the inquiry was part of an elaborate CIA scheme to recover stolen biotechnology, which it intended to resell to generate cash for a secret black ops slush fund. Chalmers' boss was currently doing a long stretch in a federal penitentiary for masterminding it all, but somehow his number two here had dodged the bullet. Basically, I trusted Chalmers as far as I could throw him with my hands S&W-ed behind my back. Speaking of S&Ws, the introductions wrapped up, the three of them just stood looking down on me. "Do you mind?" I asked Gomez, presenting my wrists to him.

"I don't know about anyone else here," said Chalmers, "but this is *sooo* making my day."

Gomez glanced at Arlen, who gave him a nod. The Ranger crouched to unlock them and said, "Don't try to escape, Vin."

To which Arlen added cryptically, "At least not until we tell you to."

"I'm prepared to let bygones be bygones once you return my weapon," I said to Gomez, standing and massaging my wrists.

The Ranger glanced at Arlen who gave the okay, so he removed it from the back of his pants and passed it to me, grip first. The weapon felt a little light.

I gestured at Gomez to give 'em up – he knew what I meant.

Digging into a pocket, he came out with six rounds of 9mm ball ammo in the palm of his hand. I took 'em, fed 'em into the magazine with my thumb, racked one into the chamber, reached around and holstered the weapon. "Now," I said. "Someone care to tell me what the fuck this is all about?"

Seven

"So this warrant for my arrest is genuine?" I asked Arlen after he'd given me the main points.

"Afraid so."

"It's one of those shoot-to-kill warrants, Cooper," said Chalmers, grinning like a simpleton.

I took a seat on the edge of the bed.

Arlen glanced at Chalmers. "Let's get on with it, shall we?"

"What about the Ranger?" the spook asked. "This is a national security issue and he's not ..."

"I ain't going nowhere," said Gomez. "The warrant was issued by DPS, which makes Cooper *my* responsibility. You want me to leave the room, he'll have to be re-cuffed."

"And I'll shoot the first person who tries," I promised. "How about it, Chalmers? Like to give it a go?"

"Let him stay," Arlen said, exasperated. "If you can't trust a Ranger, then we might as well just throw in the towel."

Chalmers didn't like it, but he had little choice. He turned to Gomez. "Nothing you hear in this room leaves this room."

"You're talking to a shadow, pal. I'm not here," he said, sitting on a chair by the front door, resting an ankle on the top of his knee, hands behind his head like he was settling in for a good show.

"Okay, Cooper," Chalmers said, facing me. "What do you know about FARC?"

Ordinarily I'd have smacked something like that into the stands; but, still not sure I wanted to play, I answered by folding my arms.

"I'll take your silence as ignorance," he said.

"Take it any way you like, Buzzby. And if your imagination's not up to it I've got suggestions."

Chalmers looked to Arlen as if I'd just said something that proved his point.

"Can we just get on with it?" Arlen said, exasperated.

The spook took an iPad out of his brief case, muttering to himself, tapped in a code and propped the device on the bench over the bar fridge. Photos taken with long lenses appeared on screen. They showed a series of armed men and women who were mostly under the age of twenty-five, dressed in jungle-pattern combat gear, berets on their heads and ammo bandoliers across their chests. They were mostly *mestizo* faces wearing serious-business-to-attend-to expressions.

"FARC, the Revolutionary Armed Forces of Colombia. The Marxist–Leninist militia claims to represent Colombia's rural poor in its struggle against wealthy landowners and industrialists. In reality, though, it's a guerilla organization made up of thugs and murderers, prepared to sell their services as assassins and mercenaries to Leftist governments in the region. Washington has designated it a terrorist organization."

The display on Chalmers' iPad moved through a voyeuristic parade of gruesome killings.

"A few years ago, FARC was all but wiped out, chased from Colombia by successive government crackdowns that began with the victory against drug lords Pablo Escobar, José Gonzalo Rodríguez Gacha, Carlos Lehder, and the demise of the Medellín Cartel. Today, while restricted to the Ecuadorian jungle bordering Colombia to the east, the mountainous jungles and forests on the Panamanian border in the north and the ismuth known as the Darién Gap, FARC has found a new reason for being. It's now Colombia's biggest reseller of cocaine and marijuana. And its primary customers are the Mexican drug cartels – the Beltran-Leyva, the Sinaloa Cartel, the Chihuahua Cartel, the Gulf Cartel, the Tijuana Cartel, the Juárez Cartel, Los Zetas, La Familia and so on. We –"

I interrupted: "And all this is somehow relevant to me because … ?"

"There's something big going on," said Chalmers. "And that's why the CIA has been called in."

"Golly gee willikers," I said. 'The CIA?'

"Are you *sure* this jerk's the right man for the job?" Chalmers pleaded.

"There's no one righter," Arlen replied.

"Righter for what?" I asked.

"You're a cop killer, Cooper," Chalmers sneered. "And where you're going, credentials don't come any better than that. Now, can I get on with this?"

Credentials? Where you're going? I had a sudden feeling that being cuffed by Gomez and put into the care of the Texas Department of Public Safety might not be such a bad option after all.

Chalmers squeezed his remote at the iPad and continued the show-and-tell. "The war on drugs launched by former Mexican President Felipe Calderón in '06 has claimed more than seventy thousand lives to date. That number is greater than all US combat fatalities in the Vietnam War. Mass graves are continually being discovered, children are being used as hit men, beheadings and dismemberings are commonplace. Just across the Rio Grande, kidnappings, murders, maimings and revenge killings are being committed on a daily basis, and in pretty much all population centers big and small. Americans of Mexican descent are being targeted by the cartels and used to commit a range of violent crimes on both sides of the border. Within Mexico, whole police forces have either capitulated or been wiped out; entire units of the Mexican Army have deserted to the cartels ..."

I yawned.

"Keeping you awake, Cooper?" Chalmers snapped.

Aside from the fact that none of this was news to me, I *had* been up since 4 am. And pretty much from the moment I opened my eyes I'd been assaulted, chased, shot at, framed, hunted or cuffed. "It's been a long day and the real shitty part is – it's barely half over," I said.

"Then why don't I just go and ask room service parked in the Charger outside if they'll go get you a pillow?"

"Can we get to the meat?" Arlen suggested to Chalmers.

I wasn't sure I appreciated that allusion.

The spook took his annoyance out on the remote and stabbed it at the iPad. One file closed, another opened.

"A few weeks ago, El Paso CBP and DEA agents intercepted a shipment of cocaine worth around thirty million dollars."

The screen illustrated Chalmers' narration with some shots of the raid itself, mostly agents slicing open bags of chicken shit to reveal the packages of cocaine within, tightly wrapped in clear plastic with warehouse batch numbers clearly visible.

More old news. I stifled another yawn.

"Forensic analysis confirmed that the cocaine was Colombian and Ecuadorian, and the chicken manure Mexican," Chalmers continued. "Unconfirmed HUMINT on the ground in Panama has traced the shipment back to this man, Juan de Jesús del Los Apostles de Medellín, alias Juan Apostles, alias the Saint, alias the Saint of Medellín, alias Jesús de Medellín."

The pictures fading in and out on screen showed various photos of a tall, lean, fit-looking guy who looked forty but was probably older, with a full head of swept-back, layered salt and pepper hair, tan skin and a playboy smile. A Latino Don Johnson. All he needed was a pastel-pink suit. If the accessories in the photos were any indication, Jesus of Medellín enjoyed the company of Ferraris, Polo ponies and twins – brunettes, mostly.

"Apostles came from a wealthy Medellín family," Chalmers continued. "He was educated at Oxford University, England, where he earned honors in economics and business. On returning home he walked into the family fortune, which was made in construction. Within a year, that fortune had disappeared."

"Did you say honors?" I asked.

"A lot of that fortune went to FARC. My friends at MI6 say that, while at Oxford, the Saint was involved in several underground Marxist–Leninist organizations."

"I don't believe it," I said.

"Don't believe what?" asked Chalmers, warily.

"Forget it." I doubted that Chalmers had friends but I wanted to know where this was going and where I fitted into it more than I wanted to wind him up some more, so I asked: "How does a garage full of Ferraris fit with the whole Marxist–Leninist thing?"

"At last, a reasonable question," Chalmers said, his voice dripping with condescension. "The Saint is a man of contradictions. He donates money to various orphanages in Mexico and Colombia on the one hand while he kills mothers and fathers and fills the orphanages on the other. In this regard, he's following in Escobar's footsteps. He's also a practicing Catholic who's been married three times and divorced three times. His first wife was Miss Venezuela. She came in second in the 1988 Miss Universe pageant." He fumbled with the remote and found a picture of the woman – tall, bikinied, blond and centerfold material. "We don't have photos of his other wives."

"Does Miss Venezuela have a twin?" I asked.

"How is that even relevant, Cooper?"

"Move it along," I suggested.

"Late in 2006," the spook continued, "at the start of the crackdown on the Colombian cartels, Juan Apostles disappeared for a while before turning up in Mexico, working for the Gulf cartel, where he came into contact with this man."

Various other photos appeared, none of them as nice to look at as the ones of Miss Venezuela. These showed a Mexican male with a shaved head, broad nose, thick neck and small black eyes that could have been plastic buttons stitched onto tan leather. Blue tears tattooed on his face ran from the outside corner of his left eye, the droplets growing bigger as they ran down his cheek so that the tears on his neck were the size of chicken eggs.

"His name is Arturo Perez. He is also known as the Tears of Chihuahua. He deserted from the *Grupo Aeromóvil de Fuerzas Especiales* – Mexican Army Special Forces – and was recruited by the Gulf Cartel in 1999 to join their private army, known as *Los Zetas*, shortly after returning from training at Fort Benning."

"*Our* Fort Benning?" I asked.

"You know of any others?" Chalmers replied.

"What did we train him to do?"

"Locate and apprehend cartel members."

"So he located them and having located them asked them for a job?"

"Seems so," said Arlen.

"Fort Benning and Oxford should hook up. What came first? The nickname or the tattoo?"

"The tattoo is apparently a celebration of his favorite pastime."

"Which is?"

"Pain. His thing is flaying people, mostly while they're still alive. The people who know about this kind of practice say flaying exposes raw nerves resulting in the most excruciating pain there is. It was a popular punishment in the Middle Ages. People would die from heart failure during the process."

Several photos played on the iPad showing a number of deceased, the skin on their thighs, arms or stomachs removed to reveal the raw muscle and fat beneath.

"Shit," I murmured.

"This guy's a prince," said Arlen. "We think Tears of Chihuahua led the attack on Horizon Airport."

A photo of Gail Sorwick appeared. Her eyes were closed and she seemed asleep, except that the bed beneath her was a cold hard stainless-steel autopsy table and the sheet covering her body was plastic. A succession of shots came and went with the sheet progressively pulled back. Eventually, photos showed the deceased's body turned over. Close-ups revealed deep cuts in her skin in the small of her back, beneath her buttocks and down across her hips – long knife cuts in the shape of a square.

"Oh, man," Gomez said under his breath.

"This is why we think it was Perez. Sure looks like his handiwork. The theory goes that he was about to flay her when he was either interrupted or simply ran out of time. Uncharacteristically for Perez, the cuts were made post mortem, hence the lack of blood."

"And – lemme guess – the reason you're not sure it was him is connected somehow to the comment about me having those unbeatable cop-killing credentials."

Arlen nodded. "Vin, if this was in fact a Mexican raid on US soil by a cartel, it represents a dangerous new phase in their strategies. We need intel. We need to know who and we need to know why. Juan Apostles is a Colombian with direct ties to

FARC. The DEA thinks Apostles and Perez are using those ties to forge a super cartel, seamlessly linking supply and distribution. Apostles and Perez have no respect for American law enforcement. If they succeed in their venture, raids like yesterday's might well become commonplace, and that will rapidly escalate into a full-scale border war with Mexico. We need someone on the inside down there. Perez and Apostles are always looking for new recruits and you'd be a special prize. You're an ex-combat controller so you know US airspace procedures, you've had all kinds of Special Forces training and –"

"And after the *El Paso Times* hits the streets tomorrow morning with your picture on the cover and the headline, 'Cop killer wanted, dead or alive', they're the only people in the world who'll want to know you. Gotta ensure your legend's authentic, right?"

I liked Chalmers even less when he had the upper hand.

"You're perfect for the job, Cooper," he continued. "I've spent some time going through your records. You like to kill. You've developed a taste for it. How many people have you put down? Can you count them? Do you see their faces in your sleep?"

"That's enough!" Arlen snapped.

"In all the ways that count," Chalmers continued, "you're really no better than this Perez character."

As much as I feigned disinterest, Chalmers' comments had reached in and twisted something in my gut. He was right. I *had* lost count and, now that he mentioned it, very few of the people I'd planted had faces I could recall, though their shadows haunted my dreams. Sure, every one of them might've deserved it, but I'd appointed myself judge, jury and executioner in most instances and that wasn't how it was supposed to be. "Assuming I succeed in buddying up to these psychos," I said to Arlen, doing my best not to seem affected by Chalmers' comments, "What do you want?"

"If it was Perez who led the raid, we'll need evidence that'll stand up in court. Only then will governments in Mexico and Colombia cooperate with us in capturing him and Apostles and extraditing them to US soil."

"What kind of evidence?"

"DNA. We have blood and semen and other DNA material recovered from the scene. We need a match."

"You want me to pick up a urine sample?"

"Or hair or clothing ..."

"Or a mouthful of cum," Chalmers interrupted, smirking.

I had six rounds in the Sig. And I could get by just as easily on five.

"Not helpful, Chalmers," said Arlen.

"No, but it makes it easier," I said.

My supervisor frowned. "Makes what easier?"

Chalmers had started packing away his gizmos, the grin on his face telling me that he was happy the scoreboard had him ahead on points.

Arlen forgot about my comment and put an envelope and a Spanish phrasebook on the bench, along with a cell phone and charger. "What's your Spanish like?"

"Incomprehensible." I picked up the booklet and flicked through it. There wasn't a section on dealing with cartels, or phrases like, "Can you please help me dismember this?" I tossed it back on the bench. I could understand Spanish. Speaking it was a problem. "What's in the envelope?"

"Your passport along with some cash, mostly in fifties and hundreds, and a couple of thousand in pesos. Keep your phone on so we can track you, and withdraw money from ATMs whenever possible so we can confirm that you and your phone haven't been separated."

"Why don't I just call you?" I said, pocketing the phone and charger.

"You're a fugitive. Let's keep up appearances."

I checked the envelope. "What good will this do me?" I asked, plucking out the passport and giving it a waggle. "I'll be on stop-and-detain lists everywhere."

"The media will get the story as it breaks, but the person who takes care of these things will forget to notify immigration."

"You mean you'll leave it to the CIA," I said with one eye on Chalmers, stuffing the envelope in my pants pocket. "What about ammo? You got cuffs?" I heard the rattle of various objects placed on the bench as I took the three steps to the front door, edged around Gomez, and opened it a couple inches. The EPPD Charger was still out the front, but it had moved – a new shift on duty, perhaps. What I had in mind was going to be tricky unless I could maximize the size of the blind spot.

"Who do I contact, and where?"

"An ex-FBI agent in Panama City, Panama, owns a bar called the Cool Room," said Chalmers, producing a small mug shot of a man in his late fifties. "His name is Panda. Big guy, looks soft but isn't. Panda has his own network of informants. He'll be able to tell you where and when you're mostly likely to find Apostles. He keeps homes in Medellín, Bogotá, Mexico City, Juárez, Buenos Aires and several other cities around the world. Lately, our information is that he's mostly commuting between Medellín and Juárez setting up his empire."

"Keep your cell phone charged up and switched on, just in case," said Arlen.

It sounded to me like this operation was barely thought out, and that the only part squared away had been nailing me for crimes I had nothing to do with. "So, let me get this straight. As far as local law enforcement is concerned, I'm a wanted killer, a fugitive from the law with a price on my head."

"No bounty as yet, but that's only a matter of time." Chalmers' smirk turned into a private chuckle.

"If things get tight down there, Panda will get you out," said Arlen. "He's also to be your first point of contact. Within a couple weeks, your name will be officially cleared, though if you're still in-country, that will remain secret."

I repeated my comments about the trailer park at Horizon not being properly searched and cleared and that an investigation into why it wasn't might yield results.

"The Sheriff's Office is already onto it," said Chalmers.

"Right. Commander Matheson and his brother, Kirk, will see to it."

"The deputy you shot, Kirk Matheson, is the nephew, not the brother," Chalmers replied.

Brother, nephew – family was family. "So, if we're done … ?" I said.

"We're done," Arlen replied.

I picked up the two full mags for the Sig and a handful of 9mm rounds, which included a couple of blanks. "What are these for?" I asked, examining a casing with the business end pinched together.

"Left over from a training exercise," Arlen said. "Don't want 'em, leave 'em."

I took them on the basis that you never know when something apparently completely useless might come in handy, and also picked up a pair of Smith & Wessons. "Any suggestions about how I might get across the border?" I glanced at Gomez.

"Don't ask me," he said. "I ain't here, though watch out for kids with cell phones."

"Because …"

"Because the cartels use 'em. *Halcones*, they call 'em."

"Falcons," I translated.

"Yeah. They give 'em the phones and a few bucks and tell 'em to call in if they see anything interesting. There are a lot of kids running around with phones over there. It gives the cartels one of the best-informed real-time intelligence systems going. Any gringos coming into Juárez at official crossings, at the moment, are considered interesting."

Chalmers was grinning like the village idiot's idiot brother, enjoying himself altogether far too much. But the smirk disappeared when I slipped the cuffs on one of his wrists, yanked it behind his back and cuffed the other wrist, much like Gomez had done to me.

"What the … ? What are you doing?" he yelped. I jammed him against the common wall with the adjoining room and he shot a plea for help at the Ranger. "Gomez!"

Gomez remained in his chair, raised his hands and reminded him, "Ain't here …"

Arlen, too, stood back.

I patted the spook down, flipped his wallet and keys onto the bed.

"Cooper!"

"Quit complaining. Gotta ensure my legend's authentic, right?" I went back for the gun my fingers detected in an ankle holster. Out came a Taurus stainless-steel .357 revolver, hammerless. "Cute," I said, holding it up. "These things come with a purse, don't they?"

"Fuck you."

I spun him so that he was facing me, grabbed handfuls of his shirt, pulled him toward me and then shoved him backward. As the pace picked up I put my elbows into his chest and pushed him hard into the wall and kept shoving when he hit it. With our combined weight, the sheet rock gave way like it wasn't there and we burst through into the room next door, landing beside a bed in a cloud of dust, shredded wallpaper and wiring.

I jumped to my feet and dragged Chalmers to his, the guy too shaken up to resist. Eyes closed, he gasped for air and then coughed and tried to snort the dust out of his face.

Marching him to the door, I noticed a scrawny middle-aged guy in his underwear and shorts sitting up on the bed with a computer beside him. A rhythmic grunting sound was coming from its speakers. His mouth was open.

"Thin walls," I said. "It's like your neighbors are in the room with you."

His eyes popped open wider, if that was possible, and he snapped the laptop closed.

I pulled the spook across the room and leaned him beside the door.

"Cooper ..." he said a little groggily.

"Just don't blow this, Chalmers," I told him, and flicked a chunk of sheet rock off his shoulder.

He lifted his head. "Fuck you."

"Maybe, if you had nicer legs," I said and opened the door an inch to check on the position of the surveillance vehicle. It hadn't moved. I slipped the chain, opened the door, pulled the Sig from the concealment holster behind my back and jammed the muzzle hard into his ribs so that he flinched. That made the weapon essentially useless, but he couldn't have known it.

"Don't make me use this, Brody. I'm a wanted fugitive."

I pushed him in front of me as we approached the Dodge Charger from a high angle in its four o'clock area – the driver's blind spot. Bending down, there were those two silhouettes in the front. The one in the passenger seat was drinking from a large cup. I ran the last ten feet, pushing Chalmers in front of me. He hit the panel over the rear wheel, jolting the car. Snatching the rear passenger door handle, I pulled up and prayed it wasn't locked. Prayer answered in my favor: the door sprang ajar. I ripped it back and virtually threw Chalmers inside. The two officers jumped in their seats. The guy with the cup flung it upwards and doused himself and his partner with hot coffee, which added to their fright as they swore and twisted this way and that like a couple of cats caught in a shower.

"HEY!" I shouted. "I've got a gun and I'm gonna use it. Follow my instructions and no one gets hurt." They turned around, fear and anger on their faces. I pressed the Sig hard into the side of Chalmers' neck so that they'd believe I meant business. The officer behind the wheel was an older guy with corporal's stripes; his partner, the one with the coffee, was young, a rookie most likely. This was a dangerous game. The longer we sat here, the greater the chance the pendulum could swing back in their favor. We needed to move fast before another cruiser wandered along. But first, some necessary housekeeping. "Show me your firearms!" I shouted at them. "Now!" There was movement in the front seat. "Easy ... easy ..." I told them.

"*You* take it easy, mister, okay?" the corporal insisted. Both officers slowly raised their Glocks where I could see them through the steel mesh divider. Their hands were shaking.

"Throw 'em into the floorboards."

Hesitation.

"Do it! You know I'm the guy you're looking for and you know what I'm capable of." Bringing my inner gangster out for some exercise, I said to the young officer, "Don't do nothin' stupid, junior. What about your backup, the one you keep in an ankle holster?"

More hesitation.

"Keep it moving, people. I don' got all day. Nice and slow. Let's use our left hands." They bent down. "Slowly, slowly," I told them. The corporal's hand came up with a .40 Smith & Wesson. The rookie had a Springfield Armory XD-S .45 ACP Micro-Pistol. "Present from dad?" I asked him.

"How'd you know?" he replied.

"The slide's inscribed, 'Love from Dad.'"

"Oh, yeah ..."

"Into the floorboards," I instructed them.

"Any flick knives, knuckle-dusters, nunchakus? Now's the time to get rid of 'em before I pat you down. I find anything on you, I'm not gonna like it. I might use it on you."

Both men emptied their pockets and tossed a variety of buck knives, brass knuckles and blackjacks into the diminishing space around their feet.

"Where's the shotgun?" I asked.

"In the trunk," said the rookie. "There's an AR-15 back there too."

These guys were packing enough heat to take on a platoon. "Keep your hands where I can see 'em – on the glove box. And you, corporal, put your hands on the wheel and keep 'em there. I don't see your hands, I ventilate Joe Citizen back here. We clear?"

"Take it easy, okay?" he said.

"So you keep saying. Just do what I tell you."

"You all right, sir?" the corporal wanted to know, eyeing Chalmers in the rear-view mirror. This guy was a good cop: even scared half out of his mind, he was still concerned for the hostage's welfare, and maybe also a bit curious about why he was covered in all that white dust.

"Yeah," I said. "Casper the Friendly Ghost here is having a super day. Now keep your eyes out of the mirror or you'll see something you won't like."

As far as these officers were aware, I was fresh from shooting four SO deputies and four witnesses. I was a cold-blooded killer. And now I was in the back seat of *their* company car with a hostage, a loaded gun and a full mag of attitude.

I hadn't closed the rear passenger door behind me. Once it was shut, there was no way to open it from the inside, not without a little modification. I changed my grip on the Sig and smacked the heel of the handle backhanded into the windowpane. The third hit shattered the glass, which became a saggy matt of crystals held in place by tinted film. Slamming the matt with my elbow a couple times finally pushed it out of the framework and onto the sidewalk. That was easier than I thought it would be. Now I could open the door by reaching out and pulling the latch, or, if I had to, slip out through the window NASCAR-style.

Refocusing on the two in front, I couldn't see Junior's hands on the dash. I had only marginal control over the situation and it could turn nasty on me at any stage. "Hands where I can see 'em," I snapped as I pulled the door closed. "Drive. Get to I-10, eastbound. Don't flash your lights, stay off the radio. Stick to the speed limit – no faster, no slower."

Nothing happened.

"*Now!*" I barked. "And don't forget I've got a gun pressed into the ribcage of a hapless, innocent bystander back here."

The officer behind the wheel turned the ignition on, signaled and accelerated into traffic. The ramp to Patriot Freeway was close. He took it, nice and gentle.

"What do you want?" the corporal asked me.

"I want you to stop with the questions. You and the new recruit will be fine, and so will Mr Average here as long as you do what I tell you." Chalmers' tie was askew. I straightened it for him.

The ramp for I-10 came up pretty fast. The officer took it and the cruiser swung to the southeast.

"Where are we going?" Junior asked.

"For a ride. Keep your hands on the dash."

The cruiser accelerated to fifty-five miles per hour and El Paso quickly gave way to desert. I glanced at Chalmers. He was glaring at me, knowing he had to play along with my dangerous little charade, quietly steaming, the upper hand he was enjoying so much no longer his.

The traffic thinned out on the Interstate, the sun a large flaming orange clipping the horizon.

"Where are we going?" the corporal wanted to know again after twenty minutes of highway cruising.

"Quit asking. You'll be home in time for dinner, providing you do what I tell you."

Another twenty minutes and the terrain was looking familiar. A gas station flashed by, a familiar battered Patriot parked in the lot. The turnoff was close. "Slow down," I said. "And keep those hands where I can see 'em."

"How you doin' back there, sir?" the corporal asked.

"I'm okay," said Chalmers. "But this gun he's got in my side is really starting to hurt. I'm gonna have a bruise there for sure."

"Shut up," I said, staying in desperado character. I had to admit, Chalmers was playing the part like a pro. "Now slow down some more," I said. The cruiser slowed to about thirty. "There's a trail coming up on your right. This one. Yeah, here. Pull into it." The Dodge washed off some more speed and turned into the trail as darkness gathered. The corporal turned on the lights. "Don't stop. Keep going straight ahead."

The rookie and the corporal were exchanging glances. They'd cooked something up for sure. Hell, I'd given them enough time to serve a three-course meal. I needed to re-establish control.

KER-BLAM!

I fired the Sig out through the window. The Dodge swerved in the dirt, clipped a bank.

"Shit! Hey! Whadaya doin', for Chrissakes!" yelled the corporal.

"We're nearly at the place where you're gonna drop me off. I just want there to be no doubt in your minds that the weapon I've got trained on my hostage back here is the real deal. I see your hands move off the wheel, or your partner's leave the dash, and the next shot will be tickling some ribs. Maybe yours."

"Okay! Okay! We're just driving!" the corporal yelled. "We weren't gonna try and jump you or nothin'."

Not anymore they weren't. Hands were back where I wanted them, where I could see them.

"We're getting close. Veer off to the left."

The Dodge bumped over the rough dirt road, taking the fork, the corporal wrestling with the wheel, the rookie bracing himself against the dash. Ahead, suddenly, was the barrier fence. But the hole cut out of the mesh … Where was it?

"Why are we here?" the corporal wanted to know, looking left and right. "What are you looking for?"

"Put your headlights on the fence," I told him.

He brought the vehicle around. The high beam picked out a section of mesh that was black instead of the usual all-over rust red.

Shit, yesterday's breach had been efficiently welded back in place.

"Someone seal up your escape hole, loser?" ventured the corporal. "Why don't you just hand over the gun and give yourself up now, and I promise you I won't stomp all over your head when you're in my holding cell."

"Very kind of you," I said. "But some idiot judge is gonna give me a stainless-steel ride to hell for sure. Why don't I just kill you all now, leave your bodies here for the coyotes, take the car and run? Dead men ain't gonna testify, yo." Channeling gangster chic, I was almost enjoying myself.

"Th … there's a gap in the fence," said the rookie, swallowing loudly.

"Shut the fuck up, Roy," the corporal told him.

"You were saying, Roy. Something about a gap in the fence?" I said, nice and pleasant.

Silence.

"Roy?" I cocked the Sig's hammer – there's no mistaking that sound.

"Ten miles down the road, further east," Roy blurted. "The fence just comes to an end. No guards, nothing. You just walk around the end of it and you're in Mexico."

"Roy!" the corporal snapped.

"Do tell. How big's the gap?" I found it hard to believe. What was the point of having a fence at all if there were gaps in it?

"'Bout fourteen miles long?"

"What?"

"Yeah. Friend o' my pappy has a ranch on the border there. Sits on his porch with a cold beer and waits. He got the southern property line bordering Mexico rigged with seismic and motion sensors so he can detect the couriers coming across at night with backpacks full of cocaine and whatever else."

"What's he waiting for?"

"A clean shot. Um, I forgot to mention he sits there with an old M1 Garand equipped with a night scope."

"I said *shut the fuck up!*"

Eight

Around twenty minutes later, by my reckoning we had to be almost there. "How much farther?" There were almost no streetlights out here where the cotton fields bordered the roadway on local Route 20. And pretty much the only traffic was the passing of Border Patrol vehicles every fifteen minutes or so. A sign announcing the town of Fort Hancock slid by. From what I could see, that's all the town consisted of – a sign.

"There's a track coming up on the right soon that'll take us across the irrigation channels," said Roy the Rookie.

"Y'know, all this accommodating you're doing," the corporal told the kid, "it might be considered aiding and abetting."

"Actually," I countered, "by being cooperative while I hold a loaded gun to the head of this extremely average man I have here in the back seat, Roy's just guaranteeing that I let y'all live. So Roy, no doubt there'll be some inquiry about all this. You just make sure you tell 'em how threatening I was and you'll be okay."

"Yessir."

The corporal grunted.

"We're close, now," said Roy. "Slow down ... That's it there." He pointed and the corporal eased on the brakes and turned off the main road.

We drove along the narrow unsealed track crowning the irrigation canals. We cut ninety degrees left and right half a dozen times before coming out onto a broader track that ran along the bank of a dry sandy canal.

"Where does the fence end?" I asked.

"Just coming up on it. Mexico starts the other side of the Rio Grande out the window there." He nodded to his right at a dry, sandy depression.

"*That's* the Rio Grande?" I said.

"Yessir."

"What happened to all the water?"

"Cotton's thirsty."

On the far side of the riverbed, on the Mexican side, lay a network of irrigation channels and, around half a mile beyond it, a large farmhouse commanding several fallow fields, its old whitewashed walls supporting what appeared to be a thatch roof. Nothing moved that I could see.

"Looks peaceful."

"That's because the Sinaloa Cartel has killed all the law enforcement and murdered or run off all the farmers so that they can occupy the farmhouses and use them as staging posts for the drug couriers," the corporal said. "If they catch you, as I'm sure they will, they'll laugh while they rip your arms and legs clean off your torso, and then they'll leave all your bits and pieces scattered on the freeway for the crows and vultures to pick over."

"So what you're saying is that my only option is to turn myself in to you before this goes any further."

"I'm glad you're comin' round to my way of thinking," said the corporal. "No one's been hurt. You've been nice and reasonable. You got no alternative from where I sit."

"And you've got a severe case of goldfish brain. You seem to have forgotten about all those deputies I gunned down at Horizon."

"You okay back there, sir?" the corporal enquired of Chalmers, changing tack.

"He's still breathing, aren't you?" I prodded Chalmers in the ribs with the Sig maybe a little harder than I needed to.

Chalmers bared his teeth and snapped, "You'll get yours, asshole. I'm just praying I get to see it."

"Okay," said Roy. "This is it."

I glanced out the windshield and saw the end of the fence. The rookie was right. No guards, no razor wire, no lights. It just ... ended. I recalled it looking like a freight train. Edge on, it seemed almost flimsy. A single, hopeful camera sat perched on top of the mesh aimed at the fourteen-mile gap that yawned beyond, which was almost funny. Almost.

"Pull up on our side of the fence," I said. "Keep those hands where I can see 'em. You too, Roy." I reached out and had the door unlatched before the Charger had come to a halt. I backed out of the vehicle and kept the weapon trained on Chalmers. "Out of the car," I told the officers, "or the guy in the ten-dollar suit gets it."

"We're gonna hunt you down," the corporal promised me.

"What? Over there?" I asked him, gesturing south. "Sure you are. Now get out." I opened his door. The corporal stumbled onto the dirt and placed his hands behind his head, his face white with rage. "Walk where I can see you, past the front of the car, and keep walking till I tell you to stop." I kept one eye on the rookie. His hands were still welded to the dash. "Your turn next, Roy. You know the drill."

"You're not going to kill us, are you?" he asked.

"You, no." I nodded at Chalmers. "Him, maybe."

The officer carefully took his hands off the dash like it might suddenly all fly apart beneath them, opened his door and got out.

"Follow your supervisor," I said. "Hands behind your head."

When he started to walk, I breathed easier. The setting sun had become a red-hot coal plucked from a forge, smoldering moodily on the horizon. The night to come would be cool.

"Go join your friends," I instructed Chalmers.

"There'll be payback for this, Cooper," he hissed as he shuffled out of the back seat on his butt bones.

"You're taking this way too personal," I said as I helped him to his feet. He shrugged his elbow out of my grasp. "That's far enough!" I called out to the officers and then leaned in and removed the Charger's ignition keys. Ten yards away the officers stopped and turned, hands still behind their heads.

"You really murder all those people?" Roy called out as I approached. It was my first opportunity to get a good look at him, the corporal, too. He was a kid of no more than nineteen with glasses, acne and teeth that reminded me of a beaver's.

"That's what they say," I replied. I walked up to him, removed the cuffs from his belt, then took the corporal's, a jowly man in his mid-fifties with a gut and a flat-top haircut.

"You're gonna regret this, son," he said.

"Maybe," I said. "Gimme the keys."

"In this pocket," the corporal said, motioning with his chin to the pocket on his shirt.

I reached in and took them. I looked at the kid. "Yours?"

"Same, same," he replied.

With their keys in my possession, I removed Arlen's cuffs from Chalmers' wrists, then handed the officers' cuffs back to them.

"Now let's put these on and make a nice daisy chain, shall we?"

I grinned at Chalmers. He ground his teeth back at me.

No one moved so I leveled the Sig at the spook, which won some compliance. "What's your eyesight like?" I asked Roy.

"Long sight's okay," he answered, "now I got these here glasses."

"Good." I lobbed the Dodge's ignition keys and the cuff keys twenty or so yards down range and watched them kick up a puff of dust beside a dry bush. "You got that?" I asked him.

"Think so," he replied.

"Oh yeah, one last thing ... Drop your pants. All of you." Chalmers' lips were as narrow as his eyes when I looked at him and said, "*This* is the personal bit."

Nine

Okay, so it wasn't purely about embarrassing Chalmers, though how was I to know the guy favored pink undershorts with red rockets on them? The main reason for the parting request was that the officers' belts bristled with various items including cans of pepper spray and Tasers. I wanted those things beyond easy reach, and around their ankles seemed easiest.

I jogged back to the cruiser as the three of them cuffed together struggled to work collaboratively to dress themselves. Away to the north, the local road tracking the fence, Route 20, was clear for the moment, but a Border Patrol vehicle would be along presently to help them out. Maybe that's why they seemed in such a hurry to get their clothes back on. A mile and a half beyond 20, traffic streamed steadily along a major road, headlights beginning to penetrate the twilight.

"That I-10 up there?" I asked Roy.

"Yeah."

"It's close."

"The closest it comes to the border for hundreds of miles."

"Opposite the break in the fence. That's convenient."

"For who?" he asked.

"Figure it out, Roy."

I opened the trunk. The shotgun, a Remington 870 pump, was where the corporal said it was, along with the AR-15, the semi-auto version of the M4 carbine. I took the bolt from the rifle and threw it into an irrigation channel, and put the rifle back in its rack. The Remington I used to blast a hole in the radio before jacking out the shells and grinding them into the dirt with my heel. Then I removed the mags from the deputies' Glocks and Colt. 45 in the floorboards, scattered them a distance away, ejected the chambered rounds and gave them the same treatment before tossing the weapons back where I found them. The bullets from the Smith & Wesson followed. I considered taking a knife, or maybe a blackjack, but decided against it. I did, however, souvenir a bottle of water. Bridges now well and truly burned, I jogged down to the riverbed.

"We'll get you, Cooper!" the corporal called after me.

I was thinking he could get me a cold beer because, even though the overhead griller had dropped below the horizon and the temperature would eventually drop, the air was still warm and the sweat was streaming down my face.

As I walked, dried-out cotton stalks crunched underfoot and the kicked-up dust smelled of manure and dirt. The farmhouse beckoned maybe a klick to the south, its solitary light a magnet. I wasn't sure what I'd find there, though hopefully it wouldn't be armed and looking for me. Picking my way across the open ground, the comments Chalmers had made about my killer personality began to echo in my head. Was Chalmers right about that? Was I just a killer, no better than many of the people I killed? Was I no different to this Perez character, for example? Was the fact that Uncle Sam paid my salary the only difference between him and me? The woman I loved, Anna Masters, was also dead because of me, as were a couple of other women I'd met recently. The truth, if I were to be honest about it: I was bad news, plain and simple.

I halted in the middle of the field, taking a moment to put a stop to the self-analysis and assess the situation. All was quiet, except for my own doubts. What the hell was I doing, aside from heading toward more death and destruction? Not much, only I couldn't go back. The shootout at Horizon had taken that option off the table. I could only go forward. Toward the farmhouse.

Hazy mental images of the people I'd killed were replaced by ones of the ghosts who needed me to speak for them. There was Gail Sorwick, flayed post mortem, her killer's semen in her mouth. There were her husband, her two kids and the other twenty-four innocent people at Horizon Airport murdered to cover an incoming load of cocaine. And yeah, even Sponson. The guy had deserved a prison cell. He hadn't deserved to be killed in cold blood. Someone had to have the last word on their account; balance the books for them. Like it or not, that someone would be me, Vin Cooper – unmarried, childless, motherless and fatherless. No ties and no tears. Maybe it wasn't much in the way of balance, but it was *something*, wasn't it? The internal debate was unconvincing, especially as the side looking to justify my presence in Mexico knew that I really didn't have a choice.

I got moving again and took to some night shadows when I came to within a dozen yards of the farmhouse. Its windows were open, but the light had mostly been blocked by black plastic taped over the openings. Dim yellow light leaked from a crack here and there. Music and the low hubbub of people murmuring escaped along with it, carried on the smells of tobacco and pot smoke. I circled around the building. Up close, it was less house and more combined stable, storehouse and garage. The doors were all closed. A beat-up delivery van, an old Toyota Land Cruiser and a newish black Hummer H3 were parked out front. As I was considering whether to break cover and attempt to steal one of them, some double doors were flung open and a big group of men ambled out to the vehicles. A quick headcount set the number at twelve. One of the men moved like the *jefe* or head guy. He was tall and sinewy the way addicts get when they're more interested in a fix than food. He wore a cowboy hat over the greasy ponytail down his back and held a pump-action shotgun in the crook of his arm. His round buddy, who was maybe eating the boss' helpings as well as his own, wore a dirty sweat-stained trucker's cap and carried a large-caliber black revolver in a holster slung low on his thigh. A long knife held in a scabbard kept his other hip company. The eleven men with him appeared unarmed, though it was impossible to be certain about that in the low light. They were, however, all carrying backpacks and the way they carried those packs told me they weren't light. Couriers.

Tubby with the revolver opened the side door in the van and the men with the backpacks piled in, the vehicle sagging low on its axles with the extra weight. When they were all squeezed in, the revolver guy slammed the door shut. He then ran around to the driver's seat, climbed behind the wheel and fired up the vehicle, which spluttered into life like someone had their hands around its neck, choking it. The *jefe* waved his pal goodbye and went back into the shed, the van chugging off and coughing smoke, all lights doused.

I kept an eye on the vehicle till the night threw an invisibility cloak over it. The couriers were heading for the border. Once across Route 20, assuming they managed to slip between the clockwork-like border patrols, it was a short walk to the I-10 where, no doubt, there'd be a rendezvous and the drugs handed over. There was nothing I could do about it. Maybe that friend of Roy's "Pappy" would get lucky. Strangely, I felt a pang of concern for the couriers, maybe because they seemed a different animal to the *hombres* with the guns – poorer, shorter, more compliant. They moved like men who had no choice. Maybe we had something in common.

The music playing inside the barn was part folk, part rock and all Mexican. Someone turned up the volume, which suited me fine. I left the darker shadows for the lighter ones around the vehicles and tried the door to the Toyota. Unlocked. I pulled it open and a wave of old beer, sweat and cigarettes rolled out. The interior light flickered on. The ashtray was stuffed with a mound of butts, and in the floorboards Oreo wrappers, empty potato chip bags and Corona bottles. The Sinaloa Cartel had to be pretty confident that its territory here was nice and secured because the keys were in the ignition. I backed out and went over to the driver's door on the Hummer. It too was unlocked, but no keys in the ignition. Leaning in, I felt around under the dash for the hood release, pulled it and heard a *clunk*. Lifting the hood, a handy light came on. Sparkplug leads beckoned so I grabbed a handful, wrenched them out like weeds and quietly re-latched the hood.

No one came out of the barn to see who was stealing the Toyota when I fired it up. Maybe they were just sitting around in there sucking on Coronas, listening to tunes, pulling bongs and gorging on Double Stuf Oreos and Lays barbecue chips. My foot found the gas pedal, and I crept outta there, keeping the speed to around ten miles per hour till the tires found themselves on something more than a driveway.

The main road I eventually located was dark with only occasional lights, which made me wonder if it was, in fact, a main road. But then a federal Highway number 2 sign flashed by, along with a sign that said fifty kilometers to Juárez. So now I had a car to go with the destination: a bar called the Cool Room down in Panama City, Panama. Exactly how far did I think I'd get in a stolen cartel car? I opened the center console and found a box of twelve-gauge double-aught shotgun shells, the dregs of a packet of nuts, a greasy US ten dollar bill and a screwdriver. I kept the screwdriver and shoved everything else back in the console.

A few miles farther along, the highway bisected a rat hole called Práxedis G. Guerrero. Compact single-story bars, convenience stores and repair shops crowded the roadside, almost all of which were darkened and/or abandoned. I turned into a side street and kept driving till I found what I was looking for, parked and grabbed the screwdriver. A listless dog appeared from nowhere to watch me pull the tags off an old Chevy, but didn't hang around to see me exchange them with the Land Cruiser's. I figured the swap might inject the Toyota with an extra twelve hours of life before either a cop or a cartel road-block stopped me to ask uncomfortable questions.

The drive to Juárez was uneventful and gave me time to go back to thinking about the circumstances that had conspired to maneuver me into this mission. In particular, I thought about Commander Matt Matheson and his nephew, Kirk, the deputy who murdered his work chums at the Horizon Airport truck yard. Were the two men cut from the same cloth? And what about Bradley Chalmers? I didn't like the guy, and I sure as hell didn't trust him. What game was he playing at? What was his angle? There was no doubt in my mind that the weasel would have one. I smiled at the way I left him, pants around his shoes, both cops looking at his ridiculous shorts, the rage on his face amplified by the realization that if he said anything, he'd blow my cover. Now there was a memory to cherish.

*

Juárez began with a long stretch of cheap diners, poles and overhead wires. There wasn't much light to see by, and I figured there probably wasn't much to see anyway, so instead

I drove around hunting for a place to hide out for the rest of the night.

I woke just on sunrise, laid out on the Toyota's bucket seat with my knees pointed at the roof lining like an astronaut on the launch pad. I'd been dreaming that I was in El Paso with an earthquake shaking the road. My eyes opened at pretty much the same time as the Land Cruiser jolted an inch or so vertically skywards. My fingers reacted, digging into the seat upholstery. Maybe the earthquake was no dream. But then, just outside, I heard someone dredging up phlegm from around their toenails, which altered my suspicions somewhat.

Sitting up, I saw three kids in the process of jacking up the back of the car in order to pilfer the wheels. I cracked open the door, which initially gave them a fright. But then the Artful Dodger, their leader – a kid with oversized jeans, white Nikes the size of loaves of bread on his feet and a purple tank top with the number 93 on it – began shouting at me and spitting on the car, creating a diversion so that the other two could recover their hardware, the jack. I opened the door wider and they all immediately took off, running across a vast expanse of gray concrete servicing a rundown mall, hurling the Spanish equivalent of four-letter words behind them as they ran.

I stifled a yawn and closed the door.

The parking lot had been a broad black void of darkness when I arrived during the night. And it wasn't that much more inspiring now that the soon-to-rise sun was throwing some light around the place. The lot was an empty wasteland around the size of four football fields. Several other abandoned vehicles dotted the area like turds dropped by mechanical giants. Directly in front of my parking spot was a Mickey D's, a Sears towering behind it. As I watched, feeling sorry for my aching back, two vehicles pulled in off the main road and slotted themselves between the faded parking lines closest to the restaurant's entrance. The drivers, a short square man and a woman of similar proportions, both wearing McDonald's uniforms, got out of their cars and shuffled toward the Golden Ass sign lit up out front. The man squashed his face up against the glass to see who was inside, but he needn't have bothered as he was the first to arrive. He unlocked the door and held it open for the woman behind him.

I was hungry, but I figured it would probably take them half an hour or so to warm up the machines, or whatever they did before opening to the public. But then a new Ford Taurus turned up, a guy in a gray business suit got out and went inside, and my stomach growled. "What are you waiting for?" I told myself.

The air inside the restaurant was cool and smelled of sugar and cleaning solvents. The businessman had already placed his order and was walking back to a table. I approached the short square guy behind the counter. A badge on his shirt said *Gerente* – manager.

"*Buenos días,*" he said, raising his eyebrow at me, which I understood to mean "what can I get you?"

I replied with a *buenos días* of my own and ordered a *huevo y salchicha* burrito by pointing at the overhead picture with egg and sausage in it, and a *café negro*.

He said, "*Sí.*"

I said, "*Gracias.*" Easy. Who needs a phrasebook? I paid and loitered, waiting for the order to be filled. But before heading off to see to it, Señor Gerente aimed a remote at a TV monitor installed for the restaurant's customers and it came to life with an ad for shampoo. It began with a woman flicking her hair around. Then she smiled seductively at the male mannequin now inside her personal space. There appeared to be more on her mind than split ends and dandruff, but her male companion looked about as feminine as she did so good luck with that, I thought.

I was distracted from this doomed mating ritual by the arrival on my tray of a burrito and coffee. I hustled the tray back to a table and sat, the guy in the suit seated roughly opposite.

On the TV behind me the ads ended and the news began. I took a large bite out of the burrito and, while I chewed, watched absently as the businessman produced a newspaper from his briefcase. He checked the front page first, which gave me a look at Sports on the back. The main story featured a guy by the name of *El Bruto*, a *lucha libra* wrestler in a black latex mask with long pointed silver teeth drawn where his mouth would be and angry silver brows over silver-outlined eyes. He looked fierce and pissed about something. I wondered what the face was doing beneath the mask, other than sweating. In the photo, *El Bruto* was dressed in a business suit, suggesting that he never took his disguise off. Did he take a shower in it? I took another bite of the burrito and pondered my next move, a drive to the airport and a flight south to Panama.

I lifted my eyes from the burrito and found myself staring at a face I recognized staring right back at me on the front cover of the *El Diario* newspaper, the businessman having turned the paper round to check out the exploits of the Brut. It took around a second before I realized that the staring face was mine. Maybe the delay was unfamiliar context. Maybe it was the fact that I was smiling, not something I do all that much – smile for the birdie. But this was the photo snapped a number of years ago on the occasion I made captain, back in the day when I believed taking on more responsibility was worth faking a smile for. Apparently, just as Arlen and Chalmers had planned, the news about what I'd supposedly done at Horizon Airport was out.

I turned to check on whether the guy at the counter could see the newspaper and what he intended to do about it if he observed that the customer he'd just sold a sausage and egg burrito to was a wanted felon, but he'd disappeared back into the kitchen. I did see, though, having turned around, that my face was now also up on the TV. Jesus, I was surrounded by me. A photo of Deputy Kirk Matheson replaced my picture. Footage of El Paso Police Department cruisers with their lights flashing outside Thompson Hospital came next, overlaid by a photo of a Sheriff's deputy whose face I didn't recognize, followed by a portrait of Arlen. Much of this was a new development, as far as I could tell. Something had happened at the hospital, and not something good. The volume was low and it was difficult to pick words out of the report, delivered in rapid-fire Spanish, accompanying the photos and the footage. I heard *policía, Aeropuerto, matanza* or massacre and *que mata* or killing. But it was a single word spoken over the picture of Arlen and the deputy that made the burrito, sausage and egg jag in my throat. The word was *muerto*, Spanish for "dead".

What the hell had happened? The conclusion I could draw from what I'd just seen and heard was that Arlen had been killed at the hospital. Was that right? I stood to go to the counter and ask if the volume could be goosed when movement out in the parking lot distracted me. A black Mercedes sedan with big chrome spinners accompanied by a Silverado crew cab had stopped out front and a bunch of unsavory types were piling out of the pickup. They were having a pow-wow with the kids who'd tried to boost the Land Cruiser's wheels from under me. Maybe those kids were *halcones*, intelligence gatherers paid by the cartels that Gomez had warned me about. If so, I was in trouble. And then I realized that the kid's ringleader, the Artful Dodger in his purple tank top, was pointing at me. Several of the men who were gathered around him immediately skipped and jogged to the restaurant's front door, hooting with delight and not 'cause Mickey Dees was making hotcakes. I was now well and truly awake. Scoping the joint quickly, I hoped to spot another exit. There had to be a door at the back of the kitchen and maybe windows in the johns. But before I could make a move, several low-lifes had burst through the front door, cutting off any attempt at escape. One held a mace, not the chemical in a can type, but the type they used to wield back in the days when men sat on horses dressed in metal armor: a length of heavy metal pipe with a perpendicular spike through the end of it. His pals carried a more modern assortment of weapons: semi and automatic firearms and so forth. I didn't like the way this was shaping up. One of the men, a short wiry type in an Abercrombie & Fitch tee and loose jeans with fuzz on his top lip walked up to me and stuck a submachine gun in my nose, but I couldn't take my eye off Sir Galahad with the mace. He was looking at me and then back at the businessman like he was saying eenie meenie minie moe to himself, making up his mind one way or the other.

"Go the other, Bub," I thought.

Ten

I braced for whatever was coming next. The guy with the machine pistol pushed me in the chest with his free hand, backing me up against the wall. When I got there, the two Mickey D's employees were already lined up, hands above their heads. The businessman was still seated, now surrounded by the new arrivals. The man with the mace seemed to have made up his mind, circling him.

The leader of this little mariachi band appeared to be a guy in his early twenties: shaved head, loose-fitting tank top and covered in tattoos – even on his bald head. I recognized several iterations of MS-13 inked on his skin, indicating that he was a member of *Mara Salvatrucha* 13, the organization that boasts it's the world's most violent gang. He was yelling at the businessman. I got the impression they knew each other. He took the man's briefcase, opened it and quickly rifled through the contents before tipping them over his head. Pens, magazines and other stationery items rained down. The bald guy then jerked the businessman to his feet. He stood hunched on the spot until several of the gangbangers started pushing and pulling him toward the restaurant's front door. They kept this up till they reached the guy's Ford and then the thug with the mace went to work, using it on the vehicle's doors, the spike leaving craters in the metalwork.

And just when I thought this was going to be the end of the show, the mace guy turned around and swung the weapon into the businessman's chest. Blood erupted from him, a red gusher, horizontal like an opened fire hydrant. The businessman dropped to his knees, one hand trying to staunch the blood, the other held out in front of him to maybe stop another swing. The assailant walked behind him, limbered up with a practice swing and then launched the mace two-handed into the businessman's temple. In baseball terms, it was a textbook hit, the batter following through on the swing so that his hands ended up around the region of his opposite shoulder, the bat pointed down his back at the ground. If it'd been a ball he'd have knocked the skin off it, but it was skull and brains whacked in this instance and most of them were now sliding down the stolen Land Cruiser's duco ten feet away. A couple of pals patted the killer on the back, all of them grinning like he'd just upped his average.

The kid in my face with the machine pistol also grinned and, satisfied by a job well done, sauntered to the counter. The *Gerente* rushed to serve him – a Big Mac, and five cheeseburgers, essentially everything that was in the rack. The kid tossed some bills on the counter, leaving the change, and walked out with a spring in his step to join the guys who, bloodlust spent, were now all climbing slowly back into the Silverado like they were a little exhausted. I watched the burgers get handed around, the *jefe* with the all-over ink taking delivery of the Big Mac. He got into the Mercedes and both vehicles drove off together, leaving the dead businessman on the asphalt as shoppers and employees began to trickle into the lot.

The woman who worked at the restaurant was shouting at the ceiling, angry and distressed – in shock. I flicked through the phrasebook before opening my mouth and, though I could guess, asked the manager who those people were: *"¿Quiénes eran esas personas?"*

With a look on his face like he was chewing something rotten, he said, *"Cartel de negocios. Quizás Sinaloa. Que el hombre, él era un contador – vino aquí a menudo."* I took that to mean: "Cartel business, maybe Sinaloa cartel. He was an accountant and came here often. I shit on all of them."

Maybe it wasn't an accurate translation but I gathered he wasn't a fan of either the businessman or the visiting breakfast club and didn't see much difference between them. He then got on the phone to the authorities, the *Federales* probably – the army, the law hereabouts. Time to bounce.

I abandoned the remains of the burrito, snatched the front page of the paper, stuffed it in my pocket, and went outside and watched shoppers giving Mickey D's a wide berth, not even stopping to gawk. There was nothing to be done for the remains of the dead businessman on the asphalt except perhaps throw a blanket over him, if only I had one. I wondered what his crime was. Did he maybe forget to add all the zeroes? Was he skimming? Or was he just working for the opposition?

I took another look at the Land Cruiser. I had to leave it and not necessarily because its door panels looked like the meat department at a supermarket. It no longer had its wheels.

*

I paid the woman from Mickey D's fifty dollars to give me a ride to the airport and another fifty to say to anyone interested enough to ask that she'd dropped the gringo off at the bus terminal. A hundred bucks was a lot of money in Juárez. I hoped it would buy me a little silence.

At the airport I bought a suitcase and some random clothes to throw into it. I also bought a ticket for the first available flight to Panama City, Panama. I'd just missed the direct flight, but I could make the Copa Airlines flight with a stopover in Mexico City. I took it and put my Sig through checked luggage, the reason for buying the suitcase and the crummy clothes. From a tourist concession I also bought a trucker's hat with I ♥ MEXICO on it, passed immigration and security without any problems and headed for the gates. Once inside, I hung around in the departure lounge for an Aeromexico flight headed to Houston as there was a TV monitor in the lounge tuned to CNN. My clean-shaven happy face was soon on screen again although, fortunately, the face currently below the I ♥ MEXICO hat was far from clean-shaven and happy. The volume was low but audible: "... *the US Air Force officer then took two police officers and a bystander hostage and forced them to drive him to the border, where he released them,*" the reporter said. "*El Paso Police are working on the assumption that he has gone into hiding in Juárez and are working with authorities there to apprehend him.*"

I hoped not and pulled the peak lower over my eyes.

"And in the latest development, El Paso law enforcement is also looking for this man, Sheriff's Deputy Kirk Matheson, wounded in a shootout with the fugitive Air Force officer earlier last night." A current official photo of Matheson appeared, clean-cut and ready for duty in front of the Star of Texas flag. "Matheson is believed to have fatally shot a fellow deputy, Renaldo Ortiz, a 21-year-old rookie, and wounded US Air Force Lieutenant Colonel Arlen Wayne during a daring escape from El Paso hospital where he had been placed under guard ..."

Hey, wait a minute – Arlen shot and Matheson split? I wanted to find out more about it but a couple of *Federales* showed up in the lounge, sniffing around, which forced me to retreat. Arlen was wounded, which meant he was alive. Saying that he was "wounded", however, covered everything from a scratch to quadriplegia and the report said nothing about what kind of condition he was in. I fought off the desire to call his cell as he'd be in the hospital himself now and the call would go to message bank. And what was I gonna say? I'll be over later with a box of chocolates and a dirty magazine?

The other big news – Matheson was on the run. Or more accurately, given his wounds, a slow painful lurch.

A female voice over the loudspeakers announced in Spanish that this was the last call for passengers on the Air Panama flight to Mexico City. She was talking to me. I went to the gate and found the lounge empty, the passengers apparently already on the plane. The middle-aged female flight attendant said, "Lucky last, Mr Cooper," cracked a smile and let me pass.

The flight to Mexico City was uneventful on account of I slept from wheels up to wheels down; two hours of dreamless recovery time. At Benito Juárez International, the airport at Mexico City, I had an hour to kill and murdered it in the departure lounge sawing a few more zees off the log.

This time I was one of the first aboard the Boeing 737 and dropped into my allocated aisle seat over the wing. Feeling refreshed and wide awake, I flicked through the airline magazine while my fellow passengers filed in and found their places. There was an article on Montego Bay, Jamaica. I've never been to Jamaica. It looked like my kind of place. The featured resort had my favorite kind of bar – it was in the pool, the barkeep serving bikini models. There was an unoccupied seat between a blond and a redhead and I mentally put my name on it. There were more pictures, mostly of beaches and golf courses so I went back to the bar. The girls were still there, waiting for me but, second time around, it just wasn't the same. My brain wandered again to the situation in El Paso with Arlen. He must have gone to the hospital to check on Matheson; maybe to ask the bent deputy some questions. How had Matheson managed to get hold of a gun? Maybe he created a disturbance, tipped over some equipment, the guard poking his head in the room to see what was up. From there, a little faked distress and the guard could've come close enough for Matheson to grab his sidearm. I could visualize the scenario like I'd witnessed it.

I glanced up at the passengers coming down the aisle. And that's when I saw Kirk Matheson. I couldn't believe it. Did the guy have a doppelganger? It just seemed so odd to see him ambling sideways down the aisle, dragging his carry-on behind him. I gave myself a mental shake. Had I conjured the guy up out of my own mind? I was thinking about him and, poof, suddenly the fucker was right in front of me. Could the same trick possibly work with Victoria's Secret models?

Our eyes met. Mine slid off his face and out the window. Did he recognize me? I took another glimpse. He wasn't staring back so I figured not. Instead he was attempting to wrangle his carry-on into the overhead locker, his seat a row in front of mine and on the other side of the aisle. He was doing this one-handed – right-handed – on account of I'd fired a bullet into his left shoulder before breakfast this morning. I hadn't been sure about the location of the wound, but now that he was close I could harden up on some of those details. Everything about Matheson – from the exhausted way he moved to his washed-out pallor – told me he was in a world of pain, the analgesics administered in the hospital long since worn off.

A flight attendant came up to help him stow his bag as he was obviously in a bad way; no color in his face, the sweat beaded across his forehead and cheeks. The rim of his blue shirt collar was dark with absorbed perspiration. The guy could barely keep his eyes open, his eyelids hanging heavy and his jaw slack.

Speaking from first-hand experience I knew that pretty much all movement for him would be excruciating. An innocent bump from a passerby would be enough to send him to the edge of unconsciousness. Taking a deep breath would be enough to make him want to faint. I gave myself a mental pat on the back. And now the asshole was right here, helpless as a baby, a fellow fugitive headed south. I got up from my seat, went over and sat heavily down beside him, my shoulder banging into his. Oops! I heard the suck of air between gritted teeth and felt the flinch shudder through his body. I gave him a great big smile. "Hey, sorry about that," I said. "Not a lot of room in here, is there? They keep building 'em smaller and smaller. Or maybe it's me getting bigger and bigger. Ha ha. A few too many Buds, right? Say, you're American, ain't you? Me too. Where you from? I'm from all over …"

Matheson turned away from this physical and verbal onslaught, showing me his back.

"Sir, do you have the right seat?"

I turned and saw the flight attendant from the air bridge back in Juárez, furrows through her dry, powdered forehead. A Mexican woman with a stern face that looked like it had seen everything and would prefer not to see any of it again accompanied her. Both of them were staring down at me. Damn it, I was just getting into the swing of things here with Matheson. I pulled my boarding pass and made like I was checking it. "Oh, gee … Musta got confused. Sorry 'bout that." I bounced out of the chair, giving Matheson another good jostling on the way up, and crossed the aisle back to my rightful place.

It was no big deal. I had the next three hours to play with the guy, time enough to figure out what I was going to do with him and maybe exact a little payback for Arlen and the several members of El Paso law enforcement who were now checked into the morgue on account of him. But it wasn't going to be all fun and games. The fact that he was free and headed in the same direction I was presented a problem: he was the only survivor, aside from myself, of the shootout in the truck yard. He knew the truth about what had happened and could blow my good-cop-gone-bad cover to any interested party.

I kept my eye on Matheson but, as far as I could make out, he hit the hay instantly and didn't wake till the plane was on descent to Panama City International. The jerk hadn't even given me the pleasure of accidentally on purpose bumping into that wounded shoulder of his on his way back from the head.

He pressed the button for service. A flight attendant came up to him, went away and came back a moment later with a plastic cup of water and waited for him to drink it.

Matheson had escaped from lawful custody in the hospital, I figured, because he believed he was safer south of the border. (I wondered if he'd still believe that if he'd caught what I'd seen in the Mickey D's parking lot.)

He threw back some pills and washed them down with the water. He handed the cup back to the attendant, slumped in his seat and closed his eyes. Not long after that, we'd landed and were taxiing to the gate. I decided to stay on this fucker's tail and see where it led. Panda and the Cool Room could wait.

Most of my fellow sardines were in the aisles shuffling forward with their carry-on when two uniformed men with the word INMIGRACIÓN on their shoulder tags fought their way in against the tide, looking for someone. They stopped at Matheson's seat and asked to see his passport, which he handed over. They checked it quickly, retrieved his bag from the overhead locker, helped him to his feet and led him away, the passengers parting in front of them like maybe Moses had a hand in it.

Hopping across the aisle, I tailgated the threesome as it hurried to the front door and only just managed to get there in time to see Matheson whisked away in a wheelchair. I kept following. If the overhead signs were any indication, the uniformed escort was speeding him to Inmigración. Walking fast, I managed to keep them in sight, at least right up to the time when they opened a door marked DO NOT ENTER and disappeared behind it.

I gave the door a push. Locked from the other side, damn it. A female Inmigración officer materialized and waved me on. Not having any alternative, I joined one of the lengthy queues leading to a bored passport clerk, filled out the paperwork and waited my turn. Matheson was gone, his escape aided by the authorities. There was no reason to be surprised about that. The folks he worked for had multi-story houses full of cash and almost everyone has their price.

The Cool Room was back at the top of the list. I collected my Sig from baggage and took a cab to a place called Casco Veijo, the Old Town, where this former CIA agent Panda had put down some semi-retirement roots.

Speeding along the waterfront, I had a mind that there were at least two Panama Cities. One was a vaguely futuristic steel and glass version that could have been a set in a cheesy sci-fi flick. The other was a partially renovated old Spanish settlement across the bay. Neither seemed occupied by the people living in Panama City who, from what I could gather, appeared to collect in the spaces between the two, like plaque.

It was pushing ninety degrees by the time I reached the Cool Room, a hideaway occupying the ground floor of a three-hundred-year-old building, tropical plants sprouting from cracks in its ancient external walls. The bar itself was a cavernous dark room with exposed wood beams and raw stucco walls. Beneath the bar's swirling ceiling fans, away from the sun, the temperature dived fifteen degrees or so. Louisiana swamp blues and ice-cold beer were being served, the latter pulled from buckets of crushed ice for tourists sitting at tables or perched at the bar.

A local girl worked the bar – full lips, big brown eyes, dark skin, short-cropped black wiry hair, athletic. She wore loose gym shorts and a thin mauve undershirt that advertised her nipples as she jiggled along to 'Polk Salad Annie'. She could take a seat at my pool bar any time she liked.

"¿Qué te gustaría?" she asked me with a little head and shoulders movement, timed to the music.

"Un cerveza, por favor," I said, motioning at the bottles of Atlas keeping a pair of English tourists beside me company.

She bobbed behind the counter and came up with the beer, ice sliding down its frosted sides, and popped the top of it reverse-handed with a bottle opener hanging from a hook. She placed the beer on the bar on an Atlas coaster. I gave her five bucks. "Speak English?"

"Maybe," she replied, implying it depended on what came next, and handed over my change.

"Keep it. Panda here?"

"Who?"

"I have an appointment," I replied.

"How is your name?"

I knew what she meant. "Cooper."

Walking away, she was on her cell a heartbeat later, I assumed, calling Panda. There were plenty of exits in case I needed to leave in a hurry. I counted seven and was working out the best lines to them when a tall guy wearing a Panama hat, smoking a cigar and carrying a beer gut supported by his belt, darkened one of them. He looked older than his mug shot. There was a telltale nod in my direction from the barmaid. The big man came over and sat in the space the English tourists had by now vacated.

"Got some ID?" he said.

I showed him my passport. He flicked through the pages, ending on the one with my photo. He told me to take off the hat. I took it off.

"Welcome to Panama, Mr Cooper," he said, satisfied, handing back the passport. "Been expecting you, but maybe not so soon." He held out his hand and we shook. It was a large warm hand as soft as bread dough.

"Nice place you got here," I remarked.

"Retirement's been good." He glanced down at his gut. "A little too good."

My eyes went for a tour of the bar and couldn't help but linger on the barmaid as she placed a glass of something clear with ice and mint leaves in front of Panda.

In case I had any ideas, he said, "That's Claudia. She's French, from our Paris station. Used to kill for a living until she started to enjoy it. The garrotte was her weapon of choice. This is the pasture they put her out to. Chin-chin." He air-toasted me and took a slurp of his drink. "Not quite the same when it's water, though," he said with a shrug. "The ol' blood pressure's stratospheric these days. Ironic now that I'm in this low-pressure existence, out of the life. You? Guessing – I'd say your BP's around one-ten over sixty and your resting heart rate is somewhere in the fifties." He nodded to himself. "Gun battles, car chases … That shit keeps you fit. Pilates is for turd burglars." Another toast. He drank, sucked on the cigar and filled the immediate area with smoke that smelled like the guts of something washed up on the beach.

"What's the latest from El Paso?" I asked. "You know anything about Lieutenant Colonel Wayne?"

"Friend of yours?"

I nodded

"Wayne ... One of the guys shot at the El Paso hospital overnight."

"Yeah."

"From what I heard, a bullet creased his head. He was lucky. The shooter must have thought your pal was a goner and left it at that. He put two rounds in the rookie on guard duty. It was the second bullet killed him."

Okay, I could relax a little about Arlen. "I just shared the flight down here with the shooter."

"Matheson was on the plane?"

"In the seat across the aisle." I flicked a chunk of ice off the counter.

"You wanna back it up to the truck park and tell me what happened?"

I filled him in on the gun battle at dawn between Deputy Matheson and me, and Panda drew the only possible conclusion – that Matheson was on the payroll of the cartel that shipped the drugs north and perpetrated the massacre. "But what I don't get," I said, "is why he's not hiding away somewhere – like in a deserted Norwegian fjord. He failed. Why confront his employer? You just know what his reward's gonna be."

Panda considered this, puffing on the burning dead thing between his lips. "Security might not have been his role. He might've been on the books just to observe and report. Fleeing south like he has – he's essentially defected. And, as a law enforcement officer, he's got the credentials being actively targeted by the cartels for recruitment. There are plenty of buyers. What he knows is invaluable to gangsters with up-coming operations over the border. And the first thing the Sheriff's Office should be doing is changing their operations and protocols to make sure whatever Matheson has is rendered obsolete."

"It gets better. Matheson's uncle is the commander back at El Paso."

"Really? At the Sheriff's Office? Well that's embarrassing," Panda observed with a grin. After considering that bit of news for a few seconds, he added, "It's also going to increase the nephew's worth."

"It's a problem for me if Kirk Matheson's boss is this Angel of Medellín. One of the first items on the list will be how the shipment was discovered by a certain OSI agent."

"Well maybe his failure to pop you when he had the chance is your best defense. The fact that he missed the opportunity is not something he's gonna brag about."

I was thinking the same thing just as it came out of Panda's mouth.

"Maybe you should'a just taken care of him on the plane," he concluded.

I didn't ask Panda how, exactly, but I suppose he was thinking I could've just asked the flight attendants to hold the guy while I shanked him with a plastic bread knife and had them open the hatch while the pilot and I threw the body out. The CIA always has the answer ... I changed the subject. "So, Juan Apostles."

"The Saint of Medellín. You wanna know where he is." Panda signaled Claudia to freshen the drinks. "The short answer is I don't know."

Singing along to Ray Charles' "Georgia", Claudia changed out the empty bottle of Atlas while I tried to picture her with someone's blue bulging throat between her hands and couldn't quite get there.

"He doesn't stay in one place too long and his schedule is random. Last week he was in Bogotá. This week ..." Panda shrugged. "But I know where you can find some of his cronies."

"Like the Tears of Chihuahua?"

"Unlikely. But you never know your luck."

"Go on."

"Have one of his people take you to him."

"Get myself taken hostage?"

"You're a fast learner, Cooper."

I wasn't sure I liked the idea, but it was a plan and that was more than I had. "So where do I start?"

"A town called Yaviza down the Pan-American Highway, on the edge of the meanest place on Earth."

"I've been to some pretty mean places," I told him, not that I wanted to get in a pissing contest with him about it.

"Yeah, right," he said, brushing my mean places aside. "The Darién Gap, where you're going, beats them all. If the drug traffickers, kidnappers, guerrillas and/or corrupt soldiers hiding out there don't kill you, the snakes, wasps, septic cuts and/or gastroenteritis will. It's the 21st century and they've sent rovers to Mars but they still haven't built a road through the Darién Gap connecting North and South America. Too dangerous."

"They've sent a rover to Mars?" I said. "Which model?"

Panda looked at me like he wondered if he'd truly heard what I just said. I could have told him that they also haven't developed an effective test for prostate cancer that didn't involve a rubber glove and lubricant, so I considered I'd gone easy on him.

"Head down the Pan-American Highway until you get to a town called Yaviza," he repeated. "The bus won't take you any further. Across the Rio Chucunaque there you'll find a bar frequented by killers, drug runners, communists, nationalist militia, smugglers, insurgents and birdwatchers."

"Birdwatchers?"

He shrugged. "The area is full of rare birds. Amphibians, too. If humans would just vacate the place, it could be a veritable Garden of Eden."

"A killer's a killer. How will I recognize the Saint's brand?"

"Ask, I guess. You carrying? For your sake I hope it's something heavy and semi automatic."

"Sig 228."

"Standard ball too, I suppose."

I nodded.

"Hmm ... Where you're going, the nice neat holes government-issue ammo makes won't do you any favors."

*

I stayed overnight in the Casco Veijo, at a hotel Panda recommended. Sometime before midnight, I was woken by a knock on my door. It turned out to be Claudia.

"I come with a present, from Panda," she said.

How thoughtful. I hoped she'd left her garrotte behind and opened the door wider, an invitation to come on in.

"Non, merci," she said, handing over Panda's actual present – a box of hollow points for the Sig, the kind of ammo governments who'd signed treaties don't issue to their militaries, the kind that leaves behind corpses with gaping wounds and minced skin and bone.

"Tell Panda thanks," I said. And then, just in case, "Sure you don't want to come in?"

Claudia was gone before I finished the question. I guessed that meant no.

The following morning, prior to boarding a bus for the border, I bought a bottle of eighty percent DEET mosquito repellent, the whining, biting critters being the worst thing about the jungle. I also bought a rucksack – easier to travel with than a suitcase and it made me look more like the tourists I saw at the bus station heading pretty much everywhere except southeast toward Colombia. The Darién Gap, around two hundred miles down the road, had a bad rap. Seemed the only folks going in that direction either lived there or hid there.

Eleven

Panamanian police armed with submachine guns stopped the bus at three separate roadblocks, boarded and checked everyone's papers. As the only gringo in sight I received particular interest, in particular what my business might be in Yaviza. I told them birdwatching and they responded uniformly along the lines that I was a crazy motherfucker with bats in my belfry. Several tried to talk me into going back to Panama City where it was less likely that I would be abducted or killed for sport. But, as I explained, there were no yellow-bellied sapsuckers in Panama City so what choice did I really have.

After one puncture and a burst radiator hose, the bus coughed into Yaviza ten hours later, three hours behind schedule. I eventually found a hotel, which was really just a cot in a room that smelled of urine, out the back of a cinderblock house with spaces in the blocks for windows and a single light bulb hanging from the ceiling, surrounded by insects. The guy who sold me the room, a *mestizo* Indian in dirty shorts with no front teeth, drew my attention to the floor where there was a mosquito coil on a plate with a box of matches and this, I gathered, was proof that this room was Yaviza's answer to the Ritz. I wasn't so sure about that until I slapped on some

DEET and took a stroll around the town to get my bearings. The place was small, poor, tired and dark, with no public street lighting. It had 'end of the road' written all over it. In fact, the Pan-American Highway, a mighty network of roads that spanned the continents of North and South America for a distance of over twenty-nine thousand miles, fizzled out in Yaviza, becoming a kind of driveway that kinked to the left and turned into a dirt path spotted with dogshit.

Cars and even scooters were rare in town, exhausted and insect-ravaged horses having taken their place. Indeed, horses had been outnumbering motorized vehicles for the last hundred miles or so giving the impression that, as the bus rolled down the highway, it was also heading back in time.

Dinner was a hand of bananas and a Coke purchased from a woman nursing a crying infant, sitting in front of a small general store stocking old products with faded packaging, the roller shutter at half-mast in front of heavy vertical steel bars. Behind the bars was an old TV sitting on a box, a soap playing. Every handful of seconds, in order to hear what was happening on the program, the woman would *shush* the baby and give it a slap on the leg, which would only make it cry some more.

And then a gunshot rang out, a rolling boom with a hard crack at its center that took me by surprise, along with Yaviza's dog population that began a howling, yapping chorus. Leaving the bananas and the Coke behind, I moved in the direction of the sound, my hand going to the small of my back to check that the Sig was where I remembered putting it. No one else was on the street. The woman quickly relocated herself and the baby behind the bars, pulling the shutter closed behind her.

Heading for the source of the gunshot took me straight to the river and a pedestrian suspension bridge spanning it. Stopping to listen, I could hear the hubbub of men talking, carried on the cool night air, but on this moonless night I couldn't locate the source. I walked across the bridge, which allowed a better view of the river bend. A couple of hundred yards upstream, a yellow light appeared, partially buried in black shadow. That had to be the place, the bar Panda had talked about. I crossed the bridge and found a pathway down by the river.

A few minutes later, crouched among the trees, I reconnoitered a shack that was part cinderblock, part corrugated steel and surprisingly large. As I watched, two men dragged a third out the door and dumped him in the shadows. Once they'd left, I worked my way over to those shadows and found a warm corpse with a head, what was left of it, turned to mush.

The windows were screens of rough cinderblock lattice that let in light, air and mosquitoes, same as my hotel. If the noise coming from inside and the number of horses tethered to the trees was any indication, there had to be quite a crowd in there enjoying itself. Someone shouted and then a couple of glasses shattered. A scrawny *mestizo* kid in a cowboy hat and faded jungle pattern camos came out and loitered in the doorway, sucking a bottle of beer, a 12-gauge Remington pump on his hip. I took a deep breath, waved the cloud of mozzies out of my face, stood up and walked out of the shadows. The kid caught a fright, almost choking on his beer when he saw the gringo with an I ♥ MEXICO ball cap emerge from the darkness.

"Mine's the chestnut bay over by the poison ivy," I said to his open mouth as I stepped onto the landing. "See she gets a carrot, will ya?" I flipped him a quarter. The kid was paralyzed with indecision long enough for me to walk past him unhindered and through the front door.

Inside, it reeked of booze, sweat, body odor, stale tobacco and weed smoke. And the dozen or so characters in the joint looked like it smelled – unwashed jungle-living desperadoes without a shred of dental hygiene between them. The furniture was rudimentary – packing crates for tables and the chairs short-cut logs stood on end. The booze being poured came from unbranded bottles. This was one bar that had never seen NASCAR or a promo girl and, on the positive side, no Canadian ice hockey either. One other point worth noting: it was suddenly very quiet in there and everyone was looking at me. I made eye contact with a man holding a bottle. Maybe he was the barman. "Miller Lite, Bub," I said, breaking the ice.

Things went downhill pretty quickly from there. Two men pulled revolvers with barrels almost as long as their arms and stuck them in my face. I heard the words *"cabrón"* and "motherfucker", *cabrón* meaning a number of things including "he-goat" and "asshole". Motherfucker needed no translation.

"Quiero ver Santo de Medellín, Santo de Medellín!" I said as I was pulled across the room, my hands above my head, and thrown down behind a table awash with booze and cigarette ash.

One man pulled my head back while another pushed the barrel of his revolver into my mouth and the Sig was ripped from the concealment holster.

"Why do you want to see the Saint of Medellín? What business do you have with him?" The voice was soft-spoken with a lisp.

Hands patted me down, found some loose rounds for the Sig in a thigh pocket and pulled them out along with my wallet and the bottle of DEET. "He's clean," someone announced in Spanish.

The muzzle of the .44 Magnum barrel in my mouth was warm and tasted of metal and gun oil. Recently fired. I thought of the body lying out in the shadows with the mushy head. I said something, or at least tried to, but it's hard to make yourself understood with a mouth full of Magnum. The barrel was removed. I spat saliva and gun oil onto the floor. "I said he needs me."

The man with the soft-spoken voice scoffed. "Why does the Saint of Medellín need *you*?"

"He's at war with Texas law enforcement. I can help him win."

"Who are you that you can make this promise?"

"When was the last time you looked at a news broadcast?" I said, trying to get a peek at this guy doing the negotiating.

Someone slapped my face.

"You answer questions," said the soft voice, lisping over the esses, "you do not ask them."

"I was a federal agent. I killed some deputies yesterday. Turn on your TV. You got a TV?"

"So you're a cop killer? Why you do this?"

"To help the Saint."

"Why?"

"Money," I said. "Only reason there is."

The man doing all the talking took the seat opposite, my wallet in his hands. He was one ugly son of a bitch. In his late fifties or early sixties, a cheek and part of his lower lip had been shot off, the old wound gnarled over with white and purple scarring, explaining the lisp. From the exhortations of his pals, I gathered his name was *El Mala Cara* – the Bad Face. That was putting it mildly.

He examined my driver's license. "So you leave your country behind, your employer, your family, Mr Cooper. That's a big move. Why?"

"You want a sob story?"

"*Si* – unless you want me to kill you right now."

Hard to refuse. "I got no family. I live alone in the burbs of DC. And Uncle Sam's not exactly forthcoming with the financial rewards so fuck him, right? I saw an opportunity. I took it."

"Kill him," advised one of the men with a permanent sneer and my Sig shoved down the front of his pants. He was looking at the cap on my head. Maybe he didn't like Mexico.

"I do not believe his lies," said someone else behind me.

"Okay, why would I walk in here otherwise?" I replied. "That would be a pretty stupid thing to do."

"*Si*, maybe you are stupid," someone agreed.

Old Fuckedface stared intently at me, summing things up, weighing the odds. He stood up. "You like games?"

I shrugged. "Hide the sausage, rummy ..."

A man was wrangled into the seat opposite me, the one just vacated. This guy was different to the rest. His clothes were threadbare and civilian. He was bearded, blond and flecked with gray. And he was clearly shitting himself. "No, no, no, no ..." he said over and over, his eyes ranging wildly around the room.

He was a captive or hostage or maybe both.

A large black revolver was slammed onto the table in front of me, sending a wave of the spilled booze off edges of the box. A Magnum .44, the Smith & Wesson Model 29. The Dirty Harry model. I didn't like where this was going. "You don't like rummy?" I asked.

Mala Cara picked up the weapon, flicked out the cylinder, ejected six rounds and put one back. He spun the cylinder, flicked it back in and cocked the hammer. At around this time I realized the room was putting money down. Amazing how fast things had gotten bent out of shape. The odds were simple – one in six that someone was gonna get their head blown off. The Magnum was handed to the man seated opposite, the captive. Mr Fuckedface was betting that someone would be me.

"Shoot. Do it," he told the captive.

One of the men pressed a pistol against the captive's head and cocked the hammer. I heard a pistol cocked against my own head. The captive aimed the Magnum at my nose, the black void of its muzzle as big as a rat hole.

"Do it," said Fuckedface.

The Magnum was shaking in the captive's hands. "No, no, no ..."

"Do it."

I was breathing hard. It had to be thirty degrees but I was cold, the temperature of fear. One chance in six. Dirty Harry's revolver was oscillating quite a bit, the captive fighting the inevitable, his finger white on the trigger. It was shoot or be shot. *Go ahead punk. Do you feel lucky?* As a matter of fact, no, not really.

El Mala Cara drew his own pistol and pressed the muzzle into the captive's temple. "Do it. I count to three. One."

Sweat streamed down the captive's horrified face along with tears, his forefinger moving the trigger.

"Two."

"Fifty to a hundred million," I said. "That's what I'm worth to the Saint. How much you gonna win if I get shot? A hundred bucks? What will the Saint do to you when he finds out how much money you cost him?"

No one bought it.

"Three."

I held my breath. Frogs croaked, mosquitoes hummed, river water gurgled, a horse blew air across it lips.

Click!

Nothing. Silence. I couldn't even hear the frogs croaking. The Magnum's hammer was resting in its seat, having come down on an empty chamber. The release of tension exploded into a cheer, winners and losers contributing to the exultant roar.

I figured I had maybe a second to act, two at most.

The guy standing over me with a pistol at my head was looking at his chums, toasting someone, a winner who bet on an empty chamber. I grabbed the barrel of his gun, which was pressed against my skull, twisted and pulled it. He reacted, squeezing the trigger, and Mr Bad Face's eye became a burst of red spray as his head flew back. The guy holding the pistol's handgrip had no idea what was going on. I re-aimed, pulled again. The barman went down this time, shot in the hip, the ultra-close range resulting in the top of his leg and buttock being blown away.

Panic swept the room. Other folks started firing just to get off a shot. Keeping my hand on the pistol, I came under the guy's outstretched arm, turned and swung my forearm into his elbow joint and heard it crack. He screamed, released the weapon and took a few steps toward one of his pals, who then shot him in the neck. Maybe they weren't friends.

And then all went quiet, a different kind of quiet to the one that greeted my entry. This one was punctuated by groans and a few whimpers.

"Okay," said a voice in English. "You want the Saint, I take you to him."

I looked over. It was the kid on valet parking duties at the front door. He seemed pretty relaxed given the bloodbath around him and was holding his shotty by the barrel, the stock below his knees. I grabbed the hostage by the collar, dragged him to his feet and made for the exit, stopping by Mr Even-More-Now *Mala Cara* to reclaim my wallet, cell and money, pick up the bottle of DEET kicked against a wall, and to prize my Sig from the hand of a dead guy lying on the floor and staring at the ceiling. The loose rounds were in his top pocket. He wouldn't be needing them either.

Twelve

The kid's details could wait. The hostage, though, was a Danish national whose name could have been Yan or Jam or Jan – my ears were still clanging from all the shooting. From what I could gather, he'd been working for some NGO on a project in the jungle on the Columbian side of the border when he'd been isolated and captured by the United Self-Defense Forces of Columbia, the organization claimed by a lot of the guys back at the bar, according to the kid. The Dane had been taken around three weeks ago. A couple of hours before I arrived his kidnappers had been told that no ransom would be forthcoming. Tonight they had scheduled him to die.

I managed to extract all this from the kid as we ran back up the path to the suspension bridge. We were running because he believed the folks back at the bar might regroup.

We stopped at the bridge where the Dane, the kid and I would be parting company. "Mr Cooper, *tak, tak*," the Dane said, shaking my hand. "Thank you, thank you."

"There was a gunfight, you escaped in the confusion," I said, coaching him. "You never heard of Mr Cooper, understand?" I patted my chest. "Never there." The last thing I wanted were headlines, if any should arise from his rescue, compromising my cover.

The Dane caught on. "Okay, okay. *Ja.* I escaped." His tone then became earnest. "I am sorry. I pulled the trigger. Very sorry."

"You'd have missed," I told him. He was shaking the gun so bad I was probably the last person who was gonna get shot, though the powder burns would've made up for it.

Over on the Yaviza side, I could see men running along the street with flashlights toward the river.

"Come on, we go," said the kid who could also see them and was impatient to move.

The Dane shook my hand so vigorously my teeth rattled. *"Tak,"* he said a final time and then ran off to intercept the lights sweeping the opposite end of the bridge.

I followed the kid. He ran a little ways back in the direction of the bar and then took a right, slithering down the steep bank to the river. There were a couple of boats moored there – canoes. He climbed into one of them.

"This yours?" I asked him.

"No, we steal it."

"A getaway canoe," I mumbled as I fell into it while he yanked the starter cord. The motor gurgled into life on the second pull. The gearbox sent a thump through the wood as he selected forward and then we were roaring downstream.

Passing under the bridge, the men on it were shouting and trying to find us with their flashlights. I heard the crack of a rifle but I had no idea if the round was meant for us. And in a moment, the lights of Yaviza were gone.

Around ten minutes later, the canoe nudged the riverbank. I jumped out and the kid followed. He then pushed the boat out into the river and the current took it away.

"You got a name, kid?" I asked him as he handed me a machete taken from the canoe.

"Marco," he replied.

"Where're we going?"

As it turned out, we weren't going far, hacking our way through thick virgin jungle strung with countless spider webs. About a klick later, we changed direction and went a hundred feet more or less vertically, up a wall of sharp volcanic rock.

"We stay here tonight. Jungle too dangerous," Marco explained.

This was his territory so I let it go and gathered some moss and twigs instead.

"Making a fire," I explained.

"No. No fire. They will find us. Kill us."

I asked him who and the answer was a shrug.

I let that go too and gathered some more moss to use as padding to sit on, the volcanic rock being about as forgiving as volcanic rock. Marco wanted to stay uncomfortable so that he wouldn't sleep. "You are taking me to the Saint of Medellín, right?" I asked, settling in.

"No. To his people. The Saint does not live in the jungle."

Who could blame him? "Where are his people?"

He shrugged. "Fifteen kilometer." He motioned behind him, indicating the direction with a flick of his hand farther into the depths of the Meanest Place on Earth.

"What's in it for you?" I inquired.

"Money, whaddya think?" He grinned, affecting my accent. "You are my hostage."

Right. And nice to see my little speech hadn't gone to waste. I had more questions, like which of the half dozen or so fucked-up organizations roaming the area did he belong to, but they could wait. It'd been a hell of a day and I'd put in enough overtime. I spread on some DEET, put my head back on the bare rock and watched Marco rack the shells out of his shotgun, clean them on a rag from his pocket and line them up on the rock, pretty relaxed about his role as hostage taker. He then set to work with the rag on the receiver, breech bolt and ejection port. There had been a lot of killing going on here. I took the blank rounds out of my pocket and jiggled them in the palm of my hand. That's pretty much the last thing I remember till the kid shook me awake, the jungle alive with frogs and birdcalls in the blue, pre-dawn light.

The following two days were spent alternately chopping through the rainforest or climbing through fast-flowing streams as we negotiated the Gap. It was tough going, but no tougher than jungles I'd experienced in the Congo or southern Thailand. There were the usual snakes, thorny bushes, stinging insects and blood-sucking leeches. Maybe I was just getting used to a different kind of normal. That was until we came across a vulture perched on a human head skewered on a cut-down sapling, and then half a dozen more like it five minutes further along. We found the bodies in a heaped pile, buzzing with birds and corpse flies and all were dressed in older-style US Army battledress uniforms or BDUs as they're called – camos. None of the BDUs carried insignia. No weapons were in evidence though the deceased had more bullet holes than a bootlegger's ride. Most of the entry holes were in their backs.

"*El Santo de Medellín*. They are his people," Marco said.

The Saint's men. "Who would've done this?" I asked.

Marco shrugged, which I read as take your pick. "Here is ..." He glanced around and didn't have the language to complete the sentence.

"... the meanest place on earth," I said, finishing it for him.

"*Si*." He nodded.

The amount of blood present on the severed necks indicated the decapitations had been post mortem. I couldn't see any further evidence that the corpses had been tampered with and none of the men's hands or feet was tied.

The birds had flown off, taking their flapping and squawking with them. An eerie stillness had rushed in to fill the vacuum left behind. I walked the scene quickly. There were no weapons or spent ammunition lying around, though there was plenty of shredded leaf litter. My conclusion based on very little was that these men had been captured, disarmed and then cut down by automatic fire as they tried to run away. Perhaps the guy we found first, out front, had been the sprinter in the group. Marco had already moved on, though he was moving with a lot more caution now. A few steps, pause, look, listen, a few steps more. And even then you couldn't be sure you weren't lined up in someone's sights. Of all the hostile terrain to move through, none is more nerve-racking than the jungle.

And as I was thinking that, I caught a whiff of body odor and suddenly the jungle beside me was carrying AK-47s and machetes. I put my hands in the air and tensed for a burst of lead in the back.

"*Hermanos,*" said Marco hugging a bush, or more accurately a squat human being camoed up, branches from a shrub stuck in his webbing. The ambush we'd just walked into was Marco's comrades – friends, *hermanos*. A couple of the men smiled at Marco and patted him on the back. And, as Marco's pal, I smiled too. But the treatment I got was a little less welcoming, catching movement out the corner of my eye. The stock of an AK.

Lights out.

*

The fog between my ears took time to clear and only then I got the picture.

"Hey!" I mumbled.

I was upside down, my damn feet and hands lashed with bark strips to a sapling, swinging between two of Marco's hermanos like I was headed for some cooking pot.

"Hey!" I said a second time, louder, more focused. My neck hurt, along with my wrists and ankles, to say nothing of my head.

Marco materialized beside me and put his finger to his lips.

It wasn't easy, but I shut up. Around five minutes later, the porters dumped me on the ground and removed the pole. I rolled onto my side and just lay there, the blood surging back into my hands and feet. Seriously, there had to be a better way to earn a buck.

I took in the surroundings. The immediate area had been semi-cleared and was interspersed with elaborate shelters fashioned from whatever the jungle could provide. Around a dozen men and a few women, all in jungle camouflage, ate, cleaned weapons and mended uniforms. No one spoke above a whisper. I couldn't hear anything other than the jungle.

Marco and another guy came over and pulled me to a seating position. Marco's friend looked about twenty-two years of age, blue crucifixes tattooed on his knuckles. He also had a large rusty knife, which he used to cut through the bindings on my hands.

"You no run," he said quietly in English as he sawed between my ankles. First putting his finger against his lips, reminding me again of the need to keep it down, he whispered, "It is dangerous. We must be sure."

I guessed he meant sure of me. I rubbed my wrists, scratched my ankles and then rolled my neck back and forth a couple of times. Bones crunched. "Who killed those men? Your people?"

"*Somos FARC,*" he said indignantly as if *his* people would never do such a thing. And now, at least, I also knew which flavor of fanatic I was hanging with. Marco continued in a low whisper: "*Ese era el trabajo de un equipo rival cártel de muerte.*" Or, in other words, the massacre was the work of another cartel hit squad, a rival to the one we found being cleaned up by vultures. He then rattled off several sentences that he believed explained the difference between his people, who were Marxist–Leninist idealists, and the brutal pro-government paramilitary scum they were eternally at war with. And then Marco's friend jumped in with his own version. I nodded agreeably as he spoke, mainly because the guy held a big rusty knife, but otherwise I couldn't see it. The commies and the fascists both provided services to the Mexican and Colombian cartels, both took hostages, both robbed and both roamed the Darién Gap looking for some financial advantage they were prepared to murder to obtain. The only difference that I could see between them was that I happened to be surrounded by the Marxist–Leninist variety and so therefore that currently made them righter than the other guys. At least for now.

Marco's pal pulled something from his pocket, a wad of newsprint, and opened it. It was my introduction letter to Juan Apostles: the front page of the *El Diario* with my smiling face and the headline, "Killer". I'd completely forgotten I'd had it and ol' Fuckedface back at the bar hadn't found it on me.

"This you," Marco's pal stated.

"*Si,*" I replied.

He patted me on the shoulder as if acknowledging I was in the same club he belonged to. "So, you wan meet Juan Apostles, eh?"

"Yeah."

"Eduardo," he responded, introducing himself, and we shook on it.

"Marco say you think you work for *el Ángel.*"

"Uh-huh."

"Maybe you say nice thing 'bout us."

"Sure. You scratch my back ..."

He nodded and kept nodding, but I could tell he thought I just asked him to scratch my back.

"Now, you pay cash," said Marco.

*

I spent that night asleep on a bed of palm fronds and saplings laid across a fork in a tree, a black wool blanket over me that smelled of sour milk and campfires, and thanked every god I could think of for the bottle of DEET in my pocket.

The following morning, which began before dawn, I ate some kind of bitter-sweet fruit the size of a tomato that could have been tamarillo, and chewed on a length of sugar cane. Marco, his pal Eduardo and two other men accompanied me through the jungle. We took it slow and steady, stopping to listen for human sounds and taste the air for human scent. That cartel death squad was out there somewhere.

Eventually, around mid-afternoon, Eduardo stopped to pull the fronds off a patch of jungle and revealed another of those getaway canoes. The escort changed out of camos and into old jeans and T-shirts, then all of us dragged the canoe into a small nearby estuary, climbed in and continued the journey.

The air quickly became tangy with salt and, within minutes, the dark jungle canopy was replaced with bright sunshine and the water opened out into marshland. Two fuel stops and three hours later, the sun sinking into haze above the jungle, the canoe motored up a slate-gray tributary clogged with bottles and plastic bags and a variety of old work-horse boats, the black mud on the riverbanks thick with rundown homes, bars and warehouses.

"Turbo," said Eduardo, providing the name of the place as Marco tied us up against a pier behind a tired old coastal cargo boat.

If you've experienced a backed-up toilet, you've pretty much got Turbo pegged. The water around the canoe bubbled with methane percolating from rotting sewage pumped into the bay. The town's reason for being, from what I could tell, was to provide boats for the ride to Capurganá, the last stop before the jump around the Gap to Panama. Turbo was also the terminus for the Pan-American Highway on the South American continent, the Yaviza of Colombia.

The streets hummed with old motor scooters and vans blowing clouds of carcinogens into the evening. Relaxed and no longer in the jungle, Marco lit up a cigarette. I took it out of his mouth and snapped it in half. It felt like the right thing to do. The kid had a chest like a bird.

The first order of business was a stop at the local internet café so that I could transfer ten thousand dollars from my account to Marco's. Arlen wasn't going to like it, but FARC's opening bid for my ransom was a million dollars even, so I figured Uncle Sugar had been let off easy. And I could position it as payment for guide services. An ATM was next, where I withdrew some cash and, by doing so, marked my position as per instructions.

"So where do I find Apostles?" I asked Marco, getting impatient as he and his pals casually dunked cheese in mugs of watery hot chocolate.

"Medellín," he replied.

I wasn't prepared for that. Medellín was at least three hundred klicks down the highway. "I thought we were going to find him here."

"His people, not him. Maybe we get lucky. We go look."

This entailed bar hopping from one dirty glass of moonshine to another. There were a lot of bars. After half a dozen of those glasses, I could see very little. After a dozen, I couldn't care. Late in the evening, we stumbled toward a bustling establishment down on the waterfront where fellow drunks were spilling out onto the road. There was something different about this place: it was the presence of a couple of well-fed sentries out front wearing jackets. This looked promising and I sobered me up. I nudged Marco and Eduardo and our party walked farther on down the road.

"Back there. Angel's men?" I asked Eduardo, stopping against a stack of old crates.

He shrugged, then belched. I took that as a maybe.

Whoever they were, they watched the comings and goings like they were waiting for trouble. They were *someone's* men. I walked a dozen steps down to the water and scanned the back door to the bar. A sweeping veranda, groaning with drunks, was built over the water. A jetty adjoined the establishment and a white RHIB, powered by a couple of high-performance outboard motors, bobbed against it. The boat's own floodlights lit it up. A couple of heavies loitered on the jetty, wearing jackets like the two at the front door.

'Let's go have a drink,' I told Eduardo, who was swaying like a tree that's not sure which way it's gonna fall.

The bar's front entrance exhaled a cloud of steamed alcohol, sweat and tobacco haze as Marco and I followed Eduardo inside. I avoided eye contact with the security on the door, but caught a glimpse of a machine pistol stuffed in the back of one of the men's pants, hitching up his jacket. Inside, the bar was clogged with customers, nearly all of whom were black. The uniform was stained singlets and shorts, working men who rarely shaved or showered and whose dark bodies had been turned to gristle by a diet of hard work and *aguardiente*, the local firewater.

The place turned out to be both a bar and a whorehouse – booze on the first floor and a good time on the second. Against the walls were tables and chairs where women, who ranged in age from way-too-young to toothless grannies, sat on laps and tried to raise some interest with their hands from the men they were sitting on. A chubby middle-aged woman in a pink slip stood up and led away a drunk who shuffled behind her like a zombie. A young man immediately filled the vacated seat and accepted an auntie on his knee.

In a corner, a couple of old blind guys sat strumming ancient scratched guitars and sang for pesos. While I watched, one of them fell off his stool onto the floor. Several admirers laughed and applauded, helped him back onto his stool and rewarded him with a slug from a bottle. He picked up where he left off, barely missing a beat. Maybe it was all part of the act.

Marco materialized with a couple of bottles of *aguardiente* and a handful of glasses. We moved through the main bar. I couldn't see anyone of interest. The veranda over the river was the last stop and I saw immediately that this was the place. Compressed drunken bodies crowded one side of the veranda while a man in a clean blue shirt and blue jeans, sitting on an old comfortable lounge chair with arms, occupied the other. A couple of guards like the ones out front and on the jetty, one on each side of him, kept watchful eyes on the locals while two young girls from upstairs took turns giving the seated man a blowjob. His head was tilted back and his eyes were closed.

"*¿Qué estás mirando, gringo?*" asked one of the man's guards.

It took a moment to realize that I was the only gringo around and that the question, "What are you looking at?" was directed at me. In fact, it wasn't that the guy's clothes were clean and pressed, a novelty in these parts, or the fact that the girls plying their trade on him were still girls. It was the tattoos on his face that had caught my fullest attention, tears that began small at the corner of his left eye and grew in size as they ran down his face, growing as big as eggs. This was Arturo Perez.

"Your boss, the Tears of Chihuahua," I said in bad Spanish. "I've been looking for him."

The bodyguards exchanged a nervous glance and their hands found their shooters.

"Easy, fellas," I said as, nice and slow, reaching around to my back pocket. I was aware of the Sig, but that wasn't what I was after.

Guns were pulled. The veranda emptied.

My thumb and forefinger gripped a folded sheet of newsprint, brought it around. I held it out to them. One of the men took it and shook it open.

"I heard you're hiring. I've come for a job," I said indicating the front page of *El Diario* they were looking at. "That's my letter of introduction."

The girls tried to run off but Perez grabbed them by their necks and refocused them on their task.

This made me think about Gail Sorwick and the way she'd fought back, biting down hard. Maybe Perez was a fast healer. Maybe Gail had bitten down on someone else. Maybe Perez hadn't been at Horizon Airport at all. Maybe someone just wanted us to believe he was there. It was a lot to suppose on the strength of a blowjob, but it reminded me why I was there and what the folks back home wanted.

Perez's eyes fluttered open, black holes of hollow nothingness. He stared at me for a few seconds. "*Mátalo*," he rasped with a voice that was dry and hard – *kill him*.

Thirteen

"Is it the hat?" It had to be the hat. I removed the I ♥ Mexico ball hat and flicked it into the river. One of the bodyguards cocked his Steyr machine pistol, and came toward me. Maybe it wasn't the hat, but I was done with it anyway. "Your shipments to the US are getting nailed," I said, doing my best to keep the fear out of my voice. "I can help you get them through. I know the El Paso police procedures, the Sheriff's Office procedures, I've worked with the Texas Rangers, US Army Special Forces, the Air Force ..."

The guy with the Steyr kept coming. It might have all ended there, except for Marco, Eduardo and their two FARC buddies who pulled weapons on the bodyguards and everyone suddenly got a little more thoughtful.

"You need me," I said into the quiet. "The Saint needs me."

No one breathed for too many seconds. And then Perez laughed. No sound came from him, but there were creases in the corners of his eyes, the side of his mouth lifted and this gut twitched a few times so I figured that's what he was doing. He shooed the girls off, tucked himself in and closed his fly, and then gestured to his men to take a step back. I indicated to Marco and the others to likewise stand down.

Perez's eyes were polished black pebbles – hard, cold and inscrutable. Damned if I could read anything in them.

"You came prepared," Perez said in English, that harsh, dry voice of his reminding me of a throat cancer survivor. "That is good. *Continuar ...*" Continue.

I tried to get my heart rate under control. "Your cartel sends cargo across the border in aircraft. That's what I'm trained for – controlling air traffic in war zones. I can get you in and out of the US, thread your aircraft through Texas airspace. I'll get you in deeper, safer, closer to your markets. Your last big shipment was a bust, and so was the one before that. You've lost how many millions?"

Perez shifted in his seat and I saw a scabbard on his belt, a mother-of-pearl handle protruding from it. Was that the knife used on Ms Sorwick? Perez motioned for the page of newsprint. "What do you want for this service?" he asked as the bodyguard handed it to him.

"Same as everyone – a big house, a Ferrari, women I currently can't afford. Maybe a little revenge."

"Revenge?"

That got him interested. I slowly unbuttoned my shirt and took it off. "Yeah, for a total lack of appreciation. I've given whatever was asked for the fight for freedom," I said as I turned around. "I've got nothing to show for it except for what you see here. I'm 34 years of age, got maybe twenty more years if I'm lucky before the wheels fall off the wagon. I figure it's time to put what I've learned to use for an employer with a better benefits plan."

"So you're a killer," said Perez, holding the front page away from his face, those hard flinty eyes of his showing signs of frailty. "You like to kill?"

"I wouldn't say it's a hobby." It wasn't the answer Perez wanted to hear. I hardened the fuck up and rephrased. "If it needs to be done, it gets done."

"How many you kill here?" He nodded at the newsprint.

"Read it," I said.

"You tell me."

"Two, maybe four."

"Was it two, or four?"

"It was a gun battle," I replied. "People might have been killed in the crossfire."

"What happened to the cocaine?"

"It was found."

"Who found it?"

"A Sheriff's deputy who died at the scene."

"The deputy you killed?"

I put my shirt back on. "It says so right there in the newspaper, don't it?"

He snorted, ridiculing the notion. "When you own the newspaper," said Perez, "the news is a toy to play with."

I never would've figured Perez for a philosopher.

"Why were you at this airport taking part in a gun battle?"

"Aircraft delivered the drugs. The Sheriff's Office wanted to know how they did that undetected. I just happened to be there." I shrugged. "Luck ..."

"Luck." Perez nodded almost imperceptibly. "If you want to work for me, you must first serve ..." He looked for the right word. *"Un aprendizaje."*

"An apprenticeship?"

"Sí."

"What sort of apprenticeship?"

"You hand over your gun and come with us."

"That kind," I said. My throat moved involuntarily, swallowing a big lump of fear, the way I had felt when I was back playing Russian roulette. The fact that I had a Sig keeping my spine company was reassuring. I wasn't happy about giving it up.

Perez stood. He might have been taller than a garden gnome, but it'd be close. He took the pearl-handled blade from out of its scabbard, the blade long and thin and hand beaten so that it appeared to be crawling with tiny worms – Damascus steel. He twisted it in the air so that the blade's edge caught the light. I had no doubt that it could split a hair. *"Dile a tus amigos … Si siguen primero te mato, y luego matarlos."* Tell your friends if they follow, first I kill you and then I kill them.

From the look on the faces of Eduardo, Marco and the others, who had all been keenly following proceedings, I knew it was something I didn't have to repeat.

The bodyguard with the Steyr patted me down, took the Sig and the spare mags. He tried to take the DEET. "Hey!" I said, attempting to snatch it back. Perez gestured for the bottle, holding out his hand. The bodyguard gave it to him and the boss took a sniff. He squeezed some into his hands and rubbed it on his neck, then indicated to the bodyguard to return it to me. If I was going to be taken hostage, I wasn't gonna do it scratching bites and slapping at insects.

Perez led the way through the bar, the place falling silent, and picked up his men working the front door. We then went down the side of the bar, onto the jetty. The boat's motors were fired up before we got there. My FARC buddies stayed on the veranda, Marco, Eduardo, nor any of the others making any gestures of farewell. I'd seen faces like theirs before, gazing down on a coffin as the dirt was shoveled onto the lid. As far as they were concerned, I was already dead.

Fourteen

The trip north, back to the Gap, was long and uneventful, except for a brief moment when the engines were set to idle and we drifted with the current. Perez got up, stretched and then shot two of the bodyguards, the men working security on the bar's front door. Perez stretched again. One of the men rolled into the water of his own accord, pulled by gravity, and sank. The other slumped where he sat, severely wounded. Perez gripped the overhead bar and started kicking him in the head. The man slumped sideways, his head on the seat, and then Perez really went to work, stomping on it again and again and again. He just kept stomping. The man was dead several times over. Somehow I had the impression that the show was for my benefit. No one said anything, but I assumed this was punishment for allowing me and my FARC friends uncontested access to the veranda. Perez finally pushed the bloody mess overboard, took out a handkerchief, wiped his hands and shoes on it, and also tossed it over the side. While he wiped, his head was angled in my direction. No smile, no frown. I assumed he was giving me the death stare, his eyes hidden behind Ray-Ban sunglasses, the seventies retro ones with large square frames.

The remaining bodyguards seemed not to notice any of this, like it was standard operating procedure, and just went on with whatever they were doing, which was to watch the world float by. Wouldn't they be thinking that next time it could be them rolled into the river? I was. I assumed that was the point.

Eventually, one of the men produced a black bag and placed it over my head. My hands were also pulled behind my back and cuff-locked. The bag was reassuring. They'd hardly bother if I was gonna follow the other two into the drink, right?

The boat changed direction several times, and the salt smell of the sea was replaced by the damp decay of the jungle. Around an hour later, sweat streaming down my face, the bag came off. It had to be well after midnight. Up ahead, movement. We pulled up to a floating pontoon where a couple of armed men wearing US Army BDUs and night vision goggles stood watch. They came to attention and saluted Perez as the boat drifted near and tied us up while the boss disembarked. He had a quiet word to one of these men, who immediately shoved an AK in my face. "Turn around," the man ordered in Spanish. I did as I was told.

In English, Perez said, "Before your apprenticeship starts, first we must examine your credentials."

"Be my guest," I said.

"If you have lied, I will cut you and the pain you will endure will far exceed any pain you have felt before."

Arlen's briefing about what it was like to be flayed came to mind and I swallowed involuntarily. I knew my bona fides would be checked sooner or later, but that didn't make me any less nervous. Through Juan de Jesús, the Saint of Medellín, the cartel would have access to reliable news sources at *El Diario*. And then there were all the people supposedly on the take in El Paso. The barest hint that I wasn't a genuine fugitive from justice, a killer who'd crossed to the dark side, and things would get ugly in a hurry.

The sentry accompanied me through what appeared to be a military-style, semi-permanent forward operating base crawling with armed guards and dogs, to a cluster of portable buildings set in a clearing hacked out of the jungle. The buildings were all draped in camouflage netting and painted with what I guessed was probably some kind of infrared-defeating coating. The sentry unlocked the door with the key, motioned me inside, and turned on a red light set on the wall beside the door. The smell of the place reminded me of the docks back at Turbo. The centerpiece was a floor-to-ceiling welded steel cage, a massive padlock securing the door. There was a bucket inside the cage, which accounted for some of the smell. On the floor outside the cage, a plastic-wrapped bundle of bottled water.

With my face up against the cage, the jailer patted me down and this time the DEET was confiscated, no ifs or buts. Then he shoved me into the cage and tossed a couple of bottles of water in behind me, pulled a knife and stuck the blade through the bars at waist height. I turned and offered my hands and he sawed through the cuff locks. That was something, at least. He departed, pulling the door shut behind him. The air hummed with mosquitoes.

Great.

There wasn't much to do except sit in a corner, pull my collar up around my ears, close my eyes and hope that whoever said things always looked brighter in the morning wasn't just making shit up.

*

He or she was making shit up. The sun rose an eternity later and turned the prison into a steam room. Midges flew in under the eaves and finished what the mosquitoes left behind. The bucket was full and the water bottles were empty. "Hey!" I called out. "HEY!"

The door opened almost immediately. Maybe I should have complained earlier. An armed man came in, a different guy to the one who'd put me in the cage. He cracked the lock, opened the door and pointed at the water bottles. I took one, opened it, poured water over my head and grabbed a second for drinking. Standing at the doorway, the guard grunted, wanting me to follow.

Out in the bright sunshine, I could confirm that this was indeed a military-style FOB, but with a few interesting differences. Most of the people, all of whom were dressed in jungle camouflage, were getting around on dirt bikes. There was also a runway obscured from above by netting and moveable floats sprouting vegetation. It was a reasonably long strip – over two thousand feet was my initial guess – long enough for medium-size, multi-engine aircraft. Off to one side of the runway, hidden under netting, were a couple of large hangars and several smaller ones. A platoon of armed men in BDUs jogged past, sounding out some unfamiliar verse in Spanish, interrupting my low-level snooping. They ran toward the jungle, all in step. Where the bush seemed impenetrable, the troop stopped and peeled back a mass of camouflage netting, revealing two lines of Yamaha dirt bikes. The men hopped on the machines, kicked them over and then roared off to tackle an obstacle course.

Another grunt from the guard told me to catch up. He led the way to a portable building not unlike the one that housed the cage. The guard knocked on the door and opened it. I wasn't sure I wanted to go inside but the options for exercising free will were limited. I walked in. Perez was sitting behind a desk, a laptop in front of him. He waved me at the chair on the opposite side of the desk. The guard left, closing the door as I sat.

Perez opened a drawer, pulled out a pistol and aimed it at me. I flinched, which he seemed to enjoy, his features assuming their imitation smile, and then he let the weapon swing down, his finger in the trigger guard so that the handle faced me. It was my Sig. Reaching forward, I took it. Perez placed the spare magazines on the desk, the ones confiscated, along with my cell and wallet. I figured my status as a cop killer had checked out.

"How about the mosquito repellent?" I asked him.

He frowned, hesitated, then went back into his drawer and the bottle of DEET was placed on the desk beside the magazines. He seemed reluctant to hand it back. Maybe weapons were easy to come by here but relief from flying insects not so much. "Okay," I said, feeling reassured. So far, so good. I looked over the Sig, finding a round in the chamber and the magazine fully loaded, just as I'd last seen it. I leaned forward to re-holster the weapon in the small of my back. "Does this mean I'm in?" I asked.

"You make a delivery," Perez said.

Hmm, that didn't answer my question, but at least that knife of his was still in its scabbard. He stood up and stared at me a moment. I couldn't help but notice that there was no light in those eyes, no reflection, no humanity. They were the eyes of a living corpse, if such a thing were possible; gateways straight to hell.

I stood too, towering over him, and then as he walked past I fell in behind him, shortening my stride. Outside, over the last five minutes, activity had ramped up some. Around fifty men were clearing the runway, rolling the camouflage to one side, and the doors of the larger hangar had been pushed back. Guarding the skies were a couple of sport utility vehicles with .50 anti-aircraft guns mounted in their trays. Only one was manned by a young woman, dressed in BDUs. She yawned and flicked a cigarette butt onto the ground.

A small tractor towed an aircraft from the deep shadow within the hangar. My heart rate spiked when the aircraft it was towing revealed itself in the sunshine – a King Air, painted buzzard black. I pictured Bobby Macey, the sole survivor at the Horizon Airport massacre, burned raw by the desert sun, lying in a hospital bed with her raised broken leg. And that made me recall the sight of Gail Sorwick sprawled under a tent on the apron with her dead husband and kids around her, the cuts in her back and CSI's breakdown of her final moments.

The King Air was heading for the threshold where half a dozen men stood around, all of whom were dressed in non-military clothing and carried an assortment of small arms: AKs, H&K light machine guns and so forth.

"Wait," Perez told me.

I stopped and he continued walking toward the gunmen. The men gathered around him and a hurried briefing ensued. Some of them looked over at me a couple of times during their chat like I was the topic of the discussion. Perez gestured me to join them so I wandered over.

"Your *aprendizaje* ..." Perez growled. "It starts."

"What do I do?" I asked.

"You help."

He handed me a machete and walked off. I looked at the rusting blade, then over at the men. They all had them in long scabbards over their shoulders. Were we going somewhere to clear something? I had questions, mostly about my job description, "Help" being pretty open-ended, especially where these folks were concerned. I sensed asking for specifics wouldn't lead to answers. In my hand, the machete's wood grip was already slick with sweat.

The tractor arrived and did a one-eighty with the aircraft, bringing it around so that it pointed down the runway. One of the gunmen disengaged the tow bar connecting the plane's undercarriage to the tractor, which then roared off back to the hangar.

"Gringo," one of the gunmen snarled in Spanish, nodding at the aircraft's open cargo door. His tattooed head was shaved and cratered with infected bites, possibly mosquito but maybe something nasty and tropical, something that laid eggs. Maybe that accounted for his mood. His name was Carlos.

I went over to the plane and climbed aboard. Inside, strapped to the floor beneath netting, were two pallets of what appeared to be plastic-wrapped bricks of cocaine, maybe eight hundred pounds of the stuff, a barcode attached to each brick.

Most of the gunmen took seats along one side of the fuselage. I took a seat opposite. Up in the cockpit, a pilot was already at the controls, running through checks. A high-pitched whine shivered through the metal against my back. The propeller began to spin. It picked up speed fast and the aircraft quickly filled with jet turbine roar and kerosene fumes. Then the second engine went through its start routine.

The door slammed shut. We sat there for a minute or two, the heat and humidity in the close confines soaring while the pilot waited for the gauges to show the right numbers. And then he released the brakes, the engine note sharpened and the plane surged forward.

A minute or so of steep climbing later, we leveled off at around fifteen hundred feet and hooked several aggressive turns. We flew around like that for maybe ten minutes before the pilot set the aircraft up in a steep descent. Wherever we were going, it was local, somewhere in the Darién Gap. For all I knew, given the erratic flight path, we could have been no more than a few miles from Perez's base.

The King Air's propellers screamed a high-pitched snarl. The jungle filled the porthole opposite and I braced for impact, guts churning, but then the aircraft leveled out and the wheels kissed the dirt an instant later. The pilot hit the brakes, reversed propeller pitch for a full emergency stop, and the aircraft bucked and jumped on the uneven ground before suddenly pirouetting on its axis to eat up some energy and finally coming to a dusty stop. The pilot cut the engines and looked back at us with a grin. Asshole.

The door in the side of the plane opened and three armed men with dirty faces stuck their black-bearded heads in, grinned and jauntily said, *"Hola, amigos!"* The leader of our party, Carlos, the guy with the bites, likewise made some friendly noises, went up to them, shook a hand and climbed out. The rest of us followed. I heard some talk exchanged with our hosts about this being a quick turnaround job and were there any other folks around to help unload the cargo? One of our guys walked to the edge of the runway where the jungle began and took a piss. Seemed like a good idea. I followed, found a tree of my own and used the time to scope the place. I wondered where we were exactly. The jungle here was thick. It reminded me of the territory Marco and I had hacked through. The landing strip was short, surrounded by triple canopy, the tallest trees off either end towering green skyscrapers. The pilot hadn't been showing off. Much.

A shed the size of a double garage was set down one end of the strip – the far end. The three young Fidel Castro lookalikes were joined by half a dozen more just like them who came from the shed toward us, two of them pushing a trolley. Our guys had taken the netting off the cargo in the King Air and were starting to stack the bricks closer to the cargo door. One of theirs picked up a brick and felt the weight. He seemed okay with it. And that's when the shooting started. Carlos just started unloading on the people pushing the trolley. It was a signal and suddenly all our people were shooting.

A Castro clone, one of those who welcomed us, put his hands up, eyes wide and frightened, and started begging for his life. The response was a strike from a machete, a horizontal swing from behind that almost but not quite took his head off. It toppled to the side, hanging weirdly on his chest by tendons and tangled black beard, swinging back and forth, blood spurting in gouts from severed arteries in the neck as the body toppled slowly to one side and twitched.

The assault was over in seconds. My mouth was open in shock. Carlos was yelling at me. He wanted to know why I didn't shoot. I looked around, distracted, in a daze. Blood was everywhere; on the ground, on the trolley and the bricks of cocaine stacked there, on the side of the plane, over the corpses and the living. Perez's men were drenched in it. Two of them were high-fiving, high on murder. I looked into Carlos' face. "*¿Por qué?*" I asked him – why? He spat on my shoes and just walked off like the reason was obvious. First corpse he reached he drew his machete and started hacking off an arm at the shoulder.

One of Carlos' men strolled past, a dismembered leg in each hand. "*Matan los nuestros, matamos los suyos.*" He shrugged like he was carting luggage – they kill ours, we kill theirs. Maybe he thought I hadn't understood and added, "*Ojo por ojo*" – an eye for an eye. Which eye? Was he meaning the pile of fly-blown decapitated bodies Marco and I had earlier stumbled across in the jungle? According to Marco they were cartel men, and they wore BDUs identical to the ones worn around here. Were they Perez's men who'd been murdered? This was payback?

The corpses were hacked up where they lay. The place increasingly smelled of copper, shit and urine as the victims began to soak the earth with their fluids. I heard a man singing a little ditty as he hacked his way through a shoulder. Still in a state of shock, it took several long seconds to register that Carlos was again yelling at me, pointing at a corpse on the ground. A few more seconds passed before I realized that he me wanted to chop it up. I unsheathed the machete given to me, threw it into the jungle and then walked toward the aircraft. Carlos intercepted me halfway there, screaming abuse, spitting as he yelled, his face speckled with someone's dried blood. He pushed me backward; pushed again; pushed a third time. I ducked low on push number three, unbalancing him, and drove my fist into his gut. While he was winded, I hooked a closed fist to the meat of his jaw. He spun around half a turn before his legs gave out and he hit the ground hard, out cold.

I heard the *clack* of an AK-47's bolt and a flash suppressor was shoved in my face. The bloodshot eyes of the man on the other end of the weapon, the way they moved from me and then back to the unconscious Carlos, hunting for clues, told me he was uncertain about his next move. He could kill me and that might be a good thing, resulting in a reward, or it might be the wrong thing, in which case a different kind of reward would come down on his ass. I didn't stand around waiting for the guy to make up his mind and merely brushed the muzzle to one side. And, like that, the tension vanished. The boss was merely down for the count, but otherwise uninjured. He could resolve the issues with me himself when he came around, right? Maybe the men were secretly pleased Carlos' lights had been punched out. I knew I enjoyed it.

I sat in the King Air's doorway while the men continued their grisly task, ferrying limbs and torsos to the edge of the runway, setting them down and then moving them, arranging them and then changing their minds like fussy homemakers. The parade made me nauseous. I wanted to get away from there but I was stuck so I tilted my head back, closed my eyes and tried to go someplace else.

When the task was complete, the men returned to the King Air, re-secured the drugs beneath the webbing, and climbed aboard with a groggy Carlos supported between two of them like a drunk at the end of a night out. They sat him in a seat and buckled him in. I went over, patted him down unopposed, removing two knives and, from the back of his pants, an old revolver. He came around as the propellers spun up, saw me sitting beside him. After several long seconds of processing, he leaned forward drunkenly and went for the revolver no longer in the back of his pants. He stopped when he felt my Sig pressed into his ribs. *"Gringo coño,"* he mumbled, still woozy – gringo cunt.

"Sticks and stones, pal," I told him.

The King Air lifted off, climbing steeply, desperately, the undercarriage smacking through the uppermost leaves of the trees off the end of the threshold. Once clear of them, the pilot leveled out, pulled a tight one-eighty and made a low pass back over the runway. I turned around for a look out the porthole as the words *"Matams a todos"* flashed past down on the ground, spelled out in arms and legs – *we kill you all.* The men in the plane nodded and grinned and slapped each other on the back. These guys weren't just killers, they were illiterate killers. They'd missed the 'o' in *Matamos*.

Fifteen

I needed somewhere else to look. The wall behind Perez's head would do. There was a black and white photograph of a Mexican bandit hanging there, a large sombrero pushed back on his head and a couple of ammo bandoliers crossed on his chest. I couldn't decide whether it was an old photo or a new photo made to look old. The bandit was grinning with mischief beneath a thick black inverted V of a moustache. Also on the wall was a map of the north of Mexico and the south of the United States, Texas and the province of Chihuahua butting up against each other.

My attention shifted back to Perez sitting behind his desk. While I couldn't read anything in those black button eyes of his, the fact that he was stropping the pearl-handled knife against a leather strap hanging from a corner of his desk didn't bode well. Carlos' position, though, was clear. The guy wanted me dead. I sat in the chair opposite Perez while his lieutenant paced the room and ranted about how I'd refused to engage in the payback raid and therefore couldn't be trusted; how I wasn't one of *them*. I felt like I'd been detained by the school principal, only in this case the headmaster enjoyed separating people from their skin, most likely with that knife he was honing, while his staff's teaching method was simply to chop folks up.

Meanwhile, I had my own considerations. The base outside the door was large and the significant numbers of men I was yet to quantify were being trained for something more than security. Though the evidence would be considered circumstantial in a court of law, the black King Air and the easy brutality I'd just witnessed left no doubt in my mind that Apostles and Perez had indeed been responsible for the massacre on US soil. I was also certain that Perez himself had led the operation. But all of these pieces were yet to form any kind of clear picture about what they were actually up to. What was coming next? And I was still no closer to getting anything from Perez with his DNA on it that pathologists back in El Paso could use to either positively confirm or eliminate his involvement in the slaughter at Horizon Airport for that court of law. In short, I was getting nowhere.

With a flick of his head, Perez gestured to Carlos to leave. Carlos did as he was told, but only after throwing a malevolent glare at me as he stormed out of the room.

"I asked you to help," growled Perez in English, his face impassive, the knife sliding back and forth across the strop like he was stroking a cat.

"You have people who slice and dice," I replied. "You don't have people who do what I do."

"How do you know what I have? You would be surprised. I am disappointed. What do I do with you?"

That pool bar in the Bahamas came to mind.

"I agree with Carlos. If you will not do what is asked, you cannot be trusted. I think I will kill you and the Saint can meet with your skinless corpse."

I forced myself not to swallow. "Dismembering people might happen every other day in your world, but it doesn't happen a lot in mine. Never, in fact. So maybe after I've been around you people a little longer I'll come to feel it's like doing the dishes after dinner. Meanwhile, as I said, there are other skills I can bring to the table. But if you're not tired of US law enforcement confiscating your drugs and costing you millions, you go right ahead and do what you gotta do with that butter knife of yours."

My impression was that reckless bravado – balls – was the only language Perez understood. He kept stropping back and forth, back and forth, those unblinking pupil-free buttons fixed on me. He put the knife down with care, like he didn't want to damage it in any way, opened a desk drawer, pulled out a pen and paper and scrawled a note on it. "Wait for Juan de Jesús del Los Apostles de Medellín here," he said, pushing the folded sheet of paper across the desk toward me. "We will be watching you."

I reached for it and Perez's hand flashed out, darting like a rattler. Something lightly touched the back of my hand and a split opened out on the skin, two inches long. Pulsing veins and white tendons revealed themselves. It was horrifying and also fascinating. Somehow that asshole had picked up his knife and cut me, all in the one lightning movement. I looked again at the cut in disbelief. It didn't hurt – the blade was so sharp the nerves were yet to realize what had happened.

"Carlos!" Perez called, his voice a spray of gravel across steel roofing.

Blood began to well up out of the cut. I kept staring at it, in shock. Carlos and two others walked in. Carlos leaned over Perez and the boss said a few quiet words while the two other men moved behind me. And then the world turned black as a hood went over my head.

*

I could smell Turbo long before the hood came off. The aroma of rotting shit, sea salt and diesel oil was both unmistakable and reassuring. At least I knew where I was. With the boat secured against the quay, I was dragged up onto solid ground and the cuff locks cut away. The hood came off next, removed by one of Carlos' men, the other flunky covering me with a revolver. The cut on my hand was throbbing, hot bolts of pain shooting up my forearm. Not a good sign. Infection was having a party down there but I couldn't see much in the darkness other than the wound was caked in black blood.

Carlos grabbed my wrist and lifted my hand, I guessed to inspect the damage. I guessed wrong. "When you meet Jesús del Los Apostles," he said, "make sure you tell him we treated you well." He then spat into the wound. One day Carlos and I would exchange words. Or maybe lead. I added him to a mental list I was keeping, a list growing daily on this mission. Any hesitation I had about nominating myself his executioner, a seed planted by CIA dipshit Chalmers back in El Paso, was gone. Perhaps Chalmers' purpose in planting the self-doubt was to make me question my purpose here, even if only for a fateful second or two – just enough indecision to get me killed. Chalmers was so going on that list.

Carlos climbed back into the boat, laughing, as the flunky tossed a plastic bag onto the quay. It landed heavily not far from where I was standing. I watched the boat reverse a short distance before it accelerated forward and surged into the night. I went to the bag and was surprised to find the Sig, three magazines, my wallet – the cash replaced by the folded front page of the *El Diario* – my cell, and even the bottle of DEET. It was like I was back where I started.

The wound on my hand needed attention. Wandering into town, the only shops open were the ones that sold booze. The bar on the water, the place where we'd stumbled across Perez barely forty-eight hours ago, was heaving with drunks and guitarists belting out tunes. I went in and bought two bottles of *aguardiente* and then headed to the bus station where I was hoping to find a room with a shower in the vicinity. At the station I lucked out, coming across a lone vendor selling an array of items to late-night travelers, from bags of potato chips to sewing kits. I bought a bunch of things including said chips and a sewing kit, and then found that room with a shower.

Standing under the cold-water tap, I soaked my hand and drank *aguardiente*. I examined the puffy red skin around the gaping cut, not a good sign. With the black blood soaked away I could still see tendons and the pain was growing more intense despite the help of the local sauce. With the bottle half drunk, I got out of the shower and went over to the table, where a length of cotton thread and a curved needle had been soaking in booze. I threaded the needle eventually, took another swig of *aguardiente*, and poured the alcohol in and around the cut. It stung like a bitch and made the flesh around the wound pucker. Taking the needle between shaking fingers, I sewed the two sides of red inflamed skin together with half a dozen large, painful sutures. To finish, I smeared toothpaste on the wound to dry it out.

Sitting on the chair, naked, I looked down at myself and drunkenly counted the scars I could see. There were plenty I couldn't. What a fucking mess. I had broken a couple of fingers on my left hand a year or two earlier that occasionally gave me some trouble. Perhaps this injury to my right would even things out a little. The second bottle of liquor was waiting patiently. I opened it and drank half while I ate dinner, which was a packet of chips, and collapsed facedown on the bed, the timetable for the bus to Medellín under my cheek.

*

There was a Piper Cub mounted on top of the entrance gate to Hacienda Nápoles, Pablo Escobar's retreat in the Colombian countryside near the town of Puerto Triunfo on the Magdalena River. According to the plaque on the gate, this very aircraft flew the drug lord's first shipment to America. I've heard of self-made millionaires framing their first big check for sentimental reasons and I supposed the Cub was Escobar's variation on the theme. I stood aside for yet another minibus turning into the driveway, full of tourists come to ogle the dead criminal's lifestyle.

Drinking the last of a bottle of Gatorade, I flicked it into the trash. The jury's out on the exact number of people Escobar murdered before he was shot dead himself on a rooftop in Medellín, but it was somewhere in the thousands. The fact that he was a greedy, manipulative, murdering psychopath who turned his country into a financial basket case with stratospheric murder rates was fading from the public consciousness. Folks had short memories.

I got back into my current mode of transport, an ancient purple Kia bought for cash off the sidewalk in Medellín. The thing blew smoke like an old pothead and had to be topped up with oil at every gas stop, but at least it was free of electronic bugs. Perez's boast that he would be watching me had been on my mind from the moment he said it and I was pretty sure he wasn't being metaphorical about it. I searched all my returned possessions and eventually found a tracking device secreted in the bottom of the bottle of DEET, which was now in a tourist's backpack heading south to Rio de Janeiro.

Perez had scrawled the Saint's address for me on that sheet of paper so he knew where I was going. I just didn't like the thought of the little blade-stropping gnome sitting on my shoulder and knowing my every move.

As I drove along, the fence lining the road suddenly became new white posts and rails, which suggested money splashed around on maintenance and upkeep, something the authorities turning the Escobar place into a cheesy theme park seemed to lack. The land behind the fence was also not overgrown but a mixture of open land for grazing dotted here and there with islands of tress and thick bushes. The front entrance to Apostles' place would be coming up soon – Hacienda Mexico. I was wondering what the Saint might mount on top of his gate, other than surveillance gear, when it flashed by suddenly on the right. It was ordinary, if a heavy steel gate between two reinforced brick columns in the middle of pretty much nowhere can be considered ordinary. It was the sort of gate designed to discourage everything from ram raiders to nosy US federal agents. I drove on, unsure about whether I should make an appearance with my hand the way it was. Swabs of iodine and hydrogen peroxide were getting on top of the wound and a local doctor had replaced the sutures I put in with ones that didn't resemble a kid's shoelaces. My paw was now thickly bandaged and looked like a Casper the Friendly Ghost hand puppet.

A helicopter appeared unexpectedly from behind a hill, came in low over the road and crossed the fence into the Hacienda not too far in front of me. I watched as it climbed a hundred feet or so, cleared some trees and descended, coming in to land. Was the Saint on the way in, or heading out? I drove on, looking for a place to make a U-turn.

Around a bend an old green Renault was pulled over onto the side of the road, its rear end jacked up. A woman was standing behind the vehicle, hands on hips, a little overwhelmed. I could use some cover for additional hang time in the vicinity, right? I pulled up behind and walked over. "*Hola.*"

"*Hola,*" the woman said without enthusiasm, her car's trunk open.

"*¿Necesitas ayuda?*" I asked. Need help?

"Sorry, I don't speak Spanish," she lied with an accent that was equal parts Spanish and American.

"That's a relief," I told her. "Me neither. Need help changing that wheel?"

"No, thank you. I can do it," she said.

"You sure?"

"A flat tire is nothing."

The damsel was maybe late twenties, dark eyes, straight dark hair and olive skin. Despite the denial about the linguistic skills, her overall appearance promised that she could *olé* like a native, assuming they did that in this country. I walked past, glanced inside the car and caught a glimpse of a digital SLR camera with a high-power lens and a pair of powerful military-grade binoculars on the driver's seat.

"Nice camera," I remarked, and the look on her face suggested I'd just trodden on her foot.

"I am a birdwatcher," she told me tersely.

I smiled. Of course she was. "Seen any yellow-bellied sapsuckers?"

"What are they?"

"Birds."

"There is no such bird."

I was sure she was wrong, but what did I know? "So, you're good?"

"Yes, I'm good. Thank you."

The thankyou was an afterthought and there was no thanks in it. I happened to see into the trunk area as the woman replaced the floor mat. "Well, have fun," I said. *"Buenos días."*

"Buenos días."

I got back to my car and sat behind the wheel as the woman turned the handle on the jack, lowering the car. She had nice legs. In fact, I couldn't help noticing that she was nice all over, except for an attitude on the wrong side of testy. I started the car and pulled onto the road, doing that U-turn and heading back the way I'd come. I waved farewell and wondered what she'd changed given there was no spare in the trunk.

The gate came up quickly, diverting my thoughts away from the woman. On impulse, I turned in, stopped and pulled off the sock puppet. What the hell – unemployed fugitives like me who were keen to seek gainful employment didn't put these things off. I got out of the car and walked to an intercom covered by a surveillance camera, perched on top of the brick pillar like a robot bird peering over the edge. I pressed the button on the intercom. *"Hola."*

Nothing.

"Hola," I repeated and waited.

"Vete a la mierda," growled a male voice. Or, in short, fuck off. No doubt someone was checking out my car and deciding that any person driving a piece of crap like that had no business ringing the bell.

"Juan de Jesús del Los Apostles de Medellín. He's expecting me."

"¿Quién es usted?" Who are you?

"Vin Cooper."

Silence.

The green Renault drove past on the road behind me, the attractive non-Spanish-speaking Colombian woman with the non-flat tire. Her eyes flicked in my direction but only for an instant before they returned to the road in front of her.

"Wait there," said a different voice – an American voice – through the intercom.

I waited, keeping half an eye on the driveway beyond the gate, watching for movement. A white golf cart eventually appeared, driven by a trim blond Scandinavian-looking type in his thirties, a Colombian goon in the passenger seat beside him large enough to compress the cart's suspension so that it drove lopsided. The cart pulled up on the other side of the gate, which remained closed, and both men got out. The goon wore a coat, despite the heat and humidity. He pulled it away from his body a little to show the piece he carried in a holster below his armpit – why, I have no idea. Perhaps the warning was standard operating procedure in his line of work.

"*Buenos días,*" said the blond guy. "Can I help you?" I recognized his voice as the one in the intercom, an educated voice dressed in knitted shirt, shorts and boat shoes, no socks. We were a long way from any boats.

By way of an answer, I passed through the bars the now blood-stained note scribbled by the Tears of Chihuahua.

He scanned it. "You have some identification, Mr Cooper?"

I went for the folded newsprint in my back pocket, which triggered a response from the goon, the coat coming away from his gun in a hurry and his other hand reaching in.

"Easy, Mack," I told him, slowing my movements. Producing the folded paper, I waggled it so they could both see it wasn't going to shoot them and opened it out to show the front page of *El Diario*.

A phone began to ring, some Beyoncé tune. The guy in the boat shoes took out his cell, decided not to take the call and put it back in his pocket. "Señor Apostles is not here," he informed me.

"I was told he would be," I said and motioned the note in his hand, the details scrawled on it by Perez.

The guy returned the note through the bars. His cell rang again. He removed it from his pocket a second time and turned it off, this time without checking the screen. "Change of plans. He wants you to meet with him in Bogotá. Tonight, eight o'clock at Dry 73."

"Dry 73?"

"Go to the Marriott. There is a bar. They do martinis. You like martinis?"

"No."

He shrugged before turning and going back to the cart, the goon following. The cart reversed into a bay and then accelerated silently, disappearing quickly into the trees.

I scoped the general area. Deserted. The only noise was coming from my tinnitus. Bogotá was a four-hour drive, six in my piece of crap, assuming it was even capable of going the distance. I walked over to it, got in, reversed back out onto the road and stood on the gas. Glancing into the rear-vision mirror, I saw a black Range Rover turn out of the Hacienda Mexico gate and accelerate onto the road behind me. It came up fast in the rear-view mirror, seemingly in a hurry. Slowing down I made a passing gesture out my window; the big black off-roader ignored the offer and instead just ploughed into the back of my car. My neck snapped back against the headrest and then jack-knifed forward.

"Hey!" I yelled.

The vehicle rammed the rear bumper a second time and the Kia swerved and bucked and threatened to skid sideways.

That's when the shooting started. The window behind me shattered, filling the air with crystals of safety glass. Holes appeared in the roof, letting in daylight.

I pulled the Sig. What the fuck? Or rather, who? Was it the guy in the boat shoes? The goon? Blood was everywhere. Had I been hit? And then I realized that reaching behind for my weapon had inadvertently ripped the surgical tape and the scab clean off the wound on my hand and blood was pouring out of it, making the Sig's handgrip equal parts slick and sticky.

Whoever was behind the wheel of the Range Rover knew how to drive. And in this heap I couldn't out-accelerate, out-brake or outmaneuver it. The road ahead was clear of traffic. I couldn't see a way out. As it pulled adjacent with the Kia's boot, I shot out the front tire. A puff of dust on the sidewall indicated a bull's-eye as air rushed from the hole, but it made no difference. The damn thing had run-flat tires.

The four-wheel drive shouldered the Kia's fender, which pushed the car into wild oversteer. It skidded sideways, came up on two wheels, and hit the dirt and grass on the side of the road. A spin came next, swapping end-to-end, all control gone. Then the car was on its side, sliding, the cabin filling with dust and glass and noise. A collision with something. Sky, earth, sky. And then, for a moment, silence. Fluids began to gurgle and steam escaped from under the hood. I was dazed. Somehow the Kia had ended up on its wheels, right way up, almost swallowed by a thick shroud of unkempt bush.

"Get out of the car," a man yelled. My brain was still spinning. "I said get the fuck out!"

The door beside me was wrenched open. An arm came across my chest, the seatbelt released, and I was pulled out of the seat by my collar and dragged along the ground.

"Well look who we got here. Vin fucking Cooper."

It was Kirk Matheson, a Glock in his shaking hand. He stood over me, the sling hanging loose from his neck. He was excited, pumped up, shaking like a cop who has just caught himself someone drifting in a parking lot.

"I saw your face in the surveillance camera. How fuckin' lucky was that? I tried calling it through, but the fool wouldn't pick up. So you're after a job with the Angel?" He laughed. "You and I both know that ain't gonna happen, Mr Under-fucking-cover."

I moved my jaw around. It'd taken a hit somewhere along the way. Where was my Sig? What day was it?

"Get up!" he demanded.

I managed to roll onto my front and take a knee.

"You're coming back to the hacienda. Once the Angel finds out what you're all about, he gonna have some fun with you, my friend. Might even get Perez over, peel you like a spud."

The world came slowly back into focus.

"I said get up!" More yelling.

I got to my feet, feeling shaky. And then Matheson was gone. He had been standing right in front of me. And then he was snatched away by a green blur. I turned my head in time to see the guy complete an arc through the air and come down heavily in some thick scrubby grass and bush back from the road like a bag of trash thrown from a speeding vehicle. The green flash turned out to be the Renault driven by the woman faking a flat. The driver's door opened and the woman in question got out and ran to the body lying in the weeds. With a hit like that, Matheson should've been dead but he moved slow, like a snake shifting its coils in the sun. I gave my head a shake to clear it and walked over, drawing the Sig.

"You hit him," I said.

"Of course I hit him," she replied.

Yeah, okay, not the sharpest opener.

She looked down on the half-dead body of the former El Paso County Sheriff's deputy.

"Why'd you hit him?"

"None of your business." She flicked her hair away from her face. "You are lucky I din hit you."

I still didn't get it. "You were staking out the Saint's hacienda."

She answered by pulling a black Ruger pistol from the back of her jeans, aiming it at Matheson and almost managing to get off a shot before I snatched the pistol out of her hand. "Hey!" she snapped at me.

I dropped out the magazine, ejected the round in the chamber onto the ground and handed the weapon back to her.

Matheson groaned.

"I need him," I told her.

"And who are you?" she asked.

"A guy looking for a job," I said.

"With the Shit of Medellín?" she sneered. "Yes, I thin' I should have hit you also. You are like them!"

I thought of those CSI tents dotting the apron at Horizon and the misspelled word on a jungle airstrip and hoped to god she was wrong.

"Your hand is bleeding," she observed.

I glanced at it absently. It was. I crouched beside Matheson.

"What are you gonna do with him?"

"Take him for a little ride." I saw the 9mm parabellum round on the grass, picked it up and handed it to her. Then I grabbed Matheson's wrist, the one attached to his bad arm, and hoisted him onto my shoulder. He groaned again, semiconscious. "You mind getting the trunk?" I asked the woman as I lifted my chin at the Range Rover, straining under the load.

"Get it yourself." She flicked her hair again and strutted off toward her car. Strut was something she knew how to do. For a moment I thought she was gonna turn and pout, or maybe wink, and then walk back the other way.

The keys were hanging conveniently out of Matheson's pocket. I snatched them and thumbed the trunk's release button, dumped him in the empty space, and then went back to the wrecked Kia to retrieve my bag and cover the tunnel it had made in the bush with some loose fronds. The Renault drove off with a handful of wheelspin. I wondered what the woman's story was. She had some beef with Apostles otherwise why have his place under surveillance? She was also prepared to do a hit and run on Matheson and didn't act or sound like any kind of law enforcement I was familiar with.

I cleaned up the general area, finding Matheson's handgun in the weeds as well as his wallet. I threw the pistol into a nearby muddy pool and checked his wallet. A wad of pesos but no business cards or phone numbers so I stuffed it in his back pocket. A few cars came and went along the road, but none stopped. I pulled a couple of sets of cuff locks from my bag and hog-tied him with them. The guy was drifting in and out of consciousness but he'd come around soon enough and when he did I didn't want any trouble.

Patting him down, hoping to find his cell, all I came up with was some loose change. He must have left it back at the ranch. I trotted to the driver's door, hopped in and found a nice surprise: a cell phone sitting in a cradle. It had to be Matheson's. The lock screen showed a default pattern. Thumbing the slide revealed the request for a passcode. I shrugged. Having the cell was better than not having it, but it was no help to me.

The Range Rover purred into life at the touch of a button. Making Bogotá in the time remaining suddenly didn't seem like such a big deal.

"Cooper …"

Matheson had finally come to his senses.

"Cooper … !"

I turned on the radio. "China Grove" by the Doobie Brothers was playing.

"Cooper!"

That's what I like about these Brit cars – great sound systems.

"HEY! MOTHERFUCKER!"

Pumping up the volume, I slipped the shift into drive and wondered if this was the model rover they sent to Mars.

Sixteen

I watched a United 747 take off and struggle for altitude while I waited for Panda to answer the phone. The air was thin here. Just walking around made me feel light-headed, like being a little drunk. Not near as much fun, but free. The call went through. *"Si?"* said a tentative voice down the line.

"Panda?"

"Yes."

"It's Cooper."

My name took a moment to register while he attached a face to it.

"Cooper," he repeated aloud.

Matheson was quiet for the moment. Duct tape over the mouth and a Sig to the head will guarantee that. "Something I need picked up."

"Where from?" Panda asked.

"El Dorado International, Bogotá."

"What's the package?"

"Kirk Matheson."

After a lengthy silence, he said, "It can be arranged."

I gave him the details of the Range Rover as well as the car park and bay numbers where it would be found and told him the keys were on the front right-hand tire. Then I followed up with a brief rundown on the past week.

"Anything else?" Panda asked like I hadn't done nearly enough and really should pull my finger out. Maybe he was right. I'd had my chance with Perez and blown it. And I remained outside of the Saint's operation.

"A sweeping generalization," I said. "These people – and I use the term 'people' loosely – have opted out of the human race."

Panda wasn't interested. "When are you meeting Apostles?"

"Tonight."

"It's management that sets the tone for a corporation. Don't let the charm fool you."

He wasn't telling me anything I didn't know. With Perez as the managing director of the business, Apostles, the CEO, had to be a complete whack job. At least when he wasn't building orphanages.

I heard a groan from the trunk. "When are you gonna make the pickup? The package is about to get restless."

"On their way. Fifteen minutes out."

Fifteen minutes was fast. CIA usually needs more time to tear itself away from the mirror. Maybe it was subcontracting in Bogotá. "One last thing. Tell Chalmers I could've sent Matheson home in a bag."

More silence.

"He'll know what I'm talking about," I said. The call ended without goodbyes and I cleared the phone's history. Checking on Matheson, I could see he was in a fair amount of discomfort, which suited me fine. With a little more time up my sleeve I would have questioned him about events back in El Paso, but time was something in short supply. I doubled the duct tape, checked his hands and feet one final time, locked the vehicle with the remote and placed it on the front right-hand tire.

I bought clothes from a shop in the Marriott lobby, all of it Gant except for the Timberland boat shoes, taking my cues from the help back at the Saint's hacienda, the Yacht-Owning Hamptons Wannabe look. I didn't do a lot of undercover work but I do know it pays to blend in. The disguise was working. No one gave me a second glance.

The concierge told me that Dry 73 was tucked away beside the Marriott's restaurant. He also told me the name stemmed from the fact that it served 73 different flavors of martini – banana, strawberry, lime and so forth. I was pretty sure I wasn't going to find one I liked unless it was Glen Keith-flavored.

The entrance to the bar was roped off along with a stand that announced FUNCIÓN PRIVADA, the words *Private function* in brackets beneath. "You are a guest at the *función*, sir?" asked a young male waiter in gray suit and Marriott tie hovering beside the sign.

"Yep," I replied. He hesitated, wrestling with this matter-of-fact answer, trying to decide which was more dangerous: pull the rope aside and let me pass or turn me away. After a few seconds of inner turmoil he unclipped the rope and said, "Welcome, Señor."

The bar itself was small, a feature wall lined with black salt bricks dug out of the rock, which also accounted for the name of the adjoining restaurant – La Mina, or the Mine. Yellow boxes of light suspended from the low ceiling contrasted with the bar's seating, individual chairs of a blue so electric they almost hummed. But I was less interested in the interior decorating than I was in the people occupying a group of those chairs: a couple of exquisitely manicured Chinese bookends dressed in red satin cheongsams and the man sitting between them, the Saint of Medellín Juan de Apostles. I took a few steps toward them but was immediately intercepted by a broad Mexican tough wearing an expensive navy suit and an earpiece. His shaved brown head was so glossy I could see those yellow lightboxes perfectly reproduced on his dome in miniature. This was a shine you usually only drive off a showroom floor.

'I'm invited,' I informed him, in case he thought I was some random sneaking in for a cheesecake martini, and showed him the note from Perez. He skimmed it and then his hands were inside my jacket, searching around my beltline, where they quickly found the Sig. Removing it, he expelled the mag, ejected the round in the chamber and handed the lot back to me. In case I had any ideas, he opened his own jacket to reveal a machine pistol concealed nice and snug under his armpit. There was nothing else to interest him and the patdown finished, but he gestured to a dark corner of the bar where another man stared back, unblinking, just to let me know that the odds were heavily weighted in their favor if I was thinking about doing some bad.

I left the Mexican security goon behind and walked toward the bar. One of the Chinese women turned her head. She had light-gray eyes with heavy linework to make them appear almond. Her full, heart-shaped lips were painted bright red. If she was Chinese, I was Pekinese. Her black hair, which shone with blue highlights, was worn up and sculpted into loose coils held in place by a pair of gold chopsticks. The red cheongsam, embroidered with small gold and blue dragons, was buttoned at the base of her smooth neck and short sleeves revealed long slim olive-skinned arms. She shifted slightly in her seat, which was an arm of the chair occupied by Apostles, revealing more of a crossed leg framed by a split that ended mid-thigh. It would make my day if she had another leg just like it. On the end of her smooth olive calves were red lacquered stilettos, the heels four-inch spikes.

Those gray eyes dropped down my body and then back again, weighing up the unknown male about to invade their space. I read in those eyes that while intrigued and not altogether displeased by what they saw, she was still unconvinced. At least that's how I read it. She sipped something brown from a martini glass, managed a coy smile, and telepathically communicated my presence to the other piece of bread in the Apostle sandwich – the woman who, like the meat in the middle, had her back to me. This woman turned her head slightly and revealed the gray eyes and red lips of a twin who was, at least at first glance, in every way identical to the other. I was seeing double, a first while stone-cold sober. The only way to tell the two of them apart was that the gold dragons on this sister's cheongsam were embroidered with green thread rather than blue.

Apostles had a thing for twins. I knew that – it was in his bio. Envy isn't something I do all that much, but I was seeing it.

Apostles leaned a little forward to catch what the distraction was, and that gave me a look at his face. His hair was thick and straight and salt and pepper, layers of it swept from a high brow that suggested brains back there somewhere. The eyes were dark and framed by heavy black eyebrows yet to gray. His nose was long and generous and there was a bulb at the end of it with a vague cleft that reminded me of a head of garlic. A week of ragged salt and pepper stubble occupied his neck and cheeks, framing a thick old-style moustache. Yes, the Latino Don Johnson force was strong with this one. He wore a gray flannel suit with light-blue business shirt open three buttons at the throat – one button too many in my opinion – revealing a tuft of salt and pepper chest hair.

With one eye on the goon for reassurance, he asked "*¿Quién coño eres tú?*" Who the fuck are you?

I handed over the note from Perez. "A cop killer."

"Did I hear about you?" he said, scanning the note, switching to English with a hint of Oxford about it. "Were you at the hacienda this afternoon?"

"Yes."

"And you want a job."

"If you've got one."

"Get lost before my boy kills you."

"He can try," I said. Apostles took another look at me and so did the slices of bread in the cheongsams either side of him. The one with the blue and gold dragons glanced over at the bar and raised a finger, and a waiter sprinted over.

"I'm having a chocolate martini," she said with a vaguely Texan accent. "Would anyone care to join me? Mister ... ?" She turned those gray eyes on me fully. They were like lenses with lights behind them and I experienced a moment of vertigo like the floor had dropped away beneath my feet.

"He doesn't have a name," said Apostles. "He is nameless until I say it can be otherwise."

"Two," said Green Dragons to the waiter as she drew figure eights on Apostles' thigh. "*Cariño?*" Darling?

"*Si*, okay," he replied, not taking his eyes off me.

"Four," Blue Dragons informed the waiter and he ran off to see to them. She looked at me again but I was prepared for it second time around. "So you were saying you kill police?"

"I try not to make a habit of it," I said, wondering whether I should sit or keep standing. I was having a drink now, evidently. A chocolate martini. I shuddered.

"An associate of mine has gone missing," said Apostles. "You were at the hacienda at around the same time. Did you happen to see anything?"

"Like what?" I asked.

"He was driving a Range Rover – black. He drove off and hasn't come back."

"Maybe he ran away."

"Do you want a job or do you want my people to take you outside?"

I made out like I was searching my memory. "Yeah, now that you mention it ... A black Range Rover almost ran me off the road. Doing a hundred miles an hour, going somewhere in a hurry. He was a friend of yours?" I shook my head. "He was around the bend and gone. No way I was going to catch him, but I wanted to, you know, tell him to slow down."

"He was a cop," said Blue Dragons. "If you'd have caught him, would you have killed him?" She smiled. It was a smile I could get used to being around.

Apostles cut Blue Dragons off. "So I'll ask again. Who the fuck are you?"

"Ex-Special Agent Vin Cooper, OSI." I handed him the *El Diario* front page.

"OSI – what's that?" He held the page away from him to read it.

"United States Air Force Office of Special Investigations."

"What do I do with you? I don't have an air force."

"What do you call the planes that fly your cargo into the United States?"

He regarded me, head tilted on a slight angle, intrigued. "What about them?"

"How many do you lose? And what does that cost you?" I let those questions hang in the air for a pregnant moment, giving him time to add all those zeroes. "I can get 'em into the US – guaranteed."

He twisted in his seat to get a better look at me. "How?"

"Before I was an Air Force cop, I was a special tactics officer. They'd drop me behind enemy lines to set up beacons for the bombers. But first we had to penetrate air defenses, which was also my job. I'd say that the United States is your enemy. Pay me right and I'll get you inside, behind the enemy's lines."

He was interested.

"Go on."

"Your market's not US–Mexican border towns, it's San Antonio, Austin, Dallas, Houston ... What if I can get your aircraft safely on the doorsteps of those cities? And get them out again. No DEA, no seizures, no loss of income."

Apostles' eyes glittered. "What's it gonna cost me?"

"I'm not greedy," I said.

"Greedy gets you dead."

"How much revenue have you lost in the US over the last twelve months? Thirty million? Fifty? Now think about losing nothing. I figure five percent of every shipment I successfully take into the States is reasonable."

He gazed at me, balancing my offer in some kind of mental scale. "One percent," he said finally.

Bingo, we were negotiating. "Four percent."

"Don't waste my time. You want two and a half percent," he said. "If we were to agree on that, you'll also train several others to do your job."

"And once they're trained up, you'll make them do it for nothing and have me killed."

"Not if you find ways to make yourself indispensable."

"Is anyone?"

His features slid into a position that could be called a smile. I took that as a no.

"And what if those shipments are delivered unsuccessfully?" asked Green Dragons, her back to me but her head angled in my general direction.

"As I'll be riding in there with them, you could say I'll have skin in the game. Get it wrong and it'll be a long stretch in a federal penitentiary for me."

Apostles didn't say anything, not immediately. "I'll think about it," he said eventually. "I'm going to ask around. Get you checked out."

The waiter arrived with four chocolate martinis on a tray and offered them to the twins. Blue Dragons took two, stood up and walked mine over to me. She was tall, maybe five-eleven. It was difficult to tell – those heels were high. But I was happy to see she did have another leg to complement the other one finding its way through that slit with every step. Her perfume swept over me, an erotic caress. "You ever had one of these before?" she asked, handing me the drink, her perfect nails painted with black lacquer. She talked and moved with a venomous sexuality.

"No."

"Try it."

I took a sip. Hmm ... cleaning fluid with chocolate after-taste.

"What do you think?"

"Yummy," I told her.

"I don't believe you. What do you usually drink?"

"Single malt."

"A man who likes scotch," she said as if it was an invitation, turning to walk back to her perch. I couldn't help but notice her long back or the swell of her ass and the way it moved against the silk. I put the drink on the table.

"Come to the hacienda tomorrow," Apostles said as he placed his hand on Blue Dragons' leg and chased it up the split. "Before you leave, where are you staying?"

"I don't know," I replied, glancing at his hand, envious of it. "I'm new in town."

I toyed with the thought that Blue Dragons was disappointed to see me go, but only for a moment because crazy hit-and-run girl with the green Renault was striding into the bar, looking for trouble. I could see that the Mexican tough in the suit behind her had his weapon drawn but seemed confused about how to stop her. She looked different to the girl I remembered. Gone was the student jeans-and-an-old-T-shirt look. In its place was a fitted black satin dress that came to mid-thigh and silver strappy heels. Her eyes wore dark, dangerous makeup and her lips shone with a pink gloss. As I watched, she pulled that pistol of hers from a silver clutch bag.

"You son of a bitch," she said, low and determined, and kept coming. Her eyes were on Apostles. She was beside me, the pistol coming up as she extended her arm and took aim.

This wasn't the time or the place. I chopped down with a knife-hand strike on her inside elbow joint, which altered the angle of the gun toward those overhead yellow lightboxes. The sharp pain caused her to cry out. Smacking the base of the weapon dislodged it from her grip and it looped forward around her forefinger. I caught the weapon when it was pointing back toward her and pulled it from her grasp. That's when the Mexican tough hit her, then wrapped his arms around her and lifted her up off the ground as she swore and spat and kicked her legs.

"You!" She glared at me. The Mexican held her tighter, his buddy in the corner moving in to see if he needed assistance. 'Put me down,' she panted, struggling to breathe in the grip of a bear hug.

Apostles was on his feet, as were the two dragons. Both women had their arms folded and Blue Dragons was smiling for reasons I couldn't fathom.

"Juliana," said Apostles, taking a step toward her. "I believed things had been sorted out between us."

Juliana. Okay, at least now I had a name.

"I hate you," Juliana replied, still struggling. Her face was reddening from mild oxygen starvation.

"You already know my daughter, I see," Apostles remarked to me as he calmly watched the fight drain out of her.

"Your daughter?"

"From my first wife," he said, drawing loony-bin circles in the air beside his temple. He motioned to the Mexican goon who then set her down and released her. Juliana leaned back on an electric-blue chair and I picked her silver clutch bag up off the floor and put it into her hand. "How do you know her?" Apostles asked.

"We met in the foyer earlier. I tried to pick her up." I shrugged, suggesting the attempt had been unsuccessful.

"Yes, beautiful and crazy – just like her mother."

"You killed her heart," Juliana snapped.

"I thought you were finished with all this nonsense," Apostles countered and pulled me aside. "Do me a favor. Take her out, talk some sense into her, though I'm not expecting miracles." A roll of cash was palmed into my hand. "Buy her something nice. I owe you. Come and see me tomorrow. The hacienda ..."

Time to leave. I took Juliana by the elbow and tried to get her moving. She shook her arm from my grasp and walked unsteadily toward the exit. I glanced back at Apostles and his "angels" – angels for the Saint. Blue Dragons still had that bemused smile on her face and now I knew what it meant. Juliana's show was nothing they hadn't all seen before.

Seventeen

I retook Juliana by the elbow and led her at a trot through the hotel foyer toward the exit. "Let me go!" she hissed. "I should have killed you when I had the chance."

A group of hotel guests overheard and gawked at us. The door opened and I ushered Juliana through it. Her car was nowhere to be seen. I signaled the line of taxis, and one of them peeled off the end and sped to our side. I opened the rear door, fed her to the back seat and climbed in after. That was as far as I had thought. Bogotá and I were strangers. "Drive. *Vamos,*" I urged the man behind the wheel.

He grunted. "Eh?"

I repeated the request. He shrugged and we pulled away from the curb. I pared half a dozen notes off the roll Apostles gave me, passed them to the front and said, *"Bares, restaurantes – más caros,"* telling him to take us to expensive bars and restaurants.

"Si," he said and took a hard right.

"You want the Zona G," Juliana said, her knees almost up around her chest in the confined space, the vehicle about the size of an olive. "Let me off here." She opened the door. I pulled it shut and slammed down the lock.

"Were you going to kill him?" I asked.

"Of course."

"Your pistol was light. There was no ammo in it. Which reminds me ..." I retrieved it from my belt line and dropped it into her lap. She turned and flashed me a look of poison. "You took a big risk for no return."

"Let me out!" she demanded.

"He wants me to talk some sense into you."

"Why should I listen to you? You're a gangster like the rest of them."

"I'm just a guy looking for a job," I assured her.

"Are you a plumber, a carpenter? No."

I wondered if she was going to make the leap to Matheson and ask why I'd abducted him and lied to her father about it. Meanwhile, she chose to sit and look out the window with her arms crossed.

A short while later the cab pulled over to a sidewalk thick with folks out for a stroll. Down the road, a dozen neon signs fought with each other for attention, advertising a range of bars, restaurants and nightclubs. Music drifted through the cool high-altitude night air. I got out. Juliana pulled the door shut behind me, hit the lock and the taxi's tires squealed as it took off. I watched it accelerate down the street.

Shit.

Half a block away, the cab came to an emergency stop. The door opened, Juliana climbed out and she strutted back down the sidewalk toward me. She came to a stop inside my personal space. Her breath smelled sweet. "You lied about the man outside Father's hacienda. Why?"

There it was. "Are you hungry?"

"I need a drink."

"How about a martini?"

"They are disgusting. I hate them."

I smiled. This might just work out.

*

Over at the bar, a long and mostly empty counter, a group of what appeared to be IT professionals out on the town for a bonding session were slapping each other's backs and doing shots. I glanced at Juliana over a Maker's Mark with rocks and watched her sip a vodka, lime and soda. We sat in a booth, all the others vacant, the Latino music loud enough to cover the conversation without killing it.

"I don't understand how you fit in," she said.

"Maybe because I don't fit in," I said.

"Why are you here?"

"I'm a US federal agent who shot a couple of Sheriff's deputies in a drug bust. That also put a bullet in my current and future job prospects in the States so I flew south, looking for gainful employment." I shrugged. "I gotta eat."

"How do you sleep at night?" she replied.

"Because I killed some people?"

"Yes. You look relaxed about it."

"Does it help if I tell you they were trying to kill me at the time?"

"They were just doing their job."

"And I was just trying to stay alive." Though Juliana was hanging me for crimes I hadn't committed on that particular occasion, the conversation was making me uncomfortable, as if any moment she'd peel off her skin and reveal Chalmers lurking beneath.

"It's not just that you have killed people – look at who you want to work for."

"Your father's not so bad." I nearly choked on those words – the Horizon Airport massacre, the activities of his right-hand man, Perez …

She gave a snort of derision as if I still didn't get it. "If you work for him, you will see." She stirred her drink with a plastic straw. "The man in the Range Rover. He tried to run you off the road. Why don't you tell me about that?"

"He was a cop from Texas. He must be working under-cover, trying to infiltrate your father's operation. I guess he recognized me at the hacienda. Perhaps he saw me on the security camera. He knew that if we met face to face I'd blow his cover, so he jumped at the opportunity to eliminate the risk." I tipped my glass at her. "Thanks for your help on that score, by the way."

"He was a lawman. If I'd known all this, it's you I would have hit."

Right.

"It would have been a fitting revenge."

"You want revenge against me?" I asked.

"It's not about you."

"I keep hearing that," I told her.

"Your CIA should hunt him down and kill him like they killed Escobar – without his shoes on, running like a scared pig."

Okay, this girl had some serious father issues. "What do you do when you're not stalking your old man?"

"I am a model."

I could believe it.

Juliana scanned the room. A couple of those soused IT professionals were leering her way, working up the nerve to ask her to rumba or cha-cha or whatever they did here. "Why didn't you just tell my father the truth?" she said. "Why didn't you tell him the man he thought was his ally was actually his enemy? I would have liked to see his face."

"Because he's going to be cautious with me – your father doesn't know me. *I* could be working undercover for all he knows. Best to avoid even raising the subject."

"Did you kill him, the man with the Range Rover?" she asked.

"No. I sent him home with a note for his pals in Texas."

"What did this note say?"

"'Burned.'" By now, Matheson would be sitting in a debriefing room in a bunker, screaming for his lawyer.

"Why are you smiling?" Juliana asked.

"No reason." I changed the subject. "Girls love their fathers. And then there's you ..."

"My father is crazy."

"He said the same about you. Does crazy run in the family?"

She turned and hit me, a closed fist in the bicep. It hurt. This girl hit hard.

"I owed you that," she said, rubbing her elbow joint where I'd chopped down on it. "He will get you killed," she said. "Or he will *have* you killed."

"*Perdón, Señorita. Estás juntos?*"

It was one of the IT guys – pale skin with a wispy black unkempt beard and some kind of dermatitis around the nose, wearing jeans and a red check shirt. He looked nervously at Juliana and then at me, probably wondering what the punch was all about. He also wanted to know whether Juliana was with me. A security blanket accompanied him, a buddy who was a slightly taller version, in black pants and a waistcoat that could have come from a dump bin at a second-hand clothing shop. Their faces were shinny from too much *aguardiente* and their gyroscopes weren't working properly – both swayed and not to the music. Not that I buy into league tables, but these hombres were way out of theirs with Juliana. I figured that's why they felt emboldened to push their noses into our space – they felt the same about me.

"*¿Qué?*" Juliana snapped at them.

Politely, they informed her they had a bet with some others in the group that she was "the girl in the orange juice ad". She said they'd won the bet. Then they asked her to dance. I thought Juliana was going to decline the offer, but suddenly she was gone and on the floor being twirled and spun and handed from one to the other. Juliana could dance. In fact she danced like she walked – with the arrogance of someone who knew people enjoyed watching how she moved.

Finishing my drink, I put some bills under the glass, grabbed my bag and left. It had been a long day. I'd come to the end of mine and Juliana looked like hers was just beginning. I figured if it was meant to be I'd run into her again, or she'd run into me – hopefully not in that green Renault of hers. I wondered what the real story was between her and Apostles. Perhaps she was just naturally fiery and that performance with the gun at the martini bar was just her way of grabbing her father's attention.

Not too far down the road, I stopped opposite a hotel, drawn there by the big Hilton 'H'. Tonight, I was gonna leave the Third World behind and check into a little piece of home.

A bus went past and there was Juliana on the side of it, a twenty-foot version of her lying around in an orange shoestring bikini, sipping orange juice from an orange with a straw stuck into it. Her breasts were almost falling out of the corn-chip-sized cups. The headline on the ad said something about how even the packaging was kept to a bare minimum. I wondered how many traffic accidents the ad had caused.

"No, you don't want to stay here."

It was Juliana herself. She'd walked up behind me.

"I don't?" I said.

"No. Every Hilton is the same as every other Hilton. It is like eating a cheeseburger from McDonald's – the same wherever you go. You must try the Bogotá experience."

"Does it have a nice firm mattress, room service and small bottles of scotch in the drawer?" I asked.

"I'll show you."

I took that as a no re scotch and so forth. She called out to a cab parked nearby, waiting for Hilton guests. "Where are your friends?"

"Which friends?"

"From the bar."

"They were just boys."

It was a non answer, like the one about the mattress and the bottles of scotch, but I was too tired to play or even argue. Maybe it was the altitude. The cab stopped beside us. I opened the rear passenger door and Juliana jumped in. *"La Candelaria, por favor. Calle ocho, numero cincuenta y siete,"* she told the driver.

A moment later we were speeding through mostly empty streets. I checked my watch – just after ten. "What's La Candelaria?"

"The old town. The university is there. Many bars. The hotels are cheap and they have style."

Just as long as the style didn't have bed bugs.

"I am sorry I hit you," Juliana volunteered.

"Ditto," I replied.

"My father had my mother committed. He put her in a place for insane people."

I looked at her.

"My mother. She wasn't like that," Juliana continued. "She was so beautiful. She was Miss Venezuela."

Now that she mentioned it, I could see the similarity between Juliana and photos that Chalmers had shown me of the beauty queen wearing a high-cut eighties bikini, big hair and a satin Miss Venezuela sash, especially now that I'd seen Juliana's ad for vitamin C.

"I was three years old. He wanted her money and he had fallen in love with someone else. My mother, Adriana, she made a fortune modeling. He drugged her to make her loco and then he paid a doctor to put her away. Then she really did go *alocado*. She died in there."

After a suitable period of mourning, I said, "Who raised you?"

"Boarding school. When I came home, *he* would be there with his new girlfriends. He likes twins. The two there tonight – they are just ornaments like all the rest. He cannot have sex with one person, he must have two."

Blue Dragons and her sister popped into my head, this time without their cheongsams. Lucky, lucky bastard.

"There were different housekeepers paid to look after me when I was home," Juliana continued. "My mother wrote letters to me, smuggled from the institution. I found them a year ago. A housekeeper had hidden them. My mother warned me, told me everything about him. He is the one who is *alocado*. He thinks he is a famous general, reincarnated."

That was something the briefing had missed. "Anyone I'd know?"

"Some Mexican generalissimo. It's not important. He is mad and very dangerous."

Apostles didn't give me the impression that he'd lost his marbles, but what sane person hires someone like Perez? "Mind if I ask you something touchy?"

"What?"

"Why didn't he kill your mother and make it look like an accident?"

"Because he still loved her. He just loved her money more."

Assuming this was all true, I felt sorry for Juliana. "How often have you threatened him with a pistol?"

"Three times," she said.

I recalled the look of indecision on the face of the Mexican goon as Juliana waved her unloaded pistol about. And suddenly I saw her plan. One day, after a few more practice attempts with an empty weapon and with everyone's guard relaxed, the pistol would be loaded. "You are going to murder him, aren't you?"

She didn't bother hiding the smirk. "I want to see his face when he knows there is a bullet in his heart and that I have tricked him."

"Then you'll be no different from me, perhaps even worse," I told her. "A killer, guilty of patricide."

"No, there is a big difference. There is nobility in revenge, even beauty. I will be righting a great wrong. You kill for money or because someone else tells you to do it."

I had never been paid to kill, not specifically. And in truth I wasn't even sure that's what I was here to do. As for the people taking an eternal snooze because our paths had crossed, I liked to think the world was better off without them. That I had taken human life was easier to live with when I thought of it that way. There was no emotion in it on my part – certainly nothing *beautiful*. And of course, there had been numerous collateral deaths over the years. One in particular – Anna, my investigative partner and the woman I had been sure I was going to end up married to. But let's not get into that again ... Through it all, I've been an instrument of Uncle Sam's, employed for the good of America. And Juliana was right: I got paid for it.

The cab pulled to a stop in front of a four-story building near the crest of a steep hill. Juliana covered the fare and we got out. The name of the place was Hotel Macarana. The front door was locked up tight and only the dimmest light was visible through a thick dimpled-glass panel beside the door.

Great. I yawned.

Across the road, a couple of bums sleeping rough were packed into dirty old sleeping bags. They looked like a collection of large grubs. Above the hotel door was a surveillance camera. That figured, the area not being what I'd call salubrious. At the risk of sounding negative, the odds on bed bugs were improving.

"What now?" I asked.

Juliana pressed a doorbell. After half a dozen seconds the latch buzzed. She pushed through the heavy door and led the way down a narrow hallway. Notice boards with various fun and compromising photos posted by guests, as well as various dos and don'ts drawn in colorful crayon, pegged the Macarana as a hostel. Those odds I mentioned were now about even.

The receptionist was around twenty years of age and black with big dark eyes and wild corkscrew hair. She wore a thick woolen beige pullover and bright-red leggings. A bar radiator warming her ankles gave the darkened office an orange glow. The laptop on a side desk showed the black and white view captured by the infrared surveillance camera out front. She turned on the lights, illuminating an old threadbare chandelier hanging from the ceiling.

I let Juliana do the talking. Apparently I was a relative from the US and did they have a room for me for the night?

No, they did not. Shame, off to the Hilton. Wait ... There was talk of – I think they said a cot.

Apparently Juliana and I were to share a room. The three of us plus a cot took a slow elevator to the fourth floor where it bounced to a stop. Juliana's room wasn't much bigger than the narrow bed pushed against one of the walls.

The receptionist wrestled the aforementioned cot into the room, a metal contraption that looked like it had been made twenty years ago from scrap metal and old coat hangers. She then brought in a thin bedroll to put on top.

Double great.

"I love this place," said Juliana once the receptionist departed. "I went to the university down the road."

"Love's a pretty strong word." I took in the bare walls illuminated by a naked light bulb.

"When I'm in Bogotá, I always stay here. It's safe. Before the owner leaves for the night, he locks the front door. It stops people breaking in and stealing your stuff."

"What if there's a fire?" I glanced out the window at the hard pavement four stories below.

"This is gorgeous. So much charm."

Maybe I was just too tired to see the gorgeousness of it all. I lay down on the cot, fully clothed. It bitched and moaned. The feeling was mutual. "You have to stop following me," I told Juliana closing my eyes.

After a lengthy silence, she replied, "Why would I follow you?"

"How else did you know where he'd be tonight?"

Another moment's silent consideration. "I always know where he is. He tells me. I am his daughter."

Now *that* was crazy. I took a deep breath.

I heard a familiar metallic click. Opening one eye, I saw her pull back the slide on her pistol. "Yes, it's loaded now," she said. "So don't you try anything."

"Scout's honor."

That's what I thought I said but maybe I didn't quite get it all out because the next thing I knew it was early morning and Juliana was showered and totally naked not two feet away, smelling of fragrant soap, her brown breasts bouncing as she gave them a final rub-down with a towel a little bigger than a handkerchief. So I did what anyone would do in such circumstances and closed my eyes to a slit to prolong the show.

"I know you have been watching," she said eventually, adding: "Men are all the same."

Right on both counts and it was interesting that she'd allowed the show to go on regardless. I opened my eyes. Juliana was now in her underwear, which was nice because it was underwear even if it was on the conservative side. Her arms were folded across her breasts, a sports bra dangling from her fingers. Now she wanted me out. I sat up and swung my legs off the cot. "Where's the bathroom?"

"Down the hall." Juliana tossed me one of those handkerchief towels. "There's someone in there. You'll have to wait."

Triple great.

Eighteen

By the time I'd showered and returned to the room, Juliana was gone. No note. I checked out and ate breakfast down the road, eggs with sausage and tomato all stirred together, and a hot chocolate made with boiling water.

This time around I hired a car, a Toyota Camry Hybrid. It was another four hours' drive back to the Hacienda Mexico and I wanted to do it in comfort while I patted myself on the back for helping to save the planet. No, I'm lying. The Camry was all they had in the lot.

The drive through the lush green Colombia countryside was uneventful. Even the Kia, backed into the bush down the road from the Hacienda Mexico, appeared undisturbed. Further down the road, I passed Escobar's old Piper Cub on top of the entrance gate. A fresh busload of tourists was landing beneath it.

The Hacienda Mexico with its immaculate fenceline came along next. I pulled in, announced my arrival, and nonchalantly looked up at the surveillance camera and hoped the background checks conducted in the interim had revealed that I was indeed a person they could thoroughly trust, a wanted cop killer. This was quite possibly the only place in the world where those credentials might earn me a welcoming chocolate martini.

"*Buenos días,*" said a familiar American voice, the one I attached to fjords and boat shoes. "Please wait."

I stood around and waited, but not for long. He arrived in the golf cart, the over-sized goon again beside him. The goon was bigger than I remembered and made the golf cart look like a prop from a circus act. This time around the gate opened.

The goon got out of the cart with a telescopic mirror on a stick and checked the Camry's skirts.

"Bring your car in. Follow us," said Blondie, the formalities taken care of. "When we stop, leave your keys in the vehicle."

I climbed back into the Camry and followed. The path wound through an area of heavy bush, allowing only the barest glimpses of the fields beyond. In one of these flashes of open ground, I saw a man on horseback, a wide-brim sombrero on his head, cantering away from the path.

The path brought me out of the bush and into an area of short-cropped grass the size of two football fields. There were tennis courts surrounded by a high steel-mesh fence at one end and, down the other, a powder-blue late-model Eurocopter parked in front of a hangar, a windsock on a pole hanging limp in the wet heat. The chopper was the same one I had seen arriving at the hacienda yesterday, flying low across the road. Occupying the long axis of the large manicured grass rectangle was a sprawling grand two-story ranch house in the Mexican hacienda style – columns, arches, even a bell tower, and a roof of interlocking terracotta half pipes. Hacienda Mexico.

The golf cart came to a stop under a portico adjacent to the hacienda's entrance. The blond guy and his circus pet got out and came back toward me, joined by three other men with sidearms belted on their thighs, one of them pushing a mirror on a pole to conduct a second opinion.

"Hands on the roof," said Blondie, nodding at the Camry. I did as asked while he, the circus animal and one of the newcomers went to work on me, patting me down and pulling out my weapon, spare ammo, wallet, cell and every other object they could find on my person and collecting them all on the Camry's hood.

"When can I see Señor Apostles?" I asked once they'd finished.

"When he's ready to see you," said the blond guy.

"What about my things?"

"The weapon, ammo and cell stay with us. The rest you can keep."

"We done?" I asked, indicating my hands still attached to the roof.

"For the moment," he replied.

Retrieving my wallet and assorted papers, a movement in a window up by the front entrance caught my attention. It was one of the Apostles' dragons – green or blue, I couldn't tell. There was no welcoming smile, no recognition in her face, just general inquisitiveness. The drape swung back in front of her face. If nothing else, her presence told me that Apostles was likely to be here.

One of the hired help got into the Camry and drove it away.

"Come with me," said Blondie.

I followed him up the stairs and into the house. It was all leather couches, the mounted heads of a stag, lion, tiger and zebra, rugs, suits of armor, pikes, crossbows and flintlocks. Weirdly, a large black taxidermy horse sat in the middle of the room. No sign of those dragons. Blondie kept walking, I kept following. He opened a door and motioned me through it. I obliged and he closed it behind me. Inside, I was surprised to see Arturo Perez sitting at a desk. The tips of his fingers tapped lightly against each other in front of him. I sensed he'd been waiting for me.

"You are a killer who does not kill," he began. "This is why I do not trust you. We have people in Texas. They tell us you killed cops, just like your newspaper says. But I don't know ..." He stood and went to a window, his stocky frame all but obliterating the view, several trees, the upper branches infested with small monkeys. "There was a man staying here, a deputy from El Paso. *El Santo* trusted this man. I am told he left in a hurry after you were turned away. Now he is missing. I think you know something about this. I think he knew *you*." Perez turned and pointed at me with his stubby finger so there was no doubt which "you" he was referring to. "I tell you now, if it was up to me, I would remove the skin from the backs of your legs, and with this removal, truth would be retrieved. What do you think?"

"I think I have no idea what you're talking about. When I left here yesterday, I went to Bogotá to meet Señor Apostles. I saw no one, met no one except, as it turns out, Señor Apostles' daughter in the foyer of the Marriott hotel."

"Where is your car?" Perez asked.

"Which car?" I replied.

"I check the security footage and yesterday you drive a different car to the car you drive today. Why is that?"

"I bought that piece of shit off the street when I arrived in Medellín. Unfortunately, it was a lemon and barely made it to Bogotá. So I offloaded it and went straight to Avis."

Perez stared at me unblinking, his face impossible to read.

"I'm running out of money," I said. "All I've got are some skills. If you're not interested in employing them, I can look elsewhere."

"No matter what *El Santo* says, you must know that I disagree with him about you. *I* haven't finished with you, Mr

Cooper. You have yet to pass my test." The corners of his eyes wrinkled. "How is your hand?"

I glanced at it involuntarily. The cut was healing well, the redness of infection gone and the stiches due to come out. I looked back at the evil little fuck with his glass button eyes and teardrop tattoos dripping down the side of his face and wondered if I could kill him right here and make it out of this place alive. Just as I was eyeing a letter opener on the desk and visualizing opening up his left ventricle with it, Juan Apostles threw the door wide.

"You're here," he said. "Good! How was Juliana? Did you take care of her?"

I nodded.

"She told you some lies about her mother, didn't she?"

There was a response on my lips but it wasn't to his question. It was to ask him about the outfit he was wearing: a dusty old black waistcoat and baggy black pants, a bandolier of ammunition on one shoulder and a wide-brim hat on his head – the character I'd seen on the horse. He reminded me of someone. And then I remembered – it was the man in the photo on the wall behind Perez at their base in the Darién Gap. No, in fact he *was* that person in the photo.

He seemed tense, in a hurry. To Perez he said in Spanish, roughly translated, "There has been another seizure. This will hurt us. Enough is enough."

Coming into the room behind Apostles was Blue Dragons. I knew it was her because, unlike her remote sister, this twin went straight for eye contact, turning those gray LED on me. The cheongsam was gone. Today's costume was female action figure: tan shirt and cargo pants, black hair pulled back in a ponytail and a black drop leg holster carrying a black pistol. The pistol was surprising and disappointing. It told me she was no innocent.

"Would you prefer Mr Cooper? Vincent? Vince?" she asked.

"My friends call me Vin," I replied.

"Vin, this is Daniela." Apostles was impatient to leave. "She will accompany you to the chopper. Twenty minutes. Do not be late." Apostles then beckoned to Perez with an outstretched arm: "Arturo ..." The squat psychopath walked to the arm and Apostles dropped it onto his shoulder as the two of them strolled into the next room, leaving Daniela and me some privacy to sweep everything off the desk and have sex on it. Okay, so that wasn't going to happen, but I just knew in a parallel universe she was making me very happy.

Daniela moved to a doorway. "I need some fresh air."

I followed her outside. The grounds were a mixture of open pasture dotted with dense outcrops of jungle, horses grazing here and there. "*El Santo* likes animals," I commented.

"Horses. Yes, he does."

"Where you from?" I asked her.

"Originally? Dallas, Texas."

"How'd you end up here?"

"Followed the opportunity," she said. "Same as you."

I nodded agreeably. The sun was out and the air hummed with insects. The grass underfoot was succulent, occasional daisies sprouting from it. Apostles had a better grip on the concept of hospitality than his sidekick, Perez.

We strolled toward a river that snaked lazily through lily fields. "Did *El Santo* own this place when the neighbor was still running around?"

"Escobar? Yes. Before my time, though. Apparently Pablo was quite charming."

Tell that to the planeload of citizens he and his people blew out of the sky, I thought. Close by, something big and brown broke up through a patch of lilies and then submerged, stopping us both in our tracks. "What the hell was that?" I asked. "A submarine?"

"No, a hippopotamus."

"A what?"

"A hippopotamus. The damn things are always breaking out."

The animal surfaced through the lilies again and opened its massive, ridiculous jaws to show off half a dozen huge teeth that reminded me of broken chisels. A smaller animal appeared beside it. Daniela took a step back. "Okay, that's Magdalena," she said nervously. "She's named after the river here. Her calf is Sophie. Maggie's quite aggressive at the moment, protective. I'll have to speak to someone. They're not supposed to be here."

"You mean, as in the wrong continent?"

"Come on," said Daniela, "we'd better go. When Juan says twenty minutes, he doesn't mean twenty-five."

"You've got hippos in your back garden?"

"They belonged to Escobar. He had a zoo stocked with exotic animals. When he was killed they sold off all the tigers, lions, elephants and chimpanzees. He also had three hippos that were too big and too grumpy to move. So they left them in the river and now there are thirty-two of them."

A couple were humping away as we watched. I wondered if that gave Daniela any ideas. Sure gave me a few. Arriving back at the Hacienda, I asked her, "So where are we going exactly? If you're stuck, I have some suggestions."

Daniela answered with an imperceptible smile, which I read to mean that I was going to find out all in good time.

"And what's your role around here?" I asked, "Aside from rolling around with the boss?"

"I get to answer only the questions I feel like answering. And as for what I do, that isn't one of them."

"Okay, then I have a question about the horse," I told her as the stuffed animal perched on four rigid legs came into view in the middle of the room. "How'd you feel about answering that?"

"Ask and I'll let you know."

"It's not often you see one standing around in a living room. What's the significance?"

"His name is *Siete Leguas*. You speak Spanish, Mr Cooper?"

"Enough. And I thought we were friends – Vin, remember."

"This is *Siete Leguas* – Seven Leagues. The horse belonged to Pancho Villa." She indicated a framed portrait of Villa up on the wall. Was the man in this picture the same person in the photo I saw on Perez's wall? Now that I thought about it, I couldn't be certain. I took a closer look at some neat, compact writing penned in ink across the white of Villa's shirt.

"Is that his signature?" I asked.

"Yes, signed by the general himself. Do you know anything about him?"

"I know he attacked the town of Columbus, New Mexico, early in the twentieth century, and that the US Army chased his ass around northern Mexico for a while."

"I meant the horse." Daniela smiled, one that could melt steel. She ran her hand down the exhibit's flank. "They called Pancho '*El Centauro del Norte*' – Centaur of the North – because he was always seen riding *Siete Leguas*. This horse once galloped over twenty miles, almost seven leagues, on one of Pancho's campaigns."

I didn't know much about horses, but twenty miles was a long way for anything to run. The car I had bought in Medellín could barely manage it. On a hunch, based on a comment Juliana had made, the get-up I'd just seen him prancing around in and the fact that he had the guy's nag in his living room, I said, "How long has the Saint of Medellín believed he was Pancho Villa?"

Daniela laughed and started moving toward the front door. "Did his daughter tell you that?"

"Not specifically."

"She's the fruitcake, not her father."

I looked into the horse's glass eyes and guessed that depended on one's definition of nuts. It was an interesting family to say the least. Mum had been institutionalized, Dad ran drugs and massacred folks while parading around as a Mexican folk hero, and the daughter had cooked up an elaborate plan to shoot him that involved an unloaded pistol.

The circus act and his blond keeper were waiting on the landing. My bag, which had been on the back seat of the Camry, was at their feet. Ahead, a hundred yards across the rolled immaculate lawn, Apostles and Perez were climbing into the Eurocopter. Daniela broke into an easy jog. I did likewise.

One of Apostles' men opened the door for us. Daniela stood aside to let me go first. I climbed in and slid onto a bench seat, which ran the width of the fuselage, next to Green Dragons. She looked at me disdainfully, the way a traveler on a train who's enjoyed the seat to themselves looks at an interloper settling beside them. Daniela took the other window seat.

"Vin, this is Lina, Daniela's sister," said Apostles sitting opposite in a soft chamois-leather bucket seat, his back to the pilot. The guy was no longer in fancy dress, having changed into tan shirt and gray cargo pants, a similar get-up to Daniela's.

I glanced at Lina, who again turned her head vaguely in my direction, but only for an instant out of deference to her boyfriend's introduction. She was dressed exactly like her twin, even down to the sidearm.

Sitting on Apostles' left, also with his back to the cockpit, was the Tears of Chihuahua, his glass eyes hidden behind those square-framed Ray-Bans. Come to think of it, even though I could feel those obsidian marbles boring into me I preferred them shielded from view. At least then I didn't have to look into the soulless void behind them.

The helicopter ride was short, taking us to José María Córdova Airport, Medellín, where we transferred to a private jet, a fast Gulfstream G650. Apostles, accompanied on each arm by Lina and Daniela, immediately went aft to a compartment that took up two thirds of the aircraft and hung a DO NOT DISTURB sign on the door. I sighed deeply.

I took a seat up the front and the Tears, who could have sat anywhere, chose one directly opposite me. I swiveled, and he changed seats to maintain this frontal attack. We sat like that for the duration. I tried to sleep without much success, so feigned it much of the time. As far as I could tell Perez stared at me the whole way, probably unblinking.

I kept half an eye on the sun. It stayed more or less on the right-hand side of the plane and toward the front as it slowly dipped to the horizon. That meant we were flying roughly northwest. The pilot told us to fasten seatbelts a little under four hours after departure. At just under seven hundred miles an hour, the average cruise for a jet like this, I guessed that would put us somewhere in northern Mexico.

As the aircraft descended, I ending the sleeping charade and took in the view through the window. We were over tan desert beneath a cloudless cobalt-blue sky. The city coming into view below appeared to be pinched together in its center by two sets of gray mountains. We were coming into Juárez.

Nineteen

We taxied to gates with a neon sign announcing *Aeropuerto Internacional Benito Juárez*.

Once inside the terminal, I witnessed the kind of fawning and obsequiousness usually reserved for powerful members of state as Apostles and his entourage, of which I was one, breezed through customs and immigration. Once out in the arrivals hall, we were met by a man in a chauffeur's outfit, accompanied by a couple of bodyguards. He and his escort led us through the crowds. We passed an ATM without a queue so I stopped, fumbled with my wallet and fed the card into the slot.

"What are you doing?" It was Perez. He was right behind me.

I punched in the four-digit PIN.

"What does it look like?" I said, pressing the key for "English". "Who passes up a chance to shop duty free, right?"

"Welcome, Mr Cooper," the title on the ATM screen read.

"Get away from the machine," Perez said as I pressed the key for 2000 MXN – around a hundred and sixty bucks – then the key for savings.

A sharp pain in my ribs made me jump. "Hey, what's your problem?" I snapped at Perez.

"My problem is you," he said, showing me the pearl-handled blade hidden in the palm of his hand. "Move."

"That's twice you've cut me," I said, taking my card from the slot.

"You think I can't count?" he replied, his Ray-Bans revealing nothing.

"Do it again and I'll kill you," I told him.

"Yes, I would like you to try."

The cash appeared in the slot and I grabbed it. I could see Apostles and the rest of our party heading out the exit and hurried to catch them up, the blood welling from Perez's jab sopped up by my black polo shirt, which also hid it.

Killing this nasty little fuck was something that needed to be done, but not before I found out what Apostles was up to.

Almost directly outside the exit was our ride, a Hummer stretched almost to breaking point. A small army in Lakers, Bulls and Celtics T-shirts and sweats, packing FN assault rifles, accompanied it, crowded into a pickup. Maybe they were there to stop the Hummer's wheels being stolen. Pairs of *Federales* securing the area, armed with H&K MP-5s and wearing ski masks and sunglasses, ignored our party completely.

The drive in the Hummer was mercifully short – Perez's little hurry up hurt like a bitch. I hoped stopping at that ATM had been worth it. The destination turned out to be a gated community around the other side of the airport called the *Campestre*, the entrance guarded by more *Federales* in ski masks with assault weapons.

Inside the gates, the traffic disappeared completely. We drove through a block with Applebee's, Starbucks, Chili's and other familiar names nestled beside various strip malls. All pretty normal – almost reassuring. And then the houses began: big, flashy homes with heavily barred windows and doors, more than a few showing neglect along with signs announcing that they were for sale. Buyers weren't queuing. Ahead, the pickup swerved around a rock half the size of a small car sitting in the middle of the road. The Hummer took a slower, more careful detour around it.

"I can see you're intrigued," said Daniela, noting my eyes fixed on the obstacle.

She had me there.

"Boulders like that are all over the Campestre. The residents put them there to slow down the kidnappers so their guards could shoot them."

I guessed that accounted for all the FOR SALE signs.

Ahead, the armed escort pulled over to the curb while the Hummer scribed a big quarter circle and came in behind it, bouncing into a wide driveway. A heavy steel gate closed behind us.

"We're here," said Daniela.

That was a relief. I wanted to see what damage Perez's knife had done to my ribs and also change my shirt, though the bleeding seemed to have stopped.

"Here" was a sprawling monument to concrete and glass humming with air-conditioning motors, crawling with more of Apostles' NBL-branded security. I followed Apostles and the twins inside where the temperature dropped into the temperate zone. "Lina, why don't you show Vin to his room," he said, his arm around her. To me, he said, "We'll meet later. We must talk."

Lina led me through the place, which echoed like a dungeon with every footfall. We climbed a curved staircase to the mezzanine level. Down below, I watched Apostles, Daniela and Perez mingle with various lieutenants and their spectacularly augmented girlfriends. I spotted a man among the party wearing an expensive suit and a mask. It was *El Bruto*, the *lucha libra* wrestler from the back page. Different suit but I'd recognize those jagged silver teeth and the scowling, angry expression anywhere. Hands were being shaken, backs slapped.

Lina cleared her throat.

"You're here," she said as I turned around, opening a door and revealing a king-size bed beyond it.

I walked past her into a room. It smelled of dead air. On a chest of drawers was a bottle of Glen Keith, a glass and an ice bucket. I licked my lips and picked up the bottle.

"*El Santo* looks after his guests," she said reacting to my expression, which was probably close to rapture.

Seeing that bottle waiting for me was good and bad: good because Glen Keith was my favorite brand of single-malt scotch whiskey; and bad because Glen Keith was my favorite brand of single-malt scotch whiskey. Apostles' intelligence had to be first class for him to know that. He'd been digging pretty deep. I cracked the seal on the screw top and savored the aroma. "Care for a belt?"

She shook her head. "I'll wait for a martini."

"Don't hold your breath."

"Downstairs," she said, smiling. Up to that moment, I didn't know she was capable of it. "There's a bathroom through that door." She nodded in its direction. "Everything you need."

"And my bag?" I asked her.

"Coming."

"Where does everyone else sleep?"

"Why do you want to know?"

"It's not a loaded question."

Loaded or not, she ignored it. "Leave your door unlocked. *El Santo* doesn't like locked doors."

"Can I go out?"

"Why would you want to go out?" she asked.

"Get my bearings. Stretch the legs. Have a steak at Applebee's."

"You're in Juárez, that's all the bearings you need. There's a gym in the basement and we have a chef on staff. If you go out, you'll be accompanied."

"For my own protection?"

"Of course. And anyway, we're going out soon."

"Where to?"

"You'll see."

I let it go. "So tell me, what do you get out of this?"

"I'm sorry?"

"He likes twins. You and Daniela are not the first and you won't be the last."

"You've been listening to his wacko daughter."

"She might have mentioned it." It had also been part of Chalmers' briefing, but I wisely kept that to myself.

"Arturo doesn't like you or trust you."

Arturo? And then I remembered: Arturo Perez. Arty. I had to smile. Someone named him when he was a baby, his mother most probably. Frankly, I couldn't imagine the guy having a mother, or for that matter being anything other than a mean, tattooed, blade-wielding psychotic with dead eyes. "Yeah, well, the feeling's mutual."

"You're bleeding." She nodded at my arm.

The blood had finally seeped through the shirt and slicked the inside of my bicep and elbow.

"What happened?"

"Nothing."

She shrugged and looked around the room. The fact that Lina was satisfied with the lack of an answer told me folks bleeding profusely in her orbit was not so unusual. And if I wasn't mistaken, the woman was lingering. She had questions, or maybe she wanted to tell me something. "There are clothes in the drawers," she said. "They're your size."

If they could land my brand of sauce, I supposed a thirty-six-inch waist was a cinch. "I've got clothes in my bag."

"It's coming."

"So you said."

"I did." She leaned against the doorjamb. I sat on the bed and bounced, testing the springs. Firm. The energy in the room was odd to say the least.

"You know, when we were kids, Daniela would pull the wings off butterflies and laugh about it as their little bodies quivered and curled up in agony," she said.

I wondered where that had come from. "Meanwhile, what did you do?"

"Watched."

"If you're warning me off your sister, you don't have to. I'm here to get work, not get laid."

"I've seen the way you look at her; the way she looks at you."

"Are you jealous?"

"Are you always so full of yourself?"

"I like to test the limits," I said.

"You're way past them." Her lip curled. "The point is, if I noticed it, so have others. Arturo, maybe. You should be careful. Otherwise that –" she pointed in the direction of my punctured rib cage – "might not be superficial next time."

Before I could respond, a kid arrived with my bag. He wore ridiculous oversize convict jeans belted so tight around his knees that he was forced to walk funny. He placed the bag inside the door and waddled off with a sly backward glance at Lina.

"I have to go," she said. "Don't want people getting the wrong idea."

"What idea is that?" Lina pushed herself off the doorjamb and walked away. No glance over the shoulder, not from her. I closed the door and wondered what had been the point of the visit, then put it out of my mind.

I picked up my bag and dropped it on the bed. Next stop, the bathroom. I stripped off the polo shirt, heavy with blood, and angled the cut toward the mirror to get a look at it. The jab in my side was around a centimeter deep between the eighth and ninth ribs. Cartilage had stopped the point of the blade from entering further. Perez was a craftsman. The prick had known exactly where to stick the blade and how much pressure to use. The wound was painful and it had bled profusely for a short period of time, but it was more of an inconvenience than a danger. With the slice on my hand, Perez had left his mark on me twice. I told myself I'd do what I could to return the favor.

I turned on the shower and went back into the room to get the phone charger and plug in my cell and, in so doing, confirm with CIA that both my Visa card and cell were in Juárez. And, of course, to throw back a couple of fingers of you know what. I took the glass into the bathroom and rested it on the basin while I checked the shower's water temperature. There was a knock on the door. I turned the shower off, threw on a clean polo shirt before opening it and saw the kid in the jailhouse jeans. *El Santo* wanted me downstairs. I tossed back the rest of the scotch and followed.

*

"There have been developments," Apostles said, reclining on a sofa away from the partying going on down the other end of the room, folks getting their groove on to Latino sounds. Apostles' hands were behind his head, an ankle resting on his thigh. The body language was relaxed, but he was frowning about something.

Arty also sat on the sofa, but rigid and upright like he was skewered on a poker. Something was up.

"Your former fucking friends across the border have intercepted more of our product," Apostles continued, like maybe I'd had something to do with it. "A significant amount –

eighty million dollars' worth." He paused, took a deep breath, then screamed, "That's over two hundred million fucking dollars your country has stolen from me in just two months!"

There wasn't much I could say but I was thinking: "Go team."

No one moved while Apostles got himself under control. He glared at me, his eyes red-rimmed with fury. "Tell me more about your plan to put my sales targets back on track."

"What you need is a pilot," I began.

"I have pilots."

"I mean like the pilots who guide ships through difficult waters."

Apostles was impatient. "And ... ?"

"From what I've seen, your aircraft are state of the art. With proper planning, I can get your planes on the ground without detection almost anywhere in the States. And because US air defenses are aimed out and not in, the further you get from the border the less likelihood there is that your aircraft will be deemed hostile. Civilian airspace control has tight corridors, ceiling and base heights. You just need to know when to fly low, when to fly high and what areas to avoid. As I said, with the right navigation systems and a little professional finesse, your aircraft can thread the eye of a needle and land somewhere more convenient to your contacts on the ground. Then we offload and return the way we came in."

"You make it sound simple," said Apostles.

"'Cause it is."

"Do not trust him," said Perez.

I ignored Arty. "I can do a trial run. Maybe land close to Austin or Houston – anywhere you've got people on the ground who can take delivery."

"I don't like it." Perez wasn't going to let it go.

Addressing Apostles, I said, "Okay, yes, you risk losing a plane and its cargo, but I'll be on board the aircraft. It'll be my ass going to prison if things land in the toilet. If it works, and I know it will, you can start flying in tons of product securely, a regular service virtually door-to-door. But there's a catch."

Perez glanced at Apostles. "And that is?" the boss asked.

"No one gets killed. If we leave a mess for the authorities to clean up, they'll figure it all out and do whatever it takes to close any loopholes I find and you'll be back where you started. The deal is we tiptoe in and leave the same way. We can't have anything happening like the shit that went down at Horizon Airport."

"We had nothing to do with that," said Apostles. "I'm a businessman. That's all I care about – business."

"I don't trust him," said the broken record beside him, glaring at me with those unblinking pits.

"What do you need, apart from the airplanes and crews?" Apostles asked.

"A check on the navigation systems your aircraft use, charts to plan the route, a departure point, the delivery destination and a briefing session with the pilot."

"And what do you want for this?" asked Perez.

"Two and a half percent," Apostles replied. "Correct?"

I nodded.

"So we put twenty million dollars' worth of cocaine in a plane with him and he flies off into the sunset," said Perez. "Twenty million dollars and a plane worth whatever it's worth. That's a better return than two and a half percent. And he just has to do it once. With that kind of money, he can disappear. What's to stop him?"

Apostles turned to his pal. "We put some reliable people on board. If there's trouble, they bring him back and I give him to you. Fair?"

Perez nodded. He liked the sound of that. He showed me his teeth, small, sharp and yellow like rat incisors.

The twins appeared, their high heels clattering on the stonework like four sticks on a snare drum. I had no idea who was who. Daniela, or maybe it was Lina, wore a skin-tight burgundy dress that came to just below the knees and several carats of solitaire diamond around her throat. Lina, or maybe it was Daniela, wore the same outfit in a dark chocolate flavor, along with a similar-size rock at the base of her long neck. The makeup for both was smoldering, accentuating the lights in their eyes. Their hair was worn loose and a little wild.

"Can we go now?" asked the eye candy in burgundy.

Go? If Apostles and I could trade places I'd head straight for satin sheets and a bottle or two of chilled vintage French leg opener.

A man in his mid-twenties in a Bull's T-shirt came in behind the twins and nodded at the boss – a signal.

"*Si*," said Apostles, grunting the old-man-grunt as he pushed himself up off the couch. "*Vamos*." We go. He turned to me and said, "Tomorrow, we will have work to do. Tonight, enjoy a little more of my hospitality."

*

Waiting out front were two regular-size white Hummers with heavily tinted windows, accompanied by a pickup full of armed security bringing up the rear. Apostles and his twins got into the lead Hummer and closed the doors.

"There," said Perez, motioning at the second Hummer for my benefit. I opened the door and climbed in. Perez entered from the other side and took the seat opposite.

The Hummers rolled, the pickup following.

"Where are we going?" I asked Perez.

He looked at me, said nothing.

"If it's dancing, I'll probably hang back," I said. "I'm not a fan. How about you? You look like you could dance okay, being short and round and just a little chubby. I can see you doing the Chicken. You know that one?" I moved my arms like they were chicken wings.

No response from Perez.

"Yeah you do. Everyone knows the Chicken."

"*Creo que me voy a matar,*" he growled – I think I'm going to kill you.

Maybe he disliked dancing more than I did.

The drive across town was uneventful. Perez stared at me. But maybe he was asleep and could do it with them open, like a horse. Whatever, I tried to ignore him and took in the passing view out the window. Juárez by night was mean and depressing. It was also largely deserted, odd for a city with around a million and a half people. I guessed the cartels and the gangs owned the hours between sunset and dawn.

We eventually arrived at a bustling parking lot managed by muscle-bound guys in suits with ponytails, directing arrivals. Our vehicles were ushered to the entrance where a VIP pit stop had been set up. This was some kind of event. The vehicle doors opened. Perez and I got out and together with Apostles and the twins were rushed by Apostles' bodyguards through the crowded entrance. There was no wedge or protection diamond, which told me his security team had no real idea about how to provide close protection. Instead they kept behind our party, leaving us open to a frontal assault. Obviously Apostles had never been hit by pros. He was vulnerable.

And just then I bumped into a woman, part of the crowd heading in the opposite direction. For the briefest instant her heavily made-up eyes met mine as I felt something pressed into my hand. She was compact, wearing a micro mini that revealed smooth athletic legs. A black leather vest and push-up bra, a blond wig with large gold hoop earrings completed her look. I recognized the big brown eyes first. Claudia: Panda's friend, former French CIA assassin, with the garrotte. With everyone distracted by the jostling crowd, I took a moment to glance into my hand to see what I'd been palmed: a small biscuit with the word CHEST burned onto it in capital letters. I crushed the biscuit to crumbs and let them scatter through my fingertips. Chest? What the hell was that about?

Inside, bright overhead lights illuminated a boxing ring and ear-splitting rock music boomed in the air. The seats, which tiered up to the roof, were filled with a shouting, beer-soaked crowd. Our seats were ringside, among cigar-smoking creeps accompanied by much younger women: nieces, the high-maintenance kind. Apostles and the twins fitted right in. I had no choice but to sit with Perez and hope nobody got the wrong idea.

I looked around, for all intents and purposes to take in the unfamiliar surroundings. In fact, I was looking for Claudia. It didn't take long to find her, sitting close by, playing the role of a paid escort. I recognized her current employer without too much trouble, despite the ridiculous pin-striped suit, sunglasses and cigar – Panda.

A promoter jumped into the ring and welcomed the crowd, which went wild. A large banner dropped from the ceiling, unfurled and proclaimed that this was Death Match II. The announcer explained for the one person in the room who had no idea what was going on – namely, me – that this was an unsanctioned *lucha libra* match where two men would settle some score and literally fight to the death. But first, the preliminary bouts. The spotlight hit a door in the side of the venue and a guy in a gold cape and gold mask walked into it. Much of the crowd surged to its feet and the fighter raised his golden-gloved fist high. He walked toward the ring as the spotlight hit another doorway and a man in a black leotard with a black and white mask, the eyes outlined with circles so that the expression seemed permanently startled. His appearance was greeted with boos. He was a bigger build than the golden guy and he roared animal-like at the crowd, which didn't appreciate it. The boos flooded back at him, louder. Goldie leaped agilely up and over the ropes and into the ring, full of confidence. The black guy started to walk toward the ring and then broke into a run while still some distance from it. And then he dived under the ropes, did a forward roll and carried the momentum into a high leap. Poised seemingly in midair above his quarry for a frozen second or two, he then came down with a vicious elbow on the crown of Goldie's head. The blow took the guy completely by surprise. He stood there, not moving, and then collapsed onto the canvas as rigid as a tree, face first, apparently unconscious. The crowd, incensed, went berserk at this atrocity. Other wrestlers – all masked – surged from the doorways and charged the ring. The black guy pounded his chest and looked, well, startled. A costumed World War III was fought in the aisles by the wrestlers supporting the protagonists in the ring, while paramedics attended the downed fighter who was moving now, but as if his limbs were made from rubber.

I looked across at Apostles. He was shaking his head, as unhappy about the result as everyone else in the venue who were pretty much all baying for the blood pumping in the veins of the fighter in the black mask. The result had gone against the script. The golden guy was supposed to win – the triumph of good over evil and so forth. The guy in the black mask had caused the universe to tilt on its axis. Well, folks, not everything goes to plan. Or, in short, shit happens. I took it on board as an omen and wondered if Juan de Apostles was doing the same.

Several masked avengers went at each other over the next hour, leaping off turnbuckles, being slammed to the canvas, having shoulders pinned to the mat and then not pinned to the mat, back and forth. The fighters mostly danced rather than fought. It made me think that perhaps the opening fight had been staged too. The crowd enjoyed it but perhaps Panda and Claudia hadn't; glancing over in their direction I saw that their seats were vacant.

Before the main event began, Perez got up from his chair and walked off, I presumed to the john. The twin in the chocolate dress beckoned me to close the gap. I moved across and took Perez's seat.

"So, what do you think?" said the twin over the noise of the crowd.

"I think you'd go well with two shots of vodka in a martini glass," I told her.

"What?"

She wasn't sure she'd heard me right, over the racket, but then it clicked.

"No, not me," she said, grinning. "This – the fights."

"Is that what they're doing?" I grinned back. "So which one are you? Daniela or Lina?"

"Guess."

"I can't," I said. "That's why I'm asking."

"Daniela. We're actually easy to tell apart, once you get to know us. In the meantime, I have a mole behind my ear and Lina doesn't." She showed me, sweeping her hair to one side and lifting the back of her ear. It was more of a freckle than a mole. "I'm the imperfect one."

The announcer reached up and pulled the mike down as it descended from the ceiling. The place fell silent, the air crackling with electricity. The sound system boomed with the announcer's voice. It was main event time. The crowd jumped to its feet and roared with expectation. The challenger's legend came first. All I got was the name, "Blue Mystery". Everyone cheered. *El Bruto*'s feats came next and everyone booed.

"Do you know what's going on here?" Daniela asked.

"Someone's making a lot of money," I said.

"Aside from that."

I shook my head. "No."

The spotlight hit the door and a big man in a blue and white leotard appeared. The crowd welcomed him with boisterous enthusiasm. He held up his fist and walked toward the ring.

Daniela had to yell. "Technically speaking, this is an illegal bout. It's un-sanctioned. No rules, anything goes. *El Bruto* is a *rudos* or bad guy and the Blue Mystery is a *técnico* – a good guy. The two have battled their whole careers with neither really getting the upper hand. They are both gods in Mexico. Then about a month ago, there was a *lucha de apuesta* or 'match with wager' between them. The winner got to unmask the loser, which is a huge insult. *El Bruto* won. Today is the rematch. It's a *máscara contra cabellera* match or 'mask versus hair'. Traditionally, in this kind of fight, if the hair loses, he must shave his head to display his humiliation. If the mask loses, he must remove his mask. But this is an unsanctioned event, so there's a twist. If *El Bruto* loses the fight, he loses his mask. But if the Blue Mystery loses, then he must retire for good. Understand?"

"I'm a bit hazy on why *Blue* Mystery and not some other color."

"It's a mystery." Daniela grinned again. "As I said, he's a very popular fighter. It would be a national disaster if he loses."

Perez returned and stood in front of me. He wanted his seat back and he wasn't going to move. I shifted over, checking with Daniela as Perez's bald head settled in between us. She shrugged.

The fight went on. And on. And on some more, every hold, leap and eye-gouge choreographed. But then, just when everyone thought the Blue Mystery was going to triumph over his old nemesis, *El Bruto* turned the tables on him – actually picking up a table from ringside and slamming it against the guy's skull, which allowed him to pin the Mystery's unconscious blue shoulders to the floor – and won. It was the end of the road for the blue guy. He had to hang up his leotard and cape. The crowd didn't like it. Cans and empty Corona bottles were thrown from the back stalls toward the ring. I glanced at Apostles. He was smiling a private smile. The crowd might have lost, but *he'd* won. I wondered how much. Security materialized with umbrellas, defense against the rain of Corona, and held them over us as they jostled us toward the exit.

"Juan de Jesús del Los Apostles de Medellín!" I heard someone shout. There was a challenge in it, malice.

I turned around and saw ... shit, it was Hector Gomez. He was standing side-on, maybe thirty feet away, dressed as a local in old jeans and stained Corona T-shirt. "Juan de Jesús del Los Apostles de Medellín!" he repeated. "*Usted es un asesino!*" You are a murderer, he said. And then a black pistol appeared in his hand.

Someone screamed. Realization dawned on Apostles and Perez, and on Apostles' security. I froze along with everyone else, waiting for the shot.

And then Gomez shifted the angle of his gun from Apostles to me. I unfroze. My hand snapping back and finding the Sig. My reflexes weren't going to hang around to get shot, even if the rest of me was. There had been the bump from Claudia. The small cookie in my hand – *Chest.* I fired twice. The shots went high, shattering glass panes above and behind Gomez. Dropping the sight, I fired again – twice. Hits. The rounds ripped into Gomez. The first caught him in the gut. The second in the rib cage, spinning him around. Blood sprayed across the concrete floor and Gomez fell to the ground. After a moment of silence like a collectively held breath, a couple of women screamed and the crowd broke into a stampede. Apostles' security tried to get to Gomez but they couldn't penetrate the masses surging out of the exits. So they did the next best thing and almost carried us to the Hummers.

I found myself in the vehicle with Apostles and the twins, all of whom were nervous and anxious. Shit. I'd just killed a buddy and that buddy was a Texas Ranger.

Twenty

Apostles' cell rang as we raced out of the car park and were waved on by frantic attendants. The caller's name came up on screen: "Arturo".

"Who was he?" I heard Apostles ask. He breathed once, in and out, when he got the answer. *"Luego, averigüe."* Then find out. Apostles lifted his eyes to me and said, *"Si, él está conmigo."* He's with me.

Was Perez concerned about my wellbeing?

"I can tell you who the man was," I said. "Hector Gomez. We were partners, briefly. He was a Texas Ranger, though who he's working for now ..." I let a shrug finish it off.

Apostles passed this information onto Perez, and ended the call. Putting his phone away, the boss looked at me earnestly and said, "Thank you." He produced his hand for me to shake.

I obliged. "No problem." We were at a fake fight. The least I could do was top it off with a fake shootout. Those first two rounds I fired, the wild, poor marksmanship on my part that took out the windows? That was intentional. No way was I going to hit Gomez with a hollow point at such close range, even though he had to have been wearing some kind of vest under that T-shirt, protecting his *chest*. The third and fourth rounds were blanks, the training cartridges Arlen had thoughtfully provided back in El Paso, loaded into the mag. Who knew Gomez was such a good actor with all that spinning and falling. There'd been plenty of blood and guts accompanying the action, maybe even a little too much. Pig's blood, probably, with some hamburger mince thrown in for added realism. In all, a convincing show. And, I had to admit, something of a relief, if only because sometimes it's reassuring to know you're not swinging solo on the highwire without a net. And why would Panda, Claudia and Gomez go to all that trouble and risk so much to achieve, well, what exactly? Because me shooting Gomez and giving up his identity was something a man *El Santo* could trust would do. And Perez had contacts – Gomez's identity wouldn't remain secret for long. In fact, I suspected CIA would make the job easy, but not too easy.

I put my head back against the rest and closed my eyes, aware of Daniela's bare leg rubbing against mine as the Hummer sped along Juárez's streets, an obstacle course of potholes and disintegrating asphalt.

*

Arriving at the bunker in Campestre, Apostles made a beeline for the drinks cabinet, thereby demonstrating that at least some of his priorities were squared away. "Single malt, right?" he asked.

"When I can get it," I replied.

The rest of Apostles' entourage arrived nosily through the front door. Perez gave the boss a nod and disappeared down the hall with a couple of his henchmen to torture small fluffy animals or whatever. The rest of the crowd went suddenly quiet when Apostles gave them a look, and then made themselves scarce. All except Daniela and Lina. The twins came up to Apostles, wrapping their arms languidly through and around him like fast-growing vines. They said goodnight to him, and departed with a glance back that I interpreted as, "It's on with both of us, Juan, so don't be long. And tonight, we're bringing toys."

Okay, so my imagination can occasionally work overtime.

"You like them," I heard Apostles say.

The comment made me realize my mouth was open and salivating as I watched the twins slink down a hallway, open a door and close it behind them. "You're a lucky, lucky man," I told him, finally getting that one off my chest.

"Yes, a certain amount of luck has been helpful," he agreed as he handed me a glass of fifty-year-old Macallan and then poured himself one. He toasted me and my lips touched heaven. Fifty-year-old Macallan? Shit, just a sip of this stuff was probably worth around a hundred bucks. "You favor Glen Keith," Apostles said, holding the contents of his glass up to the light to further appreciate the Highland malt's rich honey color. "Lovely fruits, but Glen Keith doesn't compare to this."

He was right, it didn't, but then neither did the price. He walked to a couple of lounge chairs in the large relatively bare open room and sat. I followed him and took the chair roughly opposite.

"What do you think of its sherry style?" he asked once he'd gotten comfortable.

"If sherry tasted like this I'd drink sherry."

"Perhaps if things go okay for you here, you'll be able to afford to develop a taste for it."

We both sipped some more.

"Let's talk more about luck," he said. "Luck is being born into a rich family. Luck is having you beside me this evening. But Daniela and Lina are nothing to do with luck. They are the product of my determination to satisfy my desires. For that I have worked, and continue to work, long and hard. What do you desire, my friend? What do you burn for? Tell me, man to man."

No one had ever asked me that question before, but I didn't have to think about it long or hard. I burned for Anna Masters. But traveling back in time to stop a bullet tearing through her heart was something no amount of work would achieve. Beyond that, in terms of desires, I couldn't say.

"Ah, you have experienced loss," he said, reading something in my face that I wasn't aware I displayed; an imperceptible drop of the head, a dilating of the pupils, the telltale deepening of a line in my forehead. "Show me a man who hasn't experienced loss and I'll show you a man going to his grave a pauper."

The cheesy philosophy I could do without, but if that's what it took to stand around belching occasionally while I drank a bottle of ten-thousand-dollar scotch, I could bear it.

"Then that is your life's mission," he went on, taking a gulp, maybe five-hundred bucks' worth. "To figure out what you need to fill the void, eh?"

I nodded in agreement. Daniela and toys would be a good start.

"Thank you again for tonight." He put his glass on the cabinet, Macallan shamefully still undrunk sloshing about in it. "Sleep well." He put his hand on my shoulder. "Tomorrow we will try to do it your way."

I waited for him to walk out of sight down the hallway before I tipped the contents of his glass into mine and drank it. Sounded to me like I'd made the team.

*

It felt like the day had started a week ago, but there was too much on my mind to sleep. So I stood under the showerhead and went for full hot followed by a blast of cold. After the shock of the extremes, I mixed up a temperature somewhere in the middle. And that's about when I felt fingertips caressing my shoulder. It wasn't a sensation I was expecting. *Leave your door unlocked. El Santo doesn't like locked doors.*

"You're a mess," a woman's voice cooed, not one I was familiar with, her fingers delicately tracing scar tissue.

"Do I know you?" I asked, glancing over my shoulder.

"You're about to," she said.

In fact, I did recognize her. She was one of the women I'd seen hanging around looking generally hot, on the payroll, in the column for entertainment. Her accent was mid-west American and she was tall and blond in the Marilyn Monroe fashion – darker eyebrows, strawberry hair and nipples.

"Mind if I ask what you're doing here?" I asked.

"What does it look like?"

Ask a dumb question. "Let me rephrase," I said. "What are you doing here?"

"Why didn't you ask? I'm keeping you company – orders from *El Santo*. Because of what you did tonight. He likes to reward people for a job well done." She found a bar of soap in the holder and used it to lather up some circles on my back. "I joined you in the shower for a reason. We can talk in here."

"We can't talk out there?" She knew I meant the bedroom.

"We could, but the bugs don't work so well in the bathroom." Her hands worked their way around my waist and the soap circles continued on my chest. "What do you want to talk about?"

"They were going to kill you, you know. They were going to do it tomorrow, out in the desert. Cut you up and leave you for the ants. The Tears of Chihuahua doesn't trust you."

"And why should I trust you?"

"Because I saved your life. I got a message to mutual friends across the border."

I turned around to face her. She was pretty. Slim, with large fake breasts done by someone who liked breasts almost as much as me. "What's your name?"

"Do you need one? Okay, call me Bambi."

"Really?"

"Or Fiona. Take your pick."

I'd never showered with a Disney character before. "Are you CIA, Bambi?"

"You know that's against the rules."

"Don't give me the rules bullshit. Who's running you?"

"And I just give you that?" she asked.

"I need a name and it's not Thumper."

"You know everyone uses aliases in this business. If it helps, he was forty-something, a sleaze and walked with a limp."

I relaxed. "Now we're getting somewhere."

"So we're good?"

"His name is Bradley Chalmers."

"He said it was Freddie. Saving Apostles' life tonight saved yours. You know that, don't you? I made that possible – that was my doing."

Her hands washed between my legs, making sure everything down there was especially clean. "And now, because I was picked to keep you company and we're in the shower, I get the chance to tell you about it."

"You don't have to do this if you don't want to," I told her. "We can just talk."

Bambi laughed and took hold of me, and then worked her hand up and down while she nuzzled my neck. "The bugs don't work in here, but the cameras don't have a problem. I've got a job to do, and I have to be seen to be doing it. You going to make it difficult for me?"

Her lips found mine and I kissed her hard. Our wet tongues wrestled. I eventually tapped out and whispered in her ear, "I wasn't aware we had someone on the inside. No one told me."

"Need to know," she whispered back as my soapy hands found her breasts and we exchanged suds.

"If you're here, then I don't need to be," I said.

"No, I'm a woman."

"You don't say."

"What I mean is, I don't have access all areas. I'm an ornament. When they leave this place, they don't take me with them. I just get a call when the entourage is in town. And I never get to hang out with Apostles or Perez. I take care of middle management and get the occasional VIP."

"So you hear things," I said.

"Mostly just rumors," she replied. "Everyone's pretty tight with the operational stuff. I can tell you that Daniela thinks you're cute."

"Only because she knows she can't have me."

Bambi laughed.

Yeah, that was pretty funny. "Have you heard any talk about the business at Horizon Airport?"

"Not a peep. If the Chihuahua Cartel had something to do with it, they're better at keeping secrets than anyone thought."

So far, that had been my experience, too. "What have you heard about Apostles and his Pancho Villa fixation?"

"What?" She was frowning. Apparently I'd stumped her with that one.

"There are portraits of Pancho Villa hanging in various places," I said. "I've seen Apostles parading around like the Cisco Kid – at least I think it was Apostles; and Villa's favorite horse has been stuffed and stands around in *El Santo*'s lounge room back at the Hacienda. What gives?"

"He's got Villa's horse? I've never been to the place in Colombia … Maybe he's just trying to make an impression; you know, create an image. There are plenty of Mexican peasants working for him. Many of them don't have a lot of education. If that's what he's doing it's not such a dumb idea, you know. Villa is still a hero of the Mexican revolution. They'd probably go for that kind of symbolism."

"Why would he need it?"

"I don't know. Maybe that's why you're here – to find out."

"Next question: has Apostles got a couple of screws loose?"

"He's a lot of things, but crazy isn't one of them."

"His daughter thinks he is."

"I've never met her ... Can we talk about something other than *El Santo*?"

I let it go. "So where are you from?" I asked her.

"That's better." She bit my shoulder blade – not too hard, just right. "I'm from Vegas. And, yes, I was a dancer. Now you want to know what's a nice girl like me and so forth, right?"

"I don't necessarily like nice girls."

"Good, 'cause I ain't one."

Her hands certainly had an aptitude for badness. "Then I think we're gonna get along just fine," I told her.

She nibbled on my earlobe and whispered, "I discovered young that the two loves of my life were money and sex. So what I'm doing combines them. And I was never gonna be a brain surgeon, except that guys think with their dicks so maybe in a way, I kinda am. I've got two properties in Vegas and a timeshare in Palm Springs. By the time I retire, with a little help from our mutual friends over the border, I'll have double that."

I wondered who was getting screwed here.

"So you just close your eyes and think of Uncle Sam," she suggested.

I suddenly had the image of a bearded guy wearing a Stars and Stripes top hat, standing in the shower with me. "Hey, you're spoiling it."

"Sorry."

To make up for it, she did something that made my knees tremble.

"You know how some people can sneeze at will?" she whispered. "I can orgasm. So if I like who I'm with, I reward myself."

That was a novel sales pitch. It took all the responsibility for her climax out of my hands. I was prepared to give it a go. Sensing my willingness pulsing against her bellybutton, Bambi turned away from me and leaned against the tiles, still holding me in her hand. She spread her legs and I pressed myself against her. My mouth found the nape of her neck while my hands cupped her breasts.

"And I'm about due for a ... AH ..." she said, gasping as I entered her, "... reward."

Twenty-one

Bambi rewarded both of us several times. I later woke as she was padding silently from the room, having gathered her things off the bed. It was well before dawn. She could have stayed. I wouldn't have minded waking up beside her. With no one to play with, and unable to sleep, I rolled onto my back and thought about the incident at the fights. So Perez wasn't convinced about me. I hoped "killing" Gomez had also turned him around and made the exercise worth it for Hector. There'd be a mock funeral and until this case was concluded he'd be kept in a safe house, away from spying cartel eyes, of which there were plenty in El Paso and even Austin.

While it was still dark, I got up and took another shower – a quick one – and then dressed for the coming day's activities. There was an abrupt rap on the door. It was Apostles. "Come," he said, equally abruptly when he saw I was dressed, "Arturo has something to show us."

El Santo was wearing heavyweight boots, and lightweight dun-colored pants and shirt. We were going somewhere. But that was later. Right at that moment we were going somewhere closer. As it turned out, it was the home theatre. Perez was already there, reclined in an armchair. His face was a mask but there was expectation in the air. Something was up. Whatever it was, it made me nervous.

"*Tenga,*" Perez snapped, wanting to get on with it.

A big screen covering one complete wall immediately lit up with a pretty blond anchorwoman, the CBS watermark occupying the lower right-hand corner of the screen. We were watching a news report of some kind. The anchorwoman had that concerned look on her face, the one that tells you bad shit is coming down the pipe: "… News just through about a shootout down in Austin, Texas, where an allegedly corrupt Sheriff's deputy from El Paso, wanted in connection with the recent slaughter at Horizon Airport, has escaped from custody …"

I glanced at Perez who was now grinning straight at me, displaying those yellow rodent teeth of his. My collar felt tight around my throat.

"John Stevens is at the scene in Austin," continued the newsreader. "What can you tell us, John?"

The camera panned to reveal a head and shoulder shot of John, a guy in his thirties with a reassuring square jaw, holding to his face a furry microphone about the size of a large squirrel. "Yes, Penny," John began, "it's believed the deputy, Kirk Matheson, formerly of the El Paso Sheriff's Office, who, as you say, was being held in custody in connection with the recent horrific slaughter at Horizon Airport where twenty-seven civilians were gunned down in cold blood, somehow managed to escape as he was being transferred from El Paso to Austin."

A mug shot of Matheson in his deputy uniform, standing in front of a flag with the Texas star, came up on screen as Stephens continued his live cross. "It's the second time that the former Sheriff's deputy has escaped lawful custody. He shot his way out of the hospital in El Paso the first time, killing one man and wounding another. In this latest escape, it's believed Matheson got hold of a gun, which he used to shoot the driver of the police vehicle. The vehicle crashed and that's when he shot a second law enforcement officer who was riding shotgun beside the driver. Matheson then carjacked another vehicle, but this was subsequently involved in a crash when the fugitive ran a red light."

The screen showed a number of officers in black body armor and head protection, armed with assault rifles, walking quickly around a SWAT truck.

The reporter's voice continued over this footage: "Matheson escaped the scene on foot and police have initiated a manhunt that will take in a large area of downtown Austin."

Back to Stephens: "I should mention also at this point, that the Austin Police Department has asked me to stress that the man is armed and extremely dangerous and shouldn't be approached for any reason, Penny."

Cut to Penny. "Any truth in the rumor, that the fugitive is related to someone senior within the El Paso Sheriff's Office, John?"

And back to Stephens. "Yes, that has been confirmed, Penny," he said with the hint of a wry smile. "He's related to one of the senior commanders, in fact. No doubt there'll be a few red faces in El Paso tonight," he concluded.

The screen on the wall went dark.

Apostles clapped. "*¡Excelente!* Let us hope Kirk makes it safely back across the border."

"Or even just finds a phone," said Perez, still looking at me. "When he calls us, we can help."

While a few hundred butterflies hatched in my stomach and fluttered around bumping into things, I held Perez's stare and told him, "And who says the news is always bad, huh?" This is what I get for playing by Chalmers' rules. I should have fucking whacked Matheson when I had the chance.

"Así que, vamos, ¿de acuerdo?" said Apostles, now in a good mood.

He wanted us to get moving. He and Perez exchanged a few words that I couldn't catch and half an hour later Apostles, Perez and a dozen lieutenants who ignored me completely were banging across the desert in a convoy of three beaten-up Nissan Patrol four-wheel drives, heading west. Only, as far as I knew, there was nothing in that direction other than desert and rattlers.

Whatever we were doing and wherever we were going, this was men's business. The twins were left behind, as was Bambi. So to avoid uglier thoughts I whiled away some time placing the three women in bikinis and sitting them on the chairs in the perfect pool bar in my mind. But then the twins went and ordered chocolate martinis and spoiled it for me, and Matheson again hijacked my thoughts. For all I knew, having found a phone, he was speaking with Perez in one of the other vehicles at this very moment, blowing my cover wide open. My fate was in the hands of the gods and they were a notoriously feckless and vindictive lot, which caused me to sweat some more.

The first indication that we weren't alone out here on the lunar landscape that is Mexico in these parts, were rooster tails of dirt, one on either side of our convoy that began to converge on us maybe an hour out of Juárez. Having chased Doctor Whelt across the desert, I had an idea that the cause of those rooster tails were dirt bikes long before I actually saw them. Eventually the riders became a close escort, riding in formation with the Nissans, making their Desert Storm-era BDUs clearly visible. They also wore full-face helmets and motocross armor like exo-skeletons protected their chests, shoulders and shins. The riders knew what they were doing, standing up on the footpegs mostly and taking occasional jumps that way, their legs working like shock absorbers. Watching them took my mind off Matheson.

Several other riders joined our escort, but not for long as the Nissans scribed a circle in the dirt and came to a choking, dusty stop. Looking out the window, I could see that we'd come to a halt among a collection of large hangar-like structures, all beneath desert camouflage netting. A few individuals in desert camos went about their duties.

I climbed out of the Nissan with the other passengers in time to see Perez and Apostles being led off toward different structures by some of those individuals. Not far from where the Nissans had stopped, a windsock on a pole flapping in the light breeze and evenly spaced portable lighting, in two parallel rows heading off to a vanishing point indicated the presence of a runway. So at least one of those buildings had to be an actual hangar. There was also a sizable communications tower with radio-wave dishes that I could happily disconnect. I took my phone out of my pocket and checked the screen. The words *No service* occupied the space usually reserved for bars indicating signal strength. Damn Verizon, my carrier, for not putting a tower out here in the middle of nowhere.

"*Perdone, Señor.*"

It was a Mexican kid, a blue-head, his hair cropped so short his scalp showed blue.

"*Ven, por favor.*" He wanted me to come with him, all very polite. He wore a pistol on his belt, the securing strap still buttoned up. Good sign. He must figure we were cool here. He walked, I walked. We headed toward one of those hangars and entered through a side door. The interior was sectioned off into offices. But then, out the back, it turned into a cellblock. I wasn't liking where this was going – where I was going – but I kept following the leader. We went through a series of heavy steel doors, down a narrow hall and past individual cells with solid steelplate doors and peepholes. We stopped outside one of these. The guy opened it and motioned me inside. I hesitated.

"*Por favor,*" he insisted.

From inside the room, I heard a familiar voice call my name. "Cooper!" It was Perez. I sucked in a breath, took it down deep and went on in. He was wearing a black rubber apron, with a surgical mask over his face and a clear plastic eye shield pushed up onto the crown of his bald head. Rubber boots encased his feet, and in his hand a thin blade was poised in the air like a conductor's baton. He hadn't wasted any time getting here. Beside him was a short, fat naked man, duct taped onto a gurney by his arms and lower legs. He was trussed that way, lying face up. Duct tape had also been wound around his head so that his mouth was securely covered. His eyes were wild.

Perez lifted the mask so I could better see the black holes in his face, the ones from which no light escaped. "*Señor* Cooper," he said. "*Voy a explicar esto a usted.*" Let me explain this to you.

He didn't need to. I think I got it.

"What language should I use?" he continued. "Which would you prefer?"

I didn't need to think about it too hard. "Sign language," I said.

It took him a few of seconds to respond. "Not funny, Cooper."

Who was trying to be? Enough of this bullshit. "No, I mean it. Sign language because you're gonna outline what you have in store for that man there, whose life means nothing to you, as a warning to me. So there's nothing you've got to say that I wanna hear. You're sick, Perez. You need help."

Perez rolled the blade's thin handle between his fingertips, its edge catching the light, sending a flare into my eyes. "No, Cooper, his life means *everything*. Without it, there would be nothing for me to take. Do not pity him. He is a spy, from a rival cartel. It's important you see what we do to spies among us. And I think it is you who will need help."

Perez replaced the shield over his eyes, bent over his victim and calmly made an incision with the knife across the top of the pectoral muscles, below the collarbones. A scream tore through the duct tape as the man thrashed and struggled, arching his back against the restraints like a few thousand volts were being passed through him. The gurney rattled ferociously as it moved around a little, its wheels locked off. Perez cut again and the thrashing went to the next level. I checked behind me, looking for the way out. A couple of Perez's men had moved to cover the only exit, assault rifles in hand. One of them adjusted an earplug.

The air was full of the rattling of the gurney, the man's breaths snorting through the mucous bubbles bursting from his nostrils, and still Perez cut as if undisturbed by any of it. He took forceps from the line-up of surgical tools, attached them to one side of the incision he'd made, and pulled the skin back. He fed the long thin blade under the skin, working it back and forth, making smaller cuts as if filleting a large fish, separating skin from muscle. He then lifted a large flap of tissue away, grey-brown on one side and red with layers of yellow fat on the other. The victim was now mercifully unconscious. My stomach convulsed. I just wanted to get the hell out, a hot ball of bile rising in my gorge.

I heard the door open, the hinges squealing, tortured like everything around here. It was Apostles and a couple of the men from hereabouts in Desert Storm get-up. "Arturo!" Apostles called out. "I need Cooper. Can you spare him?"

Perez made a dismissive action with his hand, the one holding the blade. A drop of blood flew from its point and landed on my boot.

"*Bueno*," Apostles said.

I never thought I'd be pleased to see *El Santo*. Though I wanted to run, get away from there, the smell of blood, shit, sweat and fear, as fast as possible, I walked to the doorway nice and slow. I wasn't going to give Perez and his team that satisfaction. But I'll admit, I was in shock. The calm cruelty of the monster was outside my experience. I thought of the twenty-seven lonely bodies under those tents, curled up on the scorching asphalt. And now the guy on the gurney. No one deserved what he was getting, except maybe the monster holding the blade. I'd already made a promise to Gail Sorwick. It was time to get specific about it. I stopped at the door. "Hey, Tears of Chihuahua. One day I'm gonna give you something to cry about. I'm gonna pop those black wormholes out of your face and stuff them down your throat. That's a promise."

Perez held his knife, rolling the handle delicately back and forth in his fingertips. His yellow teeth revealed themselves as his lips slid back from them. "You see, Cooper," he replied, "how quickly you have become one of us?"

The guards had their fingers inside the trigger guards. This wasn't the time or the place. I walked out. Slow.

Once out in the hallway, Apostles said, "You and I – we have trust. This you have yet to earn with Arturo. He doesn't believe your story. He thinks you had something to do with our friend's disappearance." I supposed he meant rogue Deputy Matheson. I had nothing to say.

Exiting the building, the clean dry heat of the desert hit us. Apostles stopped and looked me in the face. "Cooper, it would be a mistake for you to think that Arturo and I are different. We are as one on many things, even though we differ on what should be done with you. If it happens that his suspicions about you are justified, you must know that I will let him practice his hobby on you. And he will take the skin from your body, your hands, your feet and your face. He will hang it in his closet like a suit." He put his arm around my shoulders and, with a broad grin, said, "Come, there is something I want you to show you."

I hoped it wasn't another hobby.

Apostles led the way to one of the larger buildings. I glanced out toward the western horizon where a long line of dust rolled above the heat haze. A sandstorm looked to be heading our way, though a windsock snapping back and forth said that we were upwind of it. Strange then that the storm still seemed to be coming toward us.

Apostles opened another door and we went inside. I was right – at least one of these oversized sheds was a hangar. Parked on the floor was a Piper Comanche, a couple of Cessna Caravans and those two black King Airs. Beside one of the King Airs, a man was throwing brown, plastic-wrapped parcels from a pallet into the doorway of the plane, where they were caught and stacked by a familiar shitbag – Carlos.

"Hey, Spiderman," I said cheerily. "Nice to see bugs are still laying babies in your head. Seeing you has made my day."

Carlos' English wasn't great. He might have missed the nuances, but from the sneer on his face he'd caught my drift.

"How your hand, *puto*?" he replied.

As far as insults go, I definitely got the better of him on that exchange, but the comment did remind me about the last time we parted, when the prick had given me something to remember him by – spitting into the festering slice Perez had cut into the back of my hand. Carlos was on my list. I bumped him up a spot.

Apostles acknowledged the love in the air. "Good. You have met. Cooper, your *aprendizaje* continues." He slapped the tightly wrapped bundles yet to be thrown into the King Air. "You will take this product to Austin. Carlos and two others will go with you."

"Now?" I asked.

"Now."

"It has to be planned."

"There are people waiting for delivery. I cannot disappoint them."

"There's a dust storm on its way."

Apostles looked at me, a furrow between his bushy eyebrows. And then something clicked. He waved the furrow away with a sweep of his hand. "No, that is no dust storm ..."

I waited for him to elaborate. He wasn't forthcoming so I asked, "Is the pilot around?"

Apostles gestured to Carlos to provide the answer. "He is in the front, *El Santo*," Carlos said in a tone full of greasy obsequiousness.

"I'd like to see what navigation gear the plane carries," I said.

Apostles motioned to me to go aboard. "Please ..."

Carlos stepped aside.

I climbed in and went forward. The pilot was sitting in the left-hand seat, filling out a logbook. The way he snapped it shut told me he was hiding some other material within it that his mother probably wouldn't approve of. "*¿Qué?*" he barked.

I ignored him and eyeballed the navigation gear occupying the center console. It was a military spec unit with a redundant system. There was also a radar altimeter and backup. Accurate instrumentation like this was a must when you spent most of the time flying under the other guy's radar. I sat in the jump seat and pulled some maps out of a pouch in the door. I wanted to look at Austin for the simple reason that I'd never been there. The maps showed plenty of canyons out to the west of the city as well as a lake – Lake Travis. Canyons were tricky to negotiate without pilots experienced in flying nap of the earth. I figured Apostles had to have a few of those. I took a moment to consider what I was about to plan and hoped Chalmers and Arlen knew what they were doing.

El Santo was standing patiently outside, ignoring Carlos and waiting for me to appear in the doorway. "Sorry, but you're gonna have to disappoint your friends," I informed him as I jumped down. I sensed from the gathering storm twisting his eyebrows in a knot that "no" was a word he didn't hear a lot. I held up my hand traffic-cop-style as he opened his mouth. "Skipping across the border and dropping a load in the middle of nowhere is one thing. If you want me to fly this load deep inside US territory without raising suspicion so that it can be done again and again, it has to be done right."

He was listening, which was surprising.

"To start with," I told him, "while this type of aircraft is perfect in terms of its performance, avionics and instrumentation, this particular example is just too badass. When we're on the ground, other pilots will ask too many questions. You might as well paint a Jolly Roger on the fin. A King Air painted up in the colors of a company with a significant operation in Dallas/Fort Worth is what I need. Even better if the company actually does have a King Air registered in its name. And if it does, then the aircraft should also display the current registration of the plane it's supposed to be a facsimile of. If you've got internet access here I can find some reference for exactly what's required."

"No internet," he said.

I wondered if he meant they had no internet or just that I wasn't getting access to it. If I had money to bet, I'd put it on the latter. That comms tower had internet written all over it. And while I considered that, I also reminded myself that Kirk Matheson was out there somewhere. And if the jerk could get a message to Apostles' people in Colombia, or even, come to think of it, in El Paso, my skin would soon be joining whatever else Perez was hiding away in his closet.

Apostles had come to a decision. "Your plane will be here this afternoon."

"Great," I said, enthusiasm faked. AmTrak could learn a thing or two about efficiency from Apostles. Maybe they should try flaying the odd executive. I showed him the maps. "Do you have an office? I have to work out a flight plan. And I'll need an aviation weather report for the south Texas area."

"You will also be making a pickup," Apostles told me.

"Where from?"

"Anywhere you think will be suitable."

"What am I picking up?" I asked.

Apostles seemed suddenly suspicious. "What does it matter?"

"Size and weight. Aircraft have limits."

"You tell me," he said. "Fifty million dollars in one-hundred-dollar bills."

Twenty-two

I spent an hour and a half in a hot airless room, a couple of armed guards on the door, with the maps, a ruler, and a pen and paper, plotting waypoints, noting elevations, towers and other features along the route. The only significant military airspace worth noting was around Del Rio where Laughlin AFB was situated. There was no real skill required in doing what I had planned, just balls. I had no doubt that every other day organized crime did a version of what I planned to do.

Transponder on standby, we'd take off after sunset, fly nap of the earth southeast, tracking the US–Mexico border, crossing it with a turn to the north at Heath Canyon and continuing more or less north as we climbed to fourteen hundred feet to be five hundred feet above ground level over Fort Stockton. We'd hook a right-hand turn there, skirt around that military airspace centered on Laughlin AFB, maintaining five hundred feet over the Ozona gasworks, and make a beeline via Mason for Lake Travis west of Austin. From there, it would be a northwesterly heading, avoiding Waco, to Brownwood Airport, a mostly general aviation facility, for refueling. That was where, if convenient, I intended to pick up Apostles' chump change. Taking off from Brownwood with the transponder switched on, we'd fly to Dallas Love Field, another general aviation airport, in the heart of Dallas. At Love Field I intended to lodge a night VFR flight plan noting our destination as Houston, which we'd then completely ignore once in the air and beyond the airport tower's visual range. The flight south would be less circuitous. We'd look like we were heading for El Paso before turning off the transponder, dropping down to five hundred feet and hooking a left turn for a run to Mexico airspace, again crossing over in the vicinity of Heath Canyon. The distance flown would be around 1780 standard miles and, allowing for a combined thirty-minute stop in Brownwood Airport and Love Field, total time for the round trip would be about six and a half hours.

There would be a gibbous moon and zero cloud for much of the route, though there was a thirty percent chance of a thunderstorm in the Austin area. Winds weren't going to be a factor. A walk in the park.

Accompanied by the guards, I went outside for some air. The camp was around three miles from the base of a spur of mountains, rising gray and black a thousand feet high or more from the cookie-colored desert. They shimmered in the afternoon heat beneath a blue sky. There were no clouds or birds in it. Out to the west, the rising tan dust of the inbound storm that never seemed to arrive still hung on the horizon. The camp was quiet. As they say – too quiet. What the hell was this place all about?

I decided to take a tour of the various buildings, but was prevented from doing so by the guards who wanted me back into the office. I was considering whether to take the rifles out of their hands and introduce one of the stocks to their teeth when four men in BDUs, helmets and goggles on dirt bikes interrupted this thought, riding around the side of one of the hangars and disappearing inside the main door, swallowed by the dark shadow within.

Dirt bikes. Apostles was big on them for some reason. There was the escort that accompanied our arrival. And dirt bikes were a big feature of the other camp down in the Darién Gap, Colombia.

The four men who'd just ridden inside strolled out of the hangar and into the sun, coming toward me.

Agitated, one of the guards said, *"Ven conmigo."* And then, when I didn't move, repeated more assertively, *"Ven conmigo! Ahorita!"* Come with me! Now!

The riders kept walking toward me. Three were short and Mexican. One was much taller than the others, and of a completely different build. He was Caucasian. They strolled right past me, doused in sweat and water, joking among one another. The taller, rangy white guy looked at me. There was a momentary assessment, a what's-your-business-here look, but no recollection or familiarity. But while he didn't recognize me, I knew plenty about him. The last time I'd seen this guy, he was sitting on a motorcycle gesturing *fuck you* with his middle finger extended. Senior Airman Angus Whelt, alias the Doctor, AWOL from Lackland AFB, wanted for questioning in relation to the supply and distribution of narcotics. What the hell was he doing here? Had there been some prior connection between him and *El Santo*'s operation? Did he know what had happened to his pal at Horizon Airport?

I'd seen Whelt's service record with a mug shot included, but there'd been no reason or opportunity for him to have seen mine. And we'd never actually met. At our last meeting, I was just an unfriendly silhouette behind the wheel of a Jeep Patriot leaking oil from a smashed sump, chasing him across the dry desert as his rear knobby tire threw rocks at Gomez and me. He'd won the chase and sometime later jumped the barrier fence, Steve McQueen-style. Now he was here in *El Santo*'s camp on a dirt bike, doing what? I wondered.

One of the guards nudged me in the back with his AK and motioned in the direction of the hangar. I had a few things to think about and didn't have to be basting under the desert sun to do it, so I walked. A quick scan of the horizon told me that the sandstorm was definitely getting closer though the wind-sock still said it should be moving in the opposite direction. Strange, to say the least. A few things weren't adding up, but I was getting some more figures to play with.

Arriving at the hangar, the familiar sound of approaching turboprops made me stop and turn. An anonymous cream-colored King Air arrived from out of the desert, flying low and fast. It rocketed over the strip and dipped a wing that almost skimmed the ground as it turned hard and climbed. One of the guards opened the building's door and pushed me inside. The bricks of cocaine had been taken out of the black King Air and restacked on the pallet and the aircraft itself had been moved down the far end of the hangar. Carlos was nowhere around. A couple of men materialized and manually opened the hangar door, sliding one half back and then doing likewise to the other half while the cream King Air flew down its glide path on final approach, its propellers snarling and slicing the air on full fine pitch. I saw its tires kick up balls of dust on the dirt strip as it touched down adjacent to the hangar's open doors, but in an instant it was gone from my view hidden by the rest of the hangar. I heard the engine note become more aggressive as the propeller pitch reversed and full power was applied to slow the machine.

Half a minute later, the aircraft arrived at the open hangar doors and the pilot killed the turboprops. The men who had opened the doors ran to the plane with a tow bar. They fitted it to the front wheel and dragged the King Air inside, bringing it alongside the cocaine on the pallet. The fuselage door opened, a ladder came down and out stepped Daniela and Lina, dressed in Desert Storm BDUs showing plenty of cleavage and with pistols in drop leg holsters worn low on their right thighs. Both saw me and ignored me as they strode to the hangar doors, which were being closed, and slipped out through the narrowing gap.

I went over to the plane as a number of mechanics went to work on it, pulling off engine cowls and so forth. The door in the fuselage was open so I climbed inside. It was a corporate aircraft with the center seats and some of the paneling over the fuselage removed. Also, there was no pilot or co-pilot, which led me to conclude that, given I hadn't seen anyone else leave the plane, Daniela and Lina must have been at the controls. While I pondered that, I checked the navigation set-up – military specification GPS and radar altimeter, both with redundant systems. I had to hand it to Apostles, he knew how to do it right.

The sudden overwhelming roar of four-stroke single-cylinder engines filled the hangar and made it tremble as countless numbers of dirt bikes roared by the narrow gap left in the hangar door. This was interesting – I made a move toward the opening to get a better look, but those two guards materialized and barred the way.

"So now you have your aircraft," said Apostles behind me, having entered by another door. I turned and saw that the twins were accompanying him, looking like a couple of pinups from *Girls & Guns*.

"What's with all the dirt bikes?" I asked.

"Ask me tomorrow after your flight," he said, smiling, putting his arm around my shoulders and steering me back toward the plane.

"As you requested, we're going to paint her up in the corporate colors of the Hunt Oil Company, which has its headquarters in Dallas," said … don't ask me which twin. The only difference between them that I could see was that one had a pink push-up bra framing her cleavage, while the other twin wore blue. Okay, so I'll go with that – Pink Bra was doing the talking. "That's a couple of dark-blue stripes on the vertical stabilizer," she continued, looking at a print-out in her hand. "Registration number November seven four Victor Romeo." Pink Bra handed the printout to one of the men who raced off with it while some of his flunkies wheeled a cherry picker up to the aircraft's tail assembly, getting ready to mask off those stripes, I guessed.

"It shouldn't take them more than an hour to get the job done," said Blue. "In the meantime," she looked at me, "why don't you brief us?"

Apostles answered the obvious question. "The twins, they will be your flight crew tonight."

"We know the territory," said Blue.

"Dallas was our hometown," Pink added. "We were Cowboys Cheerleaders."

Apostles wore the hint of smirk, his arm around Pink and his hand on the ass of Blue. "Spiderman still joining us?" I asked to take my mind off a pang of jealousy.

The twins glanced at each other.

"Carlos," I translated.

Pink smiled.

"Carlos and one other. Security," said Blue, who by now I pegged as Lina by her no-nonsense demeanor.

"You expecting trouble?"

Lina shrugged. "You tell me."

"Hey," I reassured everyone, "I got a lot of money riding on this."

"You've got more than money riding on this, Mr Cooper," said Apostles.

"Okay, well then you might think about wearing more conventional pilot's uniforms," I replied, motioning to the twins. "While personally I think what you've got on is, well, pretty great, you're supposed to be working for a god-fearing Texan oil company, not doubling for Lara Croft."

The briefing took less than half an hour to conclude.

"We could have done this." Lina observed when I was done.

"Then why haven't you?" Neither twin had an answer for that.

Twenty-three

Thirty percent chance of rain in the vicinity of Austin turned out to be one hundred percent heavy thunderstorm activity with horizontal wind shear down on the deck that threw the King Air around like a twig in a washing machine. Carlos and his flunkie had their faces buried in barf bags, which they gripped with white knuckles either side of their faces. I enjoyed watching them struggle so much I almost forgot my own fear of striking the ground in a burning fireball of aviation fuel and shredded aluminum airframe. Well, almost.

Somewhere down on the churning waters of Lake Travis, there was a boat awaiting delivery from the sky.

"We'll have to make another run," Daniela yelled into her mike as the King Air bucked and jinked in the turbulence barely fifty to one hundred feet above the white caps, depending on the aforementioned effects of wind shear. Given our altitude and the conditions, I was nervous about a sudden downdraft turning the King Air into a submarine, but then I watched Carlos push his face into the bag a little too hard, tearing it in half so that the contents slid onto his knees, and I completely forgot my anxiety. Laughter will do that.

I felt the plane go into a steep climbing turn, the turbop-rops screaming. Carlos and his pal were shitting themselves. That made three of us, but they had it worse than me.

"C'mon!" I called at Carlos to do like we planned. "The door! Get it open ..."

Carlos sat buckled into his seat, his eyes wild, a beard of bile hanging off the hair on his chin and a slick of corn and beans sitting in his lap. He either didn't hear me or he was too scared to move. Lightning struck the plane with a loud bang. The engines surged again. I hoped Lina and Daniela knew what they were doing. Honestly, my levels of faith in that department were stretched. Maybe I was doing them a disservice but how much flying can you honestly do jumping up and down on the sidelines for the Cowboys?

Speaking of the twins, Daniela shouted over her shoulder, "Hey, we're coming around!"

I gave up on Carlos, unbuckled my restraint and somehow made it to the door. Once there, I struggled into a harness attached to a lifeline and checked that said lifeline was attached to a hard point.

"Slow us down!" I called forward.

I heard the pitch of the propellers change and sensed the nose of the aircraft come down, the flaps lowering.

"Okay, do it!" said one of the twins.

The aircraft wasn't pressurized, which made possible what I was about to do. I pulled the emergency release and, using my shoulder, pushed the door out into the airflow. The door's weight did the rest. It dropped down on its gas strut, the wind and rain howling through it at a little over one hundred miles per hour, shrieking as it whipped through the integrated handrails.

"On the count of ten," one of the twins shouted.

I grabbed bags of cocaine off the pallet and pushed them toward the opening in the side of the aircraft, the rain outside lit up red by the port-side navigation light before flashing briefly silver when the strobe on the T-tail fired.

"Seven! Six! Five … !"

I started throwing the bags out into the airflow on "two", and then dropped to my butt and started kicking them out the door to get it done faster. I saw the waiting boat flash by below. With Carlos and his pal glued to their seats, too scared to assist, it took another two frightening runs to get the cargo out the door.

"Clear!" I shouted over the screaming turbines when there were no more bundles to toss.

"Strap in!" Lina called back.

I buckled into a chair as, moments later, the King Air began to climb and roll on its side, the turboprops wailing. We kept rolling, the maneuver sickening, until the open doorway was facing the underbelly of the storm cells. Lightning forked, framed by the black rectangle open to the violent sky. Rainwater surged in, rivulets of it running from the doorway's leading edges. And then suddenly the open panel in the side of the plane was open no more as the doorway swung upwards on its hinges and slammed into place, closing decisively. Comparative silence.

The King Air rolled back onto a more conventional attitude and climbed. Some big hills between us and Brownwood.

*

"Nice night for flyin'," said the middle-aged balding guy from Texaco as he clipped the earth wire onto the King Air prior to fetching the hose from the truck. "But then I s'pose flyin's a bit like sex and pizza. Even when it's bad it's good, am I right?" He laughed.

I joined in. "Yeah."

He watched Lina walk around the aircraft, checking it over, and liked what he saw. He said as much with a conspiratorial look like I was one lucky bastard to be flying around with that. And I could guess at the look he'd give me if he saw Daniela, especially in a cheerleader's outfit.

"So where are you folks headed?" he asked as he unscrewed the cap for the main wing tank and sank the nozzle into the filler hole.

Headlights appeared on the apron. A courier truck. "Allrighty, here it is," I said. "Right on time."

"You expecting a delivery?"

"Parent company's being audited by the IRS." I gestured at the truck. "Those will be tax records. We're delivering 'em to head office in Dallas, then flying on home to Houston."

"What business you in?" he asked.

I nodded at his tank. "Oil, oil exploration, gas ..."

"The IRS? It's not right. Oil companies built this country," he said, shaking his head. "I bet it's them communists in DC. They don't like oilmen. Tryin' to take away our second amendment rights. Don't know where it's gonna end."

"Yeah," I said again, unsure about how he managed to find a link between a tax audit and the right to bear arms.

The truck pulled up beside the aircraft. Carlos and his little helper jumped out of the King Air and ran to the back of the vehicle. A moment later they reappeared, each carrying two filing storage boxes. They placed them in the King Air's doorway, pushed them in and jogged back for another load.

I gave the refueler a shrug. "No one argues with the tax man."

"I guess not," he said as he stopped pumping the gas and checked the level in the tank with a pencil flashlight. Satisfied, he replaced the filler cap.

"The captain asked me to get both tanks filled," I told him.

"No problem." He motioned at Carlos carrying another load. "A lot of paperwork you got there."

"Big company. And these days you gotta keep records for the air you breathe. Let me know when you're done. You take cards?"

"No problem."

"Might go lend the boys a hand."

"Sure, don't let me get in your way." He jumped down, hoisted the nozzle and hose to the opposite wing and repeated his process. His inquisitiveness apparently sated, I left him to it, joined Carlos at the back of the truck, and picked up a couple of boxes and carried them across to the King Air. The load in my arms was unexpectedly heavy. I wondered how much money I was carrying. Fifty million was a lot of cash. Judging by the number of boxes, assuming the weight of each box was roughly equal, I guessed the total weight to be around a thousand pounds, well inside the King Air's maximum load capacity.

Brownwood went off without a hitch. Half an hour later, we were on descent into Love Field. I went forward and crouched between Lina and Daniela, the lights of Dallas sliding under the nose.

"Love tower, this is November seven four Victor Romeo," said Lina. "VFR, one five nautical out, level five thousand, heading one-niner-zero; looking for vectors to your active. Say local altimeter. Over."

Daniela put her hand in front of the mike. "Pretty, isn't it?"

I nodded. Yep, it looked pretty, but then so did Dar es Salaam at night from five thousand feet. "Who's logging the flight plan?"

"Lina's already called it in," Daniela informed me.

"There's no need to land," Lina joined in. "The tanks are topped off, we've done what we came to do and you've proved your point. We're gonna use Love Field as a way point and turn for home."

"Being on the ground is a risk," Daniela pointed out. "Fake registration, fifty million on board ..."

They were right, of course. There was also the risk, though remote, that someone might recognize me as a cop killer from El Paso. "Okay," I said, "Let's go."

"Do we need your permission?" Lina said as she banked to the west, answering her own question.

I went back to my seat, which faced aft, and gazed at the boxes of money. At least now I couldn't see Carlos. I closed my eyes so that I couldn't see anything and wondered if I'd be able to get to sleep.

Seconds later – but maybe it was longer – they snapped open. Something was seriously wrong. The side door was open, the airflow howling past it, and the naked sound of screaming turboprops filled the cabin space.

Movement behind me. I raised a hand to protect my face. A belt was thrown over my head and pulled back. My hand was inside the loop, jammed back against my windpipe. I shifted, tried to turn, change the angles, find a way out. Choking ... Pressure against my neck ... Then Carlos' man was in front of me. He had a knife; heavy blade, curved. A bowie knife. I kicked out at him, which only dropped me lower in the seat. Carlos' face was over mine, his teeth clenched, straining. I kicked up at him again. This time my toe caught him by surprise, slammed into his nose. I saw it collapse, felt it crunch, the cartilage and bone smashed. Blood exploded from it. He howled and let go of the belt. I went down, onto the thick beige carpet. Drops of blood there. I coughed; throat scorched, dry. Carlos' pal was crouched, blade in hand, about to strike. I moved, grabbed a box, got my back up against the fuselage. The guy with the knife came at me, thrust the blade. I parried with the box. He thrust again. The blade buried itself in the box, struck something hard within – compressed money. He pulled the knife out, destroying the box. On the end of his blade, a wad of ... newsprint?

I gave him a front kick. It caught him in the sternum and sent him flying backward into the curved fuselage opposite. But all I'd done was make him mad. And now Carlos had a gun.

"No guns!" Daniela screamed, coming back from the cockpit. She hit him in the side of the head with a flight manual and sent him sprawling.

The guy with the knife attacked from the side. I twisted, felt the blade slice the skin over my ribs. I twisted some more; the blade caught in my clothes and he had to let it go. I punched him, a left jab to the teeth – felt them rattle. A right cross found his chin and his head jerked back. Punch number three came from my left, collected his jaw on the right, snapping his head in a circular motion. One, two, three. I could see his brain spin in his skull, anchored by his spine and the optic nerves attached to the back of his eyeballs, pulling them left then right. Four: an uppercut, the bottom teeth smashing against his top teeth. He staggered to the left, the wrong way to stagger.

And suddenly he disappeared through the hole in the door. He was there, and then ... gone.

Carlos charged. This time I was ready and, using his momentum, slammed him against the fuselage. The wind shot out of his mouth along with blood and spit and bits of nose bone. The bowie knife, no longer caught up in my clothing, dropped onto the carpet. I picked it up. The weight of the handle was comforting, the balance felt good. I owed this guy ... So I spun around, generating extra force, extended my arm and swung the curved blade. I felt it jar against something hard. Carlos started screaming. I glanced over and saw why. The blade had skewered his hand, pinning it fast against the plane's aluminum skin.

As I turned, there was time to see one of the twins and the butt of a raised pistol. Too late to –

*

I regained consciousness duct taped into a chair, jolted awake by the King Air's landing gear striking the earth. My head hurt, a blinding pain somewhere behind my ear. There was a trickle of dried blood that ran down my neck and into my shirt. The props screamed in reverse pitch, the plane braking hard as I pieced together the events of the night. The delivery and pickup had been a success, except that there wasn't any money in those boxes, which also told me there probably hadn't been cocaine in the packages kicked out over Lake Travis either. I didn't believe that Apostles would have sent the twins on a dry run into the United States. Why risk them when there was nothing to gain? That led me to Perez. Carlos was *his* man. I lifted my head. The exit door was closed. I glanced over at Carlos. He was unconscious, his body strapped to the fuselage and his arm outstretched like he was waving, except that the hand on the end of his arm, pinned to the fuselage and covered in clotted blood, wasn't doing any waving. Maybe Perez really believed that I'd try to hijack the flight and take off with the drugs or the money, as he'd earlier suggested to Apostles. If so, Carlos and his pal were on hand to make sure I didn't get away with it ... No, that didn't work. I was being a model of good behavior for once and had done nothing to warrant being attacked. Perez just didn't want me to return – simple as that. Carlos and his buddy had come along to kill me. I had to believe, therefore, that there was a good chance Apostles didn't know what Perez had had in store for me. And the same went for Lina and Daniela.

The King Air came to a jolting stop and the engines died. The propellers windmilled for a brief period and then came to rest altogether. I heard a thump against the fuselage and the door swung down as Blue Bra – Lina – cut me out of the duct tape with a pocket knife. "Sorry," she said.

"Yeah," I replied.

Portable lights flooded the apron with hard white light. A couple of men came onto the plane, hauled me out and brought me in front of Apostles and Perez. Half a dozen other men, all in Desert Storm BDUs, accompanied them.

Apostles drew his pistol and pressed the muzzle into my cheek.

I tried to turn away but I was being held. "Hey! What –"

"No," said Perez, placing his hand on the pistol's barrel. "You promised me."

Apostles thought about it, then raised the weapon and un-cocked the trigger.

I had no idea what was going on, but I took a shot at it anyway. "Carlos and friend jumped me," I explained.

"Shut up, Cooper," Apostles snapped, his anger on show. He moved to one side and I immediately saw the problem. Cold fear grabbed my guts and a clammy sweat bloomed between my shoulder blades. The stupid blond curls and the red, bloated face – Kirk Matheson was standing there, an arm still in a sling, grinning.

"Hey, Cooper. Fuck you, asshole."

Twenty-four

A couple of men grabbed a hold of me while a third ripped the Sig out of its concealment holster in the small of my back. I was thinking maybe I should start hiding the thing someplace else.

"Oh, c'mon," I said, focusing on Apostles, my brain racing. "You're not gonna fall for this shit, are you?"

His face was a mask of distrust.

"Matheson would have been detained by the FBI. He was linked to the Horizon Airport massacre, a suspected cartel-related event. That means CIA would have been involved in his detention," I continued, grabbing at straws. "Ask him how the hell he got away. How many people have you ever heard of escaping from CIA custody? Answer? None. That's because it *never* happens. The CIA drugs, trusses, hoods and disappears *people they like*! When it's alleged cartel cop killers?" I shook my head. "The Company gets serious about shit."

Apostles glanced at Perez.

"Surely you can do better than that, Cooper," said Matheson. He faced Apostles. "*El Santo*, like I told you, those cops he's supposed to have killed back at Horizon Airport, the ones in all the news reports? *I* killed 'em. That was me. It was Cooper who tried to stop me."

"That's not how it went down and you know it," I snapped at Matheson. "You think these folks are idiots?"

"Give Cooper to me," said Perez in Spanish. "I will get the truth."

"Hey, why me? Why don't you flay the truth outta him? Seriously, ask yourselves how he got away. We all saw the news report. The whole thing looked staged – a big bad shooting match, SWAT called out, helicopters in the sky, the coordinated media coverage ... You do realize that killing cops is far easier to fake than killing civilians, right? They can control it when cops are killed – the victims aren't buried, they just go to a safe house. If you ask me, we saw a show played out to provide Matheson with the kind of story that's gonna confirm he's your kinda guy."

"You just described your own story, Cooper," said Matheson, the confidence waning, his eyes shifting between Perez and Apostles, gauging their reaction. "And I've been working for these guys two years now. They *know* me."

At last, the shithead had given me something I could work with. "Then let's look at the last two years. A lot of big shipments over that period, right? How many of them have been seized?" I addressed Apostles. "So he lets one go through here and another there to protect his cover. And then there's a call made on a disposable cell phone and a big load gets intercepted. Sound familiar? Think about how much you've lost since Matheson joined the team. What's the figure you told me? Two hundred million?' I checked with Apostles for his response. He was half buying it. I eyeballed Matheson. "And you don't think they're wising up?"

I could feel the momentum shift, and so could Matheson. "If I were you," I said to Apostles to put the icing on the cake, "I'd be asking myself why they had Matheson in the first place. Maybe they needed to bring him in for a spell, get debriefed on your activities here."

"Just kill this *puto*," Matheson blurted.

"Cooper saved my life," Apostles reminded Perez.

"And you believe that?" Perez asked, the two of them switching to Spanish.

"I saw what he did. I would be dead now if not for him."

Matheson flared. "Aw, c'mon! This is bullshit!"

"Perhaps you should take them both," Apostles suggested to Perez.

"Actually, your pal Matheson here is right," I said. "This *is* bullshit. I searched you out, believing I might find gainful employment for my skills. But so far, despite having proven my commitment and loyalty, all I've got are threats, intimidation, incarceration, a couple of lacerations and the occasional beating. I've had enough. Maybe your competitors will appreciate my abilities."

I looked at the King Air. At first glance the plane appeared to have bled. A good four inches of the blade that pinned Carlos' hand extended beyond the smooth skin of the fuselage and a yard-long slick of dried blood trailed from it.

"Oh for Christ's sake," Matheson exclaimed, exasperated.

"Hey tonight, asshole, I delivered! Yeah, I dropped a load of what was probably baking soda, believing it was coke, to a waiting boat in Lake Travis. Then I flew to Brownwood and picked up a thousand pounds of newsprint, under the impression that it was fifty million bucks. What would've happened if there'd been an emergency landing, or I'd been recognized on the ground? That's right – in making that run I accepted enormous personal risks and I did it with the expectation that I'd receive two and a half percent. On the cash alone, that would have been one million, one hundred and twenty-five thousand dollars." I looked at Apostles. "So how much do I get for a dozen boxes of *El Diario*? But wait, there's more." I laid on the indignation. "On the way home, your people tried to throw me *out of the plane* and when I land, there's this shit." I glared at everyone. "I mean, *c'mon!*"

Everyone's attention shifted to Carlos being carried out of the King Air unconscious. The blade of the bowie knife speared through the fuselage was no longer poking out.

Apostles suddenly turned and punched one of his men in the face, pulled his pistol again and waved it around while he swore, mostly at Perez. That I'd just been on a worthless dummy run must have been news to *El Santo*. His men ducked and flinched while he ranted and fired off rounds. Apostles then shot the weapon a couple of times into the ground before tossing the pistol into the dirt. I chewed some skin off the inside of my mouth to stop myself grinning. Perez had hoped to reveal my true allegiance, but all he'd succeeded in doing was prove my commitment. And meanwhile his partner had genuinely wanted the coke delivered and the money picked up, but neither had happened.

"Lock them both up," Apostles snapped as he marched off. "I'll deal with it in the morning."

*

Our cells were adjoining.

"They're gonna find your car, asshole," said Matheson, his voice coming through the breezeblock wall. "I'm gonna tell 'em where to look. You took me out because I knew the truth about you. You lied about what happened. I know you did."

Matheson had a point. All I could do to mitigate the potential damage was try to make him less certain about what he thought he knew.

"Hey, listen ..." I said.

"No, *you* listen. I'm gonna get you whacked, motherfucker."

"Look, I just figured it out."

Silence.

"Figured what out?" he asked eventually.

"You ever had an argument with someone, a real heated argument? You go at it, no holds barred, and then suddenly you realize you're both on the same side of the argument, arguing for the same thing? You ever experienced that?"

"What the hell are you talkin' about?"

"Look Matheson, either we're both genuinely working for the Chihuahua cartel, or neither of us is. And I know I'm working for Apostles, trying to make some serious cash for once in my life, so that has to mean you are too. We're on the same team here, buddy ... Think about it."

Silence.

More silence.

"Kirk ... ?"

"I'm thinkin'," he replied.

"When you were chasing me in that Range Rover – you thought I was working undercover and I thought you were. We tried to take each other out. It's all been a misunderstanding, starting with that little shootout between us at Horizon."

"Thanks to you I woke up in a prison cell back in El Paso. Explain that misunderstanding, asshole."

Yeah, that was gonna be tricky. "Hey, I don't know how that happened, but look ... Apostles and Perez killed all those people on US soil and the authorities know it even if they can't prove it. So there have to be folks down here working undercover. That wouldn't surprise me. It's reasonable, right? Maybe these undercover agents saw what happened between you and me, and an opportunity opened up when I put you in the trunk and they took it."

"And on the plane?"

"What plane?"

"On the plane, motherfucker. You sat beside me. I was wounded and you kept bumping my arm. I didn't realize it was you until I saw your picture."

Hmm ... the only way through this one was denial. "Me and you on a plane? And I was bumping into you? Really? I don't think so. I'm pretty sure I'd remember."

"It was you."

"You were wounded."

"What's that got to do with anything?"

"Were you medicated?"

"I didn't imagine it."

"But you were drugged up on painkillers."

"I said I didn't imagine it."

"Well, I'm sorry, Kirk."

"So you admit it."

"No."

There was a sudden *clang* against the cell's steel door. Then came the sound of metal on metal as the cover of the peephole swung open. A flashlight beam swept over me as a guard yelled, *¡Callese!* Mexican for shut the fuck up. And a second or two later in the cell next door, Matheson got the same demand.

Lying on the hard floor, hands under my head, I stared at the black ceiling and tried to sleep. Half an hour later I hadn't succeeded. Sleep was palming me off and not because the floor smelled of old urine and I could feel the fleas jumping onto my bare forearms. In laying things out for Apostles and Perez, I had the overwhelming feeling that I'd hit on a significant truth, only the conscious me couldn't figure out what the hell it was. So instead I closed my eyes and tried to put myself in that pool bar ...

Shit! I sat upright, dragging myself back from the brink of sleep and Daniela, or maybe it was Lina, sitting at the bar in a skimpy shoestring bikini. She had turned to me and said, *"It's believed Matheson got hold of a gun, which he used to shoot the driver of the police vehicle ..."*

What?

The subconscious me was again proving to the part of me that walks and talks, and all too often shoots itself in the foot, that it was running this show. The Daniela in my dream had reminded me about a half-remembered television report.

Matheson *got a gun* ... ? How and where he got it hadn't been answered.

"Hey, Matheson," I said.

Silence.

"Matheson ..."

"What?"

"You shot the two cops in the transfer vehicle."

"What about it?"

"Where'd the gun come from?"

"What difference does it make to you?" he whispered.

"It wasn't one of Apostles' people because no one knew where you were. Who gave you the gun?"

"Don't know. They were walking me to the van and then I feel this peashooter pressed into my hand."

"*¡Callese!*" the guard shouted, banging against my door.

Why hadn't I seen it right away? Firearms don't just wink into existence. Someone wanted Matheson to bust out. Why? Because he'd find his way back to Apostles and Perez and the first thing he'd do would be to blow my cover. Now who would want that?

*

The day dawned like they all do out here in the desert at this time of year, dry and hot with the promise that you ain't seen nothin' yet. Breakfast was non-existent. No last meal for the condemned. I wondered how long before they came for me. The thought had barely formed when guards opened the cell door and ran me outside with a pistol pressed firmly into my earhole. The only pleasing aspect of this was that Matheson was receiving similar treatment.

We were dragged to a sort of parade ground where something black and red was arched over low posts. Coming closer to it, the blackness lifted off in a humming cloud to reveal the flayed corpses of a man and a woman infested with fat wriggling maggots. And then came the smell. My stomach heaved. This had to be the guy I'd seen Perez working on, though I couldn't recognize him with his face removed. It was the corpse of the woman, though, that filled me with a seething horror. It was Bambi, the skin on her face left so that she could be recognized. By me?

"No, no, no ..." Matheson groaned over and over.

"In the Chihuahua Cartel, this is what we do to undercover agents," said Perez proudly.

"Either both of you are undercover agents or neither of you are," said Apostles who had arrived unseen behind us. "That is our conclusion."

"*El Santo* – we worked that out too, right Cooper?" Matheson agreed, relieved as he slobbered, eager to please and seeing a way to slip the noose.

"As we can't be sure one way or the other, we believe we should kill you both as a security measure," Perez growled in Spanish.

"So tell us the truth and perhaps we will let you live," Apostles said. "Do you work with us or with someone else? Are you working undercover?"

"Tell them, Cooper," Matheson blathered. "We both work for you, don't we?"

I nodded, unable to take my eyes of Bambi. Her makeup was smudged by her tears.

"Cooper, you have skills that can make us money," said Apostles.

"But now he has shown us how to do it, do we need him?" Perez asked.

In different circumstances, I might have said I told you so. I took my shirt off and placed it over Bambi's face. Had Apostles and Perez thought all this through? Was this demonstration in their minds all along? Did they know she was CIA? "What?" I asked.

"You are in shock," said Apostles. "I understand."

"Somewhere in Texas, there's the body of a dead Mexican covered in tattoos squashed into the ground," I said, picking up the thread of what Perez had pointed out. "It won't take a genius to figure he's cartel and that he fell out of the sky. Two and two will be added together and you'll have to change tactics. You sure your people are up to that?"

"*Llévelos!*" Perez snapped, answering my question. Take them!

I looked up over my shoulder as a shadow passed across me. It was Apostles, only there was a broad sombrero on his head and bandoliers of ammunition crossed over his chest.

"I am sorry, Cooper," he said with a shrug. "I liked you."

As Matheson was dragged away I heard him pleading for mercy. No, wait, that was me.

*

Twenty-five

How long did I have before Perez showed up with his pearl-handled unpleasantness? This time I had my hands cuff-locked together, and a chain around my ankles. The cell was no more lavishly appointed than the last one I was in – four obscenity-covered walls painted brown, and two plastic buckets, one filled with tepid water. It wasn't built for extended incarceration, which made me figure on having a day here, maybe two. However, through a small steel-mesh-covered opening about six inches square, this cell did have a view across a narrow path to another cinderblock building a yard or so away. Somewhere reasonably close, I could hear Matheson yelling to be let out, calling for the Saint. I heard a door rattle open and the muffled sounds of a beating with something that rang like a bell when it struck the floor, presumably after missing the mark. Matheson stopped shouting after that.

I checked the mesh. It was welded to a frame and concreted into the cinderblock wall. Moving to the door, a quick inspection revealed it to be quarter-inch plate steel, the hinges inconveniently on the outside. A small gap between the ceiling and the walls to let air circulate and keep the temperature down briefly caught my interest. I pulled myself up to have a look and found that the ceiling was pressed steel and the pillars that kept it raised off the walls were short square-section steel posts. I let myself back down, stood in the middle of the ten-foot-square space, feeling trapped. And if by some miracle I did manage to get out, I told myself, what then? Juárez was at least 30 miles away across the open desert.

Shit.

It occurred to me that it was getting noisy outside. Small four-stroke engines and lots of them were milling about. I went back to the mesh. Pressing a cheek against it and peering off to the side, I could see a twenty-foot-wide corridor across what was some kind of parade ground. Dirt-bike riders in camos were motoring slowly across my field of view. The riders kept coming. And coming. Eventually, two phalanxes of these riders were lined up in the corridor, their engines turned off. And then, driving through this view, kicking up palls of billowing dust clouds, came a couple of trucks fitted with what appeared to be large scoops angled diagonally across them, low on one side near the area of the rear wheels and angled up over the cabin where the driver sat. What the hell were they all about?

Engines were all turned off and someone began speaking through a megaphone. It squawked with feedback a couple of times and I couldn't hear what was being said, but the riders all seemed to be listening intently. Suddenly, all the guys I could see raised a gloved fist and cheered. The voice kept speaking. Another cheer. And then I caught a glimpse of the speaker. It was Apostles, dressed in sombrero and crossed bandoliers, mounted on a horse. He cantered into view, turned and trotted out of it. I heard him say, *"Estás cerca, ahora ..."* or in English, "You are close, now ..." before he rode out of earshot in a burst of feedback.

Close to what?

The riders on the dirt bikes that I could see were all armed, assault rifles held in scabbards mounted on the front suspension forks. Apostles had himself a mobile army. I wondered about numbers. From the sound of all those engines, they weren't insignificant. The storm that seemed to move independent of the wind – it was all these dirt bikes maneuvering out there in the desert.

I took a seat on the floor and rested my back against the wall. Arlen suggested that the attack on Horizon Airport might be a trial run for something bigger. The strength of the assault force on the airport that killed twenty-seven people was estimated at between fifteen to twenty gunmen. What kind of hell could Apostles and Perez unleash with an army?

And then it came to me. Columbus, New Mexico, the town raided by Pancho Villa. Was it possible? The town was pretty close to this encampment – maybe only fifty miles to the north. Surely not ...

But there was Apostles' fancy-dress outfit, the photos of the *Generale* and his horse in his lounge room – maybe *El Santo* was nuts after all. Did he really believe he was Pancho Villa? Was he seriously going to recreate Villa's attack on US soil? A modern, fast-moving cavalry; soldiers on dirt bikes. I got up and took another look through the mesh but there was nothing to see other than dust settling.

*

I heard nothing more from Matheson during the day. A guard came in during the afternoon, holding a pistol in one hand and a plate of rice and refried beans in the other. Did he think I was gonna criticize the menu? He told me to step back against the far wall while he put the plate on the ground. I asked him to change the poo bucket but he ignored the request and backed out of the cell. I was hungry so I ate and, yeah, if he brought that shit to me again he'd better bring the damn gun.

Sometime before sunset the riders came back from the desert and the place livened up a little until around 10 pm. I even heard music, Mexican-style folk – two guitars and two voices – floating through the night. My stomach was churning, partly because of the water, partly because of those beans, but mostly because I couldn't get the image of Bambi and the remains beside her out of my head. I'd seen Perez at his work, completely oblivious to the agony he was inflicting. He could have been spreading peanut butter on toast.

Around midnight a drunk was brought into the cellblock. He sang and shouted and called out from his cell. This went on for less than two minutes before a guard went into his cell and beat some quiet into him. Maybe noise made the guard nervous. Or maybe the neighbors made the guard nervous. That gave me an idea. I sat in the middle of the floor where I could be easily seen through the spy-hole and started murdering "The Star-Spangled Banner". The hard walls, floor and ceiling amplified the racket. By the time I got to, "perilous fight", the guard was banging on the door with some kind of bar, yelling, *"¡Callese! ¡Callese!"* At the "rocket's red glare" the guard came in and, from the look on his face, he was scared.

I got up and backed against the wall and wailed about the star-spangled banner yet waving and the guard's pal entered the cell, gun in hand. The guy with the baton raised it and swung it down on my head. It was now or never. I caught it between my wrists with the cuff locks, jumped up onto his chest, wrapped the chain from between my legs around his throat and pulled him down onto the floor. That hurt my back, but it hurt his face far more as it smashed into the cinderblock wall. It happened fast. The guy with the gun hesitated, not knowing where to shoot. But when he finally got a reasonably clear shot, pointed the weapon and pulled the trigger, nothing happened. The safety. It was still engaged. The baton was on the floor. I picked it up and swung it into the guy's knees and one of them made a noise like a mouth chomping on potato chips. He'd forgotten about the pistol by then and was protecting his face from the concrete floor rushing toward it. I was over him before he realized how bad the situation was and bounced his forehead against the concrete a couple of times until I was sure he wasn't going to remember enough to complain.

The blood roaring past my ears was louder than my appalling singing. Other than that, the cellblock was quiet. The two guards on the floor were too badly injured to even groan. I bent down and picked up the gun, a Smith & Wesson M&P 9mm. I checked the safety. Yep – stuck. I *tsk*ed at the poorly maintained weapon but kept it in my hand because I felt safer that way, and patted down pockets for keys. None.

I poked my head out the door and checked the narrow corridor. The place was dead. My chains rattled and clinked as I part hopped, part shuffled down to the guards' security station, an alcove just inside the main entrance door. A bunch of keys hung from a desk lamp illuminating half a bag of corn chips, half a bottle of cheap tequila and assorted slutty hot-rod magazines. Among a litter of papers, I also found a flashlight and a pair of snips. I sat on the chair behind the desk and used the snips to cut off the cuff locks, then took a swig of tequila and stuffed a handful of corn chips down my throat while I went through the keys. Dammit, none of them fit the locks on the leg chains. I took another belt of tequila, finished off the corn chips and went through the desk drawers. In the top one I found another set of keys, assorted locks, pens, batteries and other junk. I took the keys and left the junk. Opening the second drawer I found my old pal, the Sig. I exchanged it for the S&W, hunted around in the other drawers and found my concealment holster and spare mags. I rewarded myself with a final mouthful of tequila.

Key number three fit the leg chain locks but didn't turn them. Key number five set me free. My boots, socks, belt and other personal effects were mixed in with Matheson's in a pile on the floor. I separated mine, finished dressing and put my watch back on my wrist. The tequila was working its magic, making me believe that being reckless was a good strategy, so I had one last belt to make sure. Maybe this stuff wasn't so bad after all.

There was a desert camo cap on top of an empty filing cabinet. I put it on, along with a military-pattern jacket hanging on the back of the chair. There had to be sentries posted throughout the encampment so it was important to fit in. The jacket was a tight fit, the cap loose. Maybe that said something about me. Maybe I should read more and pump iron less. Lastly, I took the keys on the chain as well as the flashlight. I figured if the keys didn't open the leg chains, perhaps they'd fit something else useful around here. And the flashlight would come in handy – it was dark outside, a dirty moon low in the sky, and almost none of the encampment was lit.

I weighed up the best course of action: steal something and leave right away or reconnoiter the place first. There were questions about numbers. And maybe I could find some intel on timings, plans of attack and so forth. In fact, the more I'd been thinking about it, the more I couldn't believe the audacity of Apostles and Perez. Attacking a United States township and slaughtering its inhabitants? That would send the US Army into Mexico, just like it did the first time Columbus was hit. Maybe they'd touch off that border war no one wanted. And just maybe that was exactly the intention.

I buried my hands in the jacket pockets and found a half-empty packet of *Faros*, a crumpled book of matches from some bar in Juárez and a couple of loose pellets of gum. Having fresh minty breath was not high on my list of priorities. I tossed the gum. Sticking to the shadows, I made my way across to one of the hangars whose internals I hadn't seen. The sentries took some of the risk of discovery out of this for me by occasionally turning their flashlights on and sweeping a door or a generator or some other piece of infrastructure, letting me know where they were. I arrived at the hangar without incident and tried the side access door. Locked. On the off chance the hunch about the keys was on the money, I found two that looked like they might do the job.

"Hey," said a voice close by that made me jump.

I pocketed the keys, turned and got ready to reach for the Sig. It was a sentry. He turned on his flashlight briefly so that I could see where he was.

"*Es una noche cálida noche,*" he said. It's a warm night tonight.

"*Sí, muy caliente,*" I replied. Yeah, real warm. I for one was sweating bullets.

As he approached, he asked if I was having problems with the door, because this one often stuck. The key in the lock turned.

He knew something was wrong when he saw how short the sleeves on the jacket were. "*Hey, ¿quién ...*"

I pulled the door open hard, bashing him in the face with it and the question of who I was never got completed. I hit him a second time with the door, just to make sure of it, then dragged him inside the hangar and closed the blunt object behind me.

With no windows, the building's interior presented a thick, impenetrable blackness and the air smelled of gasoline, dirt and rubber. The numerals on my watch glowed as bright as deep-sea fish. I fired up the flashlight and dragged the unconscious sentry to a clear space on the floor, away from the door.

He groaned and moved his head so I hit him again with the base of the flashlight. The guy was gonna end up with a hell of a headache. I straightened up and swept the flashlight beam over the hangar floor, revealing row after row of 250cc motorcycles – Hondas and Yamahas. There had to be over five hundred of the things, all lined up like they were on parade. I took the cap off one of the tanks. Full. The key was in the ignition. I checked a few more bikes. All of them were gassed and rarin' to go. There were three other hangars identical to this one from the outside, not including the hangar where the aircraft were housed. How many of these were full of motorcycles? How many dragoons did Apostles and Perez have?

Reconnoitering the rest of the space, I made a rough count of over six hundred bikes. Down one entire wall was an area dedicated to maintenance where over thirty machines were having chains replaced, punctures fixed, engines serviced and so forth. I picked up a roll of duct tape and some rags.

Going back to check on the sentry, I found that he was still counting canaries, but for how long? Tidying things up there, I taped his hands behind his back, stuffed a rag in his mouth and taped it shut. I wondered about the guards at the cellblock. They wouldn't be waking up any time soon, but unconscious, bruised and battered people discovered lying around military installations tended to make everyone else nervous. And there were plenty of guards with flashlights checking on things. Sooner or later the alarm would be raised and, of course, dawn was just around the corner.

I found the access door on the hangar's opposite wall and slipped out. All was quiet so I moved quickly to the next hangar, found the key and opened the door. The flashlight revealed more bikes, maybe another five hundred or so. Also housed in this space were half a dozen mobile vehicles with mounted .50 caliber machine guns. Further back in the building were more of those odd-looking trucks I'd seen earlier

with the offset scoops, except that a closer inspection revealed the scoops to be ramps. There were also half a dozen
horse floats. Mobile ramps, a thousand motorcycles and horse
floats. WTF?

One more hangar to go and twenty minutes or less until
predawn lightened the sky and made sneaking around undis-
covered impossible. The keys unlocked the necessary doors
and I found myself in a garage full of B-double trucks –
Macks with covered load areas. I counted twenty rigs. I found
parked among them a couple of prime movers attached to
gasoline tankers, a dozen hoses with filler nozzles on each side
of the vehicles for refueling multiple machines out in the field.
Another rig had a big tank of diesel on the back. All made
sense. Mobile infantry requires mobile gas. But what were the
ramps for? And then it hit me. The ramps would be driven into place to launch the bikes over the goddamn fence. Maybe
that's also where Whelt fit in – to teach Apostles' men how to
get their Steve McQueen on.

I swept the flashlight across the trucks, then over one of the
… twins? "Cooper – how did you escape?" she asked.

"The usual way – tied some sheets together."

"I've just come from the cellblock. You left a mess back
there."

"And what were you doing there?" I asked her, checking
my watch. "Dropping off a loaf of bread with a file in it?"

"Y'know, all I have to do is call out and back you'll go."

"I'm not ending up on Perez's table. I'm fond of my shallow exterior."

"Is that why you're escaping?"

"Can you think of a better reason?"

"You're not CIA?"

"So now it's insults," I said.

The twin lowered the torch and walked over. She was
wearing track pants, Nike runners and a puffy jacket, the

identifying push-up bra no longer visible, if indeed she was still wearing it. Her hair was loose. She looked like she was on her way to the gym, or returning from it.

"Who am I talking to, by the way?" I asked, her face close to mine. I moved her hair and looked behind her ear. No freckle. "Morning, Lina." I was surprised that it was Lina.

She reached up and grabbed me around the neck and pulled me into a kiss, her lips warm and salty.

The lights in the hangar came on, white overhead lights as bright at mini suns. The light revealed Apostles accompanied by half a dozen men armed with assault rifles. I glanced at Lina. She shrugged with the slightest of smiles.

"You want to tell me what you're doing in here?" Apostles asked in Spanish.

"Looking for a jack," I replied in English. "You're sitting on a fortune in wheels here."

"Your intention was to escape. Why didn't you take a motorcycle from one of the other buildings?"

"You're talking to a Harley rider. Those things you got back there aren't real motorcycles."

"But you are going somewhere?"

"I told you already – to another cartel who'll appreciate my skillset."

"Unlike my associate, Cooper, I don't believe torture reveals truth. People will do or say anything to make it stop. You had the perfect opportunity to provide your true allegiance to Lina just now, but you didn't change your story. The only thing that concerns me is how willing Lina was to volunteer for this job. I think she is more interested in you than she'll admit."

Lina repeated her smiling shrug.

Did I buy any of this? "Where's Perez?" I asked.

"Laying out his instruments," said Apostles. And then, with a flick of his head, *"Mantenlo!"* Hold him!

Twenty-six

Lina turned, a pistol now in her hand, aimed at my face. Odd thing to notice but her smile was gone. I snapped a hand out and deflected the barrel as she pulled the trigger. *BANG!* Powder burns stung the skin on my neck but the round missed. A sudden kick in the back of my leg sent me down on one knee. I looked over my shoulder and saw Daniela. "Morning," she said all sing-song happy, moving a KA-BAR from one hand to the other.

"I warned you about her," said Lina.

Apostles was holding back his men, apparently getting ready to enjoy the sight of his women kicking my ass.

"Cowboys Cheerleaders?" I asked, the sciatic nerve in the back of my leg sending shockwaves of hurt into my hip.

"Camouflage," said Lina with a smirk. "That sent you off into a world of cliché schoolboy fantasies, right?"

I couldn't argue with that.

"*En efecto* they were Special Operation Command," said Apostles. "They taught self-defense to Ranger candidates. But then the US Army put the integration of women into special forces on hold so Lina and Daniela searched around for another challenge. And came to me."

"And how do you know they're not working undercover?" I asked.

Daniela feinted with a thigh kick and a strike to my windpipe, both of which I saw coming and blocked. But then I felt a slight pressure on the side of my waist. Daniela took a step back and pointed at my leg with the KA-BAR. I glanced down and saw a red stain spreading down the front of my pants. She'd cut me across the ribs and the slice had been deep, aggravating the wound Perez had put there at Juárez airport. I hadn't seen that coming. A searing pain began to spread up and down my side.

The twins began to circle, looking for a way in. Eventually, they'd find one. This wasn't a good situation. My back was always going to be exposed so I reached around for the Sig but before I could pull it out, Lina came at me capoeira-style, down low, twirling, changing direction, feinting. Daniela poised, waiting her turn, the knife held two-handed for a downward strike. I crouched and moved, keeping an eye on both of them, but I moved too slow and Lina's ankle caught the side of my head. The strike left me dazed, poleaxed. Lina kept spinning, this time the opposite way. Another strike. Time – but only just – to protect my head with a raised arm and elbow but the bicep was corked and my left arm went dead. Daniela leaped at me for that two-handed knife strike. I shifted and rolled, and blood from her knife slash spattered across the concrete floor. Daniela had time to pull her strike, but when she came down, she slipped on the blood from the cut she'd put in my ribs and landed on her back, all balance gone. The knife clattered out of her hand toward me. I picked it up and swung at it at Lina as she made a move, a wild, range-finding air swing. But the follow-through took the blade through an arc that ended at Daniela's neck and the knife stuck fast in her twin's oesophagus.

"Danny!" Lina cried out, forgetting about me completely and running to her sister's side.

And then the door behind Apostles burst open. It was Matheson. He stood there attracting a lot of attention, swaying with anger, his eyeballs red and protruding. He was looking right at me, a pistol by his side. "I'm going to fucking kill you, Cooper," he rasped.

The Sig was suddenly in my hand. Pure reaction as he raised that pistol. Matheson's dirty blond curls dancing behind the Sig's front sight. The barrel leaped. An ear-slipping *BLAM!* as, in a burst of red, a hollow-point round sucked Matheson's face clean through the back of his head. I got off a second shot in the noise and confusion and one of Apostles' men, who was crouched in front of the boss, sprayed everyone with meat and cartilage as his chest exploded.

I didn't stick around for the response, diving beneath the nearest truck. I crabbed my way back beneath the coupling and stopped beneath the trailer. Lying down, looking for targets, I shot out the knees of three guards as they ran back and forth, waiting for orders.

I could see Lina tending to Daniela's injury, pulling her sister onto her side so that she didn't choke in her own blood, the knife sticking up out of her throat.

I heard doors opening and plenty of shouting. Options were diminishing by the moment. I scuttled to the back of the hangar, beneath a succession of trucks. Two men came running down the narrow passage between the vehicles. I shot out their legs and both went down screaming. An FN clattered to the ground and lodged between a tire and the floor. I made a dash for it, but one of the wounded men with no knees had a pistol and began firing. I retreated all the way to the back of the hangar, putting a wall of truck rubber and metal between Apostles' men and me. There were floor to ceiling doors here, but they were locked. A quick inspection revealed them to be thin aluminum panels hung on an aluminum frame.

I ran forward and jumped onto the running board of a turbo-diesel-powered battering ram. The driver's door was unlocked. I swung it open. The damn thing was heavy. I tapped the glass in the door – thick and bulletproof. Figured. These Macks were armored, built for battle. There was no key in the ignition so I ran to the truck beside it, a tanker. Same situation with the ignition key. Third truck along, I saw keys dangling from a sun visor.

I leaped down, crawled under the vehicle to the tanker and pulled one of the filler nozzles off the rack. There was no lock on the filler trigger to keep gasoline flowing. I looked around for something I could use. Paperclips! I dug into my pockets, pulled 'em out, straightened one and then wound it around the handle and trigger mechanism to keep it locked in the open position. More shouts. Jesus, the whole damn encampment was bearing down on me. I turned the master lever on the main fuel cock in the direction of the arrow and gasoline began to flow, gushing out of the nozzle under pressure, a miniature Niagara, splashing wheels, tires and trailers, and spreading across the floor.

I ran back to the Mack with the key in the ignition, gunshots ringing out in the confined space and rounds crackling past me, sparking and ricocheting off the metal trailers. One round tore through my jacket. I tried not to think about it, climbed into the rig and fired it up. The book of matches. I took them out of the pocket. In the door mirror I could see fuel spraying everywhere and the air was thick with choking gas fumes. Jumping across the wide seat and lowering the passenger window, I fired up the book and tossed it back toward the spreading pool of gas on the floor. I braced for the explosion, but nothing happened. A wave of gasoline had surged over the flames and extinguished them.

Fuck, fuck and triple fuck. Machine-gun fire had joined in with all the pistols and carbines. Time to motor. I jammed the rig into gear and booted the go pedal. In the mirrors I saw Apostles' men sprinting down the aisles between the vehicles, holding their weapons above their heads, firing wildly. A round smashed one of the mirrors on my door. Slugs sparked off metal like crazed fireflies all around as a fusillade of lead was unleashed at the departing rig.

As I hit the wall at the back of hangar and smashed through it, those fireflies must have touched off the fuel. A pulse of air rushed into the hangar behind the trailer and a massive explosion erupted, the heat reflecting off the remaining door mirror searing my face. A mighty fireball blew the roof and one of the walls clean off the aluminum framework and they sailed high in the dawn sky.

One problem that took the edge off my pleasure at all this mayhem: the back end of the trailer attached to the prime mover I was escaping in was also on fire. Another problem – I was so busy gloating over the destruction raining down on Apostles and his people that I ran right into the main fuel dump positioned behind the now destroyed hangar. I pulled hard on the steering wheel to avoid crashing straight into a large storage tank raised off the ground, but desert sand doesn't provide the best traction and the rig ploughed more or less straight on through regardless, taking out some pipework. The smashed and buckled plumbing sprayed diesel oil all over the back of the trailer as it barreled on by. I was now pulling a roaring gout of flame across the desert.

I scribed a lazy turn, keeping the rising sun on my right, set a northerly course and planted my foot. As far as I knew, there was nothing but thirty miles of sand and those rattlesnakes between the encampment and Texas.

Looking back, things had livened up considerably over in the encampment. Trucks and tankers were being driven out of the pool of flames and doused with foam. Men were running around everywhere. And then a stream of motorcycles surged out of one of the hangars, along with a couple of those pickups with mounted .50 caliber Brownings in the rear. Shit. I had a good head start and sixty mph showing on the speedometer, but the bikes could go faster. And meanwhile I was pulling what looked like a flaming comet and sooner or later those flames would reach my own fuel tanks.

A fire extinguisher was mounted on the side of the passenger's floorboards. I let go of the steering wheel and reached across to grab it, but not at a great moment. The rig barreled into a shallow gulley, the prime mover grabbing some air and the towed fireball bucking and weaving dangerously. The truck crashed up the other side, booting a pool of dirt skyward before sliding sideways. My heart crowded into the back of my throat as I wrestled with the wheel. At the speed I was traveling, it wouldn't take much to roll this rig on its side.

But as Apostles' daughter Juliana had pointed out, it's not always about me. In this instance, it was also about the men on those motorcycles who were gaining faster than I expected. I shouldn't have been surprised. This was their turf and they trained on it. Also, the rig didn't have the turn of speed I thought it might've had with an empty load.

There were at least a hundred dirt bikes cutting the corner, closing on the truck. And then I saw why. The sun was coming through the passenger window, which meant I'd drifted around to the east. Shit.

And just like that, the riders were on the left and right of the truck. Several of them pulled assault rifles from their scabbards and began shooting. The rounds pounded into the window and bodywork and made a lot of noise, but not much else. I thanked Apostles for the armor. When the riders saw what little effect their bullets had, they went for plan B and began shooting out the tires. I heard them blow and the rig's speed dropped back around ten miles per hour and the control became mushy, but the tires were probably anti-terror units and filling them with holes didn't have the usual effect.

The riders dropped back. I wondered why until .50 caliber rounds began pounding the cabin. The heavy slugs made a hell of a racket and cracked the armor in the door window, but it held. I swerved into the pickup, which pulled away, and the machine gunner in the back shifted his aim and had a crack at the tires. The truck sank on its axles a little more, but still the rig thundered on.

The machine-gun RV came in still closer, going for point-blank range. I swerved toward it and then pulled away. The RV likewise veered, but not until some burning fuel splashed off the back of the trailer and spattered the guy behind the gun. I watched him try to shake it off, but the stuff must have soaked through his clothes. He let go of the gun and frantic-ally patted himself down as flames consumed his arms and torso. He jumped off the back of the vehicle, perhaps to roll in the dirt and put himself out. But as I watched, two guys on dirt bikes hit him. Their front wheels collapsed with the impact and the riders went over the bars into a puddle of burning fuel discharged by the trailer and the bikes caught fire and exploded.

Maybe hanging onto this trailer wasn't such a bad idea after all.

The gun truck fell back as, in the passenger side door mir-ror, I saw one of those mobile ramps. And then two dirt bikes sailed off the end of the ramp and disappeared somewhere on top of the trailer close to the prime mover, out of the burning fuel. The slightest jarring through the steering wheel told me they'd impacted with the trailer roof. The ramp increased its speed and came closer as two more riders jumped. One of the bikes slammed into the rear of the cabin where the engine was housed, the resulting jar through the back of my seat feeling like a strike with a sledgehammer.

A boarding party? I swerved the truck left and right to dislodge the men, but nothing fell off. A noise on the roof above me. Holes suddenly appeared in the roof lining, daylight showing. Shit, no armor in the roof! I kept maneuvering the Mack from side to side, but too violently and it lost speed. More holes appeared. Rounds shattered the speedometer and fuel gauges, and shards of plastic, glass and metal filled the cabin, nicking my face and arms. I pulled the Sig, waited for a shadow to flit across those holes, fired upwards twice and heard a thump. An arm slumped in front of the windscreen, and then a smear of blood. I swerved and saw a body fall off the roof and get consumed by the sliding inferno behind me.

The passenger side door suddenly flew open and someone was suddenly in the cabin, covered in dust and black greasy soot, waving a pistol. I jerked the wheel to unbalance him as he fired. The round missed and buried itself in my door. I fired the Sig at him. The top of his helmet blew off and he seemed to go to sleep, slumping forward. The pistol in his gloved hand came to rest on the seat beside me.

And then I noticed something that had been trying to get my attention. It was a different engine sound. The truck was losing speed, the revs dropping. The turbo-diesel was running on fewer cylinders. Someone was back there fucking with the powerplant. I dragged the deceased guy beside me, fed his inert arms through the spokes in the steering wheel, and then pushed the rest of him into the floorboards. The steering now locked in the straight ahead, an improvised dead man's switch provided by a dead man, I engaged the cruise control, grabbed my gun off the seat and kicked the door open.

No sooner was I outside when the truck rammed through a collection of cacti that tore my pants to shreds and lacerated a leg. The flora would've swept me off the running board had I not been holding onto a grab rail with white-knuckled fear. A fall at this speed would be fatal. I took a moment to catch my breath and observed that the same cacti had also forced the bike riders on a wide detour, so there were benefits. I edged down the running board, fingers hunting for another hand hold, stepped over the fuel tanks and came around the vertical exhaust stacks. A wrecked motorcycle was entangled in various hydraulic lines. One of Apostles' soldiers was standing over the engine, trying to rip out any lead he could get his hands on.

His goggles were up on his helmet but I still needed a second look to make sure.

"Hey, Whelt!" I yelled at him. He turned around. "Been looking for you."

"What?"

"You're AWOL. Special Agent Cooper, OSI. I've been looking for you."

"Are you fucking kidding?"

About what?

Whelt went for the pistol on his thigh, but I didn't have to reach for anything, the Sig already in my hand. I shot from the hip, the round hitting above the knee and dropping him onto the space beside the engine. He wouldn't be going anywhere in a hurry. Loose leads whipped around over the engine, one of them sparking. Diesels have no spark plugs. From the way the cylinders were firing, my guess was that the power leads were for the fuel injection system. A quick inspection confirmed it. I got them back into their sockets, my hand jumping around with all the vibrations, and the motor instantly leaped back into life.

Looking back at the trailer, I could see that cover over the framework was largely burned away, the wood decking on the tray well alight with several wrecked motorcycles smoking and smoldering on it. Down the back was where the real action was happening. The rear tires and wheels were flaming Catherine wheels spitting molten rubber in a wide spray that made the riders keep their distance. One of the tires exploded. Once they'd all blown and the back end was running on rims, the trailer would become a massive dragging weight. Movement was keeping me alive. If the rig was made to stop, I'd be surrounded and shortly thereafter I'd be in the hereafter, no doubt checking into a nice suite in hell.

I had to lose the trailer. How did that work? It rattled, clanked and bucked on top of what looked like a turntable. A heavy locating pin was locked behind steel jaws. Maybe that's what had to be released. But how? I figured it couldn't be done while bashing across the desert at sixty mph, give or take. Checking beneath the turntable, I saw a handle. Maybe that was how to do it. I got my hands on it and tried to shift it. Nope, too much pressure. I scanned around, looking for what I wasn't sure. But then I saw it – a hammer. It was clipped against the back of the cabin. I leaped over Whelt and reached for it. But then something made me look down, a movement. It was Whelt at my feet, grinning against the pain, a pistol in his hand aimed upwards into my groin. This guy had real bad timing. I swung down and felt his collarbone collapse under the hammer as the weapon clattered out of his hand.

I stepped back to the turntable and struck the handle with the hammer. It budged, but only a few degrees. I hit it again – nothing. It only released when the trailer's weight wasn't resting on the turntable. I just had to get lucky and hit it at the right moment as the rig bucked. I struck it again and moved the handle half a turn. The jaws had opened, but not all the way. I swung the hammer again, harder this time. Maybe a little too hard. The handle snapped off, fell through the metalwork and dropped onto the ground racing away beneath the truck. Shit.

Another tire exploded.

I retraced my steps back to the cabin, the truck's bodywork puckering around me a couple of times when random percentage shots fired by riders out wide almost got lucky. The opposition seemed to have lost heart. I opened the driver's door and kept it open while I disengaged the dead man's switch and threw him out. Just maybe I'd make it over the line after all.

The engine was running smoothly, all gauges that weren't smashed either in the green or yellow. The barrier fence was only thirty miles north of Apostles' encampment and I'd been motoring now for over thirty minutes at sixty mph. I had to be close. I peered forward. Something was out there ... Whatever it was, it didn't feel right. Mexican desert slid into Texan desert without so much as a bump or ripple on the other side of the narrow dry ditch that was the Rio Grande. And yet, there did appear to be something *on* the horizon. I leaned forward and squinted. Maybe it was the fence itself.

The Mack ate up the desert toward it and the line soon came into focus ... Right. It wasn't a bump or a ripple or a fence at all but at least five hundred motorcycle riders, shoulder to shoulder, stretched out in a line with support from those RVs with 50. caliber Brownings. Shit. Perhaps this was the end of the line. A rocket-propelled grenade arced out from the line, but there was time at this distance to turn the steering wheel a few degrees and avoid the ground burst. So now Apostles and Perez were getting serious. They didn't want me escaping to pass along whatever they thought I might know, that a modernized Pancho Villa–style raid on Columbus was on the way. Dropping Matheson at their feet would've confirmed their suspicions about any holes in my story. According to Chalmers I wasn't supposed to be the judge, jury and executioner, let alone feel good about it. But maybe Chalmers was just laying the groundwork to protect his own skin, because it was going to take plenty to stop me busting a cap in the jerk's ass when I saw him next.

The outriders departed the area as more RPGs arced from the line, fingers of supposedly smokeless propellant leaving smoke trails in the morning sky as they blasted toward the truck. I kept coming, but made things difficult, putting in turns, some of them more aggressive as the distance closed. Small arms and .50 caliber rounds joined the crescendo of metal hurled at the Mack. Lead peppered the bodywork, grille and windshield – a thousand high-velocity steel fists. The Mack just shrugged it off. Damn, you gotta love American built. It just works, right? I turned the wheel and the truck skidded sideways. I put in another turn, evasive action required to avoid a couple of RPGs with flat trajectories fired from dead in front, and things suddenly got interesting. The truck veered to the left. I corrected. It skidded violently to the right, the amplitude of each skid more extreme with each correction. Oh shiiiit ... Losing control here. More lead slammed into the truck, smashing lights and mirrors, Apostles' men realizing that the end was near. In the last vestige of the passenger side door mirror remaining, I saw the problem: the trailer. It had almost unhitched itself and was swinging around off the back of the prime mover like a giant counterweight. So I spun the steering wheel to the opposite stop, massively over-correcting. The forces suddenly unleashed flicked the trailer around like a giant, multi-ton pendulum. The center pin must have ripped clean out of the base plate jaws because suddenly the trailer was on its own, free to tumble, rolling and burning across the sand, *smash* into the line of motorcycles and support vehicles. The launch of RPGs suddenly dried up in the panic as riders rode over each other to get the hell out of the way of the flaming steel juggernaut tumbling toward them.

The trailer flattened two of those .50 caliber RVs and at least twenty riders were swamped by it. Other riders, their clothes on fire, careened into others who caught fire, just like a bad smash at the Indy 500.

The Mack, now freed from the weight of its load, leaped forward with a burst of acceleration and punched through the pall of black smoke marking where the line had been, and shunted a burning vehicle out of the way.

With no mirrors, I had no way of knowing what was going on in my wake, but up ahead, maybe half a mile away, I could see the barrier fence. This was going to present its own problems. Like how the hell was I going to punch through it, a wall of reinforced steel eighteen feet high? The Mack was heavy and it was also powerful. Hell, just maybe I could batter my way through. I pulled the seat belt over my shoulder, buckled in and pushed the accelerator pedal to the boards. But at the last moment, I thought better of it. The damn fence was constructed to prevent exactly what I was about to attempt, fool, I reminded myself. I stood on the brakes and grabbed a handful of steering wheel. The Mack responded better without the trailer, but not good enough. The wheels all locked up, it skidded sideways and collided with the fence, throwing me savagely against the belt.

I sat there for several seconds, doing nothing except maybe groaning a little. Steam poured from the Mack's radiator and the air reeked of hot water, scorched rubber and diesel fumes. I unclipped the belt and pushed open the door. The Mack was tall. Perhaps if I could make it up onto the roof, I could vault the fence.

My body wasn't working so well as I climbed out onto the running board, stepped up onto the cheese grater that the mud guard over the front wheel had become, and stood on the Mack's hood. From there it was a running jump up onto the windscreen and then onto the roof but the fence was still too high and too far away. I took a deep breath, pulled the Sig and checked the magazine. One round plus one in the chamber and two full mags in my pocket. Time to change mags. No way was I going to let Perez practice his hobby on me.

I turned to look back at Apostles' front line, expecting the worst. The trailer had done a good job, but there were still a lot of tangos out there. No doubt they'd be regrouping and heading my way. But in fact the opposite was the case. They were retreating, heading south, kicking up those familiar rooster tails of dirt. Something had spooked them, and then I saw what it was. In fact it was two of them – a couple of Predator drones armed with Hellfire missiles flying figure eights overhead, slow and menacing.

"Hey Cooper," a familiar voice called out behind me, on the other side of the fence. It was Ranger Gomez, a Border Patrol SUV parked behind him. "So lemme guess ... the truck's a rental, right?"

Twenty-seven

An Air Force Black Hawk turned up and landed nearby. The loadmaster hopped out and jogged toward the Mack. I hopped down off the hood and went to meet him. He gave me the thumbs up, wanting to know if I was okay. I nodded and he patted me on the shoulder, wanting to get back to the aircraft. Sure, but first there was something I had to check. I walked back past the dented, scorched, pockmarked, twisted hunk of metal that had transported me across the desert, and climbed up into the engine section. Whelt was still there, jammed between the engine housing, the cabin and sheets of gnarled metal. His right foot was bent around so that it looked like it had been attached to his leg back to front. He might have seemed dead but his wounds were bleeding, which suggested otherwise. I felt for a pulse. All things considered, it was strong. I pulled his arm and hoisted him across my shoulders.

*

"Where do you think you're going?" said a scowling, petite nurse with a cute button nose and big brown eyes, determined to complete the examination. "Sit. I'll be back in a minute."

I showed her both hands palm out, capitulating, sat quietly on the gurney and waited for her to return with the X-rays. Before my eyes, a diagonal bruise began to materialize across my chest where the Mack's seat belt had stopped me smashing into the armored windshield. The slice above my waist delivered by Daniela's KA-BAR had already been cleaned up and sutured closed. The stab to my ribs delivered by Perez had scabbed up nicely of its own accord and needed no attention. There were quite a few small nicks, cuts and bruises, but I was surprisingly okay given the wringer I'd just been through. I didn't need an X-ray to tell me that nothing was broken. I guess I sat there nice and peaceful because I got a thing for nurses. Who doesn't?

Speaking of which, she came back in with the chest X-ray and stuck it up on the lightbox.

"I can't see. Did the surgeon leave anything in there?" I asked her.

She glanced over her shoulder and grinned.

Gomez stuck his head around the door. "How's the patient?"

"He should spend the night," said the nurse.

"I will if you will," I told her.

"I'm not on tonight," she said.

"Then where are we going?"

She grinned again as she walked out. "Okay, I think you're good to go. Just check with the desk."

I fed my arm through the shirt sleeve and said to Gomez, "That would've turned out differently if you weren't here."

"Dream on. Had a look at yourself lately?"

I caught a glimpse of my face in a mirror over a basin in the hall as we walked out. It had been bathed in the yellow-orange disinfectant, like the one used on the KA-BAR slash, and the cuts and abrasions showed a deeper crimson. I looked like a daisy that had lost all its petals. Moving right along, I said, "Where's Whelt? He's here, right?"

"Upstairs. Arlen and Chalmers are with him."

We took the elevator to the third floor. I could guess which room was his by the four uniform El Paso SWAT cops in helmets and body armor standing outside the door. They seemed serious and nervous, a reasonable state of readiness given that the Chihuahua Cartel had reached into this hospital on a couple of previous occasions. Once Apostles and Perez knew of Whelt's fate – and I had no doubt that they'd learn of it fast – I was sure they'd come for him and they'd come armed. He would have to be moved.

Gomez and I showed IDs and one of the guards opened the door. Inside were two more armed cops as well as Colonel Arlen Wayne, CIA dipshit Bradley Chalmers and several other blue-suited flunkies I didn't recognize. Arlen's head was shaved above the ear, the patch mostly covered with a bandage. Chalmers I'd like to put in bandages.

"Hey, Vin," said Arlen, beaming, coming over to shake hands. "You made it. From what I hear it was a miraculous escape."

"I'm taking the act to Vegas. How's your head?"

"Oh, this?" He touched the dressing. "This was stupid. Matheson took the gun right out of the security guard's holster and shot him. The same bullet got me. But I was lucky. Can't say the same for the security guard."

"Cooper," said Chalmers by way of greeting.

"I wondered if you'd show up," I told him. "You and I need to have a little get together. I'll let you choose the weapons."

"Get over yourself," Chalmers replied.

"You lost a good agent working undercover in the Chihuahua Cartel. She didn't die well. Her name was Bambi."

"Bambi … Bambi …" Chalmers acted like he'd never heard of her. "Cooper, if Bambi was one of ours, and I'm not saying she was, she would have known the risks. Is that what you seem so upset about?"

No, it wasn't. I took a deep breath and let it out to keep my anger under control. The issues between us would have to be resolved, but not here. "Where's Bobbie Macey?" The pilot who had survived Perez's strike on Horizon Airport had been in a room down the hall, but that was weeks ago.

"WITSEC," said Arlen.

"What about her co-pilot?"

Arlen frowned. "His family turned off his life support day before yesterday."

All I could do was shake my head at the senselessness of it.

There was a sharp intake of air from the other side of the room. "Director, sir," said one of the men in thin ties and navy suits to Chalmers. He was drawing his boss' attention to the fact that Whelt had regained consciousness. Chalmers went over to the patient, whose leg was on top of the covers and in a cast with an exoskeleton of metal keeping everything straight. Like mine, much of his exposed skin was colored disinfectant orange.

"Senior Airman Angus Whelt," said Chalmers, taking a position beside the bed.

Whelt looked at him, doped up and defiant.

"Just to let you know," Chalmers continued, "you're going to be charged with everything from desertion, to accessory to murder, to trafficking illegal substances, to being a member of a cartel, to driving on the wrong side of the fucking road and everything in between. At last count, there were up to a hundred and fifty separate charges. It's likely you won't get out of jail this side of your two-hundredth birthday. Maybe they'll stop raping you by your sixtieth birthday, but only because by then, on the prison diet, you'll have lost all your teeth and your mouth won't be as loose as your ass. And that's just a small window into your life going forward unless you cooperate."

Whelt stared at Chalmers and said, "Who the fuck are you?"

"Someone who can help you, if you play your cards right."

"Fuck off," was Whelt's reply.

Listening to the way he dealt with Chalmers made me feel that perhaps Whelt wasn't such a bad guy after all. Seriously though, the defiance suggested he was mentally strong and that could be a problem. We needed him to give up whatever he knew because Apostles and Perez had a plan and we didn't have all the details.

Whelt looked at me as I moved toward the bed and his agitation soared. "What's *he* doing here?" His eyes were suddenly wide. "Get him away from me. Get him away!"

Was it the orange coloring? Whatever, perhaps it could work for us. "Actually, why don't you clear the room?" I suggested to Arlen. "Just give us ten minutes alone."

Whelt was horrified at the suggestion.

"Would you like that, Whelt?" asked Arlen, reading the play.

"No, don't do that," Whelt pleaded, his eyes searching the faces around him. He reached for Chalmers' hand and grasped it. "Stay, okay?"

"We've got questions and you've got answers," said Chalmers, pulling his hand out of Whelt's grasp and wiping his palms on his jacket.

"I'll cooperate. I'll tell you everything," he promised. "Just get him outta here. He's fucking crazy."

I glanced at Arlen and noted the barest hint of a smile at the corner of his lips. I leaned in closer to Whelt, who tried to climb backward out of the bed away from me. "If I hear you're holding back on us, you and I are gonna go for a ride, you hear?"

Whelt nodded, tears bursting from his eyeballs, chin quivering.

I gave Gomez a shrug as I walked out past him. In the hallway I found a seat. Blood was seeping through the side of the shirt, oozing through the sutures and the dressing.

A couple of minutes later, Gomez, Arlen, Chalmers and his followers burst out of the room and came toward me. I stood. "Well?"

"July 20; Columbus, New Mexico," Chalmers announced.

Columbus was no surprise, but the date? It was familiar. I just couldn't recall its significance. "Why July 20?"

"Whelt didn't know," said Arlen. "We threatened him with a little more of you, but that didn't change the answer. You've given him a bad case of post-traumatic stress disorder. In short, we believe he told us the truth. July 20 is the date and Columbus, New Mexico, is the target. Whelt said they've been training to hit it."

The elevator doors were open on our floor. We all rode it to the basement. I didn't need to point out that it was July 15 and that the 20th was just around the corner. And then the significance hit me. "Pancho Villa died July 20, 1916."

"What's Pancho Villa got to do with anything?" asked Chalmers.

"Whelt didn't mention anything about him?" I asked.

Arlen shook his head. "We just got the top line. A full debrief will begin tomorrow. We got professional army interrogators coming. The attending doctor was concerned about his mental state. And as I said, that's your bad."

Gomez smirked. "What the hell did you do to him?"

"Villa is a symbol," I said.

"Of what?" Chalmers wanted to know.

"Mexico kicking American butt. On March 9, 1916, Pancho Villa crossed into the United States and attacked the army barracks at Columbus, New Mexico." I recalled the glimpse I had of Apostles with crossed bandoliers and a sombrero, riding around the desert parade ground on a horse. *Estás cerca, ahora* ... "He uses the symbolism to rev up his men."

"Then I don't get why he isn't attacking Columbus on March 9." Gomez observed. "Wouldn't the anniversary of the original attack be a more auspicious date?"

Arlen shrugged. "Perhaps March 9 didn't suit his overall timetable."

Down in the basement parking lot, Chalmers' minions flitted away on important CIA business as the asshole himself paused at his rental to give us his verdict. "It all fits together."

Maybe and maybe not. Gomez was a long way from stupid – an attack on Columbus on a March 9 date would've made plenty more sense.

"What's he trying to do?" asked Arlen. "Start that war?"

"Wars bring troops and troops bring money and buy drugs," Gomez said.

"Maybe we just got up his nose for intercepting so many of his drug shipments. He ain't been happy about it."

"If he attacks a US town, every disaffected misfit spoiling for a fight will rally to whatever he says his cause is," Arlen pointed out. "It'll give him the kind of credibility no other cartel has had."

Gomez rubbed his hand across the two-day growth on his cheeks. "Might just let the guy forge some kind of super cartel."

"What about the Tears of Chihuahua, Vin? What's his role?" asked Arlen.

"As far as I could tell it's fear and intimidation, which he's very good at."

"Oh, I meant to show you this." The colonel reached into his jacket's inside pocket, pulled out a folded sheet of newsprint and handed it to me.

"What is it?" I asked, unfolding it.

"Welcome back. That's tomorrow's front page. Should stop you being accidentally arrested or shot at around here."

I held a picture of my smiling face beneath the *El Diario* banner. Not my favorite photo. The last time I'd seen it, the headline above it had screamed, "Killer!" That was now replaced with the word, "Innocent."

There was a blurb beneath the photo that I assumed elaborated on the headline. I folded it up and put it in my pocket.

"And meanwhile," said Chalmers, unimpressed, "your escapade has been a waste of time and resources. You were supposed to bring back something with Perez's DNA on it to compare with evidence collected at Horizon, were you not? So where is it, Cooper?" He smiled his oily, perfect-hair smile at me. "You got maybe a sweater with stains on it for us?"

"Has anyone noticed whether there are any surveillance cameras down here?" I asked.

Gomez looked around. "Haven't seen any."

Arlen shrugged. "Why do you ask?"

I turned and buried my fist deep in Chalmers' solar plexus. His eyes popped out of his head as his sank to his knees, unable to breath.

Gomez and Arlen exchanged a glance.

I looked down on Chalmers. "I want this guy arrested on charges of ... let's see, aiding and abetting, attempted murder and conspiracy. Kirk Matheson shot his way out of lawful custody a second time. From *your* custody, Chalmers. You had one of the police guarding him slip him a gun, which he used to shoot his way out. He even killed the guy who gave him the gun. How nice and neat for you."

"We lost you, Cooper," said Chalmers, gasping for breath, down on all fours. "We believed Matheson would know where Apostles was and thus lead us to you, which he did. I saved your fucking life."

Gomez and Arlen were horrified by Chalmers' admission.

"I rest my case," I told them.

Twenty-eight

Chalmers stood beside the white Suburban parked on the apron, arms folded and wearing a scowl. I didn't need to see his eyes behind the dark sunglasses to know they were following me.

"What's he doing here?" I asked as Gomez and I walked toward the waiting Mexican Army Black Hawks.

"If anyone asks, US State Department oversight, according to Arlen," Gomez replied.

"That's not what I mean."

"You know what he did and so do we but where's the proof?"

"We all heard his admission. How many excuses do we need to lock him up?"

"You slugged the guy. You can't have us witnessing the confession on the one hand and turning a blind eye to the assault on the other."

"Why not?"

"If you bring him down, he'll take you with him, at least temporarily, and Arlen wants you on the case. He's a distraction. You know who and what we're dealing with better than anyone. Forget Chalmers. Sooner or later, we'll get him. Or he'll get himself. The system eventually flushes out guys like that. On the subject of flushing, we had to release Kirk Matheson's uncle Matt, the SO's operations commander. He was being held on suspicion of aiding and abetting his brother's escape. Did you know that?"

I didn't. I'd been away. "Who oversaw the search at Horizon, the one that missed the coke and the homies stuffed into the trailer?"

"No one's taking the rap for that. The organization of the crime scene was over-complicated by the presence of so many agencies. It got extra messy when the press started snooping around, trying to pin the blame on the donkey. Think of a roomful of law enforcement types each pointing the finger at the other and you've got the picture."

Commander Matt Matheson wasn't one of my favorite people, but innocent is innocent. Apparently you can't lock someone up for being an ass.

Heading out on the day's mission was a ragtag collection of hastily thrown-together anti-drug types: *Federales*, Mexican Army Special Forces, agents provided by SIEDO – the Mexican Attorney General's Office for Special Investigations on Organized Crime – US DEA special agents, a bomb disposal team, an OSI special agent, me, and an observer from the Texas Rangers, Gomez.

Frankly, I knew it would be a waste of time going in. The Mexican President was pissed at the US authorities for sending armed drones into Mexican airspace, and the Mexican Army paid us back by processing the request for this mission when it felt like it. And it didn't feel like it.

So now we were arriving three days after my noisy escape, long after the horse, with Apostles on top, had bolted. We were also departing from Juárez International, the airport servicing Cartel Central and crawling with *halcones* armed with cell phones, so while the Black Hawks were all painted low-vis green, they might as well have been painted with pink and white polka dots for all the stealth that provided.

The four choppers dusted off in a cloud of grit and flew out to the west, a column of black smoke rising into the clear blue desert sky marking the spot. The flight time was less than twenty minutes. Arriving at the encampment, the pilots flew an orbit of the destruction below and then landed.

The law enforcement and military potpourri all disembarked and fanned out through the smoking rubble at a crouch, M4s and AR-15s raised and at the ready. I stayed back, took my helmet and vest off and left it all in the Black Hawk.

"What are you doing?" asked Gomez.

"There's no one here but us chickens. We're not going to find squat."

"What about booby traps?"

"Why would they bother? Half the folks here are probably on the take anyway and Apostles won't want to randomly kill a possible asset. Not his style. Like I said before we took off, this is a waste of time. If we do find anything, it has been planted for us to find."

"Then what are we doing here?"

I could only see one good reason. "We're here to be nice and predictable. Coming all the way out here to search the encampment is what we *would* do."

"I think you're giving Apostles too much credit," said Gomez. "He's no super villain."

"Perez might be a straight up and down sociopathic killer with a need that has to be stoked, but Apostles is different. He comes off in some ways like an uncle, someone you can like and trust, but all the while he's weighing you, judging you, assessing your likely reactions, and feeding you stimulus to guide your actions." I looked at the armed soldiers and law enforcement hunting through the rubble but getting nowhere. "I dunno … I just have the feeling I've been played. We've all been played and the strings are still being pulled. Three days ago I escaped a prison cell guarded by a thousand guys on motorcycles, in a truck. Apostles was even there to wave me goodbye. I like to think I'm good. But am I *that* good?"

The men were starting to wander back toward us, their weapons no longer at the ready, the body language relaxed. Like I said, there was nothing doing.

"So what have we missed?" Gomez wondered.

I needed time to think about that so I went for a stroll through the rubble of the encampment on my own. And then I took a tour around the circumference of the place, while several of the men back at the Black Hawks shifted their weight from leg to leg, impatient to get going. On the ground, the breeze had shifted the sand and the dust around since the camp had been evacuated and destroyed, but there were still tracks. It intrigued me that none of them were bike tracks. Looked to me like everything and everyone had been packed into those trucks.

"They're out there somewhere. Unfortunately it's a big somewhere," Gomez said when I rejoined him. His foot rested on a lump of scorched cinderblock while he squinted into the horizon wobbling in the midmorning heat haze.

"They could've left us a forwarding address," I said.

"So what now? We can't search the whole of north Mexico. Do we wait for them to come to us?"

"That's what worries me," I said.

"What does?"

"We're counting on Columbus being the target. What if it isn't?"

*

US Army 1st Armored Division Lieutenant Colonel Dwight Needleman commanding the 1st Stryker Brigade Combat Team's 4th Battalion, 17th Infantry Regiment, chewed on a toothpick while he checked the map. The colonel's baby face, immaculately pressed uniform and hair parted crisply low on the side of his head made him look like this was his first day at school.

"Mendoza, what do you think?"

The colonel's adjutant, Captain Manny Mendoza, a young, fit man with three fingers on his right hand apparently left behind somewhere in Afghanistan, summed it up pretty quick. "No problem, sir. We dig the battalion in here, here and here. With support from three or four Bradley Fighting vehicles, the threat as we know it should be easily contained. And for insurance, we can get a couple of AC-130s put on standby out of Cannon AFB. Can we expect any cooperation from the Mexican Army?" Mendoza asked.

"In a word, no," Chalmers replied. "We believe they're enjoying watching us sweat. Not that they'd ever admit it."

"What do you think, gentlemen?" Needleman looked at Arlen and me and exchanged his toothpick for a fresh one from a silver case lifted from his breast pocket.

"Sounds good to me," said Arlen. "Cooper?"

"No problem, as long as Columbus is the target. But what if they hit somewhere else?" I said. "Somewhere like El Paso?"

Needleman seemed indifferent. "Not my problem. CIA said the target was Columbus."

"It's Columbus," Chalmers reconfirmed. "It's certainly not El Paso. You think the cartel would hit the home of Fort Bliss?"

"Doesn't look to me like we've got alignment here," said Needleman, nodding in my direction.

Chalmers shook his head, running out of patience. "We've been over this at least a dozen times, Cooper. Everything you've told us – everything debriefed from Whelt – points to Columbus. And there's the Pancho Villa connection, let's not forget that."

"What Pancho Villa connection?" Needleman asked, an eyebrow raised. "I was led to believe CIA had this one nailed down."

Yeah, like Jell-O to the ceiling.

"We have good reason to believe that what the cartel plans is a copycat raid on Columbus that mirrors an attack by Pancho Villa on the town," said Chalmers. "And, I might add, there is no intelligence that points to the target being El Paso or anywhere else. Am I right about that, at least, Cooper?"

I was reluctant to give him this, but I had no place to go. "At the moment, correct – there is no firm alternative target."

"Thank you. Then we should plan for what we do know, shouldn't we?" Chalmers was getting way too triumphant for my liking.

"Do you have an understanding of the Pancho Villa attack?" Chalmers asked the army.

Mendoza handled the reply "Sir, Villa, a revolutionary general, brought five hundred men across the Rio Grande to attack the army base there. Villa's force was badly mauled in the attack, but the general himself escaped and fled back across the border. Washington sent a thousand men after him, led by Black Jack Pershing. They never caught Villa, but General Pershing and his men caused a lot of damage to US–Mexico relations."

So in short, yes, they had an understanding.

"This have anything to do with the shit that went down at Horizon Airport?" asked Needleman.

Chalmers nodded. "The force that hit Horizon is the same one heading for Columbus, only with ten times the numbers."

"You can be sure we'll give them bastards a real Texas-friendly welcome from Old Ironsides then," the colonel said, standing. Mendoza also stood. "We'd better get a move along. The 20th is only the day after tomorrow."

"Be good to have a recon force held back for rapid reaction purposes," I said.

"And put at whose disposal, Cooper?" Chalmers wanted to know. "Yours?"

Needleman and Mendoza glanced at each other, the animosity between Chalmers and me taking its clothes off and parading around naked.

"Why me?" I smiled sweetly. "I'm not a combat commander."

"No, you're not." Chalmers had a look of victory. If he'd had a band, he'd have struck it up.

"Still not convinced about Columbus, Special Agent?" Needleman asked.

"Insurance. Couldn't hurt."

Chalmers sighed heavily and lifted his eyes to the heavens for support, and I thought right about now would be a good time for that Jell-O to drop.

Needleman looked at Mendoza, who shrugged. "We'll see what we can do, Major Cooper."

After a round of handshakes, the army left.

"Are you on this team, Cooper?" Chalmers wanted know, hands on hips, weak chin jutted forward.

"Not if it's the side of easy answers," I told him.

Chalmers couldn't hide his exasperation. "Okay then, Cooper, for the sake of unity, let's run through it again."

"After you," I said.

Chalmers believed emphatically that he was right and enjoyed laying out what we knew and what we'd been told to prove his point. And though much of the reasoning for his belief in Apostles' choice of target had come from me, I just couldn't shake the feeling that we were doing exactly what Apostles wanted us to do.

"So," said Chalmers once he'd finished his five-minute burst of condescension, "point out the flaw, Cooper. Where have I got it wrong?"

"I can't see it."

"Good."

"Which is why I think Apostles is gonna cornhole us."

Chalmers picked up his notes and limped out of the room. "You're impossible, you know that?"

I shrugged. It wasn't my job to be agreeable. There were lives at stake and I knew better than Chalmers what Apostles and Perez were capable of.

Arlen approached the map. "Vin, help me out here. I trust your instincts."

"One," I said, "Apostles positioned his base just fifty miles to the south of the town. What if he did that to make Columbus *appear* to be the obvious choice? Two, let's say he reinforced that by dangling the whole Pancho Villa thing in my face, which he did on several occasions. Three, Apostles and Perez never fully trusted me, even after those theatrics pulled by Gomez and company in Juárez. Looking back on it, they never confirmed or denied anything in my presence. Four, there was the ease with which I escaped from their base. What if they let me go just to be their messenger?" I gave up on the fingers. "Look, Whelt also readily confirmed Columbus as the target and he even gave us the date of the attack. Finally, there's Apostles himself. I thought he might be a little mad, but I've met several people I trust who think he's anything but. Add all that up and I get the picture of a man who knows what he's doing, one who wants us to believe that he's gonna hit Columbus. Conclusion? Columbus probably isn't the target."

"If he's as smart as you think he is, this could be a double-double bluff," said Gomez. "You know – he's made you think it's a target other than the one he's put right in front of you, so you run off chasing alternatives and leave the bull's-eye un-guarded."

"Thanks, Gomez," I said. "If he's that clever, we're screwed."

Arlen chewed something off the inside of his bottom lip. "Would Apostles seriously consider attacking El Paso?"

Twenty-nine

Was it warm out here, or was it nerves? The summer temperature at one-thirty in the morning on the desert floor was close to eighty degrees Fahrenheit and I still couldn't shake the feeling that we were in the wrong place at the right time, so maybe it was a little of both.

The stars were out in their billions, brilliant points of light that, in the lenses of the night vision goggles, were fluoro green. Somewhere unseen among them were MQ-1 Predator drones – unarmed – flying reconnaissance. Five hundred men dug into the desert should be enough to repel a mobile force of a thousand, but nothing was ever certain in a gunfight.

I rubbed a gloved hand across my forearm to squash something biting the exposed skin, the harvester ants doing what they do. And in the forefront of my mind the scorpions were here too, the compact super poisonous ones. Have I mentioned that I hate scorpions? The fuckers make me break out in four letter words.

While Gomez and I were armed with M4s, we were there just to observe. Assuming that there was fighting ahead, the First Armored Division, "Old Ironsides" would wage it. These were good men, well trained, veterans from Iraq and Afghanistan.

"Feeling any better about all this?" Gomez asked.

"Overjoyed," I said.

"Nothing's happening."

"They trained in daylight. They'll come at dawn."

"*If* they come," said Gomez.

"So now you're having second thoughts?" I asked.

"Doubt is infectious."

It was. There was nothing to do other than wait out the night and see what eventuated, so I closed my eyes and then suddenly came awake with a sharp intake of breath. "What time is it?" I asked.

"Two twenty-two," said Gomez. "Welcome back."

While asleep, my subconscious had sifted something important that Captain Mendoza had said out of the debris clogging most of my waking thoughts – that unconscious me at work again. "C'mon. We're getting outta here."

Gomez yawned. "Where are we going?"

"We have to reach that ready reaction force and get it in the air."

"What?" I heard him say, but I was already on the move.

He got up and followed and we ran at a crouch back through the support vehicles and jumped into a jeep, another Jeep Patriot, but this one hired from Dollar. Seemed only fair to spread the risk. Gomez threw himself into the passenger seat and buckled up. "Give me something I can believe in, Cooper. You're talking in your sleep and suddenly you're up and sprinting. Who, what, where and when?"

I fired up the jeep and stood on the gas. "We think Apostles is gonna strike Columbus because that's the town Villa hit," I shouted above the engine and wheelspin. "We didn't stop to think *why* Villa chose to attack Columbus."

"Because maybe Columbus was the only thing around here back then?"

"There was El Paso. It was bigger, richer. But he chose Columbus back then because El Paso with Fort Bliss was a nut too big to crack – like today."

The Black Hawks held on standby with a reinforced rifle platoon – about fifty guys – were only a mile behind Needleman's line and, through the NVGs, I could pick out the silhouettes of the helicopters' tail rotors against the stars. "Mendoza said Villa attacked the US Army outpost at Columbus. Remember? But the army's no longer in Columbus. If Apostles wants to emulate Villa, he's not coming here. Like I said, he just wants us to *believe* that's where he's going."

I turned in toward the choppers, stomped on the brakes and came to a sliding stop, my door open while we were still moving.

"Hey, Cooper, stop!" Gomez snapped. "Wait a minute!"

I held the door open and checked my watch: 2:32 am. "Look, the target's not Columbus because there's no longer a military outpost there. And it's not El Paso for the same reason Villa gave the place a wide berth back in the day. But Apostles still wants to use the Pancho Villa imagery, hence the 20 July date for the attack – the anniversary of the general's death. But he wants to hit something military, just like Villa did, and let's say it's something with a runway so that he can again utilize those black King Airs."

"What? Wait a second, you've lost me."

"Look, Gomez, we're wasting time here."

"What are we doing, Cooper?"

"Okay . . . Arlen suggested the raid on Horizon Airport wasn't just about dropping off a load of cocaine. Remember?" I said. "What if it was part of a dress rehearsal for something a lot bigger and badder?"

"Using the buzzards," said Gomez.

"It's a reasonable assumption. Once again they'll come in low, under the radar. But this time they'll land around forty assassins who'll quietly secure the front gate for the dirt-bike-mounted infantry that have jumped the border fence or the river or whatever. I think Apostles and Perez are gonna hit *a US military installation*. That's the missing link."

"Then all we have to do is make a phone call. If we give one base an itch, every base within a hundred miles of the border is going to be scratching, on heightened alert."

"Only this is a new kind of warfare," I reminded him. "And no one really knows exactly what's coming at them. With uncertainty on their side, the two-pronged assault like the one I believe is in the cards would be devastating."

"I'm still not convinced there's cause for alarm. Lay this insight on Arlen and, as I said, wherever the attack comes, the installation's security forces will be on alert."

"Yeah, except their primary task will be to secure base infrastructure. But Apostles and Perez are not really interested in infrastructure. They'll be going for the resource that's unprotected, the same one they hit at Horizon – *the people*."

The full audacity of it finally hit Gomez. "Oh, shit ..." he whispered.

"Like I said, it's not Bliss – that place is way too big. So give me a town with a smallish US military base that sits on the border."

Gomez didn't have to think about it too long. "You mean ... like Del Rio?"

Thirty

"It's Del Rio – Laughlin AFB," I shouted into the mike, the connection to Arlen patched through the radio and onto his cell phone as the Black Hawk climbed at an aggressive angle into the lime-green night sky.

"Laughlin's a training base," said Arlen, tired and unconvinced.

"I know. Home to the 47th Flying Training Wing, the largest primary pilot training base we've got. Big, but not too big. And all those young student pilots are gonna be tucked up nice and warm in bed when two black King Airs land, just like they did at Horizon Airport."

"Why there and not Columbus?"

"I don't say trust me very often, because mostly not even *I* trust me; but now I'm saying it. Trust me, Arlen, okay? You need to get through to the Joint Chiefs."

"What? Who?"

"The Joint Chiefs. You need to get them to release some assets. Fort Hood is closer than Bliss. The First Cavalry is there. We need men and gunships. You've also got to get onto the Wing King at Laughlin and the Security Forces commander. Apostles will come at dawn so there's still time."

"The Joint Chiefs? What do I tell them? I gotta give them *something*."

"Tell 'em Horizon was just the warm-up for Apostles and Perez. The main game is now heading Laughlin's way – a thousand armed killers."

"What? Why Laughlin?"

"Because it's the only logical target."

"That's not enough, Vin."

"You said you trusted my instincts."

There was a pause on the line, and then finally, "I'll see what I can do."

Arlen ended the call.

The pilot had already informed me that flight time to Laughlin was going to be just over two and a half hours, providing the tailwinds held up. Like any investigator, I liked to be right, but with regards to Laughlin I wanted to be dead wrong.

*

Two hours later, Arlen called back. "Just spoke with Colonel Needleman. There's an attack in progress there."

"What?"

"Yeah."

"What's happening?"

"Just like you said. Mounted infantry jumped the fence. They rode straight into Mendoza's placements."

So I'd been wrong. I almost laughed.

"I guess you can turn around."

"We'll need to stop for gas." As an afterthought, I said, "Hey, what about Laughlin. You speak to anyone there? I guess you can ring 'em up and tell 'em to go back to bed."

"Yeah, I was just on the phone to the major commanding Base Security when the line went dead."

Something in my throat tightened. "When they hit Horizon they disabled the cell tower and cut the power."

"Not so easy to do at Laughlin. More than one tower and there are redundancies. Could just be AT&T not talking to Verizon. And anyway, Apostles is getting mopped up over at Columbus. I think we can relax, bud. I called Del Rio PD a little while back. They're sending a cruiser over to check on the main gate. I haven't cancelled that request so if there's a problem we'll soon find out about it."

This didn't feel right. "Arlen, what kind of numbers are they facing at Columbus?"

"Hang on a minute, Vin, got another call coming in."

The pilot gave the hand signal – ten minutes out. It was coming up to 5 am. Sunrise was 6 am. The sky would begin to lighten in around thirty minutes.

"Vin, got Del Rio PD on the line," said Arlen. "The main gate checks out fine. All quiet. They're still at the base. You want me to ask them anything?"

"See if they've got a view of the apron. Are there any black aircraft parked there?"

While I waited for a response, I searched the sea of lights in the distance for the distinctive strobes used for aircraft navigation that would tell me where Laughlin was.

"Vin, I asked them about the black King Airs," said Arlen's voice in the phones. "They're saying it's hard to tell. There are rows and rows of aircraft parked on the tarmac. Anyway, I think we're good. When I get an update from Columbus, I'll pass it straight along. Hang on a sec ... What did you say? Sorry, I was on the other line ..."

I pictured Arlen juggling two phones. I wondered if they had any pool bars in Del Rio.

"Vin, you there?" Something had changed in the tone of Arlen's voice.

"Still here."

"The PD patrol at Laughlin. They're saying two aircraft just came in low and buzzed the runway. They're coming in to land. Vin, they're telling me these aircraft – they're black."

*

The co-pilot had called the Wing Command Post for a land-line connection to Base Security but couldn't get through. I took that to mean Security Forces were either already all dead or still engaged with the militia disgorged by the two black King Airs. I guessed we'd find out soon enough, because Laughlin AFB was in our twelve o'clock and coming up fast, its runways and infrastructure lit up in the darkness like global warming was a myth.

On the highway beyond the base was a long line of traffic for this time of the morning, headlights winking green in my NVGs. There seemed to be a hold-up at the main gate. But then, as I watched, that line of headlights began to flow down the road unobstructed, past the guardhouse. The entrance had therefore been breached, which confirmed to me that the bulk of the Base Security forces had been eliminated.

"Cooper, where you want us to put you down?" the pilot asked, his voice rasping in the headset.

"Keep us airborne over the secondary runway threshold and patch me through to Colonel Wayne," I said. A thousand militia mounted on motorcycles took up a lot of the main road through the base and snaked out onto the highway. I flipped up the NVGs, the pre-dawn light having turned the world a dull gray.

"Vin, you there?"

It was Arlen.

"Apostles is here in force," I told him. "Base Security has been overwhelmed. They're inside the wire."

"Assets are on the move, Vin. The attack on a Columbus was a feint, no more than a hundred men."

"Arlen, it's gonna be a bloodbath here. Time to target is the critical factor. We need gunships and men, whatever you can get, but they better get here fast."

"I've already called the 301st Fighter Wing in Fort Worth. They're trying to get something to you."

F-16s – *Vipers!* "Roger that. ETA?"

"No idea, but they'll contact you on Guard frequency, so turn it up. Your call sign is Oddball. Then send them to any freq. you like. Spad Ops is 252.1, if you need it."

"Spad to the bone" was the wing's motto, a bad homophone for "bad to the bone". "What else you got coming?"

"A full battalion of cavalry is in the air, along with Apache Longbows for support, but even coming across from Hood we're talking well over an hour to you."

"Jesus, Arlen, this is Texas, damn it! Guns are like screwdrivers around here – every house has got a set. What's going on here is why there's a goddamn Second Amendment. Get onto the Rangers, the DPS, PD, NRA – the PTA if you can raise 'em. Roust 'em outta bed and get 'em the fuck down here! Their sons and daughters are in need."

"On it," he said and the line went dead.

I quickly briefed the men in the four Black Hawks. "What's your loiter time?" I asked the pilot.

"Forty minutes to bingo fuel," came the reply. And then, "Cooper, we got inbound fighters for you. They know where we are. Over to you. Call sign SPAD. What freq. do you want them on?"

If circumstances were different, I might have smiled at the full circle my Air Force career had taken. Here I was again, back to being a special tactics officer calling hell down on evil-doers.

"Oddball, Oddball, this is Spad One-One," came through the headset – the pilot of the lead Viper.

"Spad One-One, Oddball. Go."

"Spad One-One inbound, VFR, five thousand descending to three, heading two-one-zero, five miles out, looking for words."

"Spad contact Oddball on two-three-seven decimal zero." This was housekeeping: we had to get off the Guard channel and onto a radio frequency no one else was using. The Black Hawk co-pilot looked back and gave me a thumbs up.

"Roger, Oddball. Spad One-Two, go two-three-seven decimal zero."

"Two," came the terse reply.

Another thumbs up from the co-pilot.

"Spad check."

"Two."

"Oddball, Oddball, Spad up your freq."

"Spad, Oddball. Local altimeter two niner niner four. Say state."

"Copy two-nine-nine-four. Spad One-One, flight of two Fox 16s, six BDU-33s and five hundred rounds 20mm TP diverted en route from Falcon Range. We have ten minutes play time; thirty if we can recover at Laughlin. Confirm troops in Contact? Over."

TP – target practice ammo. Five hundred rounds of the stuff could make a hell of a mess of someone's day.

"Spad One-One, Oddball. Negative recovery at Laughlin. Affirmative Tango India Charlie. Target is approximately one thousand, I say again, one thousand personnel mounted on dirt bikes with light automatic weapons. Civilians and friendlies in the area. How copy?"

"Spad One-One."

"Spad lead, are you familiar with Del Rio?" I asked him.

"That's affirmative, Oddball. Say intentions."

"Spad, we need to buy some time. Make your passes on the traffic down Liberty Drive, the main artery off Highway

90 on a heading of one-three zero. Same again down the secondary entrance off route three one seven on a heading of two-two zero. Any dirt bike is a target. Avoid Mexican airspace if possible. You copy? Over."

"Oddball, Spad One-One. Loud and clear. Jesus – that's my goddamn alma mater down there! Class 01–14. Over."

"Okay, Spad. Stay with us as long as you can. Oddball will remain on this freq., but we'll be maneuvering below five hundred feet. You're cleared in hot – your discretion."

"Spad One-One copies 'cleared in hot; my discretion.' Spad One-Two?"

"One-Two."

I heard the lead pilot brief his wingman: "Okay, Romeo, strafe to start. Hold on the perch at thirty-five hundred. I'll mark the target with a BDU-33. Call 'Smoke in sight', and I'll clear you in for your first pass. Conserve ammo, and be sure of your targets. Watch your altitude, and look out for small-arms fire. I'll follow with ten-second spacing. Copy?"

"Two copies."

Coming out of the west at around two hundred feet and four hundred knots, the two Vipers rocketed down the main runway, one slightly ahead of the other. I watched them hook into steep turns beyond the threshold and come onto independent divergent headings and climbing before I lost them in the haze.

Over on Liberty Drive, the headlights had thinned out a little as the attacking force had begun to disperse toward the base housing areas, where military folks lived. More headlights along Laughlin Drive indicated the road being secured by the cartel, confirming also that, as I'd guessed, it would be the invaders' intended departure route to the south.

I held my breath and everything seemed to slow. A Viper came from the east, diving at a shallow angle down Liberty. Its engines shrieked, cutting through the Black Hawk's main rotor thump. Suddenly, there was a burst of smoke followed an instant later by a row of dark asphalt spurts and a pulse of thick dust that rolled up and engulfed the traffic. A second shriek of jet engine and more geysers of pulverized asphalt followed by a cloud of dust shocked into midair.

I watched as the Vipers made two runs each over Liberty, then one over Laughlin Drive, the destruction both awesome and terrible. The dust hung lazily in the early morning air, in no hurry to settle. There didn't seem to be many headlights on those roads now.

A burst of static started me breathing again. A voice in my ear said, "Oddball, Spad One-One. The clean-up is yours. Make it personal. Over and out."

"Spad One-One. Oddball. Count on it."

"Spad flight, button four."

"Two."

The F-16s made another low pass over the Liberty Drive. They came along faster this time and from west to east, their engines howling, no doubt striking terror into the surviving terrorists who'd just experienced their fury.

"Cooper," the Black Hawk pilot asked, looking over his shoulder. "Where do you want us to put you down?"

"Closer to base housing. We'll need some cover."

"There's a big parking lot a block back from the apron, just off Liberty Drive."

"Let's do it. After we're out, dust off and give us covering fire." I noted with satisfaction that smaller streams of those headlights were leaving the base. Did I say leaving? Fleeing would be a better word to describe it. Maybe a little taste of F-16 wasn't to their liking. Also, I was happy to see away in the distance, around five miles back along Highway 90 toward Del Rio, a stream of flashing blues and reds heading our way.

The pilot brought the Black Hawk over the apron and cleared the hangars. Over on Liberty, I could see individual militia on their bikes. Many were down on the ground and not moving. But many more were still heading for base housing.

I could also see now that bikes were coming and going, motoring past the old retired aircraft planted beside Liberty Drive. A police cruiser was parked near the guard gate, large black numbers on its roof. The police who drove it there would be dead, as would any security forces manning the guardhouse. Bodies were strewn around on the ground everywhere I looked.

A couple of rounds banged off the Black Hawk's armor. The man beside me had his helmet knocked sideways by another round and I heard him swear.

"Comin' in hot, Cooper," the pilot announced as our aircraft dropped toward the vacant parking lot, its nose high in the aggressive flare. Behind us were three other Black Hawks also coming in just as fast and taking fire, the door gunners returning it with interest.

"Make for those cars," I told Gomez, pointing to several rows of them parked on the asphalt.

The ground, white and chalky where it was unsurfaced, rose up toward us. At the last instant, the Black Hawk's nose came down and the skids touched the earth. Gomez was first out, running toward the vehicles. I was right behind him with men panting and boots pounding the earth behind me.

The Black Hawks lifted off as I skidded to a stop beside Gomez, the cars around us taking random fire from dirt bikes still game enough to come along Liberty. Down at ground level, the invasion seemed anything but organized. A little further along the road to the west, back toward the main guard gate where the F-16s had concentrated their fire, where the finer dust still hung in the air, smashed and broken bodies and motorcycles lay around like discarded refuse.

But despite the death and destruction, the Chihuahua assault was continuing. I saw a man walk out of a building nearby, wearing jogging gear and white buds in his ears, probably wondering about the racket interfering with his music. A rider rode past him, firing a carbine one-handed, and the jogger was dead from a burst of automatic fire before he could scratch his head.

Three riders jumped the curb into the parking lot and skidded to a stop. They snatched carbines from scabbards and started unloading on us. I took aim and shot one through the visor. Gomez raked the second guy with a burst of full auto, which disintegrated the guy's gas tank. The fuel ignited on the hot engine and burst into a ball of flame that also consumed the rider stopped beside him.

Around fifty of us were assembled within the parking lot's little auto-fort. The platoon's commanding officer, a young black lieutenant, wanted to move. "El-Tee, get your troops into fire teams," I shouted. "The residential quarters are west and southwest of our position three blocks over, less than half a mile. The situation's straightforward. The cartel is here to kill. We're here to stop 'em. There's plenty of weapons and ammo on the enemy if you run out. The accuracy of fire from these guys when they're on the move is low, but don't take it for granted. When they stop, they're vulnerable. Questions?"

There weren't any.

"Oorah," said Lieutenant Sommers. The rest of the platoon repeated it.

"You and you," I said, nodding at two men from the weapons section armed with M249 SAWs – a couple of specialists, a Korean and a black guy. I read the names off their tapes. "Kim and Roslyn. On me." Other units were already on the move. "Gomez, cover me."

Sommers, the medic, and the rest of the weapons section went off at an angle while I ran at a crouch toward Liberty Drive and then across it, firing three-shot bursts from the hip at the riders motoring along the street. Gomez, Kim and

Roslyn on over-watch also fired. Two riders went down, half a dozen others scattered. One of those RVs with a .50 caliber Browning got off a ranging burst before a long yellow tongue reached out from a Black Hawk's M134 Minigun and virtually sawed the vehicle in half.

Ahead was a building with a sign on it that read AVIONICS. There was a parking lot out front. I ran for it across open ground. Making it to a Lexus in the lot, I turned and took a knee. Gomez jumped up and ran across the same open ground. Two riders left the road and sped off after him, firing. I shot one of them. He slumped forward on the bars and ran straight into a tree. Unlucky. Not many trees around here. Kim and Roslyn dismounted two more bikers with well-aimed fire as they rode past their cover. They got up, ran to the bikes and picked them up. The remaining rider in that group might have been in a panic at being fired on, or maybe he was just distracted, but he misjudged a turn and hit a pole, smashing his leg. Gomez changed direction and ran to the motorcycle as the downed rider rolled onto his side, holding his leg. Running up to him, Gomez booted the downed rider's helmet, connecting under the chin like he was going for three points at the Super Bowl.

"Cooper!" Gomez called out, picking up the bike. "You ride?"

Kim and Roslyn were stationary, weapons up, sweeping through the angles, keeping over-watch as I ran across and jumped on behind the handlebars. For a little while, at least until friendlies arrived and shot at anything on two wheels, perhaps being on a motorcycle wasn't such a bad idea. The bad guys might believe we were on their side until we fired on them. And, of course, we could cover the remaining ground to base housing faster. Gomez leaped on the back and tapped my shoulder, ready to go. I stomped down on the gearshift, gave it a fistful of throttle and dumped the clutch, the front wheel pawing the air as we accelerated.

The sky was fast gathering light. With more peripheral vision, my attention was caught by two joggers lying unmoving on the running track around a football field. They were probably dead. Apostles' militia were going about their work methodically, efficiently, their training and a thirst for blood kicking in.

Three riders came at us from a cross street, gave us a friendly hand signal. Gomez and Roslyn made them pay for the familiarity, ending their lives with full automatic bursts. Gomez dropped the magazine out of his M4 and it clattered onto the road as he jammed a fresh one home.

Base housing was separated into two distinct areas by an Olympic pool, a golf course, a circular park with more mounted aircraft and a baseball diamond. The ground was billiard-table flat, making it easy to see what was going on and, Jesus, it wasn't pretty. The cartel was slaughtering the residents in their homes and on their front lawns. It was like something from a medieval sacking. I pulled to the curb. Ahead, one of our teams was already at work, shooting the killers where they stood, the cartel's attacking force still unaware that there was an organized opposition among them. I did a U-turn and went two streets over, Kim and Roslyn following. Screams filled the dawn. We arrived to see a man in a motorcycle helmet ripping the nightie off a woman on her front porch, under the Stars and Stripes. The woman's husband was on his knees, the barrel of the man's rifle in his mouth. I pulled to a stop. Gomez rested the stock of his M4 on my shoulder, took careful aim and shot out the back of the man's neck. With no spine he collapsed at the woman's feet, unable to do anything other than die. The woman ran naked inside her home and slammed the door while her husband stayed on his knees and retched.

We rode slowly up the street like that, Gomez using my shoulder as a rest, shooting cartel killers. The Ranger was a good shot. I could hear more screaming and the sound of glass breaking. I tried to zone in on the source of the sound when a picture frame came flying out a front door. I stopped. Gomez leaped off the bike and ran into the home. In the house next door, I could hear a man shouting. Shots fired. I grabbed the carbine out of the bike's scabbard, let the machine fall over and ran in through the splintered front door. Inside on the lounge-room floor, a man in pajamas lay dead on the carpet in a pool of blood. A woman sobbed beside him, covered in blood, trying to make him move. Another man was standing nearby, wearing Desert Storm camos and a helmet, pointing his rifle at the woman. I shot him through the chest as he looked at me. He staggered back a step and regained his footing. I took two steps toward him and stomped him with a front kick where the blood was spurting from the hole in his clothing and the killer sailed backward through a plate glass window behind him, shattering it. Shards of glass rained down on him, slicing through his neck.

I lifted the woman off the dead man, dragged her into the bedroom. I made some noises to try to calm her but she was beyond reason. Her eyes were wild, terrified, her face covered in tears, blood and mucous. As I pulled her down onto the floor, she became hysterical so I pushed her under the bedframe and told her to stay there. Somehow the message got through to her and she calmed down in the darkness under the mattress. If there was somewhere safer to take the woman, I couldn't think of it.

Running back outside, I picked up the bike and saw Roslyn fighting hand-to-hand with a man armed with a machete. Kim was down on the ground with a bloody gash across the side of his head, holding his ear in his hand. Pulling my Sig from the holster, I walked up to the machete wielder and shot him in the mouth as he turned toward me. Kim was bleeding badly, but wounds to the ear do that.

Two riders turned into our street and stopped when they saw us. I shot one with the Sig; I'm not sure where but he fell backward off the bike and didn't get up. Kim picked himself off the ground, grabbed the machete and ran screaming at the remaining rider. The man stomped down on the gearshift lever with his boot, but I guessed the gearbox had jammed. Kim caught up with him, a downswing with two hands on the handle burying the blade deep in the meat of his shoulder. And then for some unexplained reason, the bike slipped into gear, the engine raced and the machine performed an instant ground loop, landing on top of the rider with the machete sticking out of him like a Halloween gimmick. The rear wheel spun wildly until the man's hand became tangled in its spokes and that suddenly stopped it.

Kim stuffed his bloody ear in his pocket, picked up his helmet and put it on. Roslyn got back onto a bike and Kim took the seat behind him.

"You okay?" I asked him.

"Better than them," he said, nodding at the dead cartel militia on the road.

"The bleeding's slowed," I told him. "We'll work through this street, turn right if we can, then come down the next street over."

Gomez sprinted out of the house he'd gone into and jumped on the pillion seat behind me. I rode slowly down the road, the Ranger firing at cartel militia with deadly accuracy. But then bullet holes appeared in the fuel tank, thankfully above the level of gasoline it held.

"Shit!" Gomez yelled. "I'm hit."

This was no place to stop.

"Hang on," I called out.

Several militia had set themselves behind bricked-in garden beds. One of them jumped up and raised his fist. Roslyn, coming along behind us, saw them and rode over the curb, exposing their flank. Kim mowed three of them down, emptying a magazine on full auto into their position. A fourth man got up and ran for another position of cover. I pulled the Sig and fired. The third shot rolled him into a bed of daisies.

"How bad is it?" I shouted, half turning.

"My leg's broken," Gomez screamed out, presumably as the bones moved against each other.

Down the far end of the street, where we'd just been, I saw a black Texas State Trooper cruiser race past with lights flashing. Seconds later, a Del Rio PD cruiser came around the corner sideways, siren and lights blazing. The vehicle skidded to a stop and the police inside threw their doors open and took cover behind them. Cartel militia came out of several homes and concentrated their fire on the officers wearing body armor and firing AR-15s. Another PD cruiser rounded the corner, an officer firing a shotgun out the passenger window. The militia were starting to pay as the officers took control.

I thought that maybe now might be a good time for us to ditch the motorcycle before we became mistaken for tangoes. And then ahead, I saw something strange. A man on horseback, a sombrero pushed off his head and waving around behind his back in the airflow as his horse galloped across a lawn and then the road, jumped a garden bed and disappeared between two homes. I felt the weight shift on the bike as Gomez climbed off. "You go." He winced, his voice hoarse with the pain, his leg useless. He waved me on. "Bring that fucker down."

Kim appeared. "I'll stay with him," he shouted, maybe a little deaf, and Gomez used him as a crutch to get to some cover behind an SUV parked in a driveway.

I dumped the clutch and raced after ... Pancho Villa. Or should I say Apostles. The bike's knobby rear tire tore up the lawn as it fought for traction, the front wheel off the ground as I gave chase. I shot around the side of a house and saw the horse's rump working hard as Apostles whipped it along. Dropping back a gear, I leaned over the front forks and wound the throttle to its stop. The ground was sandy and flat and I was gaining on the animal. The bike and I burst into open space between a couple of homes, and raced across a front lawn littered with children's toys, furniture and a dead dog. A State Trooper was wrestling a man to the ground, while his partner looked up and fired his service pistol at me as I flew by, thinking I was one of the bad guys, the round taking out a chunk of masonry just in front of me as I raced between another two houses.

Apostles knew I was closing. He glanced over his shoulder, tried to change direction, head left and then right, jump a flowerbed, but the horse was no match for horsepower. The animal galloped across the street and onto the golf course. Out on the fairway there was nowhere to hide. I closed the distance fast and soon overtook horse and rider. The animal's flanks were lathered. It had had enough and began to slow. And then it decided to stop altogether, throwing the rider over its ears. He landed heavily on the grass. I skidded sideways to a halt, dropped the bike from under me and, taking the last few steps at a run, launched myself through the air at Apostles struggling to get to his feet. I hit him in the shoulder with my shoulder and felt his bones give way. He hit the ground hard again, only semiconscious this time. I grabbed a handful of his fucking shirt and smashed my fist into his fucking cheek. And then I pulled my Sig and lifted Apostles' bloody chin with the muzzle.

"Freeze, motherfucker. Don't you fucking move, y'hear?"

It wasn't me talking, it was someone behind me. Red and blue flashing lights announced that we were on the same team.

"Lower your weapon or I'll shoot you dead, I promise you …"

Over my shoulder I shouted, "Special Agent Cooper, United States Air Force."

"You're on a bike. You're lucky I haven't already blown your brains out."

Yeah.

"Put your weapon on the ground," he shouted, "and your hands behind your head."

Out the corner of my eye I could see two of them, both young, both experiencing sensory overload having witnessed all the death and destruction around them, and probably having had to deliver a share of it themselves. They were jumpy and jumpy is trigger happy. I placed the Sig on the ground and put my hands where they wanted them.

"Interlock your fingers. Do it."

Yessir.

An approaching roar suddenly became deafening as an Apache Longbow gunship passed low overhead. The cavalry had arrived – the First Cavalry to be precise. I looked down at the man under me with crossed bandoliers on his chest, his beard matted with blood and bits of grass and twigs. It wasn't who I expected to see. "Who the fuck are you?"

Thirty-one

Gomez was transferred to the Scott & White Medical Center in Killeen, the state's hospital system severely tested by the numbers of wounded. Kim got his ear sewn back on by some world-famous plastic surgeon in Dallas. Casualties were ferried all over the country, everyone wanting to help. The States united.

Calling a spade a spade, the attack on Laughlin AFB was a disaster for US intelligence and law enforcement. The media went crazy, blaming the CIA, the Army, the Texas Rangers, local PD, the State Troopers, Homeland Security, the US President, the Mexican President, the Mexican Army, the *Federales* – any and all law enforcement and officialdom elected to keep America safe, and some that weren't. We'd all failed the people, according to the press. And, for once, the press was right.

The body count at base housing, where the cartel had concentrated its forces, was over two hundred and fifty with sixty more wounded, half of which were critical. If there was a consolation it was that these numbers could've been far worse.

The only folks who escaped the nation's anger and disappointment were the Base Security Squadron, whose members accounted for ninety-three of the enemy casualties while losing eighty percent of its numbers, and the rifle platoon commanded by Lieutenant Sommers, whose troops killed or wounded well over two hundred cartel militia, before the lieutenant was himself shot dead in action. The platoon sergeant who took command of the survivors said that the lieutenant killed over twenty-three himself and died protecting the medic rendering aid to the wounded.

There was talk of Sommers receiving a posthumous Medal of Honor, except that south Texas was not, technically, a declared war zone and the army's involvement in it deemed a 'police function' so there would be no medals beyond the Purple Hearts and those for saving life or service. Somehow a Soldier's Medal for Sommers just seemed totally inadequate.

This had more to do with appeasing the Mexican President than anything else. If south Texas was deemed a "hostile fire zone", who was America at war with? Mexico? And, of course, this made anyone who had been fighting the so-called War on Drugs shake their heads. I mean, was it a fucking war or wasn't it?

The number of fatalities quickly became statistics batted around by the media and politicians, a mechanism hiding the tragic reality – innocent American men, women and children had lives, loves and dreams cut short in horrific circumstances by inhumane sociopaths who resented having their supply chain interrupted.

Soon the funerals would begin. The nation was in mourning. After the sorrow, anger would set in. A desire for revenge would surely follow. Plenty of social commentators feared the worst. Bring it on, was my thought on that. Over three hundred cartel militia had been taken prisoner on the ground at Laughlin, hiding in surrounding areas or trying to get across into Mexico. There were plenty of folks out there who wanted them lined up against a wall and shot. And they were the moderates. All that could be extracted from these people was they'd been poor before joining Apostles' militia, and now they were prisoners. Few of them knew what the plan had been when they signed up, other than it involved the US town of Columbus and the leader was a great Mexican general. The naivety was breathtaking. Apostles knew exactly what he was dealing with. The thousand riders had crossed the Rio Grande west of the town of Manuel Ojinaga, using the mobile ramps to jump the river. Then they'd simply rode up Highway 90 to Laughlin while the world slept, proving again (if it needed proving) that the best plans are the most basic ones.

In some medieval sandpit where inedible food was cooked on fires of camel shit, people danced in the streets. There were commentators in Mexico who thought it was about time Americans got a taste of what they'd been living with for years.

At home, the lawyers were having a field day. This was another 9/11 event. Who were we going to invade now? Mexico? Sections of congress were all for it, which is what anyone with common sense feared. And, of course, I knew with reasonable certainty that was exactly what Apostles wanted.

I reflected on all this as my gloved hand gripped the M4, the ski mask scratching the skin on my face and neck as the sweat leaked from my pores in the dry heat, the thump of the helicopter's main rotor pounding behind my sternum. Perhaps no one had failed the public more than me. I could have killed Apostles. I could have done it with my bare hands the night we were drinking that fifty-year-old Macallan. A crushed windpipe, a pen through the eye and into the corpus callosum, a smashed glass into the carotid – plenty of ways to do it. Why hadn't I? What had I been waiting for? A fucking court of law? And then there was Perez. I could have jumped his desk, taken that pearl-handled knife off him and ran the blade across his neck. It would've been over in seconds. I wouldn't have survived, but think of all the folks who'd still be alive today if I'd turned assassin. Could've, should've, didn't.

Now, three days after the events at Laughlin, we were raiding Apostles' Juárez residence. In the Black Hawk with me and the one behind us were Mexican Army Special Forces, agents from SEIDO and CIA kill team members. Teams of similar makeup on the ground were deployed in an armed cordon blocking escape routes on the Campestre's roads and pathways. Our orders were to take Apostles and Perez alive or dead, along with any other Chihuahua Cartel members who happened to be in the house. But our chances of finding anyone significant in the Juárez house were a little less than zero. Everyone knew that – as did the politicians on both sides of the border keen to lay blame – but we were here anyway. Finally. My role in this force was to positively identify Apostles now that his penchant for using body doubles was out in the open. And of course, I'd stayed in the house so I knew something of the layout of the place. Looking back on it, I wondered if all the meetings I'd had with Apostles had been with the real McCoy. I was starting to doubt a couple of them.

The truth was, we'd all been played for suckers by a master. Psychologists and profilers picking through the disaster believed Apostles' infatuation with Pancho Villa was genuine, even down to having a psychopath for a right-hand man. The Tears of Chihuahua was to Apostles what Rodolfo Fierro had been to the revolutionary general. Perez liked to flay while Fierro just got a kick out of killing. He apparently once shot a man dead just to see which way he'd fall – forward or backward. The story goes he fell forward. Yeah, that kind of careless disregard for human life sounded familiar.

Ciudad Juárez was still asleep; 4 am according to my watch. The roofs of the city slid by in shades of NVG green.

The team leader, a Mexican Army second captain with a wide grim face, whose name was Medina, gave the signal: one minute to target. Men were getting ready to drop ropes, a hefty coil out the door on each side. No one was talking, the NVGs along with the seriousness of the task at hand forcing silence on the group.

The Black Hawk went into its characteristic nose high flare and then settled into the hover. I heard the signal to deploy the ropes and then each of us went out in turn, down the rope and onto the roof.

We stood back as the Mexican Army guys used a charge to blow the fire door off the stairwell. I followed the grunts down the stairs. The top floor housed most of the bedrooms. Doors were opened one by one. I heard a muffled woman's scream and then a man charged out of a room with a pistol. He was cut down by a silenced round to the chest and another to the head. After that, everyone else threw in the towel relatively quietly. I checked the room I had stayed in and got a surprise: two men in bed together. A familiar blue and white leotard hung from a cupboard door. It was the Blue Mystery and friend. I rousted them outta the sack, told them to get some clothes on. Mr Mystery wasn't gonna make it easy. Standing there in his bathing suit wasn't stopping him from getting some ideas – there were two of them and only one of me, even if I was the only one with a rifle. They pegged me for a gringo straight away, despite the NVGs. The lights in the hallway had gone on so I flipped the lenses up. They were talking about tag teaming, putting a sleeper hold on my ass and making me their bitch. I shot Mr Mystery, grazing the meat of his thigh, which took the steam out of that idea. As the 'hair' rolled around on the bed, wailing, I had his partner slip the cuff locks on him, and then I did the same to his chum.

One of the Mexican Army Special Forces guys came in, saw the Blue Mystery and left shaking his head. The wrestler realized what this was going to mean in terms of his image and started going on about how his career would be ruined if the TV stations got onto this. I didn't give a damn about his career or his preferences in the sack. What I did care about was the company he kept and I didn't mean his pal. That he was a cartel toy was all that mattered to me. I searched the house until I found the rooms Apostles and Perez had occupied. They were the largest rooms and left vacant. Both rooms contained personal belongings, and I recognized a shirt I'd seen Apostles wear and souvenired it for DNA purposes. In the master bathroom off Perez's room, I took several items including a disposable razor.

In all, twenty-two people were put into security or paramedics vehicles and taken away. Not one was a high-value target. Six were hookers, five were MS-13 gang members, and two were from a drug transport operation – the rest were just people who found making money off the cartel easier than making an honest living, and I included the wrestler and friend in this bunch.

I doubted anyone would be able to give us a lead on Apostles or Perez as, so far, none of the militia captured at Laughlin knew shit from macaroni cheese on that score.

*

Two days after the Juárez raid I was down in Colombia, involved in a Special Forces mission to infiltrate and destroy the Chihuahua camp on the edge of the Darién Gap. There were militia there, but again no one of high value and the place had already been stripped of most of its intel. What remained had been left for a reason and no one trusted it. The Hacienda Mexico was simultaneously raided by Colombian Police Special Forces and CIA special agents. Nothing and no one of consequence was captured. Apostles and Perez had vanished.

A month after Laughlin, the US Army was still engaged, actively patrolling the border between Texas and Mexico. DEA intelligence reported that the cartels had never been happier, business booming to new levels with corruption rampant in the military cordon. Apostles and Perez were rumored to have made the most of their statement at Laughlin, amalgamating the Sinaloa Cartel, the Gulf Cartel and the Chihuahua Cartel into a super cartel, though how and where they were running it was a mystery.

The system dealt with Chalmers the best way it knew how, promoting him to its Asia bureau with title of Director because, of course, he did such a great job of identifying Perez at the Horizon Airport massacre. The most galling aspect of this was that the disposable razor I'd brought back from the Juárez villa is what did it for him – the DNA found on it matched the DNA recovered from Gail Sorwick's nasal tract, which finally and positively placed the Tears of Chihuahua at that crime scene.

It would only be a matter of time before Chalmers and I crossed paths again and next time I wouldn't be so accommodating.

As for me, I was taken off the hunt for Apostles and Perez and put back on chasing enlisted men gone AWOL. Fuck that. I took some damn vacation time. And, of course, I packed the Sig.

Thirty-two

I retraced some of my steps, like the ones to Yaviza. Others I avoided, like those through the Darién Gap. Everything they say about that place is true and one visit is one too many.

The dockside at Turbo was still a good way to clear the sinuses even if the temperatures had come down a few degrees since I was last there. But the bar on the river was just as I remembered it – full of drunks. On the off chance that I might jag a lead, I flashed photos of Perez and Apostles around to anyone prepared to give me some eye contact. Hope over reason, you might say. Pretty soon folks started avoiding the gringo with the mug shots. It wasn't good for the health to be identifying cartel bad guys to strangers in drug-smuggling territory.

The bus ride to Medellín was uneventful. I hired a car and drove to Bogotá and stayed at the Marriott. That night, I went to Dry 73, ordered a chocolate martini for old times' sake and sat on it, watching the clientele come and go. There was nothing to see here, though I stayed in town several days hoping it would show up. Next stop: the Hacienda Mexico, Apostles' spread next to Pablo Escobar's country retreat on the road halfway back to Medellín.

The trip was uneventful. No one tried to run me off the road, shoot at me or peel my skin off. This was how most people got around, listening to music, enjoying the countryside. I could get used to it. I finished the bottle of water and threw it into the floorboards to join its pals there and listened on the radio to local Colombian folk music funked up with rap. To my ears, it was the aural equivalent of dunking cheese in hot chocolate. I could go for either on its own, but together they just seemed wrong.

The place where Matheson ran me off the road rolled along. The purple Kia was gone, as was the greenery that had kept it so conveniently hidden.

The next landmark along was the Piper Cub on top of the gate at Escobar's place. Being mid-week, there were fewer tourists and buses.

The Hacienda Mexico was ten minutes' drive further on down the road. Coming up on the familiar entrance, I could see it had a new ornament to complement the security cameras – a Colombian Army armored personnel carrier parked across the gate. I pulled to the verge and stopped thirty yards down range. Okay, not smart. This must have looked suspicious. The soldier with dark sunglasses sitting up behind the APC's turreted machine gun turned his head in the direction of the car. I could see from his body language that its arrival made him nervous. He jabbered something into his headset. I got out of the vehicle, walked toward him and gave a friendly wave. He responded with a wave of his own, shouting, *"¡Alto! ¡Fuera!"*

Technically, what he said was, "Stop! Go away!" But what he meant was, "You! Fuck off!" Who argues with a. 50 caliber Browning? I returned to the car and drove down the road a ways, pulling over again around the corner and out of the soldier's sight. Was I thinking I was just gonna drive on in there? The Colombian Army had the place bottled up. Made sense. Three months after the event, the wounds inflicted on the US, Mexico and Colombia by Messrs Apostles and Perez were still raw.

So I dialed my supervisor.

The call went through. "Hola," I said to Arlen, making it chirpy.

"Hey, how's life on the road? What's going on, bud?"

"Not a lot."

"Excellent."

"Arlen, I want you to do something for me."

Silence.

"Arlen?"

"You know, historically, when you say 'Hey, Arlen, I want you to do something for me' that usually means trouble," he said.

"Nope, no trouble."

"So what is it you want that's no trouble – an urgent delivery of suntan lotion FedExed to wherever you are, pronto?"

"I'm outside Apostles' Hacienda in Colombia."

"Vin ..."

I could feel the exasperation.

"I wanna get inside the house."

"Why?"

"I don't know."

"Great reason."

"Arlen ..."

Silence.

"What are you doing, Vin?"

"Looking around."

"Every intelligence service in the world is hunting those two."

"In that case one more set of eyes won't hurt."

"You think they're just going to move back home?"

"Crooks are creatures of habit – even super crooks. And these two have a serious arrogance problem. Who knows what they would or wouldn't do?"

"I repeat – you think they're just going to move back home?"

My turn for exasperation. "I'm doing this on my own time, Arlen. Get me inside. Please."

"And it's just to look around."

"That's a promise."

"When?"

"Now."

"Jesus." Resigned sigh. "Give me an hour."

I drove back up the road, the soldier in the APC tracking the car as I drove past. So I had an hour to kill. What the hell, I turned into the Hacienda Nápoles and joined a recently arrived busload of tourists. Together, we all ogled at lifesize dinosaur models and bullet-riddled burned-out cars and what remained of Escobar's zoo. There were some of those hippos and also a few zebras, and I heard a guide say that the grandfather of the herd had been stolen by Escobar from the Medellín zoo. The story went that the zookeepers arrived one morning to find their one and only prized zebra replaced by a donkey painted with black and white stripes. Fun guy that Escobar.

More recent additions to the deceased drug lord's seven-thousand-acre ranch was a Jurassic-themed water park and a maximum security prison where the only thing that escaped was irony.

My cell rang.

It was Arlen. "Where are you now?"

"Looking at zebras."

"Really?"

"Or donkeys painted black and white. You can't be sure around here."

"Right. Meanwhile, if you want to get into Apostles' place, I've cleared it. Get down there now. They're expecting you. You've got a twenty-minute window and you'll be accompanied."

"I'll take what I can get."

"That's the spirit."

"Let me know if anything interesting turns up."

"Will do," I promised. "Anyone in particular I should check in with?"

"Lieutenant Jimanez. J-I-M –"

"Jimanez. Got it, thanks."

"What are you driving?" he asked. "I'll tell them to look out for you."

I gave him the details.

"Vin – don't do anything ..."

"Stupid?"

"Put an adjective in front of it."

"Fucking stupid?"

"That's it. Like I said, let me know if anything turns up," he said.

"Will do."

The call ended.

*

This time I pulled up behind the APC rather than down the road and the soldier behind the machine gun didn't appear to be so nervous. He said something into the mike and the APC rolled back a dozen yards, exposing the gate, which was open. He waved me through. I drove up the cinder driveway, through the dense overhanging islands of jungle. My memory stitched Apostles into the scenery, riding around on horseback dressed up as Villa though, looking back on it, I now believed that what I'd seen back then was a body double.

Finally the view opened out on to the expansive grounds and the double tennis courts, the lush green lawn now slightly overgrown. Also ahead was the magnificent grand old ranch house in the Mexican style.

Along with a couple of golf carts, several light utility army vehicles were parked outside the main entrance, a couple of men in Colombian Army-issue camos standing around talking. I stopped behind the vehicles. A man came out the front door of the house and walked up to my car.

"Special Agent Cooper?" he asked.

I showed my OSI ID and read JIMANEZ on the tape above his breast pocket. He was of medium height and dark with narrow almond-shaped eyes. In lightly accented English, he said, officiously, "I have orders to show you around." I got out of the car. "What would you like to see? What are you hoping to find?"

"Just come to have a look." I shrugged. "Maybe there's nothing to find."

"If you don't mind, I must accompany you," he said, gesturing at the front entrance.

I nodded and went inside, past the staircase. I absently picked a flintlock pistol up off a side table, looked at it and put it down. A suit of medieval armor now guarded the doorway into the lounge room. "I met with Perez in a study," I told the lieutenant.

He knew the layout of the place better than me and led the way. "I didn't realize that you had been here before," he said.

"Yeah," I replied, trying to concentrate on what was different and what was the same because things had moved.

"And Juan de Apostles was also here?"

I nodded. The hallway off the lounge room was familiar.

"Down here?" I said to the lieutenant. 'There's a study.'

Jimanez turned and led the way. He went through a doorway. The desk. Yeah, I remembered this room. *You are a killer who does not kill.* That's what Perez had told me. He was sitting behind that desk when he said it. The letter opener he'd had that I'd fleetingly considered using on his throat was now standing innocently in a red cut-glass container with a handful of pens. I picked up the letter opener. The blade was dull, the tip of the blade a sharp point. It would've done the job like it was made for it. Perhaps I'd have gone through with it if Daniela hadn't come through the door. I wondered how she was getting on. Daniela hadn't looked so great when I'd last seen her.

"You have met with evil, Agent Cooper."

"Yeah," I agreed, taking in the rest of the room.

"My country breeds such men."

"Something in the water, maybe?"

I glanced back down the hallway and headed in that direction. The lieutenant caught up. "Yes, and the soil. They are the curse of Colombia," he said.

"Why?"

"Because of the plentiful water and the rich soil, everything grows here. Every fruit you can think of. It all grows wild. No one will ever go hungry in Colombia. The same is true of coca. It grows wild. And this leaf brings out the worst in people."

I couldn't argue with that. We walked out of the house, down the back stairs and onto the lawn, the air thick with insects, heat and tropical dampness.

"Fifteen years ago, there was Escobar and others. He killed thousands, all because of the coca leaf. My father was a policeman and his corrupt partner shot him dead. The coca leaf made everyone crazy. No one wanted those days ever to return to Colombia. And yet now we have men like Apostles. Yes, there is something in the water."

I looked out over the river. No hippos there today.

"Have you seen anything of interest?" Jimanez asked.

"A few things have been moved around. The suit of armor near the front entrance – I don't remember that being there, or the flintlock gun."

The lieutenant shrugged. "We have touched nothing."

"How long has the army been occupying the ranch?"

"Some days," he said with a shrug, giving away nothing I could build on.

"Head back inside?" I asked him and the Lieutenant led the way.

A couple of the lieutenant's men were sitting on a couch and a chair in the lounge room. One was flicking through a magazine on American country homes, the other speaking quietly on a cell phone. Jimanez snapped at them and they both jumped up and left in a hurry.

I stood in the room and took it all in: suits of armor, crossed pikes, leather couches, rugs, crossbows, the mounted heads of various animals on the wall. Something significant was missing. "Where's the horse?" I asked Jimanez.

"Horse?"

"There was a horse, Pancho Villa's horse, Seven Leagues – *Siete Leguas*. It was standing right there."

The lieutenant looked at me like I had a screw loose. "When?"

Now that I'd pulled my head out of my ass, I noticed that signed and framed photographic portrait of the general was also no longer on the wall either. In fact, quite a bit was missing: one of the stuffed heads, the lion; a crossbow ... Perhaps there was more. Where had it gone? "The surveillance cameras here are all switched on?"

"Of course."

I pulled my cell and went outside.

"Arlen ..." I said when I heard him pick up.

"You're excited about something," he said. "That's concerning."

"There are items missing from Apostles' hacienda."

"So?"

"Isn't it supposed to be locked down?"

"It's Colombia. What can I tell you?"

"Arlen, the items that are missing are specific. There's Pancho Villa's horse, a portrait –"

"Villa's horse?"

"It was stuffed."

"That's an understatement – would have been almost a hundred years old."

"Funny. Look, I think someone has come with a list and cherry-picked the things Apostles cherished the most."

"That could have happened well before Laughlin."

"There must have been some kind of inventory taken when the army moved in here."

"I can find out. Where you staying?" asked Arlen.

"Puerto Triunfo, a town down the road. There'll be a motel. Hey, also – there are surveillance cameras all over Apostles' place. Maybe they got something."

"I'll look into it, call you back."

I thanked Lieutenant Jimanez for his time and trouble, climbed into the rental and drove to town.

Eventually, I found a place that called itself a motel, but then so does the facility that lures cockroaches to their deaths. When it came time to sleep, I bunked down in the rental. And that turned out to be a good decision because if I'd stayed in a room, I might not have seen a familiar green Renault drive down the main street and stop outside the motel.

Thirty-three

I watched Juliana get out of the car and head to reception with a small rucksack, her ponytail bouncing as she walked. Was she checking in, having just arrived, or had she been staying here a while already? And what was she doing in Puerto Triunfo – staying somewhere strategic prior to visiting the Hacienda Nápoles, or hanging around for the same reason I was, hoping to pick up Apostles' scent? Reclining in the seat, I settled in for the long haul but around twenty minutes later Juliana came out, still carrying the rucksack, changed into fitted jeans and a singlet, her dark hair no longer in a ponytail but held by a bright-orange headband. I got out of the car and followed her from a distance.

She stopped at a shop and bought a Zero. I followed her down a couple of streets as she window shopped.

My cell vibrated. I checked the screen. Arlen.

"Hey," I said.

"Okay, you might be onto something, though what I'm not sure. You're right about an inventory. They did one. Nothing is supposed to have been removed from the property. That's one of the reasons the army's there – to stop looters. I've just received a copy of that inventory, dated 17 July. After your escape from Apostles' camp and before Laughlin. The inventory's long – reads like a props list for an episode for *Game of Thrones*. Medieval fighting axes?"

"He's a romantic. What about the horse?"

"It's on the list."

A tingling sensation ran up the back of my neck.

"Well it's not there now," I said.

"And you're sure it hasn't been moved to another room?"

"Not according to Jimanez. I think it has been heisted," I said.

"Risky thing to steal from a cartel boss while he's still alive and on the loose."

"You'd think. What if the cartel boss stole from himself?"

"What, he just wandered back after hitting Laughlin and removed a few of his favorite things?"

"Why not? And it could have happened before Laughlin."

"Whatever, it's still brazen."

"This is a guy who whacked a US military facility."

"Good point."

"What about the surveillance cameras?"

"I've put in a request on that front. No idea when they'll get back to me, though."

Mañana, most probably.

"It's a long shot, Vin," Arlen added.

"Got nothing to lose," I said.

"And not a lot to gain either. What matters is not what he took, but where he took it to."

Yeah. Confirming that he'd come back and run off with some of his stuff didn't necessarily take us anywhere. I looked up and saw Juliana coming my way, carrying a poorly wrapped crossbow in a bag. "Arlen, gotta go." I hung up on him and stepped out onto the sidewalk in front of her.

"*Tú!*" she blurted. You!

"I thought you were gonna stop following me," I said.

She tried to push past me, but I blocked her path again. "What you got there?" I nodded at the badly wrapped crossbow in her hand. "That a crossbow?"

A bunch of storm clouds rolled across her face. "I should have killed you."

"You've never killed anyone in your life. Take it from me, you don't want to start."

She turned away and strode across the road. I went after her. "Juliana, I've got some explaining to do. Let me buy you a drink."

"No, I don't care what you have to say. I don't do friendly chitter-chatter with my father's people," she snapped.

"I'm not your father's people and never was."

She stopped on the other side of the road and stared into my face. "You lie."

"All the time when I'm working undercover."

She scoffed. "Undercover. You?"

Was it so hard to believe? "C'mon. Vodka, lime and soda, right? What have you got to lose?"

She examined my face, weighing the pros and cons. The pros had it. "I give you five minutes, no more."

I found us a bar facing the river. We could have anything we liked as long as it was *aguardiente*. With my cover blown, I figured I could tell Juliana pretty much everything now without compromising any secrecy acts. So I debriefed her on Horizon Airport, the gun battle with Kirk Matheson and my subsequent escape across the border into Mexico. I took the spin off my reasons for sending Matheson home after she batted him into the weeds with her Renault. The events in Bogotá she already knew about, but I recapped them anyway. Then I told her about the house in Juárez and the camp in the Mexican desert that I subsequently escaped from. There were some details omitted, a few of the more challenging details such as the ones that concerned Bambi.

When I was finished, half an hour and two-thirds of the bottle of *aguardiente* later, she asked, "Why have you come back? Why are you here?"

"Unfinished business," I said.

"You want to kill Juan de Apostles – I can see it in your eyes."

I shook my head. "No, the United States government wants him dead or alive, along with his pal the Tears of Chihuahua. Which usually means the preference is to bring the fugitive home in a pine box. But killing him and Perez with a bullet is too quick and easy. I want 'em to go the hard way – have them stand trial, get convicted and spend the next thirty years on death row never knowing whether the next meal will be their last."

Juliana signaled the barman to bring another bottle. Our terms were improving. She filled the glasses with the last of the first bottle and held her glass to me to toast. "I apologize then," she said, her smile sultry and her brown eyes wandering a little with the booze.

I clinked my glass with hers. "What for?"

"I didn't say goodbye to you in Bogotá. I left when you took a shower."

"Forget about it. Tell me about the crossbow. It belonged to your father, am I right?"

"You know this already?"

"An educated guess. The ranch was full of that stuff and some of it is missing."

Juliana lifted it off the floor, out of the bag and tore the paper away. "My father is a collector of old weapons. This is a *ballista,* a French crossbow. It looks old, but it is just a copy." She handed it to me.

It was heavy, solid and obviously made by a craftsman. Half a dozen bolts were taped to the intricately carved wooden stock. The mechanism for pulling back the thick gut string was still in the bag.

"When I visited him," she continued, "he would tell me stories. I think these were used in the Hundred Years War against England, maybe around 1400?" She was unsure. "My father had this one made from original plans. It has a range of over three hundred yards. He had it made because he wanted to see how well it would work."

"What was it doing in that shop?"

"I think it was given as payment to the man who owns the shop."

"For what?"

She looked at me matter-of-fact. "The man also has a truck. He moved some of my father's possessions to his new ranch."

That electric tingle in the back of my neck returned, only this time it ran up the back of my neck, down my spine and into my nuts. *I always know where he is. He tells me. I am his daughter.* "And you know where that ranch is?"

"Yes, of course."

*

We left Juliana's Renault outside the motel and took the rental. I drove around for a while until I was sure we weren't being tailed.

"When I left you, I got a job at a bar in the Zona G and also did some modeling work," Juliana said, explaining her movements. "On the days I had no work, I would take a book, drive to the Hacienda Mexico, and just park there and wait. A stakeout, yes?"

"Did you eat donuts?"

"What?"

"Never mind."

"He has many houses, but I was sure he would come back to the ranch. Did you know that the ranch was his favorite place in the world?"

I shook my head.

"This was his true home." She glanced over her shoulder. "Are we clear?"

I checked the rear-view mirror again. There'd been no traffic in it for a while. "We're good," I told her. "Has he been in contact with you?"

"No. I have heard nothing."

I'll admit to being disappointed when I heard that, but there was something about Juliana's certainty that convinced me to just go with it.

"There's a road coming up on your left," she said. "Turn there."

It was a minor road, unsealed. We drove for a minute or two in silence until I prompted her. "So you were saying something about the ranch."

"After what happened at the American base, it was all over the news, of course. Where is the last place people would think my father would dare to go? It would be the ranch. But I knew he would come back, even for a visit. So I waited. Some nights I slept in the car. Then, early in the morning maybe four days after the fight in your country, a truck came to the ranch when it was still dark. They had the security code. The gate opened and they went in."

"What about the army?"

"What army?"

"Forget about it," I said. "Then what?"

"Around an hour later they came out, closed the gate and drove away. I followed, headlights off. And where I'm taking you now is where the truck went."

"So you don't know for sure that your father is there?"

"Yes, of course he is there."

"But you haven't *seen* him."

"He is there."

Hmm ... A joint Colombian Special Forces/CIA go team wouldn't descend on this ranch without hard intelligence. The word of a resentful dependent wouldn't cut it.

"Did you talk about your father with the guy in the shop, the truck owner?"

"No, of course I didn't. Why would I send him a warning like that? Do you think I am stupid?"

"Just checking. So what was your plan?"

"What plan do you mean?"

"You still want to kill him, right?"

"Of course."

"How were you going achieve that?" I asked her.

"I was going to steal a boat."

Thirty-four

Back from the road, unfenced bushland and open fields suddenly became permanent high cinderblock walls painted green, topped by coiled razor wire. An entrance gate came up. I slowed right down to get a good look at it. The gate was new and solid. Signs warned of surveillance and jail terms for trespassers. Someone was keen on privacy, but there was no APOSTLES LIVES HERE banner. Still not enough to get that go team off the beach volleyball court. Nothing less than a positive sighting would be required.

*

Before I Skyped Arlen, I played through the conversation in my mind. I'd tell him about Apostles' whereabouts, to which he'd say: "So you think he's moved a mile up the road?" There'd be skepticism.

I'd say: "That's what his daughter believes."

To which he'd respond: "He has a daughter?"

"Her mother was Miss Venezuela. Remember Miss Venezuela, Apostles' first wife?"

"Oh right, I understand now."

"Understand what?"

"Is that her I can see in the background there? Is she hot? Show me ..."

"What's getting a look at her got to do with anything?"

"Because, Vin, sometimes you think with your dick."

I knew Arlen and, of course, he knew me. So the end result of this deliberation was that I didn't call him. One look at Juliana and he'd think for sure my libido was running the show.

So I opened up Google Earth instead to see what it would reveal. As it turned out, not a lot. While the resolution over Puerto Triunfo was reasonable, things became blurry over the countryside. And an apparently innocent random flight in a helicopter over the property wasn't on the cards either, as the only choppers in the skies in this part of the world were flown either by drug lords, or by the police or military looking for drug lords.

That explains why I stole a boat. Yes, okay, that was Juliana's idea but, truthfully, I didn't have a better one. And while stealing it was easy, keeping Juliana out of it was a little tougher. She agreed to remain behind on dry land only after I promised I was just gonna float downstream and recce the place. Juliana believed this because, unlike Arlen, she really didn't know me at all.

She stood on the bank lit up silver as the gentle current took hold of the craft and pulled it into the center of the river. The air was alive with the sound of frogs and insects croaking and clicking at each other, and sudden louder rustlings suggestive of larger animals. That's about when I remembered there were hippos in these waters and that they killed more folks in Africa than any other animal. But this was South America, I reassured myself, another continent entirely and maybe they were better behaved here. Something large in the water moved nearby.

"Nice hippo," I whispered.

I pushed off a bank with a pole as the river rounded a bend. A night light burned brightly on the rear porch of a rambling old mansion set back on higher ground away from the flood plain. A couple of horses slept standing under the stars. The boat, more of a dinghy, kept moving with the current. Around half an hour later and past two more neighboring properties, both with cattle, I drifted into the weeds on the edge of the ranch Juliana believed now housed the most wanted men in the world. Two stories of it sprawled from left to right roughly parallel to the course of the river. Two other smaller buildings also occupied the land. All of them were running dark and there didn't appear to be any livestock in the fields, except for a few horses. Even if no one was home, the place was probably wired up with infrared surveillance. Surveillance would include motion sensors.

It was about ten minutes before first light. Mist drifted over the land, ghostly in the moonlight. An animal with what sounded like very large lips blew air across them, and then gave a succession of deep warty grunts. And it was close. Dry land suddenly seemed a better risk than the river.

"Good hippo," I whispered as I removed the Sig from the small of my back, holding it aloft with my cell as I slid out of the dinghy. I gave the boat a gentle push to send it on its way, and pulled myself through the water-clogged weeds that hid the bank from view. My boots soon found the ooze on the bottom and I slowly, soundlessly snaked up the shelf, out of the water and into a stand of overgrown bush. Off to the east, the sky was giving a hint of the coming day. I checked the cell – no signal bars.

The ranch house and other buildings were maybe a hundred yards back from the river, much of them obscured by the thickening mist. And then I spotted movement. It was a man walking across the back of the house, beside a deep veranda.

He had a dog on a leash and some kind of rifle slung over his shoulder. My heart rate leaped up the scale. A man patrolling with a rifle was pretty suggestive that Juliana might be right about this ranch's residents. And then there was the dog. That presented a problem. Well-trained K-9s were difficult customers. They had a nose for trouble and lots of snapping teeth to deal with it.

The back door of the house opened and a figure came out, met by another figure that I hadn't seen, obscured by deeper shadows. The two of them started running – no, they were jogging. They turned and turned again, on a course heading straight toward my hide. The sky was getting lighter by the moment, light enough for me to see that one of the joggers ran with a shoulder holster, light enough for me to recognize the person running beside him. Jesus – Lina. They kept coming toward my position. I didn't have a lot of time to think through the options. I couldn't spot the guard with the K-9. This was risky. My muscles were twitching, breathing short and shallow. The Sig was in my hand.

They changed course in front of me, heading away. I leaped from the hide, slid onto the ground, got my legs either side of the armed runner's legs and twisted my body. The guy had no idea what happened. One moment he was running and maybe having a nice chat about global domination or whatever with Lina, and the next his face was accelerating toward the earth at a frightening rate. He had time to reach out with one hand to break his fall and I heard his wrist snap an instant before his face slammed into the turf. Lina had stopped. She was wide-eyed at the lightning assault. I was on the ground, Sig was pointed up at her, daring her to make a move. Or a sound. She was frozen.

"Morning," I said.

"Y ... you," she replied, a whisper.

"How many guards are there?"

"Three."

"Why only three?"

"Too many would ... draw attention." Lina was still getting over the shock of seeing how fast her world could be turned upside down.

Keeping the Sig on Lina, I untangled the rifle from the fallen guard. He was unconscious, but for how long? I tapped him behind the ear with the rifle stock, just hard enough to keep him seeing stars for an extended period.

"Drag him into the bush," I told Lina, the Sig tracking her every movement.

She hesitated, looking around for rescue. None was coming.

"Do it," I repeated.

"What are you going to do?" she asked once her guard was hidden away.

"Start running," I said.

"What?"

"You heard me. You were running. Let's just keep going, have a catch-up." She started to run and I ran with her, the Sig pointed across my body at her ribs. "Where's Apostles?"

"Not here," she said.

"And Perez isn't here either, I suppose."

"No."

"You're lying."

"Why would I tell you anything? You can find out for yourself."

"How's Daniela?"

"Do you care?"

"What do you think? You're both part of an operation that killed hundreds of your fellow Americans – men, women and children – and nearly started a war. Your boyfriend is a drug lord who pedals addiction while he murders people, and his best pal is a psycho fiend who belongs in a rubber room or, better still, with a lethal injection plugged into a vein."

"She can't talk after what you did to her. She was so beautiful. I think she's going to die."

Lina altered course, jogged away from the river and headed toward a couple of tennis courts with a cabana, all surrounded by steel-mesh fencing. Beyond the courts were stables and, beyond them, the ranch house.

"What are you going to do?"

"Just keep running until I tell you to stop." That sounded a lot more convincing than, "I'll let you know when it occurs to me."

We ran past the courts and the stables.

Moments later, approaching the ranch house, the guard with the dog walked around the side of one of the detached buildings, more or less into our path. The animal saw Lina and me, got the scent, and started barking and straining at the leash. It knew something was wrong – that something with an unfamiliar scent was in its presence. The guard was too busy restraining the animal to get a good look at me. He pulled on the dog's leash, yelled a command and managed to settle it down a little. The dog was a beast, some kind of shepherd–Rottweiler cross. It had jaws straight out of some horror movie and it clearly wanted to get them around my throat. The guard apologized to Lina with a friendly wave as we ran past and gave the K-9 another good yank on its chain to remind it who was boss.

I didn't know how long I was going to keep this up. I couldn't run around with Lina all day long and every footfall she had to be thinking about how to get on top of me, in a manner of speaking. I was just one man and it was now daylight. We came around the front of the house. There was a large, fast helicopter parked on the lawn, outside a hangar. Beyond it, partly obscured by trees, were other buildings, including garages where several vehicles were parked. Three large radio dishes were perched on the roof of the garage.

Apostles and Perez were wired into the world, running their empire.

Lina changed direction again. "So you just run around and around the house?" I asked her. "What happened at Laughlin changed the game. What the hell was Apostles thinking?"

No answer.

"This is it, you know," I told her. "I found you and now Uncle Sam is gonna reach down here and squash you. You can't leave – there's nowhere you can go. You're trapped. Like they say, the jig is up."

Finding her voice, Lina suddenly laughed. "It's just you, isn't it! Jesus, you've followed a hunch and here you are. They wouldn't send one man. No fucking way. There'd be the CIA, Colombian police. Shit ..."

We came around the corner of the house. The guard with the K-9 was quite close.

"¡Ayúdame!" Lina shouted, pushing me away.

At the call for help, the dog, already wary, instantly broke from the handler and leaped at me. I shot it. No choice. The animal died quiet. The handler swung his rifle off his shoulder as the Sig came around and barked at him too. At this extreme close range, the soft-nosed round punched him backward off his feet. When he landed, there was a big hole in his heart. He wasn't moving and neither was the dog.

In the dense morning air the gunshots had gone off like bigger explosions. They were ringing in my ears. And now surprise was lost and with it went any control of the situation that I might have had.

Lina had disappeared inside the house. I stripped the rifle off the dead guard, pulled the bolt and threw it. A man burst from one of the buildings away from the house, firing a carbine on full auto as he ran. The angle was bad for him, good for me. I had time to lead him two-handed as he ran. Squeezing the trigger, the Sig jumped and the man rolled into some longer grass before he could reach cover. I stood behind the side of the house, listening. Lina had said three guards. I believed her. When she'd told me she'd been in too much shock to think about lying. Three guards were now accounted for.

I thought about alternatives to storming the house. Most of them circled the notion of calling for backup. Only who was I gonna call? There was no 1st Cav gonna be riding on in this time. And then there was the question of how I was gonna make said call. I looked at my cell. Still no bars, damn it.

I checked the Sig's magazine: five rounds and one in the chamber. Dropping the mag out of the FN FAL carbine taken from Lina's running partner showed it to be full. The Sig was a better choice in confined quarters, like inside a house. The FN would be my reserve weapon. I slung it over my shoulder. The world had gone way too quiet to be healthy. I took a couple of deep breaths to get my heart rate under control, then stepped warily to the dark doorway through which Lina had disappeared.

I put my head around the corner, in and out. A billiards room, full-size table. The room was empty. I went in. The air smelled of fresh paint. No sound, no movement. Off the room, two hallways and a spiral staircase. I took the staircase. The stairs topped out in a kind of sitting room with a spare bedroom off one end and an office off the other. On the wall in the sitting room, that familiar signed photo of Pancho Villa. The office was vacant, no paperwork or computer gear. One hallway off the sitting room. Still no sound or movement. I took the hallway. On the wall, an old oil painting of a vast sea battle – sails, cannon fire, explosions. On the wall opposite, a very large mirror in a gold frame. Beneath the mirror, some kind of antique wooden chopping block with an ancient rifle displayed on top. Further down the hall, a suit of armor. A doorway. A bedroom. I went in. The bed had been slept in. An en-suite bathroom, empty. I backed out into the bedroom.

Somewhere, a door opened. And before I had time to react, a loop of steel enveloped my arms and body and squeezed.

No, not steel – arms. They lifted me off the ground, the pressure intensifying. My ribs – they were going to crack. I struggled, slammed my head back, hoping to do some damage, but whoever had me in this bear hug was ready for it. I got a look at the human vice in the mirror. It wore a black mask, jagged silver teeth, round silver-painted eyes and angry silver brows. Jesus, *El Bruto*? Lina dashed across the hall, pistol up and aimed at me. I found the wall with my boots and pushed off an instant before she fired. The round skimmed the wall, taking off paint. I couldn't breathe. *El Bruto* roared in my ear and squeezed ever harder. I thought my head was going to burst. I gripped the Sig, pointing at the floor, changed the angle slightly and fired. The roar turned into a scream as bits of *El Bruto*'s foot burst all over the floor. He released his grip as we both toppled over, the wrestler making animal sounds of intense pain.

Sprawled on the floor, I glanced up and saw Lina run down the hallway, disappear into a room and slam the door closed behind her. The fight had gone right out of *El Bruto*, the man shaking with shock and holding his mangled quivering foot in the air, his scream almost continuous.

I got up and left the wrestler where he was. He was noisy, but out of the game. Edging further down the hall, I wasn't sure of the wisdom of following Lina. I put my hand on a doorknob and turned it. The air that came from the room was close and smelled of sickness. I opened the door. Daniela was propped up in bed, sleeping. Her closed eyes wore circles of green pallor, her throat encased in bandages. She opened her eyes and saw me. They went wide with fear. She opened her mouth, tried to call or scream, but only a dry croak escaped. I felt a pang of regret. She'd been a beautiful creature, emphasis on creature. Daniela was out of the game too. I closed the door and continued down the hall. Three other bedrooms. All were gorgeously decorated with tapestries, rugs and old weapons. The four-poster beds had all been slept in. Another suit of armor marked the end of the hall and the entrance to a dining room. A horse with a case of rigor stood stiff and dead in one corner of the room. It was *Siete Leguas* – Seven Leagues, Villa's stuffed nag.

The sound of a vase or a plate smashing distracted me. It came from downstairs. It felt like a lure. I backtracked, past *El Bruto* who was now whimpering, his bloody foot making a hell of a mess on the wall and floor, and took the stairs down from the sitting room. The billiards room was still clear. My palms were sweating on the Sig's handgrips. Along with Lina, who was armed and dangerous, Apostles and Perez were embedded somewhere in this house, waiting for me. More specifically, waiting to kill me. And by now, they would know that I'd come alone. Or maybe not.

*

I fired the rifle into the air and the three horses went through the ground floor hallway like, well, a herd of horses. They made plenty of noise knocking paintings off the walls, smashing vases, sliding on rugs and breaking chairs, neighing and whinnying in the strange environment. When they got to the front door and found it closed, the animals went seriously berserk, bucking and turning, and kicking out with their hooves, skidding on the wood floor. I came in behind them and ran to the side, into a library. I figured Apostles was into horses more than humans. He'd be worried about them. I heard him calling out to them, trying to soothe them and horse-whisper them back out the way they came in. One of the animals got the message, reared up and twisted around, galloped down the hall and out the rear entrance, the other horses following. I snuck into a room, came through an adjoining door and, in a mirror, saw Apostles' back, a machine pistol dangling from his hand. All the noise and distraction hid my movement. Apostles sensed me behind him too late. He spun around but now the Sig was barely inches away, aimed at the bridge of his nose.

"I'll take that," I told him as he hesitated, relieving him of the machine pistol, pulling the weapon out of his hand.

"I don't think so," said Perez in Spanish.

What? I froze. Jesus – the man was behind me! He'd done to me what I'd done to Apostles. The short vicious little fuck stepped around where I could see him. He had a H&K pistol, blue-black with pearl grips, pointed at my chest. The stupid gun matched that stupid knife of his. Maybe it was a boxed set.

I held my nerve. "Don't think about moving." To Perez I said, "This trigger only needs two point two pounds' pressure to release the hammer. I'm squeezing it now – gotta be close to two pounds' pressure on the trigger. Shoot me and the shock will make my finger twitch." I took a glance at Perez. His head was no longer shaved smooth, a band of scraggly salt and pepper fuzz running around the back of his head from ear to ear. The tear tattoos were mostly gone, expensively lasered off I guessed, the skin still mildly scarred from the burning. The color of his eyes had also changed. Dung-beetle black was now cow-brown. He was changing his appearance, getting ready to disappear or perhaps start afresh. "Had a makeover?" I asked him. "Going for that paedophile accountant look, I see. Suits you."

"I am going to enjoy killing you, Cooper," Perez growled.

"Don't count your chickens." I sounded tough, if a sentence with chickens in it could sound tough, but I was compensating – the momentum had shifted out of my control.

Perez switched to English. "What is it you gringos call this? A Mexican standoff?"

And then Juliana walked in through the back door, hands behind her head. Coming in behind her was Lina, armed with that crossbow, the bolt aimed between Juliana's shoulder blades.

"Ah, Juliana. How nice to see you, as always," said Apostles. "And look, you're returning my ballista. Can you believe those *putas* stole it?"

Juliana's eyes met mine, and there was an apology in them. She must have simply stolen another boat and drifted along down the river behind me. But however she'd managed to get herself here was academic. Juliana was now their prisoner and this changed things, the balance now firmly in Apostles' favor. Once upon a time, I might have taken a gamble in a situation like this, had a crack, shot first and worried about the consequences later, but I'd learned my lesson. This was how Anna Masters had lost her life. Experience had taught me this standoff shit never ends well.

Perez relieved me of the machine pistol as Apostles turned and took the Sig from my hand. "I liked you, you know that? We could have done some good business, you and me. Pity."

Plan A was busted. My mind raced through plans B, C, D, all the way to Z, and came up empty. I couldn't see a way out. Apostles had my pistol, Perez was behind me with a pistol and Lina had an iron bolt that could kill out to three hundred yards aimed point blank at Juliana's back. Tears of frustration ran down Juliana's face.

Apostles checked that there was indeed a round in the Sig's chamber. Satisfied, he cocked the weapon, brought it up and pushed the muzzle against my forehead.

"Move," Apostles suggested to Perez, who was in his line of fire if my brains didn't stop the bullet.

I taunted him. "What's the matter, afraid you'll miss?"

Apostles smiled a pleasant smile, pushed the weapon hard into my forehead. And then he pulled the trigger.

Click!

The hammer hit home but nothing happened. Apostles looked at Perez and took the gun away from my head, confused for an instant. An instant was all I needed. I reached out, snatched Apostles' hand, jammed it under his chin and pulled his own finger against the trigger. This time, with no backward pressure on the slide, the Sig roared as it coughed up a round. The barrel jerked up and back and Apostles' skin and blood and gray matter flew in all directions as the soft-nose bullet did its job.

Lina looked on in horror at her lover's brains hitting the ceiling. Juliana dove for the floor as Lina's finger tightened automatically on the crossbow's trigger. The weapon's string made a sound like a musical note as it discharged. A moment later, from down on the floor, Juliana fired her own pistol up at Lina, the bullet smashing the girl's hip and spinning her around. Lina screamed and toppled to the floor.

Something was missing: Perez. He'd gone. "Where is he?" I yelled.

"He's wounded – the crossbow," Juliana yelled back, the gunfire and Lina's screams ringing in our ears, and pointed out the door.

I sprinted for the back door and saw him. He was running toward the river with an awkward gait, clutching his bloody side, the kidney area. A long smear of deep crimson on the grass said the wound was bad. I ran and caught up with him trying to drag a heavy wooden canoe off the weeds and into deeper water. I hadn't seen this boat earlier. I guessed it was the one Juliana had arrived in. Weak from blood loss, not to mention the pain, the task was beyond Perez and he was puffing, exhausted, staggering like a drunk in the shallows.

"What do you want?" he panted in that dry voice of his. "Money, a share of the business?"

"You could take that fancy pistol of yours out of your pants – using your left hand – and throw it into the water," I told him.

He did as I asked and tossed it into the weeds between us.

"Good. Now your knife."

He removed it from inside his jacket pocket and it went into the drink, roughly where he'd thrown the pistol.

"Any other weapons?" I asked him, covering his movements with the Sig.

"No," he said and then coughed. "Tell me, what do you want? I can make anything happen for you."

That was some claim. It took my mind back through a jumble of nightmarish images. "I want you to pay for the people you killed at Horizon Airport. There was a woman. Her name was Gail Sorwick. You remember her? You killed her husband and children after you forced yourself on her. And then you cut her. Remember?"

Perez stumbled to keep his footing and coughed some more. *"Por favor ..."* he pleaded.

"There was a girl by the name of Bambi, and the hundreds of men, women and children you killed or wounded at Laughlin. Can you bring them all back, asshole?"

I placed the Sig's front sight on Perez and followed him with it as he stumbled around in the weeds, in the grip of a minor coughing fit, hacking up blood. I'd made a promise to Gail and to Bambi. To hell with Chalmers and his guilt trip. That shit had almost gotten me killed anyway. Monsters like Perez should never have been born. I could do this. It would be so easy. It's what I'd been paid to do. I kneaded the Sig's handgrip. No witnesses. Just pull the trigger on this piece of shit. Do it.

A sudden depression appeared in the water close to Perez, followed by a bow wave like a submarine surfacing. Shit – a large animal surged out of the water, stopped still in the weeds and waggled a bizarrely cute set of ears on top of its head. It scared the crap outta me. Jesus, a hippo, one of the descendants of Escobar's zoo. It wasn't a full-sized one – an adolescent or even a baby. It might even have been the animal I'd seen at Apostles' ranch on my first visit there. What was its name? Sophie?

If its arrival startled me, it gave Perez the shock of his life. He lost his footing and lurched a few steps toward it, off balance. That's when a second hippo the size of an M1 main battle tank charged out of the water. If the smaller one was Sophie, then the big one had to be Sophie's mother, Magdalena. Maggie trotted to Perez with her mouth open wide and snatched him up, impaling him on those huge chisel teeth and shaking him from side to side several times before throwing him up onto the bank, broken and bleeding.

Mother then nuzzled daughter affectionately and herded her back into the water.

I blinked. A wheezing Perez groaned at my feet.

Epilogue

It's a core belief of mine that you can't trust advertising. It's all retouched, right? But then I got a look at Juliana naked and I have to admit that the reality was every bit as desirable as the orange-juice fantasy on the side of the bus. Put it this way – if she were a Big Mac, I'd eat Big Macs.

I gazed down on her tan body, the blue-white sheet twisted into a loose column that lay across a hip, a breast and an arm. She enjoyed the attention and gave me her 'blue steel' look, part pout and all seduction. "This would make a great picture for your portfolio. You want me to get a camera?" I asked her.

"No." She shook her head and smiled that knowing, over-sexed smile I was becoming familiar with. I took her lead, leaned over the exposed breast and traced the edges of her aureole with the tip of my tongue, which hardened pretty much instantly into ridges of coffee-colored pleasure crowned with a chocolate nipple. And then the playtime turned into something else as she grabbed me, rolled her tan leg to one side and, keeping her eyes on mine, guided me inside her.

I wasn't going to fight it.

Sometime later, when the sun was well and truly overhead and we needed to come up for air and sustenance, we hit the pool, slipped into the warm water and waded up to the bar overlooking Montego Bay.

I gave the barman a nod, a young black guy by the name of Innocent with dreads and a silver skull hanging from his earlobe, and made the multi-lingual gesture for two drinks. Already regulars, a vodka, lime and soda and a Maker's Mark materialized on coasters in front of us.

"What shall we toast?" Juliana asked me.

"Indecision," I suggested.

"Still haven't made up your mind?"

I gave her an ambiguous smile and took a long sip.

My phone started ringing, one of those waterproof models. I took it out of my back pocket. It displayed a photo of Arlen and Marnie, Anna's sister, on the screen. Marnie's arm was casually draped across Arlen's shoulder.

"Hey," I said to my boss and pal.

"Hey yourself," Arlen replied.

"So you got it?"

"Just hit my desk."

"How's Gomez?" I asked.

"Fine. No long-term damage. He told me to tell you that next time you need a partner ... ask someone else."

"What about Perez?"

"I heard he's gonna pull through well enough so that we can kill him all nice and legal with a lethal injection."

"Where they holding him?" "They" being the feds.

"It's a secret. There's been a move to reinstate public hangings. People want to throw garbage at him while he swings."

The depth of feeling was understandable. Perez was the very worst example of the human species. Apostles wasn't much better, but he was entertaining worms and beyond reach.

"What about Daniela and Lina?" I asked.

"They won't come out of it much better than Perez."

They didn't deserve to.

"You still with Apostles' daughter?" Arlen wanted to know.

I turned to look at Juliana. She was chatting to a slim Asian woman who'd swum up to the bar. My keen powers of observation noted that the newcomer's bikini was as brief as Juliana's, though not as full in the cup area. "Yeah."

"I'm sure you know what you're doing," he said.

"That's a first."

"You know how the media would react to it if they ever found out you were sleeping with the enemy's daughter?"

"Why would they care? I'm no one."

"I care."

"You haven't met her. Don't judge."

A black woman swam onto the seat beside me, her hair piled up on top of her head and held in place by her sunglasses. She ordered a mojito. A small diamond stud twinkled in her nose. She caught my extended glance summing up her figure – tall, lean and dangerous. "Hi," I said to be neighborly.

"*Bonjour*," she replied, all smiles.

"What?" said Arlen.

"Nothing – just doing my bit for international relations here."

"Getting back to this letter ... You seriously want to resign your commission?"

"That's what it says."

"We haven't talked about this. It's out of the blue. I'm going to do you a favor and sit on it a while. You take your time. Think about it. I'll clear things here. And when you're ready to come back, you let me know."

"Don't hold your breath."

"I know you, Vin. You'll get bored and restless."

"I doubt it," I said as another Maker's Mark materialized on the bar in front of me.

"From the lady," said Innocent, nodding at the Asian woman who was looking at me, giggling about something with Juliana. I gave her a nod.

"So what are you gonna do?" asked Arlen.

I leaned back in the seat with drink in hand and enjoyed the view to my left and right. The black woman caught me feasting on her a second time. Busted. I shrugged her an apology. She reacted with a smile, shrugged right back, sipped her drink through a straw and I felt her leg brush against mine under the water.

"Arlen, I think I'll just live the dream for a while, you know? Live the dream."

Acknowledgments

To start off with I'd like to thank Mike "Panda" Pandolfo, Lieutenant Colonel, USAF, (Ret.) for organizing field trips, interviews, managing the technical editing, proofreading, and providing the odd good idea here and there for this book. I couldn't have written it without him.

In researching *Standoff*, I spent some time in El Paso, TX, hanging out with Deputy Manny Marquez from the El Paso County Sheriff's Office on a ridealong (organized by Panda). Now that was an eye-opening experience. Thank you for that, Manny.

Thanks also to EPSCO CSI for some interesting insights, and for providing some equally interesting introductions. (I met this one guy through them who sat on his veranda on the American side of the border with an AR-15, waiting for the drug couriers to trip the sensors on his property. Yeah, like I said, interesting!)

Of course, thanks to Sheriff Wiles for approving the time I spent with Deputy Marquez and the folks in CSI. Thanks also go to Christina Acosta, EPCSO Public Affairs Director, and to Deputy Eileen Lopez, the acting PIO at the time.

Thank you Texas Rangers for an enlightening briefing session (and a delicious "Texas friendly" lunch). And thank you El Paso Police Department for some invaluable insights.

And of course, thanks also to a significant number of other law enforcement officers and private individuals in El Paso who freely gave of their knowledge and experience, but were reluctant to let their names appear in print. Again, thank you – you know who you are.

Bruce County Public Library
1243 Mackenzie Rd.
Port Elgin ON N0H 2C6

CPSIA information can be obtained at www.ICGtesting.com
Printed in the USA
LVOW08s1544270314

379216LV00003B/658/P

9 781760 080938